THEY WERE SWEPT UP BY A RAGING RIVER
OF RAW PASSIONS AND DEADLY DESIRES

TED HENDERSON—Heroic leader of the band called Henderson's Scouts, a soldier in the prime of his manhood, expert with a rifle, deadly with knife . . . and facing an enemy that threatened his land and his life.

KIT CARSON—Legendary frontiersman, now heeding his country's call to lead the most audacious battle plan of a bloody war . . . and kill whoever jeopardized his mission.

JUDY HUBBARD—Beautiful and headstrong wife of a Union officer, her mistake was trusting a Confederate scoundrel . . . and the price was a rendezvous with shame and blood.

KEVIN O'REILLY—Young, handsome Cavalry rider, he would love one woman in defiance of the world . . . and hate one man with the fire of an Irish temper ignited by outrage and vengeance.

WIND FLOWER—Provocatively lovely daughter of the Navaho chief, she would be torn between her heritage and heart.

CHOSHAY—Ugly in body and mean of spirit, he would betray his own people to take what he wanted—Wind Flower and the scalp of a Cavalry man.

D1011752

WINNING THE WEST
BOOK I

RIO GRANDE
DONALD CLAYTON PORTER

Created by the Producers of
Wagons West, White Indian,
and Stagecoach.

Chairman of the Board: Lyle Kenyon Engel

BANTAM BOOKS
TORONTO • NEW YORK • LONDON • SYDNEY • AUCKLAND

RIO GRANDE

A Bantam Book / published by arrangement with
Book Creations, Inc.

Bantam edition / December 1986

Produced by Book Creations, Inc.
Chairman of the Board: Lyle Kenyon Engel

ISBN 0-553-24535-X

Published simultaneously in the United States and Canada

Bantam Books are published by Bantam Books, Inc. Its trade-
mark, consisting of the words "Bantam Books" and the por-
trayal of a rooster, is Registered in U.S. Patent and Trademark
Office and in other countries. Marca Registrada. Bantam
Books, Inc., 666 Fifth Avenue, New York, New York 10103.

PRINTED IN THE UNITED STATES OF AMERICA

KR   0 9 8 7 6 5 4 3 2 1

AUTHOR'S NOTE

In 1861, after the old West was spanned by telegraph wire, the Pony Express was disbanded, having served out its glorious—if brief—role in history. But the struggle to win the West was far from over. The region became a pawn in the Civil War, as North and South competed for the strategically important western territories. Meanwhile, Indian tribes harried the soldiers of both sides, seeing that the white man was determined to bring to their lands his alien civilization and warfare.

This is the story of one man of the old West, Captain Ted Henderson, former Pony Express rider and now an army regular. It is also the story of his war, and that of his fellow army officers and men on both sides of the conflict. And it is the story of the Indian tribes whose lands lay helpless before the white man's incursions.

Donald Clayton Porter

RIO GRANDE

RON TOELKE '83

I

Splashes of gold from aspens rippled among the many shades of green in the pine forest, the colors bright under a cloudless autumn sky. Ted Henderson eased his stallion to a stop atop the ridge overlooking the valley, and he realized it would not be long before winter snows blanketed the land.

It was one of the few luxuries the lean man in buckskins allowed himself, this habit of pausing before starting the final part of his ride home. Nestled in the valley below was the familiar, sturdy house, modest but comfortable, protected from the howling blizzards of the high country by the surrounding mountains. A few head of cattle nibbled the tall, dun-colored grass that waved green in spring and summer and provided forage in leaner times.

The stallion shuffled his front feet, ears pointed toward the barn below. Ted touched the animal's neck just above the withers. The horse stilled at the familiar signal for quiet. "I know, boy," Ted said in a quiet and steady voice, "you're just as anxious as I am to get home. But let's enjoy it for just a minute more."

Even as he absorbed the tranquil beauty of the scene below, Ted studied each clump of trees, then examined the slope of the mountainside and the valley. His instincts were the result of living in the mountains and his experience as a Pony Express rider on the treacherous South Pass route. Finally, satisfied that all was well, he touched a knee to the stallion's side. The horse needed no further encouragement to head toward the ranch and broke into a running walk, a gait that could cover miles without tiring horse or rider.

There were, Ted thought, many rewards in a man's life. A

1

job done well. Finding the one telltale bend in a single blade of grass that brought the trail of a fugitive into sharp focus. But nothing was more rewarding than this—coming home to Wilma.

At first the returns to the ranch house had been filled with dread. Flashes of the horror and pain of coming home to find his wife and little daughter savagely slaughtered had raised the hairs on the backs of his hands. But now those memories had been beaten. It was Wilma who had helped him put the past where it belonged and move on to the present, planning for the future. Wilma had helped him recover from the searing grief and from the bottle, which had been his near-ruin. She had made him a whole man once more.

Only a few yards from the house, Ted stood in the stirrups and returned his wife's wave, warmth and pride washing away the final traces of his long ride. A mild autumn wind stirred Wilma's full, long hair and pressed the simple cotton dress against the curves of her body. The corners of Ted's mouth lifted in an involuntary grin. Standing there in the slanting rays of the late afternoon sun, her arm upraised, Wilma Henderson seemed more like a painting than a real woman.

But Ted knew better.

Automatically, he pulled the stallion to a stop, dismounted, and draped the reins around a hitchrack. Then his arms were full of Wilma, and his heart was full of peace. She smelled of rose-scented soap and fresh-baked bread. Ted was pleased that he had been able to find a deep pool on the high creak to wash the dirt of the trail from his own body.

Their kiss was long and hungry and deep. Finally Wilma pulled away and led him into the delicious smells of baking bread and burning wood that turned a house into a home.

Ted's very being settled into the neat, comfortable surroundings, where small flames danced in the fireplace. Ripples of late-afternoon sunlight played over the small statue above the mantel in its own specially carved niche of the native stone wall. It was a bronze, a Pony Express rider firmly astride his *mochila* and saddle, the horse stretched out in a determined gallop. Beside it was a document, framed in fine-carved, hand-fitted cedar and protected by a thick pane of glass. Bearing the signature of Abraham Lincoln, the letter had been sent along with the bronze statue to Ted, in acknowledgment of his extraordinary accomplishments as a rider for the Pony Express. The phrase *I know of no one more deserving of this gift than you* made the White House parchment stationery Ted's second greatest treasure. The first leaned comfortably against his side. He felt the warmth of her body penetrating the buckskin he wore.

"What is your pleasure, Captain? Bed, supper, or"—her eyes sparkled in the fading light—"both?"

Ted smiled and took her hand. "A man must be in love when he's away for less than a week but feels as though it's been years. But first things first. I have a hungry horse outside who's probably wondering why he's been left standing there so long." With a loving squeeze of her hand, he went outside to tend the animal.

Wilma watched him loosen the cinch. As he led the horse from her field of view, she swallowed the lump in her throat. She realized just how lucky a woman she was. Most western men felt that expressing deep feelings of sentiment was a sign of weakness. But her husband was a man who had fought Indians, had battled mountain blizzards, had doggedly stood his ground and put a bullet in the chest of the man who killed his first wife and daughter. And he also had won the hardest battle of all—the one in his heart and mind—and still he was not ashamed to say the word "love."

She heard his shrill whistle calling the horses in for the night. With Indians and horse thieves still making mischief sometimes, the most valuable animals had to be kept in stalls and corrals at night for protection. She brushed back a stray strand of hair as the door swung open, and once more she took him in her arms, savoring the smells of horse and hay and man, the campfire odor still clinging to his buckskins.

Ted smiled down at her. "I'm not that hungry at the moment," he said, grinning. "After all, I did eat dinner. Yesterday."

"Then, sir, you may have your choice of any woman in the house." Wilma snuggled her cheek against the solid muscle where his neck met his shoulder, and smiled to herself. This running jest had done much to purge her mind and spirit of the stigma of her past life as the operator of a saloon and fancy house.

Ted pulled away, forcing an intent scowl on his weather-lined face, and in mock seriousness began to prowl each room of the small house. In a few moments he returned and stood before her, the glint in his eyes betraying the teasing. A warm glow begin to spread throughout Wilma's body, and her own heartbeat quickened.

"I can't say much for the variety of your stable," he said, "but in quality, it can't be surpassed. I demand the most beautiful, the most passionate woman here." He jabbed a finger at her. "I want you," he said.

Her answer was the rustle of cloth dropping onto the polished hardwood floor.

Ted pushed himself away from the dinner table, the elk steak pleasantly heavy in his stomach after a few days on field rations, and lifted a cup of steaming coffee. They sat in silence for a moment, satiated, savoring each other's company. Wilma's soft violet eyes studied the lean man across the table. The broken nose and wide-set eyes gave a rugged but still handsome appearance to the face. A few strands of gray streaked the dark hair above the temples, a few small scars on cheekbone and jaw testified to the demanding, often violent, life he had lived. But when he smiled, he had all his teeth, and that in itself told something of the man's ability in a fight.

Wilma sighed. "You, sir, are disgusting."

Ted raised an eyebrow. "I beg your pardon?"

"You eat like a horse and never gain so much as an ounce," she said, her tone scolding. "I can walk by an oven full of bread baking and the smell alone puts another inch on my hips."

Ted grinned. "Woman, you have a long way to go before your figure is anything short of fantastic."

As his brown eyes devoured her, she felt the warmth of passion begin to rise again and decided to change the subject. "How was the scouting mission? Did you catch them?"

"Second day out," he replied. "Just two Ute youngsters playing at being braves. They had terrorized a housewife on an isolated ranch, whooping and hollering and putting an arrow or two into the door. But as soon as they found out Henderson's Scouts were after them, they just sat down on a rock and waited to be caught."

Wilma saw the glint of pride in his eyes. "What happened to them?"

"I outlined the choices. The could be sent back to their tribe to let the elders decide the punishment—which would have been based on their stupidity, not their actions—or they could go to Fort Bridger, where Colonel Wild Bill Robinson has moved his headquarters, and accept the sentence handed down by the colonel himself. They might have been young, but they weren't dumb. They decided to go see the colonel."

"What will happen to them?"

Ted shrugged. "I'm sure Colonel Robinson will tailor the punishment to the crime," he said. "They probably will be given a lecture they won't soon forget. Then he'll feed them for a couple of days while he sends word to their elders to keep an eye on the youths or be held personally accountable. Then he'll turn them loose."

"They're lucky," Wilma said matter-of-factly. "Neither you nor Colonel Robinson is an Indian-hater like some people in this area. In other hands they might have been hanged on the spot."

Ted nodded. "The white men who see Indians as animals are the cause of our problems. Without them—with my scouts and Robinson showing the way—a lasting peace could be brought to the frontier. There should be room in this vast wilderness for people of different colors and different cultures to live side by side." Ted's voice changed, taking on an edge of sadness. "But more and more white men come, invaders into Indian territory. They're destroying Indian hunting grounds, disrupting the movement of the buffalo herds, and worst of all, trying to tell the Indians that the customs and religion that have served them so well for centuries are wrong." Ted snorted in disgust. "It's a wonder we don't have more incidents than we do. And one day, Wilma, I'm afraid the entire frontier is going to burst into flames. . . ." His voice trailed off.

Wilma could think of nothing to say. She knew that Ted thought as much like an Indian as any Cheyenne chief, and he was seldom wrong in either his forecasts on the trail or his assessments of the future.

"Any word from Yellow Crow?" Ted's question brought Wilma back to the present. She shook her head.

"I have to admit that I'm becoming concerned," she said. "He should have been back by now. Are you sure it's a good idea to send him out on these scouting trips alone? There are a lot of white men out there who hate Indians—all Indians—and other tribes are constantly looking for the scalp of the Cheyenne who rides with Henderson's Scouts. Even some of Yellow Crow's own tribe would not wail at his death since he has become a blood brother to a white man."

"Don't be worried on Yellow Crow's behalf," Ted reas-

sured his wife. "My Cheyenne brother is probably safer alone
than he would be with a full platoon of cavalry tagging along."

Wilma sighed. "It will be nice to have you both back home
again. I don't fear for my safety, not with one of your scouts
staying in the vicinity of the ranch in your absence and a
loaded shotgun nearby. But I can't help worrying about you
both."

Wilma pushed her chair back from the table and began to
gather the dishes. Ted pitched in, a sight that never ceased to
amuse Wilma—her rugged frontiersman with weather-beaten
hands carefully drying a stoneware dish as though it were fine
china.

"Any problems here while I was gone?" he asked.

Wilma laughed. "None except with Bertha—the old
floozie kicked the milk bucket over twice. That cow must have
something against being milked by a woman."

Ted suddenly stiffened, a hand instinctively going to the
pistol at his belt.

"What is it?" Wilma whispered.

"I heard something near the barn. You know what to do."
Ted reached for his rifle and cocked it as Wilma plucked the
shotgun from its rack above the sink and disappeared into a
back room.

Ted eased himself through the front door, his step
soundless. He stood for a moment, letting his eyes adjust to
the faint illumination from the rising moon, and listened
intently. He heard the sound again, the soft snuffle of his
stallion, a warning sign from the animal that something was
amiss. Ted slipped into the inky shadow at the side of the
house, his view of the barn and corrals unimpaired.

Then he saw it. A flicker of movement in the shadows at
the corner of the line of stalls. The stallion had sounded no
challenge, so the intruder was not a predatory animal. Unless
it was a man.

Suddenly the shadow took shape. A short, powerfully
built Indian, his arrow notched against his bowstring, turned
in Ted's direction as the arrow point moved upward. Ted
rushed his shot, firing by instinct. He knew he had missed
even before the sound of the slug striking wood reached his
ears.

He dropped the rifle, rolled to one side, and tugged the
pistol free. He had the sinking sensation born of experience
that he was not going to be in time. The warrior had the arrow

at full draw. Ted could only hope it would not strike him in a vital area, that he could still fire one accurate shot.

Ted felt the air sing by his ear, the distinct whistle of an arrow, and a split second later came the solid sound of missile striking flesh. The brave at the barn staggered, his arrow fluttering harmlessly to the side as the bow fell free. The Indian grasped at his chest. Ted had the pistol lined up now but eased the pressure on the trigger. In the growing light of the rising moon he could see the shaft of an arrow protruding from the brave's chest. The Indian slid down the side of the barn, one hand grasping the arrow for a moment, then the arm dropped and his head fell forward, chin resting on chest. Ted would have bet a lot of money that the Indian was dead.

He called over his shoulder, "Good hunting, brother!"

Yellow Crow stepped from behind the woodpile nearby, another arrow notched and ready. Ted rose, brushed the dirt away, and turned to face the Cheyenne. He was startled momentarily at the sight; Yellow Crow, tall even by Cheyenne standards, was in full war paint.

"This one I have tracked for two days," the Indian said in English. "He came here to steal horse. I found his dead horse a sun ago."

The two men approached the downed warrior, the white man with pistol cocked, the painted Cheyenne with bow drawn. Neither was needed.

Yellow Crow grasped the dead man's hair and roughly yanked the face upward so that the moonlight fell on the slack features. "It is as I thought," he said, studying the face carefully. "This one I know." The Cheyenne reached down, grasped a thong about the dead man's neck, and yanked. He handed a small leather bag to Ted. "Medicine pouch. Mescalero Apache go nowhere without it. We study it, maybe learn something, maybe not." He turned back to his search of the body and soon found a thin, deerhide scroll stained with body sweat and bear grease. He glanced at it, then handed it to Ted without comment.

They dragged the Indian's body inside an empty box stall where no animal could get at it and where it would remain until it could be buried. They started back toward the house.

"Yellow Crow," Ted said, "once again you have pulled your brother's skin away from the fire."

The Indian shrugged, moonlight dancing across the heavy shoulder muscles. "Brothers not keep count," he said.

Inside, Wilma quickly recovered from the unexpected shock of seeing the Cheyenne in war paint, greeted Yellow Crow with a warm embrace, then promptly excused herself to prepare something for him to eat. Ted and the Cheyenne emptied the dead Indian's medicine bag onto the table. Yellow Crow sorted through the small bones and pebbles and the dried plant leaves. After a long moment, he turned to Ted.

"You look. Tell me what bones say."

Ted studied the contents carefully. "Mescalero Apache, all right," he said. "Far from his home range in the south and carrying his strongest medicine talismans—what an Apache would carry if he knew his chances of returning home were slim."

Yellow Crow nodded. "For white man, you read medicine pouch well. When this one left his tipi, he was prepared for a long journey and for the crossing into the other world." Abruptly, Yellow Crow snatched the pebbles and bones from the table and hurled the objects into the fireplace with a vengeance. Both Ted and Wilma knew why the dead Apache caused Yellow Crow to show such fury. Mescalero braves had killed Yellow Crow's parents when he was very young. And both Ted and Wilma knew the reason for the destruction of the medicine bag's contents. Without them, the soul of the dead Apache would wander for eternity in the dread Darkness Between Worlds.

Ted turned his attention back to the deerskin scroll. It was covered with strange symbols, a language or code he had never before seen. The symbols appeared to have been burned into the soft, flexible material with the red-hot point of a hunting knife. Perhaps a more careful examination of the weapons and clothing of the dead man would explain why an Apache would be carrying such a document. He called to Yellow Crow. The Cheyenne seemed to shudder, then returned to the table.

"Are you familiar with any of these signs?" Ted pointed to a string of characters on the deerskin scroll.

Yellow Crow shook his head. "Not see before. Not Apache signs." A strong finger traced a line of symbols. "Indian writing, but not make words," he said.

Ted nodded. "It seems to be some kind of code. I think we had better leave tomorrow for Fort Bridger and deliver this to Colonel Robinson." He turned to Wilma. "Would you like to come, Wilma?"

Wilma, placing a platter of food before Yellow Crow, readily agreed. "I'd love to! Since Colonel Robinson and the Third Cavalry moved to Bridger from Laramie, I haven't had a chance to visit my friends and do any shopping. But who will watch the stock and milk old Bertha?"

Yellow Crow, who could crouch behind a tree and gnaw the raw meat from the bones of a freshly killed rabbit if need be, deftly sliced a piece of steak, lifted it with a fork, and chewed thoughtfully. "Yellow Crow come back, tend place," he said. "Maybe more Mescalero come." Ted thought he detected a faint trace of hope in the final words.

In the first hours of the new day, Ted and Yellow Crow buried the dead Apache, despite the Cheyenne's mild objection, "Better that coyotes and wolves get full bellies from Mescalero; not deserve grave." Only after the Apache was buried did Yellow Crow finally wash away the war paint from his face and torso.

By the time they had finished the task, the efficient Wilma already had a small bag packed and tied securely behind the Mexican-made, high-horned saddle she rode. Her split riding skirt was tucked into the tops of cavalry-style boots. Watching as she checked the bridle to make sure the bit rode properly in the mouth of the rangy, dun-colored mare, Ted smiled. He was proud of his talented wife, for she was now as comfortable on horseback in the wilderness as she once had been in the opulent sitting room where he had first met her.

"The ladies back East would be shocked at you, Mrs. Henderson, riding astride like a man instead of sidesaddle."

"The ladies back East don't face having to make a wild run over rocky ground with a band of Indians after them," she said matter-of-factly. "And besides that, the idiot who invented the sidesaddle obviously hated women. He probably designed the corset, too—anything to make a woman uncomfortable."

Ted nodded toward the double-barreled shotgun tucked into the oversized saddle boot he had made for her. "Check the loads?"

"Yes, sir, Captain. Buckshot. Ugly, but highly effective if need be. Now you get yourself ready while I go shutter and bolt the windows. It won't keep an Indian or a dedicated thief out, but it will keep trespassers at bay until Yellow Crow gets back." She went into the house, and he could hear the muffled sound of bars sliding home behind the shutters.

Yellow Crow appeared beside him, and they quickly mounted their horses, the burn-etched deerhide firmly tucked inside Ted's belt. After a last-minute check of their weapons, the trio moved out at a nod from the Cheyenne. Ted was painfully aware that the woman and the horses would be prime catches for some ambitious brave—if the Indian should happen to get lucky.

In the narrow pass five miles out, a flash of movement registered in the corner of Ted's eye. His handgun was half out of the holster and at full cock before he recognized the darting jackrabbit for what it was. Feeling a bit foolish, he holstered the pistol and then grinned. Yellow Crow's war ax was raised, and Wilma's hand was on the butt of the big shotgun. They exchanged glances. Wilma's laugh and the glint in the Cheyenne's eye broke the tension for the moment.

At the midpoint of their journey, Yellow Crow, who was riding a few yards ahead, raised a hand as he pulled his horse to a stop on a ridge. Ted kneed his stallion forward.

Several hundred yards away, a band of Indians rode a trail roughly parallel to their own. Ted squinted slightly in the bright, midmorning sun.

"Arapaho?" he asked, studying the barely visible tips of what seemed to be a forest of spearpoints rising above the distant horsemen.

Yellow Crow grunted his agreement. "Not hunting party. Too many braves find no deer. Arapaho in bunch like skunk in lodge. Not good."

They watched in silence as the procession of Indians suddenly swung northward. "They seem to know where they're going," Ted said.

"I follow?"

"No, Yellow Crow. Let's get this message to Colonel Robinson first. I know of no white settlers in that direction who might be in immediate danger. I'm sure the colonel will want to send out a patrol, or maybe a few of the scouts, and at least we can tell him where to look."

Colonel Bill Robinson probed among the clutter of the scarred and aging desk, searching for his ever-elusive pen. The calluses on his hands and fingers from years of handling reins and weapons marked him as a working soldier more comfortable afield than in his office. "Easier to keep a bronco Ute buck in sight than to keep up with that infernal writing instrument," he grumbled to himself.

He looked up as familiar footsteps sounded on the narrow walk outside his door. "Come in, Captain," he called. "You know I never lock the darn thing."

He got to his feet, a broad smile creasing his weathered face, as Ted and Wilma came in, followed closely by Yellow Crow. But Ted noticed the quick flash of concern in the colonel's eyes. Robinson bowed over Wilma's outstretched hand, then impulsively leaned forward and gave her a quick peck on the cheek.

"You're just as lovely as ever, Mrs. Henderson," he said. "I'm delighted to see that this husband of yours is not overworking you. I'd hate to have to punish a full captain by sending him out to clean the stalls."

Wilma laughed heartily, as though she would not be surprised to see the leather-tough colonel doing exactly what he said.

"Vi! Come on out here! We have a visitor!" At the colonel's call, a door connecting the commander's office to his living quarters swung open, and Vi Robinson swept into the room. She said hello to Ted and Yellow Crow, and her greeting to Wilma was the solid embrace of longtime friends.

Wilma stepped back. "Marriage agrees with you, Vi," she said. "You're looking very well."

"I feel wonderful," Vi said, and took Wilma's arm. "Come—let's fetch these men some coffee, and we'll go shopping and catch up on the post gossip while they get into soldier's talk. It appears to me this may not be a completely social visit."

Ted watched the two women leave the room, chattering like a couple of schoolgirls, and realized that his admiration for Vi Robinson and her courage had grown stronger. When her first husband drank himself down, Vi had to run the Pony Express station alone. Loyal to the end, she stood by her previous husband and sincerely grieved when he was killed in cold blood by the Confederate agent attempting to use him to keep the Indians stirred up along the Pony Express route. *Bill Robinson is a lucky man*, Ted thought, *almost as lucky as I am*.

"Vi's right, Ted," Robinson. "I don't think this is a social visit, particularly since you left this office only a few days ago." He waved toward a straight-backed bench, comfortably worn and horsehair-padded. Vi and Wilma returned with steaming mugs of coffee, then retired to catch up on the news from both ranch and fort.

Yellow Crow sipped the coffee, admitting to himself that some of the white man's ways were good. Cheyenne herb tea might be needed at times to settle one's stormy insides, but its bitterness remained long after the ailment was forgotten, and its taste was no match for the flavor of the black water in the heavy cup. He listened as Ted briefed the colonel on their sighting of the mounted band of Arapaho.

Robinson turned to the Cheyenne. "Anything you can add, Yellow Crow? Did you recognize the leader?"

The Cheyenne shook his head. "Riders too far off, tracks not cross. To guess no better than try hit flying quail with tomahawk."

The colonel strode to the door, his slightly rolling gait that of a man more accustomed to riding on the back of a horse than to walking across the rough-hewn pine floorboards of an office. Briskly, he issued instructions for a party of four of Henderson's Scouts to be dispatched to trail the Indian band. Ted nodded in approval. Four men could accomplish more than a full platoon, especially if the four were crack frontiersmen and veteran Indian fighters from his own company.

Robinson came back inside, shaking his head. "Every day it seems we have more and more trouble with the Arapaho and the Ute, even though their leaders have agreed to live in peace," he said. "Within the past week, we've had four ranches raided, one settler killed, and a dozen horses stolen." The officer sighed. "In a way, I can't blame the Indians. They were here first, and now they're taking advantage of the fact that the size of my force is being depleted as entire companies are being called back East to fight in this blasted civil war. But that's beside the point, Ted. You must have had good reason to ride back here so soon after your last scouting assignment."

Ted handed the soft deerskin scroll to Robinson without speaking. The colonel shoved aside some papers on his desk and unrolled the scroll. He studied it for a long moment before looking up.

"What do you make of this, Ted?"

"I don't know for sure, sir. But it was taken from the body of a Mescalero Apache—alone—as he was trying to steal one of my horses." Wasting no words, he related the circumstances that led to the killing of the Indian.

Robinson's heavy eyebrows almost met as he frowned at

the deerskin. "Mescalero Apache don't have that much use for symbol writing," the colonel said, as much to himself as to the other two men in the room. "Almost unheard of for a single Indian, particularly a Mescalero, to make such a long trip north when the buffalo aren't moving."

"One more thing, sir," Ted said. "From the contents of his medicine pouch, it appears that the Apache knew he was embarking on a dangerous trip, one from which he might not return."

The colonel turned away, paced three or four strides, then retraced his steps to study the document again. "It would appear to be some kind of code," Robinson finally said. "But I've never known Indians—Cherokee, Choctaw, and the others belonging to the Five Civilized Tribes—to use a written code." Abruptly, he strode to the door and issued a quiet command to the corporal on duty nearby. "Perhaps we'll learn in a few moments whether it's just idle doodling or whether it might be more significant than that." Robinson again turned his attention to the deerskin.

At a knock on the door, he called out, "Come in," then returned the salute of a young, slender lieutenant wearing the crossed cannon pin, which marked him as an artillery officer. Ted sensed an intensity and a considerable intellect in the new officer's eyes.

"Captain Ted Henderson, Yellow Crow, I'd like you to meet Lieutenant Chad Clark," Robinson said. The artillery-man's grip showed a surprising strength in the slender fingers as Ted and Clark exchanged handshakes. Ted was pleased to see Clark also extend his hand to Yellow Crow. "It's a pleasure to meet you gentlemen," Clark said. "I've heard a great many complimentary things about both of you."

"Lieutenant Clark has been with me about three months, gentlemen, and I'd like you to know you'll never meet a finer gunner in this man's army," Robinson said.

Ted caught the faint touch of red on the lieutenant's face and admitted he was impressed; Wild Bill Robinson was not one to offer an unearned compliment. "Coffee, Chad?"

"No thank you, sir. The corporal said you had something to show me?"

Robinson motioned toward the scroll on the desk. "Take a look at that, please, and let me know what you think."

The lieutenant produced a pair of reading glasses from his pocket, slipped them on, and stared intently at the deerskin.

Robinson turned to Ted and Yellow Crow. "Lieutenant Clark is something of a specialist in subjects other than where to point a howitzer. He's a graduate of William and Mary College, where he studied languages, ancient cultures, and mathematics. When the war broke out, he joined the Union forces, and it was a good thing for us that he did."

Clark, oblivious to the conversation, shook his head as he studied the scroll. "I can't make any sense of it, sir, but it appears to be a deliberate form of gibberish." He removed his glasses and wiped the lenses with his neckerchief. "Perhaps if I knew something about its source?"

Robinson nodded to Ted, who sensed a growing excitement in the lieutenant's blue eyes as he recounted the story behind the acquisition of the scroll.

Clark turned to the colonel. "Sir, it is my initial impression that what we have here is a coded document," he said. "May I have it for a while to study? And with your permission, sir, I'd like access to your library in addition to my own."

"Certainly, son. We don't know if that scroll is meaningless or important. It's in your hands now. Find out whatever you can. Anything you need to help you in this project is yours. And you are excused from gunnery duty and practice"—a wry smile formed on the colonel's lips—"which we would have if we had enough ammunition to waste on targets that don't shoot back."

"Thank you, sir. I'll do my best."

"That, Lieutenant, is all I ask of any man," Colonel Robinson said kindly.

Scroll tucked under an arm, Clark said his good-byes and left the room, his stride light and quick.

Robinson watched the door close behind the lieutenant. "If any man in the West can make sense of that thing, aside from the man who wrote it, Chad Clark will. Only problem with that young man is that he keeps apologizing for being right. Well, gentlemen, if there's nothing else you need from me, I'll let you get on about your business." A heavy hand thumped down on a sheaf of papers. Robinson sighed and Ted thought he heard a touch of disgust in the sound. "It's been said that an army travels on its stomach," Robinson said, "but the command part of it travels on paper. If I could spend as much time in the field as I do writing these endless reports, I might get something done."

Ted and Yellow Crow turned toward the door but were

stopped by the sound of the colonel's voice. "Ted, do me one more favor. Try to find that woman of mine and send her back home before she spends next month's pay!" Ted grinned. Vi Robinson was one of the most frugal women he had ever met, and her husband would be the first to admit it. "Incidentally," the colonel continued, "Abel is back from patrol, and I'm sure he and Judy would be delighted to share dinner with you two and Wilma.

Ted Henderson pushed back his plate, thoroughly stuffed, and waved off the offer of more deep-dish apple pie. It took some effort because such treats were rare in the frontier country. "Judy," he said, smiling at the young woman across the table, "you have become a superb cook."

"Why, thank you, sir," she said, obviously delighted with the compliment. "Such flattery will keep a place set for you in this humble house at all times. Besides, I have some good teachers—Wilma and Vi can nurse more variety and flavor out of simple foods than any two women I've ever met."

Ted studied the young woman at some length. Judy, the daughter of Colonel Robinson, seemed to have bloomed even more since marrying Abel Hubbard. Ted had served as best man at their wedding, and Wilma, once treated as a pariah in Fort Laramie because she owned a bawdy house, had stood as honor attendant. Judy had never looked lovelier than she did tonight, Ted decided. She was radiant in a daringly low-cut gown. Yet he still could not put down a vague feeling of unease about the marriage of the colonel's daughter and his good friend, even though the glances they frequently exchanged with each other left no doubt they were still wildly in love. Even so, Judy was impetuous and headstrong, spoiled by her widowed father, who had indulged her every whim, and she was not hesitant to take advantage of the privileges accorded the offspring of a cavalry colonel and post commander. She seemed to have accepted Vi Robinson as her stepmother, though on previous visits Ted had sensed an undercurrent of jealousy flowing from Judy toward the woman who now shared her father's life.

Declining Judy's offer of a glass of wine and accepting a final cup of coffee instead, Ted glanced at his friend and saddlemate. He and Abel Hubbard had shared long and hazardous rides in their Pony Express days, which had strengthened the bond between them. Over the rim of Abel's cup, his face reflected tension and strain, and the normally squared shoulders drooped slightly. Perhaps, Ted thought, it was only the fatigue of the long scouting assignment and patrol from which Abel had just returned.

Judy drained the last of the wine from her long-stemmed glass, and said, "I wish Yellow Crow had joined us."

Ted waved a casual hand. "Yellow Crow's tastes in food are simpler than ours. He intended no snub, I promise you, because he's fond of you both. And there's the possibility," Ted added with a grin, "that Yellow Crow just might have a friend in town as charming as you two ladies." He did not add that the Indian had already headed back to the ranch.

Judy's cheeks colored slightly, but Wilma's laugh was full of affectionate enjoyment. She put a hand on Judy's forearm. "Don't forget, dear Judy, that Indians are men, too." Wilma abruptly stood. "Let's get the dishes cleaned up while the men trade stories of the good old days before their lives became cluttered up with women. And there's no sense wasting good lamp oil while there is still enough light in the kitchen for domestic chores."

"Come along, Ted," Abel said. "It seems a good policy never to get in the way of a woman at work. Otherwise, you're sure to get recruited to help out, and the dishwater keeps my calluses so soft I have to wear my campaign gloves even during the summer heat."

Ted had to smile. At least his friend had not lost his sense of humor, he thought, following Abel into the adjoining room. Originally it had been an ample storehouse but had been converted to living area by a judicious cleaning, installation of oil lamps, and placement of a few pieces of furniture. Abel sank into a heavily upholstered chair, his dusty cavalry boots outstretched. Ted picked a less opulent but equally comfortable chair.

Refusing Abel's offer of a cigar, Ted listened to the muted voices of the women and the rattle of plates. It should have been a comfortable setting, but feeling of tension nibbled at the edge of his mind.

"How did the scouting mission go, Abel?"

Hubbard shifted in his chair. "Troublesome," he replied grimly. "We saw the signs of several bands of Indians roaming about, but never caught up with any. We arrived at one sheepherder's dugout just about two days late to help. It wasn't a pretty sight, Ted." He sighed. "It's like chasing ghosts. They're out there somewhere, but they have the advantage. They know where they are, and we don't—until they want us to know."

Abel fished in his pocket and tossed a metallic object to Ted. The shiny cartridge case sat heavily in Ted's palm. He raised an eyebrow in Abel's direction.

"I found that just a few feet from the shepherd's front door," Abel said. "The business end of the cartridge had taken off a big chunk of the old man's head. It's a fifty-six caliber. A Spencer. I'm wondering where an Indian could come up with a weapon that powerful, and even more accurate than our best Springfields. It certainly didn't belong to the shepherd. All he had was an old musket."

Ted turned the cartridge over in his fingers, examining it with care. "Cartridge brass—especially for a Spencer—is pretty hard to come by out here."

Abel nodded. "Which indicates—and this thought scares me plenty—that someone's been supplying the Indians with expensive rifles and ammunition."

"And," Ted added, "I would suspect the weapon was new to the Indian. Otherwise, he would just have driven a lance or an arrow into the shepherd. That's a frightening thought, Abel. If a quantity of weapons like this gets into the hands of the Indians, we've got a bear by the tail and no way to let go."

The two men sat in silence for a moment, each with his own disturbing thoughts. "Any indication where it might have come from?" Ted finally asked.

"No," Abel replied. "Could have been traders. A few scoundrels around here do provide weapons to the Indians, along with whiskey, blankets, and the like. But a rifle like that would cost more than any Indian, even a chief, could pay. What's more, I doubt that any traders in the area even have a Spencer. No, I don't know how the Indian got the rifle, and I'll be honest, Ted—it has me concerned."

"Colonel Robinson said there had been an increase in the number of Indian raids lately. But he didn't mention anything about them being equipped with arms of this type."

Abel stretched his lanky form in the chair, releasing tension from leg muscles not long out of the saddle. "It doesn't surprise me that the colonel didn't mention it," he said. "That's the first one that's turned up in Indian hands, and the colonel has enough worries as it is."

Ted detected a note of wariness in Abel's tone of voice. "Are the Indian raids that troublesome?"

"It's more than that," Abel replied. "The war has been difficult for both sides. The strain on men and supplies has been great. Colonel Robinson's force here has been badly depleted as regular army troops are called back East. He's always fighting to get powder and lead for the cannon, ammunition for the troops, medical supplies—you name it, he needs it. Everything except more troubles."

Ted shook his head, partly in disgust and partly in sadness. "The politicians and some of the generals always think they'll win a quick victory. Both of us know there is no such thing as a short war, particularly when each side has competent leaders and good fighting men. After all, there is almost as much West Point talent wearing gray as wearing blue. I've been somewhat isolated, I admit. Is the Union effort going that badly?"

"We've had some setbacks, and so have the Confederates," Abel said. "So far neither side has managed to gain a great deal of ground, even though the battles have been as intense and as bloody as any military campaign in history."

Abel snuffed the remnants of his cigar into a corn-grinding stone that had been moved from Indian campground to ashtray duty. "In fact," he said, "it would not surprise me if I and my men were transferred east to join the fight against the Confederates."

The sudden sound of breaking glass brought both men to their feet, alert and startled. Judy Hubbard stood in the doorway, eyes wide, the back of her hand against her mouth, shards of the dropped wineglass at her feet. Abel started toward her. "I'm sorry, honey—I didn't mean for you to learn of it this way. But it is a fact we will have to face."

Judy drew back from his touch, her pale skin flushing as the initial shock gave way to growing anger. "No!" she said. "Absolutely not! I will forbid Daddy to send you away, and I will forbid you to go!" Then her voice softened slightly, and she flew into Abel's arms. "We've been married such a short time, darling. I—I can't—bear the thought of your being away from me." Tears welled in her large eyes, smearing the faint green makeup she used to emphasize them and staining the upper portion of a cheekbone. "Daddy wouldn't do that to us, Abel, He just couldn't."

Abel held her at arm's length, his hands firm but gentle on

her shoulders. "Be realistic, Judy," he pleaded. "You know how much I love you, and how much I miss you even when I'm gone only for a few days on patrol. But remember that I am a soldier. I must follow orders."

As quickly as it had vanished, her temper flared again. Slipping free of his grasp, she turned away to face the far wall.

"Abel Hubbard, there are dozens of officers available. *Unmarried* ones. Daddy can send them, but not you! I won't permit it!"

Abel grabbed his wife's arm and spun her about. Anger tinged his own cheecks. "Judy, you're being childish! How much respect do you think my men would have for me if I were excused from active duty just because I'm married to the daughter of the commanding officer? They wouldn't even follow me to the mess tent, much less into the field. And Colonel Robinson cannot afford to have a favoritism charge on his conscience or on his record."

"Then resign your commission! Don't be a soldier anymore! Then nobody could tell you where to go or what to do!"

Abel shook his head. "Next to you, Judy, the army is my life," he said, his voice tight. "It's my career. You knew that when we married. Darling, please—don't make me choose between the army and my self-respect or my wife!"

"You just don't understand," Judy whined. "All I have to do is talk to Daddy—"

Abel interrupted her in midsentence, his voice sharp. "You are the one who doesn't understand! I forbid you to speak with the colonel on my behalf!"

Abruptly, Judy jerked her arm out of his grip and raised her palm as if to strike his face. Then she slowly lowered her hand, but fire still flashed in her eyes.

"Abel Hubbard, nobody forbids me from doing anything! I'm not some private in your precious army! And I'll not have you riding off in your shiny blue uniform and leaving me behind! Your first duty is to me!" She spun on a heel and started toward the door, then stopped. Over her shoulder, she said, "And what's more, if you do get sent away, I'll follow you. Wherever you go, I will be close behind!"

"Judy, I—" The slam of the door cut Abel off in midsentence. Exasperated, he turned to Ted.

"I'm sorry for my wife's inexcusable behavior, Ted," he said. "I don't understand what came over her. My being sent east is still speculation."

"Don't apologize for her, Abel," Ted replied, his voice soft. "She's just upset at the idea of a possible separation." Ted hoped he sounded more convincing than he felt. "Perhaps what seemed to you to be a temper tantrum was just Judy's way of telling you how much she loves you. Besides, if she's like most women, she will go to Wilma and Vi with her worries. I'm sure they will talk her out of doing anything rash. And as you say, it's a question which may never arise."

Abel slumped into a chair, despair obvious in his features. "I love her, Ted—"

"I know that. And Judy loves you."

"—but I will not resign my commission. I could never live with myself, leaving my command and my country in time of crisis." Abel sighed heavily. "I just hope that Wilma and Vi are able to put some sense into her head."

"I'm sure they will. I don't think you need to worry about it. Judy may have a volatile temper, but I don't think she would deliberately harm you or your career." But even as he tried to reassure his friend, Ted's own brain was spinning. If the war clouds were gathering out west, he knew one captain of scouts who might get rained on.

II

The distant rumble of thunder above the far peaks rolled through the valley, a fading memory of the brief shower that had swept the dust particles from the air earlier in the afternoon. The sky seemed to sparkle over the Henderson ranch, the surrounding mountains standing in sharp, clear relief.

Ted paced the floor, pausing occasionally before the open window to breathe deeply of the crisp, clean air, which carried the scent of approaching winter. To Ted, it seemed as though a hand stretched from the window could almost lift a clump of fresh snow from the mountains, even though the towering peaks were a day of hard riding distant.

Yellow Crow sat cross-legged before the hearth, carefully whetting his war knife with a fine-grained stone. The cutting edge of the weapon had given way before the stone so many times that its shape showed a distinct taper from hilt to stiletto-like point.

Watching the Cheyenne work slowly and methodically, Ted thought that any surgeon on the post could use Yellow Crow's knife much more efficiently than one of the crude scalpels issued by the army. Yellow Crow crushed the edge of the knife across his leather half-leggings, further polishing the keen blade, and glanced up at Ted.

"Thunder-rain when leaves all fall not good sign," he said. "Sky gods angry. Soon send snow, cold wind. Long time white before trees green again."

Wilma, busy at the kitchen cabinet putting away the last of the freshly washed dishes from the noon meal, said over her shoulder, "I think you're right, Yellow Crow. We had such a

21

mild winter last year and such a long autumn season so far, that when it comes, we may see snow up to the roof."

Their conversation barely registered with Ted. He had scarcely tasted the midday meal despite Wilma's talent in the kitchen.

"Ted Henderson," Wilma said, drying the final cup, "you have been pacing that floor all day. I know you well enough to recognize when something's on your mind. How about sharing your troubles with a couple of friends?"

Ted stopped in midstride. Leave it to Wilma, he thought, to get straight to the heart of a matter.

"What we heard at the fort has me quite concerned," he said. "There is little doubt in my mind that Colonel Robinson is hard-pressed for supplies and men, and it may be only a matter of time until his situation becomes critical. Fort Bridger is the only protection offered settlers for hundreds of square miles—from Fort Laramie all the way to Fort Critten-den, near Salt Lake City. If someone is, in fact, supplying the Arapaho and other nearby tribes with modern weapons and ammunition, the whole region could explode at any time."

"Arapaho and Ute happy," Yellow Crow said. "More soldiers go to join fight between white man and white man, fewer left to chase Indian."

Wilma stripped off her apron, stepped to where Ted stood in the center of the room, and placed a hand on his forearm. Her touch was warm and reassuring. "So," she said, "how about some conclusions?"

Ted braced himself for what he had to say. The problem was not about to go away of its own free will.

"Darling," he said, " Colonel Robinson has no choice, as I see it, but to recall all available men to active duty."

"Meaning you as well," Wilma said. "I am not exactly a blank slate on military matters, dear. After all, I have had some excellent teachers in you, the colonel, and Yellow Crow."

"I have been thinking of—"

"—returning to Fort Bridger." Wilma finished the sentence for him. "And you're going to assume full-time command of Henderson's Scouts once more." Her tone was matter-of-fact. "You are a soldier, Ted, and a good one, even if my opinion is based on personal prejudice. A man must do what he must and what he does best."

"Yellow Crow will be needed as well, should he decide to go," Ted said. "As a commissioned officer, even one on reserve status, I have no choice. If I did, I wouldn't take it. I owe a great deal to Colonel Robinson and to my country as well." He turned toward the Cheyenne, now dressing the string of a short but powerful bow with beeswax. "My brother is not bound to the United States Army; he is free to do as he chooses."

"Yellow Crow go if needed."

"That means we probably will have to close the ranch," Wilma said, her eyes softening as she looked about the room.

Ted sighed, relieved that she had brought up the subject that he so very much wanted to avoid. "Yes. I will not leave you here alone, Wilma, since I cannot promise that my scouts or anyone else will be available to protect you."

"I may be a woman, Ted, but I am a realist." Wilma gave his arm a solid squeeze. "I can't run this place alone. Besides, I have grown very accustomed to combing my own hair. I have no desire to leave this ranch, but I have less desire of being scalped."

"It will be a painful move for both of us."

"With the joys come the pains, Captain Henderson. Remember, Colonel Robinson placed you on reserve status in order to give you time to build a home. Well, we have built it. I know for a fact there were many times when he desperately needed your help. Yet he left you here. And it has been a good time for us, dear. Not only have we had each other, but our crops are good, the mares are in foal, and our yearlings are ready to go market anyway. I understand cattle are bringing excellent prices these days, what with the army and the civilians all clamoring for beef."

Ted enfolded his wife in his arms and held her tenderly for a long moment. "You are a most remarkable woman, Wilma Henderson. I know the thought of leaving this place hurts you as much as it does me."

Her voice barely a whisper at his ear, she said, "It will still be here when this unpleasantness is over." She drew back and waved a hand about the room. "This house is made of native stone, and it will be standing even for our grandchildren, should we have some. It will even withstand the torch, should someone try to burn it. What furnishings we can't take with us are not important, and I shan't miss them in the least.

"We've made money, Ted. I haven't told you, because I know that finances are far down your list of priorities. But we've not only recouped our investment; we have also reached the point at which we might be considered wealthy—at least by frontier standards." The feminine shoulders squared. "I'll remind you, sir, that I am a competent businesswoman. Even though I used to deal in a different commodity, meat on the hoof is still meat on the hoof, and supply and demand do not change."

Her lips touched his as she pulled away. "With the money we have, I see no earthly reason why we can't come back one day and rebuild this place. Even better than it is now. The land will still be here."

"Wilma speaks truth," Yellow Crow said, checking the tension on the bowstring. "People come, people go. But land always beneath feet—"

The Cheyenne suddenly flung his body to one side; at the same instant Ted heard the *whir* of the feathered shaft, the solid *thunk* as the arrow imbedded itself in the floor within inches of where Yellow Crow had been sitting. Then sound piled atop sound. The crash of shattering glass was muffled by the heavy boom of a large-caliber rifle and the piercing yells from outside. Ted silently cursed himself for his lack of vigilance as he roughly pushed Wilma against the protection of a stone wall and scooped up his rifle. He glanced out the window, instinctively ducked as an arrow ripped by his ear, then quickly shot. Over the blast of his own rifle, he heard a startled yelp. He had missed, but apparently not by much.

A movement in the corner of his vision almost stopped his heart. Wilma had left the safety of the wall and was running to the sink, ignoring the impact of a heavy slug against the cupboard as she grabbed the shotgun from its rack. Horrified, Ted saw an arrow tug at the hem of her skirt. She seemed to move in slow motion as she swung open the ammunition cabinet, scooped up rifle cartridges, jammed the spare revolver under an arm, and grabbed a powder flask and heavy sack of shot. Then Wilma crouched and tossed the box of rifle cartridges to Ted, before dashing back to the wall beside a far window. She stood there for a moment, her breasts heaving as she gulped in air.

"Yellow Crow! How many?" Ted asked.

"Two hands—" Part of the Cheyenne's sentence was drowned by the roar of the big rifle and the splintering of wood as a shutter exploded inward and dangled from its hinges. "—foot."

Ted whipped off a round through the window and saw a

form crumple to the earth. "They're going to charge!" he yelled.

The Indians seemed to rise from the ground, as a half-dozen or so made a headlong charge toward the ranch house. But at his right, Ted heard the deadly cough of Wilma's shotgun and saw one of the braves lifted from his feet and slammed backward into the dirt. A second brave went down, an arrow shot by Yellow Crow in his belly, and a carefully aimed shot from Ted's rifle sent a third brave spinning. As quickly as it began, the charge ended.

The smoke-filled room was acrid with the scent of black powder. Coughing, Ted watched Wilma quickly reload the spent barrel of the shotgun and bring both hammers back to full cock. Her face was the color of ashes, but she seemed calm and collected.

The sudden silence left Ted aware of the ringing in his ears. He watched as Yellow Crow darted from window to window, then crawled across the floor to take a position alongside Ted.

"What do you think?" Ted asked.

Yellow Crow's eyes had narrowed to slits. "Arapaho. They lose four men already. Not expect to have hard fight. They talk, maybe come again." A strong red hand waved toward the barn. "Only one in back. By post at corner of fence. You take him down, Yellow Crow sneak out, go surprise Arapaho." Ted nodded, reloading his rifle. Ducking low so their movements could not be seen through the windows, Ted and Yellow Crow worked their way to the back door, then edged it open an inch or two. After a few seconds, Ted spotted his target. The Indian was partly hidden behind the solid, thick corner post at the corral. "When I go out door," Yellow Crow said, his voice hoarse against Ted's ear, "you take head off warrior. Yellow Crow take over from there."

Ted nodded grimly, hoping his accuracy equaled what was expected of him by the Cheyenne. Then the door swung open, and the warrior at the corral looked around the post to see what the noise was. Ted's slug took him at the bridge of the nose. Ted shifted the rifle to his left hand, pulled his revolver, and waited. Nothing moved during the few seconds it took Yellow Crow to vanish into the tall grass beyond the barn. Ted closed and bolted the back door, the heavy cough of Wilma's shotgun covering the slam of the bar into its niche. He called over his shoulder. "Wilma! Are you all right?"

"Yes! But I missed the last shot! Just dusted his backside!"

Again keeping low, Ted worked his way back to the front of the house. A heavy ball ripped through the oak of the front door and thumped into the back wall. Ted quickly assessed their situation; though outnumbered, he and Wilma could hold the attackers at bay from inside the house—at least long enough for Yellow Crow to begin doing his damage. There was at least one powerful big-bore rifle out there, he knew. The report of the Spencer was distinctive—and spelled danger. One of those big slugs could do an enormous amount of damage.

As the thought crossed his mind, the Spencer fired again. Wilma suddenly flattened her body against the wall, and the half-shutter on the window shattered.

She looked across the room at Ted, a question in her eyes. At his nod, she shoved the shotgun barrel through the window, blasted away, then dropped to the floor and grabbed for the pistol nearby. Ted sent a round toward a clump of rocks where he had detected a bit of movement. "Wilma," he called, "don't take any chances! But let's see if we can keep their attention on us until Yellow Crow gets back into the fight!"

Her reply was to send three fast shots toward the rocks. Ted laid a couple more behind them, then stopped to reload as Wilma, firing more slowly now, finished emptying her handgun. When he resumed firing, she paused to reload—first the shotgun, then the pistol. Cocking the weapons, she grinned in his direction. "Maybe we're not drawing any blood," she yelled, "but we're making enough noise!"

Another slug from the big rifle outside drilled a thumb-sized hole in the doorframe, slammed into the stone of the fireplace, and ricocheted with a buzz past Ted's ear to imbed itself in the chink between two stones. Inwardly, he shuddered. That blasting Spencer, given enough time and ammunition, could eventually connect.

Yellow Crow, his breathing still even despite the long, circling run, saw the puff of smoke from the ridge ahead. A hundred yards beyond the rocks, several braves huddled as stone chips flew about their ears. By the time the sound of the big rifle reached the spot where the Cheyenne had been, Yellow Crow was already on his way up the slope. As he drew near the dead tree he had used as a marker, his approach became one of stealth, the hunter on the prowl. He slipped off his moccasins, trusting his bare feet to avoid making the telltale snap of twig or rustle of leaf. He studied the low scrub along the side of the ridge with care, then spotted what he sought. A small sapling, angled more slightly than the others, did not shake quite as much as its brothers did in the freshening breeze.

Notching an arrow against the taut string of the powerful wooden bow made of Osage orange, Yellow Crow slipped around the edge of a boulder. Barely twenty strides away, an Indian dressed in white man's clothing took aim down the barrel of a long rifle. In one smooth motion, Yellow Crow drew the bow to its fullest reach and released. The blurred flight of the broad-head arrow ended in a solid *whump*, and the Arapaho staggered, dropping the rifle. The brave stared for a half-second at the Cheyenne arrow driven deep into his chest. Then, with a strangled sound, the rifleman fell out of the tree to the ground.

Yellow Crow sprinted to the side of the downed Indian. He immediately sheathed his knife; the arrow had done its work well. At the base of the sapling stood an open rawhide case, half-filled with the biggest rifle shells the Cheyenne had ever seen. Yellow Crow picked up the heavy weapon and examined it briefly. No stranger to the white man's guns, it took only a few seconds until he understood how the weapon worked. He flipped open the breech. Satisfied that there was a live round in the chamber, he snapped the trapdoor back into place, cocked the big hammer, and sighted on the backside of one of the Indians in the rocks below. Yellow Crow squeezed the trigger and grunted in surprise at the heavy recoil of the weapon. Through the billowing smoke from the muzzle, he could tell his shot had gone wide.

He worked the action and ejected the spent cartridge, sliding another home. He snugged the weapon into his shoulder and found himself looking down the sights at a startled Indian who had turned in surprise and shock toward Yellow Crow's position beside the young tree. The heavy slug tumbled the warrior over the rocks.

The remaining Indians, caught in the murderous crossfire from the house below and the unexpected assault from above, broke and ran. A few moments later, Yellow Crow heard the clatter of hoofbeats rapidly fading.

In the house, Ted breathed a sigh of relief but immediately began coughing from the heavy pall of gun smoke hanging in the room. He crossed quickly to Wilma's window, plucked the shotgun from her grasp, and took her in his arms, waiting for the emotional storm to break. He felt her body shudder and the wet stain of her tears against his shirt. Holding her tight, he watched Yellow Crow casually cross the open ground to the house, his bow slung across his broad back, a big Spencer rifle in the crook of his elbow.

By the time the Cheyenne had stepped into the room, Wilma was beginning to regain her composure.

"You two safe?" Yellow Crow asked.

Ted nodded. Wilma, trying to speak, managed only a hiccup. Yellow Crow nodded in her direction. "First time Wilma kill?"

She nodded.

"You not like. But better than your scalp on Arapaho lodge pole."

"You did some pretty heavy damage out there yourself," Ted said.

The Indian hefted the Spencer. "Big gun make big hole. I can keep gun?"

"You earned it, my brother," Ted said.

Yellow Crow patted the side of the .56 caliber, then nodded toward the window. "They not come back," he said. "Arapaho women wail tonight. Six warriors who leave camp not ride home. No more trouble today."

Ted nodded, his eyes drawn to the Spencer. "Did you pick up any of the fired cartridges?" From the ammunition box, Yellow Crow plucked an empty case and tossed it to Ted who stared hard at its base, the sinking sensation in his stomach confirming what his eyes recorded. The firing pin had left a clean, sharp indentation on the rim of the cartridge. The one Abel Hubbard had found bore a crescent-shaped impression, obviously made by a different firing pin. This was not the same weapon Abel had reported. And the dead brave on the hill outside the ranch had been firing away as though ammunition was the least of his worries. Two Spencer rifles in Indian hands accounted for, Ted thought, and who knows how many more?

Ted became conscious of Wilma's weight resting against his side a bit more heavily than normal. He steered her to a chair, noticing that her legs were still a bit wobbly. From a small cabinet he took a bottle of brandy, pulled the cork, and poured a small amount into a cup. "Nerve medicine," he said, handing a cup to his wife.

Wilma took the drink with trembling fingers, sipped at

the cup, and coughed. "I'll—I'll be all right now. I—just seem to have—a tendency to fall apart after a crisis is past."

"Fall apart all you wish," Ted said with a smile. "During the crisis, you were as calm and collected as a deacon at Sunday dinner."

"What do we do now, Ted?"

He did not have to ponder the question for long. "I think after what happened today, there's no question we should move out. Right away. We'll load what we can on the wagon, take the horses and as many cattle as we can gather quickly, and make a run for Fort Bridger. We're having too many visitors of the wrong kind." Wilma noticed his eyes soften as he glanced around the room. "As you said, we can always come back."

"We have to bury the Indians—"

"Not this time, Wilma," Ted said. "I'm not sure we can spare the few hours that would take. As soon as you're feeling strong enough, I'd like for you to start packing. I'm going outside to take a look around."

Ted searched each of the Indian bodies with care, giving particular attention to the brave from whom Yellow Crow had taken the rifle.

Not one clue could he find as to where the Arapaho brave might have obtained the Spencer. Each of the dead Indians carried new knives, still bearing the traces of the makers' grinding wheels. More disturbing yet, no two knives displayed the same maker's mark or brand name. There was no common thread. Ted knew that to put together a virtually untraceable collection of weapons required not only enormous sums of money but a vast network of suppliers as well. "Expensive," he muttered, "and clever."

He stripped a blood-stained shirt from the body of one brave and used it to wrap all the dead Indians' weapons. Should the band return to claim its fallen members, at least they would lose a few of the arms of war. He picked up the last of the new hand axes and methodically destroyed the bows and arrows the ill-fated band had carried. Then, shouldering the bundle of weapons, he turned to leave—and abruptly halted as sunlight flashed from metal half-buried beneath a body.

Ted knelt beside the still form and carefully removed the simple silver chain. Thinking it was probably part of the spoils of a raid on some unsuspecting farmhouse, he was about to tuck it into a pocket when the curious design engraved on the clasp caught his eye. Turning it in the light, he examined the tiny engraving with care. The design appeared at first glance to be the French fleur-de-lis. But closer inspection revealed that two outward leaves of the design actually were in contact with the upward-thrusting petal. Ted realized with a jolt that he was examining a stylized and miniature engraving of a cotton boll ready for the picking.

Wilma sat on the wagon bench, reins in hand, as Ted loaded one last trunk into the back of the wagon. This time he mounted a sorrel gelding, his stallion being used to trail the mares and keep them in line. He patted his shirt pocket to make sure the small chain remained firmly in place in its soft doeskin pouch, then turned to his wife.

"I'm sorry we couldn't take all your things, Wilma," he said. "I wish I could promise they will be here when we return, but with thieves of both red and white skins about, I have no way of making a guarantee."

She shrugged. "Things can be replaced. Oh, Ted, I almost forgot! Just a minute!"

He watched as she jumped from the wagon and dashed into the house. She emerged in a moment, huffing from the weight of the bronze Pony Express Rider statue and with the framed message from President Lincoln folded under one arm. She tucked the statue into a safe place at the rear of the wagon, draped a blanket over it, then wrapped the message carefully in a bundle of rags. "Wherever we go, Ted Henderson, this goes along. And don't argue about it."

Touched by her determination to save his mementos, while leaving some of her own prized possessions behind, he could only smile his thanks. "Just be sure you don't get ahead of us on the trail. The cattle will have to move slowly, and I don't want you exposed to any unnecessary danger," he said. "And keep your rifle handy, just in case."

She snapped a salute in his direction. "Yes, sir, Captain. Anything else?"

"Yes. One more thing." He kneed the sorrel in close, leaned over, and kissed her tenderly. "Now," he said, a slight hoarseness in his voice, "you may move out, soldier."

It seemed to the tired Ted that all of Fort Bridger turned out to watch the strange procession after the lookout guard sighted their arrival. He had been especially pleased to see his good friend from the Pony Express days, now Sergeant Major Frank Armbrister, and a half-dozen members of Henderson's Scouts, appear to escort them the last mile and a half. For the first time during the tension-filled and sleepless, if uneventful, trip, Ted was able to relax and let his hand drift away from the pistol at his hip. He let Armbrister take the point, then dropped back to his place beside the wagon and Wilma.

Even Colonel Robinson and Abel Hubbard were waiting, their salutes as crisp as that offered by the corporal standing guard at the gate of the stockade.

"It is obvious there has been trouble," Robinson said, "or you wouldn't be pulling in here with your whole camp in tow." He waved away Ted's explanation before the first word formed. "Let's get you settled and rested a bit, and you can fill me in on the details later in the day."

Yellow Crow led the stallion and mares to the cavalry stables, where they would be looked after for the duration of the Hendersons' stay. Yellow Crow himself would be quartered in the soldiers' barracks while he was at the fort.

Frank Armbrister rode up, his wiry frame solidly astride an enormous bay gelding. "I'll see your stock are bedded in, Ted," he said. "We have plenty of corral space for them." At the touch of a knee, the big bay moved out, head carried low to the ground, as Frank directed the cattle toward the corral. Robinson watched horse and man for a few moments, then shook his head.

"When they first brought that horse in here," the colonel said, "I would have bet that not a man in the United States Army could ever handle him. And that sergeant, who won't weigh a hundred and fifty sweated out, has him working like a Sunday church horse in a week's time."

Ted grinned at the colonel's obvious respect. "Don't ever be surprised at what Frank Armbrister can do with a horse, Colonel. Not only is he one of the finest horsemen who ever picked up a bridle, but he has a way with animals that must be seen to be believed."

"He made a believer out of me—along with that bay," Robinson replied. "Come along, Ted. You're in luck in one way. There's a cattle buyer at the post right now. If you plan to get rid of your herd, this is a good time to sell. This gentleman is absolutely reliable and pays top dollar. I don't suppose the horses are for sale?"

Wilma broke in. "No, Colonel Robinson. Those are some

of the finest mares in all of the West. I hate to see the cattle go, of course, but they can be replaced at the proper time. Unless I miss my guess and my business instinct has gone sour, horses are where the future really lies."

"Pity," Robinson muttered. "I rather fancied the dapple gray myself. Wilma, if you will turn the reins over to our Private Graves here, he will take you to your new home away from home. Vi will be along in a moment with a pot of tea, and I suspect she knows where a woman might find a hot tub."

As the wagon drove off, Wild Bill Robinson told Ted where he and Wilma would be residing while at the fort, and also where he could find the big Irishman who would buy his cattle. "And if you strike a deal, you're welcome to leave the proceeds from the sale in my safe. If I'm not there, Abel will be, and he knows the combination. Now if you will excuse me, I must return to my office to finish those infernal reports."

Ted smiled at the retreating colonel's back. Wild Bill Robinson might never make general's rank because of his dislike for political games and paperwork and parade-ground soldiering. But as a field commander, no one was better, Ted thought.

He set off for the farrier's shop located near the corral to meet with the cattle buyer. The two men shook hands and then the red-haired, burly Irishman studied the newly arrived cattle with care. The cash offer he made Ted was more than satisfactory, and Ted signed a bill of sale. A handshake wrapped up the transaction.

Walking back toward the colonel's office, Ted found himself thinking he might be out of the cattle business for the moment, but the roll of U.S. currency in his pocket provided its own reassurance . . . unless the Confederates won the war, and from what Ted had heard so far, he admitted to himself it was too close to call at the moment.

The lowering sun had impaled itself on one of the rough-cut logs of the fort stockade, casting strange patters of shadow across the compound. When Ted stepped into the colonel's office, he breathed a sigh of relief, happy with the prospect of soon being rid of the conspicuous bulge of the money in his pocket.

Colonel Robinson had already left the office, and Abel Hubbard rose from behind the colonel's battered desk. "Doesn't take you long to sell a herd of cattle," he said.

"When the price is right and the buyer doesn't waste time

on small talk, it doesn't take long at all." Ted pulled the roll of currency from his pocket as Abel turned his attention to opening the safe. He took the money, tucked it into a corner, and closed the strongbox. He went to the desk, picked up a pen, and started scribbling. "Your receipt," he said over his shoulder. "How much was there?"

Ted told him. "Don't you want to count it before you sign that receipt, Abel?"

The lieutenant completed the small document with a flourish of the pen and grinned at Ted.

"The day you lie to me about money," he said, "is the day I'll have that particular Ted Henderson shot as an imposter." The lieutenant's tone suddenly sobered. "I gather there was big trouble back at your ranch, Ted."

"Big enough, if I read the signs right." Briefly, Ted told Abel about the Arapaho raid, including Yellow Crow's capture of the Spencer rifle and his own discovery of the chain with the cotton-boll engraving.

After looking at the cartridge and the chain Ted handed him, Abel pursed his lips in a silent whistle. "Sounds like we need to have a war council. But first, I expect you would like to have a bath and a fair-sized chunk of beef."

"In this part of the country, I don't see a man turning down an opportunity at either. They can come pretty far apart at times."

"You know which quarters you have been assigned to?" At Ted's nod, Abel continued. "I don't expect Wilma will feel much like cooking, so have your bath, then join Judy and me for dinner." He glanced at a large clock on the wall. "I go off watch in two hours. I'll join the three of you then."

Ted stepped into the rapidly cooling air of early evening and took a deep breath. He could almost smell the snow that would be coming soon.

His boots raised small puffs of dust as he made his way across the compound toward the visitor's quarters he and Wilma had been assigned. He stopped in midstride, listening intently—the rustling sound of a boot in dry leaves seemed to linger in his ears. He felt the exhaustion drain from his body, and a tingling sensation worked its way from forearm to fingertip. Probably just a stray dog, he told himself, and he wondered if he was getting twitchy with advancing age. Even as these thoughts formed, however, he was putting his hand on the revolver holstered at his hip, ready to use the weapon if need be. When his sixth sense spoke, Ted always listened. It had saved his hide on more than one occasion.

He stepped onto the boardwalk, alert to the sounds and smells of the fort, but his muscles were deliberately relaxed and loose. He knew from experience a split second was wasted when a tensed muscle had to be relaxed and then recoiled. The shadows had deepened into heavy dusk; flickering and feeble light came from the few oil lamps and open windows along the row of shotgun-type barracks, so called because they were long and narrow and built in a straight line. Between buildings, the blackness was like velvet, concealing anything or anyone. He felt the tempo of his heart quicken inside his chest.

Even with his body and senses poised and fine-tuned, they almost got him.

The whistling sound of a club sent him lunging to one side. The club grazed the side of his neck, sent his hat spinning, and crashed into a shoulder even as Ted flung himself into a body roll that brought him to his feet. He knew by instinct that he would not have time to draw the heavy pistol. There were two big men almost upon him, one a burly giant brandishing a large club.

Ted waited a split second until the club began its descent toward his head, then he took a quick step forward and deflected the club by raising his left arm. He clamped the club and a thick wrist under his left armpit, and swung the heel of his right hand with all his force into the back of the extended elbow. The joint popped like a rifle shot, and the big man's mouth opened as if to scream in agony—but the sound never came as Ted slammed a knee into the club-wielder's groin. Jumping back to let the man fall, he spun on his heel and caught a heavy blow just above the cheekbone.

Stunned for a moment, Ted stepped back, shook his head to clear his vision, and regained his senses just in time to avoid the next hard punch from the other assailant. Ted lashed a wicked jab into the bearded face before him and followed up with a hard right to the midsection. The man's breath left with an audible *whoosh*, as he staggered backward.

The bearded man gasped in a lungful of air and charged, head down. Ted sidestepped the rush, ducked a wild right, and put his entire weight behind a solid blow to the ribs. The bearded one grunted but did not go down. He started to turn, but Ted continued to batter him with a right to the bridge of the nose, then a left and a right to the body. Still the big man would not go down. Ted blocked a wide-swinging blow, slammed a knee to the groin, and stepped back out of reach, his own breath ragged and harsh in his throat. For the first time since the assault began, he had a chance to reach for his handgun.

Then something crashed into the side of Ted's skull, and he felt himself slipping downward, sliding through a sea of brilliant colors. In the far distance, it seemed, he heard a shout, and then the lights around the compound winked out.

Ted struggled back toward consciousness, an elusive light at the end of a long tunnel beckoning him onward. For a moment he had the sensation of floating, as though borne on a cloud, only to have the comfortable illusion dashed in a wave of pain. From somewhere near, he heard a low moan; as reality slowly returned, he became aware the sound had been his.

Something cool touched his cheek. The light became brighter, a wavering, hazy form that finally took the shape of an oil lamp on a bedside table.

"Easy, Ted. Just rest." Wilma's voice broke through the barrier of confusion in his mind. He tried to raise a hand to her, but the arm was too heavy. The taste in his mouth was metallic, as though he held a copper coin beneath his tongue.

"Well," a gruff voice said from near his ear, "it appears that nothing is broken. But from a professional point of view, Captain Henderson, I'd say you picked up a few dents." The post surgeon's touch was as gentle as his voice was rough. "I'm a little concerned over that apparent head blow, Mrs. Henderson. It could cause some dangerous effects that may not be readily visible." Dr. Mason sighed. "You won't be able to, of course, but at least try to keep him in bed for a couple of days. I'll look in on him from time to time." With this, the doctor picked up his bag and left the room.

Ted licked his parched lips and tried to speak. "Wil—Wilma—"

"I'm here, dear. Do you feel as bad as you look?"

"Hope—I don't look—that bad."

The laugh from nearby told Ted that Colonel Robinson was there as well.

"I got—stupid, Bill," Ted said. "Forgot about the man with—club." He felt the strength begin to flow back into his sore limbs and again tried to raise a hand to Wilma. He managed to lift it a couple of inches, and then he felt her fingers slide beneath his.

"Your knuckles are a mess, Ted Henderson," she scolded in a tender tone. "I hope those two who jumped you feel like they've been run over by a runaway wagon."

"Tried my best," Ted said. "What happened? Thought they had put me down for keeps."

"Ruckus alerted a soldier, lucky for you," Robinson chimed in. "He yelled, and those two took off. We couldn't find them, or at least we haven't yet, but from what the private told me, one of them was dragging an arm and neither of them was walking—or running—straight up."

"Tell the private that an officer owes him a drink and a steak dinner."

"And," Wilma added, "the gratitude of a woman who is still a wife and not a widow. I'll cook the steak myself."

"Can you think of any reason why two saddle bums might want to tear you to pieces, Ted?"

Ted moved as though to sit up. It was not worth it, he decided; every muscle seemed to have a prickly pear inside. He felt a pair of soft hands lift his scraped forearm and smooth a bandage into place. Vi Robinson patted her handiwork, gently lowered the limb back onto the bed, and moved from Ted's field of vision.

"Maybe they saw Ted sell the cattle," he heard Vi say. "Men have been killed over a lot less money."

The touch of the damp rag in Wilma's hand was both cooling and comforting. "I doubt seriously that robbery was the reason," Wilma said. "They would have seen Ted go into the colonel's office, and it is common knowledge on the frontier that a commanding officer's den not only has a safe place for keeping valuables, but also is under armed guard at all times. If they were after the money, wouldn't they have tried to take it as soon as Ted had left the cattle buyer's sight?"

"For a worried wife, the lady makes a lot of sense, Ted." Colonel Robinson's tone was reflective. "I'm inclined to think it was something else. A personal grudge, maybe."

A scene from the past flashed through Wilma's mind: Ted and the sadistic Confederate agent slugging it out back in the Pony Express days. "Could it have been a friend or relative of Beau Sampson? Blood feuds are not uncommon, Ted."

Ted shook his head. "Sampson and his men are—were— the types who settle any quarrels with rifles from the safety of a rocky hill. Besides, Sampson was a loner and a crazy man. Even the Confederates who backed his spying operations were horrified when they learned of all the wanton death and destruction he had caused."

Ted paused for a moment, gathering his strength after such an extended speech. "I have no shortage of enemies," he said at length. "But most of them could be called honorable enemies. At least they would not hire a couple of thugs to do a job they would enjoy doing themselves."

The colonel sighed. "Well, son, you spend your energies for the next few hours healing up as much as possible. We'll chew on this particular buffalo hump tomorrow."

"There is a broth on the stove, Wilma," Vi said. "Ted, if you want something more substantial, I can—"

"No thanks, Vi," he interrupted. "Broth will be just fine. I'm not really hungry, and even if I were, I'd have trouble chewing. But I would like to sit up, if someone would give me a boost."

The deceptively strong hands of the two women were quickly beneath his shoulders. The shock of sitting up left Ted's ears ringing and his head spinning, but he leaned against the tall oak headboard and closed his eyes until the sensations began to fade.

"If there is nothing more we can do at the moment, Wilma," the colonel said, "Vi and I will leave you to tend your wounded." Ted heard footsteps moving toward the door, and the sound of a door closing.

Wilma went to the stove, and within moments she was back at Ted's side, a bowl of broth in hand. She shushed his protests and fed him, a spoonful at a time, until finally he waved the bowl away. She replaced the utensils and returned, her weight settling onto the side of the bed.

"I must admit, Ted, that I'm worried. First the Indian attack, and now this. We live with constant danger out here, I know. But if someone has decided to make you a personal target . . ." Her voice trailed away.

Ted squeezed her hand gently and winced at the pain in his knuckles. "What worries me more, dear, is that it could have been just a random incident. Two drifters looking for an easy dollar or just taking out some mean whiskey on the first person who came by. I'm glad it was me out for an evening stroll and not you. You must be especially careful these days.

Move about only in daytime, and keep the door bolted when you are alone."

Touched by his concern for her despite his own aches, Wilma stroked his cheek, her fingers lightly tracing the bruises. Her lips brushed against his.

"I am supposed to keep you in bed for two days," she said. "Do I have any chance of carrying out that assignment?"

He smiled at her, aware that the swelling in his jaw twisted his grin a bit. "If I were a healthy man, honey, you would have no problem at all with that project. But in my current condition, it is doubtful."

Wilma sighed. "In that case, I might as well unpack my nightgown. I really hadn't planned on wearing it tonight. . . ."

Colonel Bill Robinson, concern reflected in the eyes beneath beetled brows, strolled into Ted's quarters in the midmorning light. "How are you feeling this morning, Captain?"

"Compared to eight hours ago, not bad," Ted answered. "Something afoot?"

The colonel nodded somberly. "This morning the telegraph lines between here and Fort Laramie were cut. Again. And just after dawn," Robinson continued, "a patrol found the body of a dispatch rider headed this way from Laramie. His horse and dispatch pouch were missing. The patrol lost the trail of the killers. The soldier had been shot by a powerful, large-caliber weapon—the type you and Abel have been stumbling over of late."

"Spencer fifty-six?"

"Could have been, according to the corporal in charge of the patrol. He was still a little pale in the gills when he described it to me. Dr. Mason is examining the body now. As soon as you are feeling up to it, I would like to bring Abel over here for a planning session."

Ted waved a hand. "Let's meet in your office," he said. "I need to move around anyway, work off some of the soreness."

"The surgeon said you should stay in bed for a couple of days, Ted. I wish you'd follow his advice."

Ted contemplated the dull throb in his temple for a moment. "I'm not going to try to be any hero, Colonel," he said, "but I'm not going to lie around when there's work to be done. Besides, I've always healed faster when I had something to keep my mind off my hurts. Give me twenty minutes?"

Ted quickly crossed the compound to the colonel's office, forcing his sore muscles to move a bit faster than his usual energy-saving pace, and by the time he had reached the narrow boardwalk in front of the commanding officer's door, he could already feel the joints and muscles beginning to loosen.

As he stepped onto the boardwalk, he heard the colonel's familiar call, "Come in, Ted," and wondered if it really was true that Robinson could identify all of his men just by the sound of the bootsteps. Reaching for the doorknob, he decided it was not surprising. Robinson's concern for his soldiers' welfare had built a loyalty among the troops that few men of his rank could claim. But the colonel paid the price, Ted thought; many times he had seen the pain in Robinson's eyes when one of his soldiers went down.

Robinson waved him to a chair alongside one occupied by Abel Hubbard. The colonel was fingering two brass rifle cartridges, obviously the one found by Abel plus the Spencer casing Ted had turned over to Hubbard the previous night. The chain with the etched cotton boll was on Robinson's desk.

"Gentlemen," Robinson said, tossing the cartridge cases and chain casually onto a stack of papers on his desk, "I think we might as well come straight to the matter. We have all suspected, I believe, that Confederate agents or their sympathizers have been stirring up trouble among some of the more restless members of the Indian tribes in this area. I think we can safely stop using the word 'suspected' now."

The colonel shoved back his own rawhide chair and stood before a map tacked to the office wall. Ted and Abel watched as Robinson studied the region around Fort Bridger. He stabbed a finger at first one spot, then another.

Turning to the two officers, Robinson said, "Each of these locations has been the site of trouble in the last few weeks. As you can see, each place is a considerable distance from the fort, but we have had reports from other areas, too. And within the last few days, the attacks have moved noticeably closer to the post. At first, the raids were minor skirmishes, a few horses stolen, a few sheep, maybe a steer or two. I would steal myself, if game were scarce and my family were hungry. So we had resigned ourselves to the fact that those few head of lost livestock were simply part of the price of doing business on the frontier."

The officer began to pace back and forth as he spoke, and from time to time, he glanced at the map on the wall.

"But," he said, "the raids have become increasingly violent. Some incidents, such as the murder of the harmless old shepherd, appear to be wanton acts of senseless violence. But the cutting of the telegraph lines and the murder of the dispatch rider are nothing less than acts of war, perpetrated by Confederates in the area. What's more, I'm inclined to believe that the attack on Ted's ranch and the attempt on his life were also instigated by the Confederates, in the hope of doing away with the one man who has caused them considerable trouble in the past—and can do so again in the future.

"These Confederate plots have to stop, gentlemen. I want no more blood spilled, red or white, and I don't want the captain of my scouts killed. We will have peace, and we will have justice. Ted, I want you to handpick a half-dozen of your scouts, each to lead a patrol in a different direction."

"Yes, sir."

"Caution them that the patrols are not to fire at the Indians until fired upon. But if they are attacked, they are to strike back hard and fast. No women or children are to be captured, injured, or killed. I want those patrols to be visible to every tribe in this territory. This isn't to be a scouting expedition but a show of force and intent. I want bluecoats to be seen at every corner of the compass, so that the Indians will know they can no longer take guns from the Confederates and strike out against us."

"Yes, sir. My scouts and I will work out the routes to be taken. They can gather their supplies and move out in a short time."

"Abel."

"Sir?"

"With the possible exception of Ted here, you speak the Indian dialects of this area as well as any white man. And you understand Indian customs. I want you and no more than five soldiers to visit every major camp to remind the chiefs that after we defeated them at Hidden Valley, they agreed not to take up arms against the army or the settlers. Tell them that you speak for me, that we have kept our part of the bargain, but they have not. Warn them that if they cannot control their young braves and their outlaws, the army will."

It's been a long time, Ted thought to himself, *since the colonel's voice has had such a hard edge.*

"Tell them I will hold each tribal leader personally responsible for the future conduct of his warriors, that punishment will fall heavily on the heads of those who raid and pillage." The colonel paused for a moment, eyes glittering. "Finally, tell them that any brave found with a new large-caliber rifle will be brought to justice on sight by my men. Each chief is to consider the medicine of whoever is supplying these rifles, and to consider the medicine of Wild Bill Robinson and Henderson's Scouts. Impress upon them that while we will be fair, we *will* have peace."

"Yes, sir."

"Pick your five men with care. I don't want some hotheaded recruit or Indian hater to do anything rash. You will be traveling greater distances than any of the patrols, so you have your choice of the best horses and pack animals."

Abel merely nodded. Ted could tell from the expression on the lieutenant's face that he was already planning his line of march.

The colonel turned back to Ted. "I want the person who shot that dispatch rider, and I want him badly," Robinson said through clenched teeth. "If anyone on this post can pick up the trail of that killer, it is Yellow Crow. I will place twenty men at his disposal. This is not a patrol or a warning party—this is to be a punitive expedition."

"Colonel Robinson," Ted said, "with your permission, I will accompany Yellow Crow. We make an excellent team."

For a long moment, Robinson did not speak, and Ted knew when not to push the colonel.

"You are supposed to be recuperating from a blow to the head, Captain Henderson. I could very well order you confined to quarters."

"Yes, sir. That is your right as commanding officer. And if, in your judgment, there is any question that I might be a handicap to the party, it is your duty as well as your right. But fresh air and some hard tracking won't do me more harm than sitting around brooding."

"Wilma would nail my hide to the wall."

"Colonel, Wilma is a soldier's wife. She knows the frontier. And she also is aware that, given the number of soldiers we have and the square miles that must be protected, we must act right away."

Robinson's glare softened. "Very well," he said, "but if you run into any physical problems at all, young man, get yourself back here—in the company of an armed escort—immediately. Don't try to be a hero." The colonel sighed. "I was afraid you might volunteer. I had hoped to lead that expedition myself. But you are a better tracker than I, and you and Yellow Crow have worked together for so long that each of you usually knows what the other is thinking."

The sun had traveled barely a quarter of its arc across the bright autumn sky when Ted and Yellow Crow set the pace at the head of the two-abreast, ten-deep column of grim-faced, veteran cavalrymen. The path from livery area to the stockade gate led past the row of barracks and officers' quarters. The few married men in the company, having already said their private good-byes, followed Ted's lead and touched their hat brims in silent salute to their wives standing near doorways.

Wrapped in a heavy shawl against the lingering chill of the morning, Wilma nodded and smiled at Ted's salute. Vi Robinson, standing at her side, half raised a hand in a farewell to Ted.

"It never gets easy, does it, Vi?" Wilma's voice was soft against the sounds of the rustling uniforms, the snorting and stamping of eager horses, and the creaking of leather as the column passed.

"No, it doesn't," the colonel's wife replied. "But each time a soldier's woman watches him ride away, knowing there is a chance he might not return, the pain of the moment is less than the pride. A soldier's job is dangerous, dirty, mostly boring, and the majority of them could make more money playing poker on a Saturday night than they make in a month on horseback. They are a special breed, Wilma. And I think we should count ourselves lucky to have them."

Wilma nodded gravely, watching the figure at the head of the column move in easy motion with the horse beneath him.

"Yes," she said, "and no woman has ever experienced a more intense homecoming than the wife or lover of a soldier. . . ."

But when Ted's company returned at sundown of the third day after they had ridden smartly from the fort, Wilma—alerted by the sentry's call—could easily detect the slight droop of tired shoulders beneath heavy greatcoats. Here and there along the line, a horse stumbled; even the pack mules were showing signs of strain and fatigue.

The seemingly tireless Yellow Crow had slumped a bit in

the saddle, and Wilma needed nothing more to tell her what these men had been through in the last three days. Yet she felt her heart beat faster and the corners of her mouth lift in a relieved, welcoming smile at the sight of her husband returning home safely and apparently uninjured. She checked the impulse to run to him; as an officer's wife, she had to follow military protocol as well. Ted's first duty was to his men, so she contented herself with watching and waiting as he dismissed the soldiers, expressing his personal thanks for their efforts and instructing them to turn their mounts over to the livery detail for care, then get a hot meal and an early bed.

"Those of you who need extra rest or wish to remain in bed a bit longer tomorrow are excused from reveille," she heard him say, his strong voice carrying well above the howl of the cold wind. "And each of you will stand down from guard duty or extra detail for the remainder of the week. Gentlemen, you have earned a rest."

Only when the last of the pack animals had been led away for care did Ted strip the rifle from its saddle boot and turn the reins of his own mount over to a young private. Then he crossed the compound to where Wilma stood. He touched the brim of his hat, and as he approached, she could see the redness in his eyes, the two narrow furrows that formed between his eyebrows when things had not gone well.

She waited until the door closed behind them before melting into his arms. After several minutes he stepped back, holding her shoulders, and she saw the tension and exhaustion slowly drain from his face.

"Woman," he said, "I don't know how you do it. Ten minutes ago I felt ninety years old. Now I'm nineteen again."

She laughed softly. "I'll not flatter myself, Ted Henderson," she said. "It's obviously the aroma of the pot roast I've prepared for your dinner that has perked you up."

He kissed her lightly. "How in the world did you know?"

"You claim to have a sixth sense about danger, dear. Women can have those intuitions as well. I just felt in my bones that you would be coming home today."

He shook his head, a look of disbelief on his stubbled face. "Are you sure, my love, that you don't have some Indian blood in your background? I've known some Kiowa and Comanche women whose medicine was strong enough to read the future."

"Sorry to disappoint you, sir. Strictly Dutch, with a

seasoning of Irish and a dash of English that my immediate family violently denied. Poor Grandmother was always under suspicion about that."

Ted reluctantly reached for his hat. "The one thing I want to do is stay here with you," he said. "But first I have to report to Colonel Robinson that his famed tracker blew the assignment."

She touched his arm gently. "When will you learn that even you are not infallible? I'll wait until you have made your report." She did not try to suppress her soft giggle. "Besides, the anticipation will only sweeten the event. I'll have some water heated for your bath when you return—and for the colonel's sake, forget the hangdog look. You're not going to the woodshed, you know."

He sighed. "You're right, of course. But we didn't catch the killer of the dispatch rider, and I hate to disappoint the colonel." A hint of a smile touched his lips. "Not many centuries ago, the bearer of bad news was summarily killed. At least we've come this far toward civilization. . . ." He clamped his hat on his head. A puff of cold air entered the room as he slipped through the door.

Ted made his way across the compound to the colonel's office, buttoning his tunic against the bite of the wind. He reached the door at almost the same instant as Yellow Crow, and at the colonel's call, the two stepped into the welcome warmth of the small office.

Colonel Robinson rose from behind the scarred desk, waved off Ted's salute, and pointed the two scouts toward the more comfortable chairs.

"No luck, Ted?"

"No, sir. We lost the trail. But we did learn something."

The colonel turned to the fireplace where a steaming coffeepot perched, poured two cups, and handed them to Ted and Yellow Crow. "Get some of this in you, then tell me about it," he said.

Ted sipped at the strong brew, letting its warmth flow into his tired body.

"Yellow Crow struck sign about a mile from where the corporal told us he had lost the trail," Ted said. "It cut through Devil's Gate, turned north toward the Bighorns, then suddenly cut east. We lost the trail as it headed toward the Black Hills."

The colonel whistled softly. "That's a lot of miles to cover in only three days."

"We had to push, Colonel, because the trail was cold and the wind was kicking up. Finally it became strong enough to obliterate the signs to the point where neither Yellow Crow nor myself could get back on the hunt."

Robinson sighed, but Ted could detect no sense of disapproval in the sound. "Any casualties?"

"Lost one mule, sir. The men are exhausted but otherwise healthy."

"Good. Now, you said you had learned something?"

"Trail was made by white man." Yellow Crow's voice was matter-of-fact. "Just one man. But he good; hide trail better than Indian."

The colonel's eyebrows arched. "How do you know it was a white man? I assumed it would be an Indian attack that killed the dispatch rider."

"Try make it look that way," the Cheyenne said. "Wear Ute moccasins. But not act like Ute."

"Yellow Crow is right, Colonel," Ted said. "I'd stake my reputation on that conclusion. The courier was killed from long range. We found the spot the ambusher fired from; it was five hundred paces from the trail. Also, the rifleman had worked spots in the sand for his toes, hips, and elbows. Indians aren't that sophisticated about techniques for firing long range with a powerful rifle. And while the feet were clad in Ute moccasins, the size of the print tells us that it was made by a tall, heavy man, much larger than the tallest Ute I have ever seen. In addition, we found the discarded pouch on the north side of Devil's Gate. An Indian would discard the papers, but keep the pouch because it has use. We found no papers; only a white man would keep written documents, at least in the opinion of Yellow Crow and myself."

Ted lifted his coffee cup, aware that the length of his report thus far had allowed it to cool somewhat.

"Whoever this man is, Colonel," Ted finally added, "he's good. He is obviously a fine marksman and a frontiersman as well, and if I were to hazard a guess, I would say he's had military training, if not actual experience."

The colonel stopped his pacing to stand before Ted. "Do you think he could be the man who has been supplying the Indians with rifles and inciting the attacks?"

Ted's shoulders lifted, then dropped. "I have no proof

either way at the moment, Colonel. But if I were a gambling man, that's a bet I would have to make. We might have had the answer now, if I had caught him—"

Robinson interrupted. "Captain Henderson, I'll have no more talk of any failure on your part. It would be almost impossible to track a herd of buffalo through the Black Hills, let alone an accomplished frontiersman, such as you describe. Now both of you go and get some rest. We will eventually apprehend the agent. Our patrols should be returning over the next few days. Maybe one of them will have some information on this Confederate bastard."

III

One by one, the patrols trickled back into Fort Bridger. Some returned through the heavy frosts that sparkled the dried grass, others in the crackling air of dusk. And with each arrival, the patrol leader went immediately to Colonel Wild Bill Robinson to file his report.

Abel Hubbard and his five men were the last to arrive; almost three weeks had passed since they had ridden from the fort. Greeting his friend at the stockade gate, Ted immediately noticed the lines of strain and fatigue in the face of the former Pony-Express rider.

Abel dismissed his men with a salute, an expression of thanks, and a handshake for each, then started toward Robinson's office. Ted fell into step with him, as he had done with the other patrol leaders, and was almost knocked over by the exuberant Judy as she hurled herself into her husband's arms. Ted excused himself and, leaving the two to their reunion on the parade ground, went to Robinson's command post.

"Abel will be here to report in a moment, Colonel," Ted said. "He sort of got himself bushwhacked on the way."

Robinson shook his head, trying to appear solemn. But the twinkle in his eye gave his true feelings away. "That girl will never learn military decorum," he muttered. "Oh, well—I was young once myself. I realize that after a few years of living together they'll get over it."

"I sincerely hope not, sir."

"Judy has her mother's zest for life, I suppose," Robinson said, "and she's just as possessive of her man as her mother was." The colonel sighed. "Meaning no disrespect to her memory, but I must admit I am more comfortable with Vi."

Abel entered, took the offered cup of coffee, and sank heavily into a chair opposite his father-in-law's littered desk.

"I don't know how much we have accomplished, Colonel," he said, "but the next few weeks should give us an answer."

Abel ticked off the names of the tribes and the chiefs he and his patrol had visited, leaving even Ted impressed with the distance the half-dozen men had covered.

"Every chief had basically the same story—it must be some braves from another tribe causing the trouble, for they themselves wished only to live by the terms of the agreement made with the chief of the horse soldiers. Obviously, some of them were lying. The Arapaho and Ute chiefs, in particular, were a bit too eager with their protests." Hubbard sighed, lifted the coffee cup again, and sipped. "Next time I'm going to pick at least one good cook, whether or not he knows a Springfield from a tomahawk. That's the first good cup of coffee I've had since we left.

"At any rate," he continued, "I think our message got through. I expect some young bucks have taken a tongue-lashing since we started our circle. And of course, not one chief claimed to know where the new rifles were coming from. They even denied ever having seen one, and most insisted no traders of any kind had been near their camps for months."

The colonel merely nodded, unperturbed. "I expected as much," he said. "But it sounds as if you accomplished your mission well, Abel."

The colonel summarized the results of Ted's expedition. "Did you by any chance run across the trail of someone who might be up to mischief and traveling alone?"

Abel shook his head. "No, sir. Of course we were making no effort to conceal ourselves, so it is unlikely our paths would have crossed if this man is as good a frontiersman as you indicate. We did come upon the tracks of one heavily laden wagon crossing a small creek leading into Blue Lake, miles from any major road. But the tracks were at least a month old." He heaved himself to his feet, crossed to the map tacked to the wall, and pointed to a spot on an obscure creek. "Just about here, if memory and map reading still serve me."

"That is within a half-day ride of where three incidents were reported several weeks ago," Robinson said. "I think we should make a note of that point. And I wonder how many other isolated creeks might have similar tracks. . . . Anyway, Abel, you and your men have earned a rest. Take yourself and your escort from the active duty roster for a few days, then go to your quarters. I think there's a lady waiting who just may have a special welcome home for you." The colonel winked at Ted as the color flared in Hubbard's cheeks.

"Yes, sir. I will file my written report tomorrow, if that is satisfactory."

Robinson waved a hand. "Don't worry about it, Abel. One officer in the family with writer's cramp should satisfy the United States Army. I'll summarize all the patrol reports, including yours. Provided, of course, I can chase that blasted pen from its hiding place one more time."

"Colonel," Ted said, "I make it a policy never to volunteer anyone for duty. But if you think it would be of help, I will speak to Wilma about fixing up the reports for you. She can write almost as rapidly as I can talk, and she has a fine hand."

Robinson grinned. "Thanks for the thought, Ted. But I have literate noncoms and privates whenever I need a clerk. Besides, she has a man to look after. And if my reports get too literate and readable, I might be transferred to a desk job somewhere, spending the rest of my days swimming upstream against a sea of paper. When I reach the age of retirement from this man's army, I want it to come on a day when I'm in the saddle on patrol, not nursing a callus on my middle finger. Now begone, both of you, before I yell for the corporal of the guard to throw you out."

After they left, the two officers paused outside the colonel's office, Abel Hubbard sniffing the air like a wolf on the scent.

"Ted, I don't know if these patrols and all this talk will accomplish any lasting peace or not," Abel said. "But if it keeps the raids in check for a couple of weeks, I think we can look for some extra help. I haven't been in these mountains as long as you, but I don't remember a single December with less bad weather than this. The low passes in the mountains are less than knee-deep in snow. But I have a feeling that when it finally breaks, we're going to find ourselves in one of the wildest blizzards to hit this country in years."

Ted scratched his chin in thought. "I agree, Abel. I've seen this pattern twice before. We've had only two or three inches of snow at a time, followed by warm air waves, so the ground cover melts away within a few hours. Like you, I sense a tension building in the air over those mountains. That blizzard is putting itself together somewhere out there. I can't say I wouldn't welcome it, in a sense. Although it's tough on men and horses, at least it keeps the Indians inside with a warm fire, a blanket, and a squaw. Which, come to think of it, is a more civilized way of spending the winter than a white man has." He sighed. "It doesn't look as if we'll have a white Christmas, but I'm not so sure of the first two months of 1862."

Inside Fort Bridger's protective walls, Christmas Day was a spartan one as far as gift-giving was concerned. It was not a lack of generosity or even a shortage of money. But with necessities becoming more and more scarce as supplies were diverted from the frontier to the beleaguered Union army in the East, luxuries and gift items were almost nonexistent.

The few children did not suffer, a tribute to the ingenuity of parents long skilled in the use of hands, leather, scraps of cloth, and wood. Carefully hoarded treats were broken out, and the table was spread for the enlisted men's holiday dinner—helped along by Colonel Robinson's contribution of a barrel of dried apples for a cobbler and Ted's timely downing of a tender young elk—helped ease the loneliness of men without families and away from home.

In early afternoon, Ted's forecast was proven partially wrong as a light snow powdered the area of the fort.

Ted's comfort came from the pressure of Wilma's side against his own as they made their way, arm in arm, across the compound after the short but emotional Christmas service delivered by the post chaplain to an overflow crowd.

Inside, a fire crackled beyond the hearth, the flames posting counterpoints of light against the faint illumination filtering through the two windows, curtains drawn aside to allow into the room such light as was available from the gray skies outside.

Their embrace was long and gentle, and finally Ted held Wilma at arm's length, realizing the tears in the corners of her eyes were signs of happiness. "Woman," he said, "today I am going to break a long-standing rule. In that cabinet along the wall are several bottles of fine German wine. If you will join me, I'll raise a single glass—in a toast to you."

Wilma curtsied. "If you will make that a toast to us, Captain Henderson, I should be delighted to join you."

Within moments, she had produced two tulip-shaped, long-stemmed glasses as he, with some difficulty, wrestled the cork from a bottle. He filled the two glasses, then winked at her.

"Miss," he said, "you may find it necessary to strain the liquid between your teeth, as your bartender just broke the cork while trying to open the bottle. And those Germans cork a bottle in a manner which will assure a sober man of staying in that condition."

Her melodic laugh seemed to brighten the entire room. Ted raised his glass.

"To a beautiful, strong, sensible woman, a delightful companion, and a friend to a rough-edged, stubborn, and very lucky man," he said.

"No," she replied, "that doesn't quite fit." She raised her glass, "To two people very much in love—"

The shattering of glass, Wilma's sudden cry of shock and pain, and a tug at Ted's sleeve followed the blast of a large-caliber pistol, the sound rolling into the room through the wrecked window. Stunned, Ted stood rooted to the spot, watching as Wilma took a slow step backward and slid to the floor, her white blouse suddenly sprouting a small, red, rose-shaped stain. Shards of glass from the broken window tinkled to the floor, jarring Ted to action.

"Wilma!" Suddenly he was in motion, flinging his own body across hers, muscles tensed for the shock of a second bullet that never came. His ears rang from the blast of the revolver fired from just outside the window. Desperately he held her to his chest, afraid to look, his heart locked in a frozen chunk of ragged winter ice. At his wife's low moan, Ted summoned all the courage he could muster and, with trembling fingers, peeled the stained red fabric away.

The knot in his stomach tightened, even as relief flooded his brain. The slug had taken a chunk from the outside muscle of Wilma's upper arm; a few inches to the right and it would have been a fatal wound. At the same time, Ted realized that had the slug actually gone to the right, it would also have hit him in the back. He whipped the clean kerchief from his breast pocket and pressed it against the wound. At the sound of footsteps outside he tensed. The familiar voice of Abel Hubbard penetrated his stunned mind.

"Ted! What hapened?"

"Get the surgeon! Wilma's been shot!"

* * *

Ted stood at the side of the bed as the post surgeon finished dressing Wilma's shoulder. She was conscious but pale. "No severe damage, Mrs. Henderson," Dr. Mason said, "and you seem to have recovered from the shock. The bullet missed any bones or major arteries. I'm sorry if the stitches caused you any pain, but we wouldn't want such an attractive arm to bear a nasty scar." The surgeon laid a hand on Wilma's shoulder. "You, Mrs. Henderson, are the best patient I have had in years of patching up bullet holes in this man's army."

The surgeon stood, poured a quantity of liquid onto a clean rag, and wiped the small needle carefully before returning it to his black leather bag. He turned to Ted.

"Captain, I think you may be in worse shape than your wife—and understandably so. She will be fine, rest assured, and all we must watch for is fever and the possibility of infection, neither of which is likely." Over his shoulder he added, "Begging your pardon, Mrs. Henderson, but you seem to have the constitution of a Missouri mule. If the pain gets to be too much, take a spoonful of the medicine from the bottle on the nightstand. Not too much, though. Laudanum, like bullets, is one of those commodities in which a little goes a long way. Your arm and shoulder are going to be mighty sore for a while. I'll stop by a couple of times a day to check on you and change the bandages. And if you should need me for anything, I'll not be far away."

"I'll be with her, Dr. Mason, if she needs anything," Vi Robinson said, lowering the lamp she had held to give the surgeon light to perform his work.

"Non—nonsense," Wilma said. "Vi, it's Christmas night. Go spend it with your husband."

"And have him boot my backside for leaving a friend? No thanks, dear. Besides, there are certain things only a woman should help another woman with."

Vi turned to Ted. "Captain Henderson, I think you need a stiff drink."

Ted shook his head. "No. That's the one thing I don't need at the moment. That bullet was intended for me, Vi. I just wish it had found its mark instead of hitting Wilma."

"Pooh! Compared to having a baby, this is only a scratch. Now get out of here, Captain, and do something useful while I help Wilma change into something more appropriate for bed rest. Shoo!"

"Ted!" Yellow Crow's call from outside the bedroom was soft yet urgent. With a final squeeze of Wilma's uninjured arm, Ted made his way into the larger room. He noticed immediately that a stiff rawhide strip had already been nailed over the shattered window; the smell of gunpowder still lingered in the room. Yellow Crow and Abel Hubbard stood by the door, brushing the snow from their greatcoats.

"We go around and over fort twice," Yellow Crow said. "Man who shoot Wilma still near. Tracks in snow outside window head toward gate."

Abel nodded his agreement. "Yellow Crow and I made a wide sweep around the fort but struck no trail. In the snow, we would have found the track of a field mouse. It is my guess he managed to get outside the walls of the fort, and at this moment is probably in a saloon or holed up in some safe place in one of the buildings around the fort. If you would like, I'll summon the troopers. The word has spread, and every one of those soldiers would like to get his hands on the man who shot Mrs. Henderson. We can sweep through the entire settlement, house by house."

Ted shook his head, the sickness and shock in his stomach giving way to a growing rage. "No," he said, surprised at the level sound of his own voice despite the emotional storm raging within his body. "This man is mine. I will find him myself, and when I do—" Ted peeled off his uniform and began putting on the buckskins he preferred when on the hunt. The uniform of a soldier would be conspicuous in the small town that had grown up around the fort, and even though most people in the area knew him by sight, he had rarely been out of his blue uniform. He checked his revolver and dropped it into the holster at his side.

"Ted, when you find this man, keep your senses," Abel admonished. "Remember, he is more important to us alive than dead. He can tell us whom he's working for and where we can find him."

Ted stared at the lieutenant for a long moment. "Abel," he finally said, "if that were Judy in there instead of Wilma, how would you feel about it?"

"I'd kill him on the spot."

Ted slipped through the door into the deepening night.

Yellow Crow stood for a moment, listening. "Wilma safe now?"

Abel nodded. "I have so many guards around this place

the Confederate army couldn't break through. And I'll be inside with a finger on a trigger."

"Yellow Crow follow Ted. Maybe help." The Cheyenne was through the door before Abel could agree.

Ted's eyes ached from the tobacco smoke and fatigue. The smell of unwashed bodies, stale whiskey, and unemptied spittoons assaulted his nostrils, and his temples throbbed with pent-up fury and frustration.

For what seemed like half the night, he had followed the same routine. He would enter a gin mill or a bawdyhouse or a late-night store, order a shot of rye, then spend a long time making circles on the bar without raising the glass as he listened and watched. And so far, nothing. Now, he realized, he was running out of places to go. Gantry's was the last of the saloons along the strip of establishments that seemed to sprout near every military post to separate the soldiers from their infrequent pay.

A loud, boisterous laugh from a table in a far corner caught his attention, then a cry:

"Hey, barkeep! More whiskey!"

The bartender, a barrel-chested bear of a man, reached under the counter and came up with a brand of whiskey Ted realized was pure skull-buster. The bartender walked to the table, returned, tossed a coin on the counter, and reached into the cash box to make change. The coin drew Ted's immediate attention. He caught the bartender's eye and motioned toward the coin. "May I take a look?"

The barkeep nodded. "Sure. Just don't forget where you found it."

Ted turned the coin in his fingers. A twenty-dollar gold piece was a scarce thing on the frontier, especially one that bore a curious mint mark he could not immediately identify. But it was so new it bore no scratches, and most currency in the West was either Union scrip or gold and silver, either nuggets or dust.

He handed the coin back to the bartender. "Can't say I've ever seen one like it," he said, his tone conversational.

The barkeep shrugged. "Me neither. But it's real gold, and that jasper in the corner seems to have plenty of 'em. He's already been through two of 'em since he came into town. Chances are he'll never make it through another one, way he's been beltin' it down."

Ted had an idea. It might be grasping at straws, but it was worth a try.

"Send another bottle to the table," he told the bartender, peeling off a couple of Union banknotes, "and make it the good stuff. Tell the loud one it's from an old acquaintance who will join him in a few minutes."

"Seems a shame to waste good stuff on a drunk," the barkeep said with a shrug, "but it's your money." He counted out Ted's change, plucked a bottle from a back shelf, and set off toward the corner table.

Ted waited for five long minutes, letting curiosity and more liquor work on the man in the corner. "You know my friend over there? The one with the big thirst and the gold pieces?"

The bartender shook his head. "Rode into town a couple days ago. But I hear talk he's somethin' else with a pistol. Local toughs walk a wide path around 'im." The bartender leaned on his elbows, eyes locked onto Ted's. "Thought you said you was an old friend," he said in a menacing tone. "You ain't plannin' to knock him in the head for his money, are you? I don't go for that kinda stuff around here. Gives the place a bad name."

Ted forced a grin. "No. Just wondering if anyone else here knew him."

Ted casually picked up his drink and, faking an unsteady weave, made his way to the loudmouth's table. He clapped his glass onto the coarse pine, making sure to give it just enough of a tilt to slosh out part of the amber liquid.

"Well, by thunder!" Ted pretended to have trouble focusing his eyes on the square, unshaven face before him. "Who'd ever thought we—we'd cross tracks again, you ol' skin—skinner."

Small, deep-set eyes above a flattened nose wavered beneath the weight of drink as the man stared back at Ted. "San Antone, warn't it?" Ted deliberately slurred the words. "Naw—mebbe Austin."

Frown lines deepened across the scarred forehead as the seated man appeared to be trying to place the face. Ted waved a hand as if to dismiss the notion, and plopped heavily into a chair at the man's left. "Don't make no diff'rence where 'twas, I reckon." He forced a short laugh, then clapped the man on the shoulder. Dust flew at the impact. "Anyhow, you sure done went and snuck one in on me. Them was some mighty fine hosses, and you done haul off an' beat me to 'em." He left a twisted grin on his face, chuckling softly at the memory of the made-up incident.

The man mumbled something; to Ted it sounded like "Lee-Bowe" with a question mark at the end.

"Hisself. An' jist to prove ain't no hard feelin's, I done ordered us up a bottle. It get here yet?"

A finger pointed unsteadily at one of three bottles on the table. Ted made a show of pouring much of the whiskey down the side of the glass, then lifted it. "To ol' times," he said, and tossed down the contents in a single swallow. He refilled the man's half-empty glass, letting the neck of the bottle clatter on the rim of the drinking utensil. "You drink up, y'hear?"

The square-faced one gulped down half the contents without coming up for air, then belched.

"Lee-Bowe," he said, grinning at Ted. "Heard they'd kilt you somewheres up to Shy-Anne."

"S'funny. I heard you got hung."

A grin twisted the square face. "Ain't nobody gonna hang ol' Boog Winnett. Whatcha been doin', Lee-Bowe?"

Ted wondered to himself who this Lee-Bowe character really was. He shrugged. "Jist driftin', pickin' up a job here'n there. Thought I had me one lined up here't Bridger." Ted felt his stomach knot from the tension and the single shot of whiskey. He lowered his voice to a near-whisper, a conspiratorial tone. "Fact is, somebody already done it. Feller wanted some army cap'n name Henderson done in. Offer was two hunnerd in gold. Easy money. But I hear talk right after I hits town today some jasper done beat me to it."

Winnett stared at Ted for a long time, then cut loose with a full-throated guffaw that seemed to rattle the bottles on the table. Ted waited until the storm of laughter subsided into a shaking of shoulders. "Whasso funny, Boog?"

The square face twisted in mirth. "Lee-Bowe, you ain't gonna believe it. I done beat you on another one. An' I got six hunnerd!"

The laugh started to build, then ended in a choked gasp as the edge of Ted's right hand slammed into the throat just below the chin. The blow sent Winnett tumbling from his chair. Ted was on him before the toppling glass reached the floor, letting the fury pour out as he pounded first one fist and then the other into the square face. Then he grabbed Winnett by the hair and slammed the back of his head into the rough timber of the floor.

"Let me introduce myself, Winnett. Captain Ted Henderson, United States Army. And that was my wife, not me, who took your bullet." He yanked Winnett's head forward and slammed his right fist over and over into the now shapeless face, ignoring the blood that spattered into his own eyes. He fed every ounce of hate and frustration into each blow. Suddenly, his wrist was locked in a grip like a bear trap, a forearm was solidly beneath his chin, and a voice in his ear said, "Enough, brother. You kill him later."

Ted felt himself lifted bodily into the air. Then his feet were on the floor again, and he turned, ready to strike. The blow never materialized as the face of Yellow Crow snapped into focus.

"Beat man to death, we not know who pay him and why," the Cheyenne said. The calm voice and pure logic gradually pushed the desire to kill from Ted's seething brain. The Indian scooped up the two hundred or so pounds of unconscious bulk from the floor, tossed Winnett over a shoulder, and gripped his friend's arm.

"We take to fort. He talk to chief of soldiers. If not talk to colonel, he talk to Yellow Crow."

Ted sat in a chair, his still sore right hand resting on his lap, and looked across the desk at Colonel Wild Bill Robinson. The commanding officer shook his head. "He won't talk, Ted. I've been at him two days, and he won't even admit firing the shot. But his pistol had one fired chamber, and it's a rather unique weapon—a Walker Colt. The slug we dug out of the wall after Wilma was shot could have come from the same weapon. How's the hand?"

"Sore as a grizzly's temper."

"Next time, use a gun butt or a rock. Easier on the knuckles. Anyway, I threatened to turn you loose on him, and still he wouldn't talk. That leaves just one chance—"

"Yellow Crow?"

The colonel nodded. "Of course, as commanding officer, I cannot condone the torture of prisoners. But these are busy times, and a man cannot be everywhere at once. I am going for a short walk; it's a pleasant day since the snow has melted, and I have a feeling it may be our last one for a while. If Yellow Crow should happen to come by in"—the colonel glanced at the heavy clock on the mantel—"say, three minutes . . ."

Ted nodded. "Thank you, Colonel."

"Just leave him alive, Ted. I can't lose a good officer through court-martial."

"Yes, sir."

The colonel rose from behind the desk, carefully placed his hat on his head, and started toward the door. A metallic clink of metal on wood—keys falling on the floor—marked his passing.

The door had barely closed behind the colonel when Yellow Crow came into the office carrying a small bundle. The Cheyenne picked up the keys, unlocked the closet, and shoved Boog Winnett into the room.

Ted was surprised, almost shocked, at the damage his fists had done. Winnett's eyes were swollen almost shut, there was scarcely an inch of skin left untorn, the nose was shattered, and a sunken spot hinted at a crushed cheekbone. The man glared as best he could at Ted.

"Ain't gonna tell you nothin'," he said. "Gonna kill you one day."

Ted shrugged. "I hadn't planned to ask any questions. I'll leave that up to my friend here."

For the first time Winnett seemed to notice Yellow Crow. The small eyes grew bright with a flash of sudden fear. The Cheyenne was carefully arranging a fishhook, a sharp skinning knife, and a bag of salt on the hearth of the fireplace.

"No—you can't—not to a white man—" Winnett's voice was a ragged croak.

"Why not?" Ted said, his voice level and calm despite the queasiness in his stomach; he could only pray the man broke before Yellow Crow went to work in earnest. "My Cheyenne friend here knows hundreds of ways of keeping a man alive even though he would rather be dead. Of course, he is a simple savage. If I tell him to stop, maybe he will. Maybe he won't."

Boog Winnett cowered against the wall, the sweat of pure terror running down the broken cheeks. Yellow Crow casually picked up a bit of salt and the skinning knife. "Take off ear first," Yellow Crow said. "Then nose." The knife suddenly slashed downward, the keen blade slicing through Winnett's belt without touching skin. "Then maybe make stallion into something else." The Indian dribbled a few grains of salt into a laceration on Winnett's cheek. The battered man opened his mouth to scream, but a brown hand clamped it shut. Winnett's eyes followed the tip of the sharp knife.

Yellow Crow changed the direction of the knifepoint. "Maybe take out one eye first. Hang fishhook in other." The Cheyenne released his hand from over Winnett's mouth. The tip of the knife neared the right eye, its needle-sharp point glinting in the light from the window nearby.

"*No!*" Winnett turned pleading eyes toward Ted. "Stop it! I'll tell you!"

The knife tip dropped away. Yellow Crow's face remained impassive.

"You shoot woman?"

Winnett swallowed and nodded. "Did—didn't mean— woman. Whiskey—made me miss—captain."

"Who paid you?" Ted's tone was sharp, probing the man's fear. "Give me a name or I will turn you over to Yellow Crow. Now!"

"Can't give name. Don't know who supplied money. Old friend brought it to me. Wouldn't say whose money."

"Who was the friend?"

"Don't matter none. He's lit out, long gone. Prob'ly in Canada by now."

Ted sighed. "Well, I guess that does it. Yellow Crow, he doesn't seem to want to tell the truth. He's all yours—"

"No! For God's sake, man! What I'm sayin' is gospel! You gotta believe me! Don't let that heathen at me!" Winnett was sobbing with terror. "I didn't mean to shoot the woman, as God is my witness! If I knowed, I'd for sure tell! Shoot me or hang me, but don't let that Injun near me!"

Ted knew the man had been broken; if he had known any more, it would have been out by now. The spreading stain on Winnett's pants and the odor of urine confirmed Ted's judgment.

"Enough, Yellow Crow," he said. "I think he is telling the truth."

The Cheyenne merely shrugged and replaced his equipment in the leather bundle.

The door opened, and Colonel Bill Robinson strode into the room. "Good thing I was passing by," he said to the terrified Winnett. "I heard your confession. You will get your trial, and it is fortunate for you no one was more seriously hurt."

The colonel turned to Ted. "That blizzard you have been expecting is about to hit. I've seen that grayish color in the sky before." He yelled for the corporal of the guard. The soldier entered, and Robinson waved toward the prisoner. "Take him to the guardhouse and see that he's put in chains."

Winnett, with one last terrified look at Yellow Crow, went meekly with the corporal.

"Yellow Crow," Ted said, "would you have . . ." His voice trailed off.

The Cheyenne shrugged. "No need. He talk."

The distinctive blast of a big-bore rifle rolled into the compound, and as they sprinted to the door, an alarmed cry from the corporal reached their ears. Boog Winnett lay flat on his back, his eyes staring lifelessly at the lowering gray clouds. A hole the size of a half-dollar was punched neatly in his forehead.

Ted took in the scene with a quick glance. The young corporal stood looking down at the body, his face ashen. Ted followed Yellow Crow's gaze toward the elevated hills well beyond the walls of the stockade. In his own mind he, too, tracked the probable flight of the fatal bullet.

Yellow Crow spun on a heel and sprinted toward the stable, pausing only long enough to dart into his barracks to scoop up the newly acquired Spencer rifle and a handful of ammunition. In what seemed only a matter of seconds, the Cheyenne swept past the growing group of soldiers, bareback on his powerful palomino gelding. Ted watched the Cheyenne pass through the gate.

"Sergeant!"

Frank Armbrister materialized at the colonel's side. "Sir?"

"Get a patrol up in those hills, double-quick."

"Yes, sir!"

"Colonel?"

Robinson turned to Ted, an eyebrow raised.

"Permission to join Yellow Crow in the pursuit?"

"Granted. But watch yourself, Ted."

Within minutes, Ted was mounted and following the tracks of Yellow Crow's horse toward the nearby hills. The freshening wind carried flakes of snow which stung his cheeks as he moved out at a long lope.

Some four miles from the fort, Ted caught up with Yellow Crow. The Cheyenne was kneeling beside his palomino, studying the earth already covered by more than an inch of snow.

"Me not follow anymore," Yellow Crow said by way of greeting. "Trail gone. Soon snow cover all tracks." The Indian swung onto his horse and kneed the animal back in the direction of the fort. Ted let his horse fall into step alongside Yellow Crow's. They rode in silence for a time, retracing their steps already drifted with small banks of snow.

"Same white man shoot Winnett and soldier with pouch," Yellow Crow said at length. "Make same holes for elbows, knees, before pull trigger. Hide trail same way."

Ted had suspected as much. The long-range shot fired with such deadly accuracy, the careful choice of footing for the horse, taking time to hide the initial trail instead of simply spurring for distance—all these were the marks of a man who knew what he was doing.

The Cheyenne said, "Man good. Lucky, too. Get away from Yellow Crow twice. Not happen again."

Ted decided he would not care to wager against the Indian. After studying the fugitive's tracks twice, Yellow Crow now knew more about the rifleman than anyone except the fleeing man himself.

As they approached the fort, the entrance could barely be seen through thick, swirling flakes. Still, Ted could make out the form of Colonel Robinson awaiting the return of his men, pacing in the elements rather than in his warm and comfortable office.

Ted quickly told the colonel what Yellow Crow had found, and as he finished his report, Frank Armbrister's patrol also rode in.

The sergeant major shifted his wiry body in his saddle, and Armbrister summarized his report to the colonel in a straightforward style: "All we found, sir, was a lot of cold."

For a few days the fort settled into a comfortable routine, only the patrols on duty suffering from the elements. There were no reports of Indian raids in the Fort Bridger area, although travelers and dispatch riders indicated Fort Laramie was hard put to keep the tribes in the immediate area in line.

Lieutenant Chad Clark doggedly continued with his study of the coded deerskin scroll that Ted had given him, but so far he had learned nothing. His reports to the colonel were always the same: He had been reading and rereading every book at his disposal, but the code still made no sense.

The routine at the fort was quickly broken when an order from the War Department came. Company K, one of Fort Bridger's seasoned, veteran infantry units, was recalled to the

East and would be replaced primarily by volunteers. All of Fort Bridger turned out to send Company K off, and despite the cheery yells of "So long, soldier" and "See you in Georgia," Ted sensed the undercurrent of loss among the troops. The soldiers who stayed behind were painfully aware they were seeing many of their comrades-in-arms for the final time.

As the reinforcements came in to replace Company K, Ted had the distinct impression that he was witnessing a rare occasion. Wild Bill Robinson usually confined his cursing to those occasions of real need, but Ted suspected the words mumbled by Robinson as he inspected the latest band of reinforcements might not have been welcomed at Vi's dinner table. Robinson's expression was that of a man who just found a bug in his stew. It was, Ted decided, understandable.

The replacements trickled in throughout the week, and Ted was reasonably sure he could count the number of experienced fighting men on his two hands and still have his trigger finger free. The few now undergoing inspection carried battered and mismatched weapons, empty or nearly empty shot-and-ball pouches, and their clothing was less than adequate for the bitter winter patrols.

Robinson concluded his brief welcoming speech and turned the men over to Sergeant Major Frank Armbrister for assignment of barracks. As the new arrivals shuffled away, the colonel shook his head.

"I give up more than sixty good, solid soldiers, and in their place I get this ragtag bunch," he said. "Farm boys who never faced anything meaner than a pregnant squirrel. A few Indian-haters, I would venture, out to collect a scalp. Here and there a real soldier, but few enough to make you wonder if the war is really going that badly back East."

The two officers, starting toward the colonel's office, stopped as the guard at the gate hailed, "Column approaching!"

Robinson turned toward the fort entrance and grunted in surprise. Where the other groups had wandered in with all the organization of a flock of startled chickens, the column now entering the compound actually looked military. A massive hulk of a black man, mounted on a rangy, big-eared bay, led the way as point rider. A half-dozen other horsemen were deployed around the fifteen men on foot. With the exception of their leader, all the men were white.

The black man touched his knee to the big bay, approached the two officers, and delivered a smart salute as he reined the animal to a stop.

"Permission to report, sir." The baritone voice, Ted noticed, held a strange undertone of Southern drawl and clipped Irish.

"Granted, soldier," the colonel said as he and Ted returned the salute. "You may dismount if you wish."

"Thank you, Colonel. Beggin' your pardon, sir, but the man who designed the army issue saddle must have been a desk man, pure and simple."

Ted felt a grin tug at the corners of his own mouth; many times he had thought the same thing.

"Are you in command of this column, soldier?"

"No, sir, Colonel. Well, not really. But nobody else wanted the job. I used to be a noncom, but I lost my stripes."

"How?"

"Gentleman back in Pennsylvania called me a nigger, sir. Now I ain't denyin' I'm a nigger, I'm just choosy about who calls me one." The huge shoulders lifted, then fell. "Nobody told me he was the commanding officer's nephew, sir."

Robinson extended a hand. "Welcome to Fort Bridger, soldier. I'm Colonel Robinson. This is Captain Ted Henderson."

"Private Albert Jonas, sir." Ted felt the controlled power in the handshake; his own fingers barely spanned the breadth of the man's hand.

"If anyone here calls you a nigger, Private Jonas," Robinson said, "you have my permission to set him straight."

Jonas's laugh was deep, almost musical. "Man can't get busted no lower than private, sir, and the next step down's the stockade. I reckon I'll control my temper."

Robinson nodded. "Just remember," he said, "that no man of any rank in my command takes abuse from another, and all except the new arrivals know it. I'll have Sergeant Major Armbrister show you and the other men to the assigned quarters, Jonas." The colonel slowly walked around the big bay, studying the animal. He judiciously stayed well clear of the back end, noticing that the horse's long ears were laid tight against its neck.

"Jonas," the colonel finally said, "that has to be the ugliest horse I have ever seen."

Jonas grinned, teeth flashing white. "Yes, sir. He's homely. Too ugly to steal, too mean to ride, too tough to eat, and can run any three other horses into the dirt. Couldn't ask for a better combination."

Ted and the colonel watched as Frank Armbrister took charge of the column and led the men away. "I think we found ourselves a soldier," Robinson said. "I'm going to see that he's promoted to corporal right away."

Ted nodded his agreement. "I would like to have him assigned to my patrols, if you can spare him," he said. "I think he can be of invaluable aid to me and my scouts."

"Of course, Ted. And I'll be mighty surprised if he doesn't live up to our expectations. Coffee?"

Ted was halfway through his cup when Frank Armbrister came into the colonel's quarters. Robinson poured the sergeant a cup and waved him to a chair.

"Colonel," Armbrister said, "we may have some trouble on our hands."

The colonel raised an eyebrow.

"One of the troopers in this last batch of replacements may not have his sympathies in the right place. He's a galvanized Yankee."

"A Confederate soldier, eh? But after being captured, he decided to serve the Union army rather than spend the war in our prison camps. Right?"

"Yes, sir."

"What's his name?" Colonel Robinson asked.

"Private Bernie Christian, sir. Personally, I have no reason to doubt the man. But some of the other troopers are likely to be pretty upset."

"Well, keep an eye on him, Frank." The colonel refilled his cup. "I don't believe in convicting a man until he's done something wrong. But changes in philosophy are not uncommon; look at the number of West Point graduates fighting for the Confederacy right now. Give him every opportunity, keeping in mind the one thing we don't need right now is a possible saboteur in the ranks."

"Yes, sir. I'll keep watch on him."

"How does the rest of the replacement force shape up?"

Armbrister sighed. "Frankly, Colonel, the army handed you the dirty end of this stick. It was about a five-for-one trade, with us getting the one and giving up the five. And it's going to just about wipe out our stores of spare rifles, clothing, and field equipment just to get them even looking like soldiers!"

*　*　*

Colonel Bill Robinson paced the floor of his small office as Abel Hubbard, sitting behind the colonel's desk, calculated the supplies remaining in the fort's storehouses. Finally, he closed the ledger and looked up.

"Colonel," he said, "it's as we feared. Outfitting the new troops has pushed us close to the danger point on basic equipment, and feeding a growing number of Indians outside the fort in a time of scarce game has cut into our foodstocks."

The colonel's brows furrowed. "Just how serious is it, Abel?"

"I figure that with what we have on hand now, we have perhaps two weeks' worth of powder and about two weeks of basics such as flour, bacon, and salt. Even counting on the supply wagons that should come in from Fort Laramie soon, we're cutting it close, sir."

"Time to tighten our belts?"

"It's approaching in a hurry—" Abel was cut off in midsentence by a shout outside.

"Fire in the storeroom!"

The two officers were through the door in an instant, sprinting toward the end of the compound where a food storage building was sending a black column of smoke toward the low-lying clouds.

Momentary confusion gave way to organization as troopers formed a bucket brigade, but the feeble slosh of the water did little to quench the inferno.

Robinson himself grabbed a bucket, scooping water from a trough and handing it to the private next in line.

"We're swimming upstream, sir!" the private yelled above the crackle of flames. "She's gone!"

"Wet down the other storehouses! Don't let it spread!"

Only after the flames had subsided and the surrounding structures seemed safe did Abel Hubbard notice the three slightly scorched bags of flour just outside the reach of the flames—and the slender figure of the one-time Confederate, Bernie Christian, firmly in the grasp of a burly trooper. Abel started toward the two men, then stopped as Sergeant Major Frank Armbrister materialized from the ranks of the fire fighters. Abel was close enough to hear the conversation.

"What's going on here, Langston?" Armbrister's tone seemed to carry a weight of authority far beyond the sergeant major's rank, Abel thought.

"Caught this blasted Reb comin' outta the storeroom right

after the fire," Langston replied angrily. "Seen a torch in the back corner, too—set on purpose, it was!"

A mutter of voices grew as the fire fighters turned from the building, which was now reduced to rubble and a few flickering flames.

Abel became aware of Colonel Robinson's presence and motioned the commanding officer not to approach any closer. "Let Frank handle it, sir." Unnoticed by the growing crowd, the colonel and the lieutenant stood and watched and listened.

"What do you have to say for yourself, Christian?" Armbrister's voice carried over the frustrated grumbling of the crowd.

Christian, held on his tiptoes by the ham-sized fist twisted in his collar, faced the sergeant major. "I was just passing by," he said with his southern drawl, "and I seen the fire and hollered and dragged out what I could 'fore it got too hot." He held out his scorched uniform sleeves. "I didn't set it, Sergeant! You gotta believe me!"

"Damn Johnny Reb!" someone yelled from the crowd. "Get a rope, and let's settle his bacon!"

The murmur grew into a chorus of agreement.

"Hold it!" Frank Armbrister's tone momentarily silenced the troopers. "Nobody's making a move until we find out what happened!"

Langston hurled the smaller Christian to the ground. "Ain't no use to ask," the big trooper said, pulling himself to his full six-foot-plus height. "Jist let's hand the Johnny Reb what's comin' to 'im!"

Armbrister stepped between the fallen Christian and the imposing bulk of the big trooper. He looked up, glaring into the larger man's eyes.

"Langston," Armbrister said, his voice taut, "if you or any man here wants to get Christian, you're going to have to get me first!"

Langston's gaze wavered. He glanced around the circle of soldiers, hoping for help but getting none.

"Come on, Langston! You've got almost a hundred pounds on me! You want Christian, you come get him! Or shut up and go about your business! Now, make your move, one way or the other!" The rage was barely checked in Armbrister's voice as he stood, weight poised on the balls of his feet, daring the larger man.

Langston took a half-step forward, then stopped. "I don't want no trouble with you, Armbrister."

One of the older troopers at the edge of the circle chuckled, then spoke in a voice loud enough for the crowd to hear. "What he really means is that he's seen Frank Armbrister in action afore, and he ain't sure he can handle 'im." A few shallow laughs broke out among the throng.

"Where are you from, Langston?"

Langston's voice dropped. "Alabama."

"Alabama, you say? Then how do we know you're not a Confederate sympathizer or spy?" The challenge in Armbrister's voice could not be denied. "You want us to show you a short rope because of where you're from?"

Langston's anger flared for a moment. "You can't hold that agin me!"

"But you can hold it against Christian, right? Think that over, Langston—while you help Christian to his feet."

The big trooper, his support from the crowd fading fast and his own knowledge of the sergeant's fighting ability working against his pride, dropped his eyes. Slowly, he helped Christian stand up.

"Anybody here see what happened?" Armbrister called.

"Christian's telling the truth, Sergeant," a voice from the ranks called. "He was just walking along when it started burning. I been keeping a close eye on him."

"Then why didn't you speak up?" Armbrister raised his voice. "I'm ashamed of all of you! You say you're soldiers? Well, if the army depends on the likes of you, the Union is in big trouble! Now get about your business!"

A few troopers walked away from the crowd, then more, until only Christian and Armbrister stood in the compound, each unaware of the presence of the two officers nearby.

"Are you okay, Christian?"

"Yes, Sergeant. Just scared a lot."

"If I were in your boots, Christian, I would be, too. Every time something goes wrong around here, you're going to be the prime suspect. And I'll be among the suspicious. You're going to have to be the best soldier in this unit, just to prove your loyalty. And if you have none—if I ever find you are responsible for an act of sabotage—I'll put a revolver to your head and pull the trigger myself. Now get out of here, Christian. Go muck out the stables. And watch your back." The sergeant turned and walked away.

Abel Hubbard allowed himself a wink at the grinning Colonel Robinson. "With men like Armbrister," Abel said, "we don't ever have to worry about the Third Cavalry."

Captain Ted Henderson slumped forward on the low dressing stool, eyes half-closed, letting Wilma's expert fingers massage the exhaustion from his shoulder muscles.

Her voice was gentle in his ear. "Ted, dear, you are pushing yourself awfully hard. I haven't seen you this tired since your Pony Express days."

He sighed heavily. "I know, Wilma. I'd much rather be here with you. But you know how hard-pressed we all are. Even Wild Bill Robinson is showing signs of strain. As fast as he sends out a patrol to repair the telegraph lines, they are cut in another place. And it seems each time I send my scouts in one direction, the Indians hit a dozen miles away. But I can't stop pushing—I won't stop—until I find out who's responsible for supplying the Indians with weapons and liquor and inciting them to harass the settlers. Eventually someone will make a mistake, and I'll be able to put an end to it."

He felt her lips brush the nape of his neck. "I know you will," she said. "If you have a single flaw, Captain Henderson, it is that almost stubborn devotion to duty. And goodness knows, the people of this area need you and your men. If it weren't for the dedication of the officers and men of this fort, not a single person inside or outside these walls would be safe, the way things have been going."

He reached up and gently squeezed her soft forearm. "Things haven't exactly been a nap in a hay meadow for you either, honey."

"Oh, they haven't been bad. I've always liked to keep busy. I've been helping Dr. Mason, and I'm learning a lot of medicine in the process—did I tell you I delivered a baby all by myself the other day?" Ted could hear the excitement and delight in her voice. "It was the most exhilarating and scary thing I've ever done. I sometimes think if every white man and woman could hold a beautiful Arapaho baby and the Indians could do the same with a white child, all this cruelty and raiding would stop." She sighed. "And yet the very day I delivered the baby, I was also melting lead, casting bullets, and reloading cartridges for the troops."

Her hands dropped lower on his shoulders, fingers working gently around the ragged scar. The bullet had taken him during his record-breaking Pony Express ride, one that had already become a legend across the nation.

A ripple of excitement in the compound drew them to a window. At the end of the parade ground, an army supply wagon had already passed through the gate, followed by a second, then a third. Ted felt Wilma's fingers slide between his own and squeeze.

"I never thought a plain old wagon could be so beautiful," she said. "I know it's probably too much to ask, but if there's a sack of salt in one of those wagons . . ."

Colonel Robinson was already moving from wagon to wagon, throwing back the coverings. Approaching at a rapid walk, Ted could see the veins swelling in the commanding officer's neck, the red surge of anger climbing toward furrowed brows. Ted stepped alongside the now-furious officer. "Trouble, Colonel?"

Robinson waved a hand down the line of supply wagons, the frustration and fury as obvious in the gesture as in the voice. "Look at that, Ted! It's bad enough we have to fight blizzards and Indians—now the army's fighting us, too!" Robinson wheeled and stomped off toward his office.

Ted glanced into each wagon, his own anger and disappointment growing at each stop. He saw only summer uniforms. There was ammunition for four-pounder cannons, but Fort Bridger had only two- and twelve-pounders. There were sacks of weevil-filled flour; grain for the horses bore the unmistakable odor of mold. There was not one spare wagon wheel or spoke, no sugar, no salt, no medical supplies—not a usable item in the whole shipment.

Fighting to control his anger, Ted approached the driver of the lead team.

"Who ordered this stuff sent here, soldier?"

The teamster, a glimmer of fear in his eyes, pawed at a coat pocket and produced a crumpled paper. Ted scanned the order list, noted the signature at the bottom, and stood for a moment, stunned—it was signed by Abel Hubbard. He folded the paper in disbelief and carefully stowed it in a pocket. He would ask Abel later about the requisition.

"Well, soldier," he said to the teamster, "at least we can use some of this junk."

The trooper's sigh of relief was almost audible.

"What we can use," Ted said, his voice tight, "are the mules and the wagons."

"But—but, sir, how d'we get back to Laramie?"

Ted shrugged. "Maybe we will hold you for ransom for a bag of fresh flour and a crate of horseshoes. Or maybe you can walk home, just to get a taste of what it is like to be afoot with no food, ammunition, or warm clothing. Or perhaps you would like to volunteer for duty as one of our infantrymen. It makes no difference to me."

Ted stared at the frightened eyes of the lead teamster and realized he was being unreasonable in his anger; it was not the driver's fault. He sighed. "Next time a patrol goes as far as Fort Laramie, they'll take you along—with my personal message to your quartermaster. Park the wagons on the far end of the compound and report to the troop mess hall for dinner. I hope you like half-rations of watery soup and dried meat, because that's what we've been living on for the past two and a half weeks!"

Ted turned on his heel and strode across the compound, telling a private to find Lieutenant Hubbard and send him to Colonel Robinson's office. As he walked, Ted muttered to himself, "Maybe we can whip the Indians with rocks—or beat them to death with rolled-up army requisitions."

Robinson was staring out the window, the muscles of his jaw bulging. The coffee, once a staple in the cluttered office, was long gone now. Ted went to a small corner cabinet, poured a shot of amber liquid into a heavy cup, and handed it to Robinson.

"I know you don't drink often, sir, and never on duty," Ted said, "but I think you need this."

Robinson downed the raw whiskey at a gulp and shuddered. "Tell me one thing, Ted," he said through clenched teeth, "how is it that no matter what you run out of on the frontier, you can always find a bottle of whiskey in one of these godforsaken fort towns?"

"You can make whiskey, Colonel, but you can't make powder and lead and flour and oats."

Abel Hubbard now walked into the office, looking quizzically at the other men. Ted quickly described the worthless supplies that had just arrived and showed him the requisition order. "It's signed by you, Abel," Ted said quietly.

"Damned if I know who made out that order," Abel said. "That's not my signature; it's not even close to my handwriting." He tossed the document onto the colonel's desk. "Must have been the work of some bungling army clerk at Laramie."

Ted nodded. "So what's our status now, Colonel?"

"Somewhere between bad off and purely pitiful," Robinson said. "We're down to a week's supply of food, out of clothing, and maybe by stretching things, we've got thirty rounds of ammunition per man. You might say our situation has just passed the desperate level!"

A gunshot rattled the bitter air of dusk.

"Horseman approaching, sir!" The guard at the gate lowered his rifle as the hoofbeats drew near the fort. "White man, sir! Riding a big palomino!"

"You don't have to shout now, soldier," Robinson said. "Just open the gate and let's see what he has to say."

Standing at Robinson's side as the horseman entered the compound, Ted admitted to himself that the rider was an imposing sight. A full-length, saddle-split coat of fine beaver fell from wide shoulders over a hand-tooled Mexican saddle that would have cost a captain six months' wages. The coat brushed halfway down the tops of expensive leather boots. The butt of a new repeating rifle protruded from the saddle scabbard. Yellow hair, almost the color of a palomino gelding, cascaded in waves from beneath a beaver hat to well below the collar of the rich coat. The wide-set, penetrating blue eyes seemed out of place in the weather-tanned skin of the handsome face.

With a single word, the rider eased his mount to a halt before the two officers. A gloved hand touched the brim of the beaver hat.

"Colonel Robinson, I presume?" The voice was rich, almost melodic. At Robinson's curious nod, the rider continued, "May I introduce myself? Colin Dibley, sir, at your service." Dibley swung his six-foot-two frame with ease from the saddle, stripped off a glove, and extended a hand.

"Welcome to Fort Bridger, Mr. Dibley," Robinson said. "May I present Ted Henderson, captain of scouts?"

The two men eyed each other as they shook hands. Then the newcomer turned his gaze on the colonel. "It is my understanding, Colonel Robinson, that you may have encountered something of a supply problem here."

"We have had some supply difficulties, just as other units have." Ted knew the cautious Robinson was not about to reveal the true status of the fort's supply problem to a stranger.

"Then, sir, I am sure I may be of help. My wagons will be

here before dark; you are welcome to whatever you need, with my compliments."

"Wagons? Through country swarming with Indians?" Ted caught the incredulous tone in Robinson's voice.

Dibley smiled, revealing a row of strong white teeth. "I don't blame you for being a bit suspicious, sir. Granted, it was an audacious thing to do. But then we Dibleys have always been audacious. Tell a Dibley something is impossible if you want it done, as my father used to say. Perhaps you've heard of the Boston Dibleys?"

"Banking, shipping, land—yes, I do believe I have heard the family name," Robinson said. "It seems to be on every major building in Boston. Are the Dibleys in the business of supplying goods to the army now?"

Dibley's laugh was throaty. "Contributing, sir, would be a better word. Whatever you find in the wagons to be of use is yours, and we will touch none of your coin. It is merely our small contribution to the war effort."

The first of the wagons rolled into view, leaving Ted slightly stunned. They were sturdy Studebaker freight wagons, riding heavily, and he could count at least six before the deepening night swallowed the view.

"Granted," Dibley said, "that my father is first and foremost a staunch patriot of the Union. But he is also a rather shrewd businessman. I doubt that he relishes the thought of the Dibley holdings falling into Confederate hands. He—all of us Dibleys, in fact—have become accustomed to the better things in life."

Colonel Robinson turned to Ted. "Captain, I think we have kept Mr. Dibley standing in the cold long enough. Would you please organize a detail to accommodate the wagons, see to lodging for the teamsters, and then join us in my office?" He turned back to the tall blond man. "I would offer you coffee," the colonel said, "but we seem to be a little short."

Dibley laughed, reached into a saddlebag as a private led the snorting palomino away, and pulled out a sack. "I think you'll find this to your liking, Colonel. It's my favorite blend." The voices of the two men faded as Ted set out organizing a detail. A sizable crowd had gathered at the approach of the wagon train. A murmur swept through the troops as the covering was stripped from first one wagon, then another.

"My Gawd, would you lookit that," he heard one voice say. "That's real salt, and here's powder and lead and blankets. . . ." Troopers, who only a half hour ago were almost dead on their feet from exhaustion, suddenly found a new spurt of energy, unloading the wagons and handling each keg and carton as though it were fine china.

Ted turned the unloading project over to Armbrister and rejoined Dibley and the colonel in the officer's quarters. The smell of rich coffee hit his nostrils as he stepped into the lamp-lit clutter.

". . . so that is the story, Colonel," Dibley was saying as Ted came in. "Most of the Dibley family's financial support is going to the troops in the East. But I have been west many times on holiday, and I keep up with developments on both fronts. It seemed to me that since I had amassed a considerable fortune myself, those funds could be put to good use on the frontier. And I must admit to a bit of selfishness in my motives as well; when the Union flag flies over all of the states once more, there are fortunes upon fortunes to be made in the West, opportunities which have long disappeared from the East. Besides, I find the political games and society functions a bit of a bore. A good horse and a fine gun feel better in my hands than a business contract. Got that from my mother's side of the family, I guess."

As he spoke, Dibley poured coffee into a cup and handed it to the captain. Expressing his thanks, Ted took a sip of the excellent, full-bodied brew and sighed.

"You will, of course, be my guest for dinner, Mr. Dibley," Robinson said. "However, I'm afraid we are running low on meat."

"Not anymore, Colonel. I had great good fortune on the hunt this morning. In the last wagon are the dressed carcasses of three fine young elk. I've instructed my teamsters to deliver a choice hindquarter to your wife."

"Excellent! Ted, you and Wilma will join us, of course, along with Abel and Judy. It's about time we had a feast and a party around here."

Despite the lack of preparation time, Vi Robinson and Wilma had outdone themselves with the dinner, and they enjoyed the sight of their men pushing their plates back at the end of the meal, sighing with contentment.

Colonel Bill Robinson sat at the head of the table. Abel Hubbard and Judy sat across from Vi and Dibley, the guest of honor, with Wilma and Ted rounding out the group. Ted had observed Wilma's fleeting frown of disapproval when Judy had entered for dinner. Abel's wife wore a seductively low-cut, form-fitting gown, and had seemed to glow at the restrained compliments Dibley had directed at Abel for his good fortune in finding such a lovely young wife.

Ted could sense the growing unease in Abel as Judy became coquettish in her rapt attention to Dibley's small talk. Abel's shoulders tensed as Robinson reached for the wine decanter, only to have Judy beat him to the container with a bright, "I'll pour." It seemed to Ted that she lingered over Dibley's glass, perhaps leaning forward a trifle more than needed. Dibley seemed unaware of the sudden exposure of feminine flesh, and merely muttered a thank you, resuming his discusion with Vi Robinson.

The colonel raised his glass. "To Colin Dibley and his supply train," Robinson said. Ted noticed that Abel seemed reluctant, yet courteously raised his glass in salute. Ted's glass of water suddenly felt heavy in his hand, but he lifted it to his lips for a sip. He wondered if his initial reservations toward the handsome blond businessman were simply jealousy on his own part, at the silk suit, the polished table manners, the obvious success. And possibly the attention Dibley paid to Wilma. Ted did not view Dibley as a potential rival, but the protective instinct was still there. For whatever reason, he suddenly became aware of a growing distrust of Colin Dibley. He resolved to give Dibley the benefit of the doubt, but he also would do well, he told himself, to keep an eye on the Bostonian's movements.

Ted joined only infrequently in the small talk, studying the undercurrents at the dinner table and wishing Judy would show a bit more restraint. He caught Wilma's eye, glanced toward Judy, and saw his wife's answering nod. Wilma was an expert when it came to the relationships between men and women, and he felt some of the weight lift from his shoulders. Perhaps Wilma could talk some sense into Judy before Abel did something foolish.

"We will be moving out in a few days," Dibley was saying to the colonel.

"Oh, no, you mustn't," Judy protested, "there are so many things we haven't discussed yet—the Boston fashions, the theater."

Dibley's smile was dazzling. "It will be a terrible shame to leave such lovely and fascinating company," he said, "but there are other contributions yet to be made to the war effort."

A sudden knock on the door interrupted the flow of conversation. Vi ushered in an obviously tired cavalryman clutching a dispatch case. The trooper saluted and said, "Sorry to bother you at such a time, Colonel Robinson, but the commander at Fort Laramie said to deliver this to you immediately. He said it was too sensitive to trust to the telegraph." He handed the dispatch case to the colonel and gratefully accepted Vi's offer of coffee and dinner.

Vi handed the trooper a heaping plate and the soldier glanced around, obviously looking for an out-of-the-way place to eat his meal. Robinson glanced up from the sheaf of papers he was thumbing through and said, "Sit down, son—enlisted men are welcome here. After you eat, pick yourself a cot in the barracks—stay as long as you like."

Outwardly, Robinson seemed unperturbed as he replaced the papers in the dispatch case and stood. "Ladies, Mr. Dibley—I must ask you to excuse us for a few moments. A rather urgent military situation has been brought to my attention. Captain Henderson, Lieutenant Hubbard, if you would accompany me to the office?"

Both officers rose, and even though Abel was reluctant to leave his wife with Colin Dibley, the lieutenant knew full well that when his father-in-law used full military titles in an informal setting, something was afoot.

Robinson carefully closed the door between the office and his living quarters, then spread the contents of the dispatch pouch across the cluttered desk. He read intently for a few moments, then rose and began pacing the floor.

"Ted, Abel, some of these messages merely confirm what we have known all along—that the Apache, some of the Navajo bands, and other Indians have apparently formed a loose alliance with the Confederacy. We also have known of the presence of a Confederate force in southern New Mexico."

Robinson stopped his pacing, pulled a pipe from a desk drawer, and filled it. He continued: "What we didn't know until now is that a column of Texas volunteers has joined the Confederates along the Rio Grande, in the Mesilla Valley. That brings the total Confederate force in the valley to almost twenty-five hundred men." He paused to light the pipe. "But here is the worst of the news: Jefferson Davis has hand-picked a leader for the Texas-Confederate joint column. Gentlemen, the new commander's name is Lieutenant Colonel Roy Simon Humphries."

Ted's sharp intake of breath was followed by Abel Hubbard's low whistle at the mention of the name.

"As you well know, the Third Cavalry and Humphries have met before at Hidden Valley," Robinson said, "and we had the devil's own time of it. Roy Simon Humphries may well be one of the South's best field commanders. I have known him since West Point, and many times I have wished he had chosen the blue instead of the gray."

"But, Colonel," Abel interjected, "why would the Confederates send one of their most highly regarded officers to the West, when their major need for experienced leadership would seem to be on the eastern front?"

"With a sufficient force and a strong leader, the Confederates could cause all manner of problems in the West," the colonel said. "It is my gut feeling that Humphries's arrival on the scene can mean only one thing. Gentlemen, I believe a storm is brewing on the Rio Grande."

IV

A weak winter sun set pinpoints of light dancing across the dusting of snow in the small clearing in the foothills of the Guadalupe Mountains. Lieutenant Colonel Roy Simon Humphries, wearing the full uniform of an officer in the army of the Confederate States of America, traced random patterns in the snow with a cedar twig and awaited the arrival of the Mescalero Apache subchief Tanaya.

Humphries admitted to himself that he had not been looking forward to the meeting. Chastising an Apache was not an easy thing to do. Yet it must be done; Tanaya had overstepped the bounds of his agreement with the Confederacy and must be brought back into line.

The Indian suddenly materialized at the opposite side of the clearing, standing by a gnarled cedar tree and glaring at the Confederate officer. Humphries merely glanced at the short, powerfully built Apache. Tanaya, clad in soiled deerskin against the slight nip of winter cold, wore the perpetual scowl that was as much his trademark as the tomahawk in his belt. Humphries breathed a silent sigh of relief as he noted the absence of war paint on the muscular body; it was an indication that Tanaya accepted this meeting for what it was, a conference between two leaders and not a confrontation.

Humphries remained in his squatting position and waited for the Apache to cross the clearing and assume a similar pose. Humphries carefully calculated the length of silence before he spoke, measuring the gesture of respect so that Tanaya would recognize it as such, yet cutting it short before the silence could be interpreted by the Apache as offering too much of an honor.

77

"Tanaya and his scouts have served well," Humphries said.

The Indian made no reply.

"With Tanaya's help and talents in the wilderness, our soldiers now know the best routes to the forts and towns of the bluecoats. We know where to find water and game and the best locations for lookouts." Humphries's praise was not hollow, but exaggerated just enough to satisfy the considerable ego of the Mescalero subchief. Of all the tribes he had dealt with—and there had been many—Humphries always found the mercurial Apache the most difficult of all, quick to anger, quick to take offense at an innocent remark, yet easily mollified with praise and gifts. He continued to choose his words with care, trying to walk the fine line between command and offense.

"In exchange for these valuable services, Tanaya and his tribe have been well supplied with guns, powder, pots, and other needed goods by the Confederacy," Humphries said. "It is a good arrangement, benefiting both tribes. Yet Tanaya has violated one of the rules of the agreement. He was to have understood that the Confederacy does not make war on women and children or take them captive."

Humphries glanced at the Indian. The scowl seemed to have deepened and the dark eyes were half-lidded; it was not a good sign. Yet the trail had been broken, and now it must be followed.

"Does Tanaya find fault with the promise of the Confederate States of America? Have we not kept our side of the blanket warm?"

The Mescalero merely grunted. The sound was noncommittal.

"It has come to my attention," Humphries said, "that on a recent raid your warriors captured a white woman and a girl-child and took them to Tanaya's camp. I know that Tanaya's word is his bond, that a promise made by the most feared of the Mescalero warriors will be kept." Humphries looked up and faced the Apache for the first time.

"Tanaya must return the woman and the girl-child. He will be allowed to keep the mules and the horses captured on the raid, and will be given gifts of new rifles and knives. The exchange will take place at Mesilla at the height of the second sun from this day. Each of us will send one man to handle the exchange. If either side violates the terms of the exchange, the other is free to punish the offender, and the agreement between our chiefs and yours will end."

The Mescalero nodded, but Humphries could easily read the resentment in the dark eyes. He knew Tanaya would comply with the terms, for the Apache needed guns and goods much more than they needed more captive mouths to feed. They also needed the alliance with the Confederacy to keep the raiding routes open to the interior of Mexico. But it had to sting when a white man told a Mescalero Apache subchief what to do and when to do it.

Humphries knew he was in no immediate danger from Tanaya, for each was bound by word of honor not to draw weapons against the other for the duration of the Apache-Confederacy agreement. But that agreement would expire with the success of the Confederacy's bold strike in this region. Then there would be no holds barred, and he fervently hoped he never had to meet the short, frowning Apache in battle. Humphries feared no man, but he walked rather cautiously around some.

And he knew, as he watched the Mescalero disappear into the surrounding dry mountain forest scrub, that he would be feeling a tight spot between his shoulder blades on the long ride back to Mesilla on the Rio Grande.

As he returned to the Confederate camp and crossed the sentry line, he felt the tension ease. But the worried greeting from his second-in-command caused Humphries to become concerned all over again.

In his command tent, Humphries sipped a glass of water from a nearby wooden keg and listened without comment as the major delivered his report.

"Sir, two of our supply ships have been sunk by Union privateer gunboats off Galveston Island. The two battalions of experienced infantry we were promised cannot be spared. Things are not going well in the southern and eastern battlefields. What do we do now, sir?"

Humphries tapped a breast pocket. "We proceed as planned, Major. The orders from President Jefferson Davis must be followed. The loss of supplies and additional men will force us to do some creative planning. Please ask all officers to report to my tent at once."

The junior officer saluted and slipped from the tent. Humphries lifted the glass of tepid water and took a sip. The lieutenant colonel's insignia seemed very heavy indeed against his body. Lieutenant Colonel Roy Simon Humphries, with fewer than twenty-five hundred men at his command and with supply lines thin, would be solely responsible for the boldest, most ingenious military campaign ever devised.

He sighed heavily. He knew he was a professional, a good soldier and a leader of men. Now he had to raise himself above his own exacting standards. The very fate of the Confederate States of America could well lie in his strong, weathered hands.

The officers began filing into Humphries's command tent, and the lieutenant colonel nodded to each one, saying nothing until his entire corps of officers was assembled. Only then did he address the men in his sonorous voice.

"Gentlemen, we are going to strike north! We are going to push the Union forces all the way up the Rio Grande, north of the intersection of the Old Spanish Trail and the Continental Divide." He touched a pointer to a map stitched to one wall of the tent. "Here," he said, "is the key. Fort Union. It is the most heavily stocked supply depot in the West this side of California itself."

He hesitated for a moment to emphasize his next point. "With our supply situation as it is, we *must* take Fort Union. Then, with our wagons full, we strike west, using Fort Union as a relay station supply dump with wagons shuttling both ways along our line of march. That march will cut off all overland routes. We are going to isolate California from the Union!"

There was a murmur of surprise and disbelief from the men who were assembled in the tent. No one had anticipated the extent and daring of this campaign.

"Gentlemen," Humphries went on, "I need not tell you that California's immense wealth has provided most of the Union Army's war chest. We will make it the war chest of the Confederate States of America!"

He let the words hang for a long moment. "Such a dramatic strike," he finally said, "will open the gold and silver mines and the shipping ports of the West Coast to the Confederacy. And it could also be a turning point of the entire war. As most of you are aware, the Confederacy desperately needs European support in the area of war goods, goods that require the heavy machinery production the South does not have. A blow such as this, a major, decisive victory, will prove to the Europeans the Confederate States of America not only can, but will, win this war! The Europeans will back a winner. It is up to us to give them one."

He placed the pointer back on his field desk and looked over at the still-startled faces of his officers. He saw their enthusiasm flicker, begin to catch fire, and finally glow. "Any questions?"

"Yes, sir. How much do we know about enemy forces in the line of march?"

"Quite a lot, Lieutenant," Humphries answered. "Some months ago, we sent out ten scouts. They have returned. The only major force to be reckoned with in the immediate area is a small contingent of regulars and volunteers under the command of General Kelly Murphy. He is a good officer, but undermanned; most of his troops are inexperienced. He is all that stands between us and Fort Union."

"How about Union reinforcements from the north?"

"There are only two major armed units available to help," Humphries answered, "and one of those has its hands full with Indians. So we can forget Fort Laramie. That leaves only Colonel Bill Robinson's Third Cavalry Regiment at Fort Bridger to contend with."

Humphries paced the dirt floor beneath the wind-whipped canvas. "Robinson is a crack field leader with superb officers and seasoned troops. Ordinarily, he would present a problem. But deep snows in the mountain passes will keep him at home, or at least slow him down enough that we can capture Fort Union and launch our campaign." Humphries allowed himself a smile. "Besides, our operatives—spies, if you will—are already working to make sure that the Third Cavalry stays put in Bridger. Or at least never makes it to our forward positions."

He raised his voice above the murmur of the gathering of officers. "Gentlemen, it won't be easy. Kelly will fight as best he can. Remember, Fort Union is our key. With it, we unlock the door to California—and to the victory of the Confederate States of America!"

Yells of enthusiasm and confidence billowed through the walls of the command tent.

General Kelly Murphy paced the floor of his spartan office at Fort Union, stopping from time to time before a makeshift wallboard that held a map and several notes. The general rolled his unlighted cigar from one corner of his mouth to the other and turned to his adjutant.

"What do you make of it, Sanborne?"

The major shifted his weight in the straight-backed chair, attempting to relieve the pain of an arthritic hip. "Don't like it, sir. Not one bit. No army puts men anywhere without a reason." Sanborne rose, limped to the map on the wall, and studied it for a moment. "Now, the Confederates have got over a thousand, maybe fifteen hundred volunteers from Texas with 'em. I can smell a dust storm before I see it, General, and I think I smell one now."

Murphy strode to the window, watched for a moment, then waved his adjutant to his side. Shuffling through the dust was a handful of civilians. The general waved a hand toward the compound.

"There they are, Major," he said, "the bottom of the barrel as far as manpower goes. We've called in every soldier from every fort within two weeks' ride of here, we've scrounged up all the volunteers we could find, and still we scarcely have enough troops to make a decent poker game." The general snorted and twirled the cigar stub with his tongue. "The First New Mexico Volunteers have little or no training in warfare, and they are without capable leadership.

"Major," Murphy said suddenly, "you're a Texan by birth, aren't you?"

"Yes, sir. Still am by blood and love of the land."

"How do you feel about going against fellow Texans in battle?"

Sanborne shrugged. "I don't look forward to it, General. But they made their choice, and I made mine. You will be facing men who once wore the Union blue like yourself." The major shook his head. "It's a damn shame, General," he said. "But when a line is drawn in the dirt, you stand on one side or the other. I've known close families split—brother in gray, brother in blue. It's an unfair war, General, but it's out of our hands now except to fight to win it, even if we do have an uphill climb ahead of us."

The general sighed and turned to his desk. "Someday, Major, this war will be known as the great American tragedy. But philosophy doesn't turn back cyclones. We're in the water, and we're going to get wet." The general turned to face his adjutant, and Sanborne thought he caught the hint of a smile. "President Lincoln and Secretary of War Stanton were most apologetic that they could spare no more troops," Murphy said, "but they did manage to find us one man."

"One man, sir?"

"If you can call a legend one man, yes."

The smell of rich, bubbling stew from the nearby hearth saturated the relaxed interior of the native stone home. In a sturdy oak rocker, a blond-haired man of slight build gently rocked a small child while a dark-skinned woman of Spanish descent tended the fire.

At the knock on the door, it was the woman who responded. She was tall, graceful, and still an imposing figure, despite the years which had touched her black hair with a random frosting of gray.

A young corporal stood in the doorway, an envelope clutched in one hand. The envelope bore the seal of the President of the United States. The young man held out the package in a trembling hand. "Message for Mr. Christopher Carson of Taos," he said. Josefa Carson swung the door wide and beckoned the corporal into the room.

"Guess that's for me," the blond man said, still rocking the child. "Come on in, Corporal. Something to drink? We have plenty of water, or Josefa could make you some coffee."

"Water will be fine, sir."

Josefa handed the young soldier a cup of clear, sparkling spring water, then took the letter from his hand. The corporal sipped at the water, noticed that his fingers still shook, and despite himself could not help staring at the slight figure in the rocker. The corporal had thought the legendary Kit Carson would be more physically prepossessing.

Josefa Carson read the brief letter aloud.

> "As a personal favor to me, I would ask you to take command of the First New Mexico Volunteers. Only in this way will we be prepared in the event of Confederate forays in your area. With lasting gratitude, your obedient servant, Abraham Lincoln."

Josefa folded the letter and returned it to the envelope.

The corporal thought he saw a quick, slight frown on the fine-boned face of the famed mountain man, trapper, Indian fighter, and scout.

"Begging your pardon, sir—ma'am," the corporal stammered, "but I have been instructed to await your reply. General Murphy is anxious to know if you will be joining him at Fort Union."

"Of course, Corporal, of course," Carson said, gently rising from the rocker and placing the sleeping child in a small daybed nearby. "Stay for supper?"

The soldier shook his head, overwhelmed at the hospitality shown to a mere corporal by this living legend of the frontier. "No, thank you, Mr. Carson. I must return to the post."

"Josefa," Kit Carson said to his wife, his voice tender, "you know I can't refuse a request from the President himself."

Josefa merely nodded, moved to a small desk at a corner of the room, dipped pen in ink, and began to write. She did not need her husband to tell her what to write; she had seen that fleeting glint of excitement and challenge in his eyes. She finished the three-line message and carried the pen to her husband. Laboriously, Kit Carson signed his name.

The scene jarred the corporal—the famed Kit Carson, the man who had opened new trails and fought Indians across more than half a continent, could barely read and write! Still taken aback, he watched as Carson blew his signature dry, then carefully folded the message and handed it to the waiting messenger.

"Tell Kelly Murphy that I will serve my country to the best of my ability," Carson said, his eyes twinkling, "and tell him he could have asked himself—didn't really have to have Mr. Lincoln do it." One sparkling eye closed in a conspiratorial wink.

On a sudden impulse, the corporal blurted out, "Sir, I would consider it a great honor to serve with you, if you can use another man."

"The First New Mexico," Carson said, "is an infantry unit. I see from your patch that you're a cavalryman. Now, I can't for the life of me understand why a young man would give up a perfectly good seat on a horse to walk through the Southwest and probably into a fight, but if it meets with your commanding officer's approval, I'd be happy to have you."

The corporal could not hold back the grin; would his grandchildren—if he had any—ever believe that their grandpa rode with and maybe fought alongside Kit Carson? "Yes, sir. Thank you, sir."

"Thank me, Corporal, after the blisters on your feet heal up. Not before." The frontiersman waved the soldier into the approaching sunset.

Kit Carson crossed the room and took the shoulders of his

slightly taller wife in a gentle grasp. "Josefa, I won't deny that I was expecting that message in one form or another. I'm no military man, but from everything I've heard, there could be pretty hard fighting around here if the Confederates at Mesilla decide to move north."

He kissed her gently on the lips. "I had hoped," he said, "that I had put all my days in the field behind me. You've spoiled me, Josefa."

His wife watched as he walked to the daybed where their youngest slept. His step was still smooth and quiet, muscles almost as wiry as they had been in the wilderness days. He reached down to stroke the dark hair of the child. "You've tamed me pretty well," he said, turning back to his wife, "and if you'll remember, I didn't put up much of a fuss. I find life here as a family man much more rewarding and comfortable than the mountains. But, Josefa, if the war does come, I must do everything in my power to make sure it does not reach you and the children. Nothing else matters to me now."

Josefa moved to his side, her long fingers stroking the stubble which had developed since his morning shave.

"Christopher Carson," she said, "you have never dodged a fight before in your life, and I'll not argue that if there is trouble brewing, there is no man I would rather have between the danger and the children than you."

"It will only be until the threat here has ended, Josefa. Then I will resign my commission and come home."

She ran her fingers through the long blond hair now streaked with gray. "If there is to be fighting, there will be need of hospitals and those to tend the sick and wounded," she said in a determined voice. "You protect your family and your flag, sir, and I will do what I can to see that the fallen warriors of both sides are attended to. Now, let's go get you packed. I'm not even sure I know where we keep your saber these days."

She felt strong fingers on her shoulder, the brush of weathered lips against her own.

"Josefa," Kit Carson said, "you are one of the most remarkable women I have ever known."

Remarkable on the outside, she thought, finally pulling away reluctantly from his embrace, but inside there is still the fear, the ache. . . .

Colonel Bill Robinson studied the map spread across the top of his aged desk. It was a chart of the nation west of the

Mississippi. Lieutenant Abel Hubbard stood at his left, and Captain Ted Henderson was at his right.

"There has to be something building in the Mesilla Valley of New Mexico," Robinson said, "but I'm a plain and simple draft mule if I can figure out what—" All three men started as the door of the office suddenly burst open.

The young artillery officer had taken two steps toward the colonel's desk before he suddenly stopped, his cheeks coloring in embarrassment.

"Sorry, sir," Lieutenant Chad Clark said. "I just got carried away and forgot to knock."

"Well, come on, son. If it has you that stirred up, it should be important enough to get our attention, too. You look pale, Clark."

"Yes, sir. I suppose I do. I've been spending most of my time with my nose in a book—but I think I did it, sir! I believe I have broken the code on that Apache deerskin!"

His voice climbing excitedly, Clark spread the deerskin over the map on the colonel's desk.

"Part of the answer came from one of my old college books, an early history of Central and South America. The real key, Colonel, came from your private library—a small diary kept by a Spanish soldier, one of the first people to reach the Texas Gulf Coast and come in contact with the natives there. It was a stroke of luck, sir, that he was an excellent observer, a man of some curiosity and literate to boot."

Clark pointed to first one symbol, then another. "It is a strange blend of ancient Mayan symbols and the language of an Indian tribe that no longer exists," Clark said. "What gave me so much trouble until I found that little diary was identifying the tribal language. It appears to be Karankawa—and it is spelled phonetically, the way the words are pronounced, for that tribe had no written language. It is a devilishly clever code, sir, and I would hazard a guess it was devised by a highly educated man, a student of history. And a military man."

The artillery officer pointed to a symbol in the lower right corner. "It begins here, sir, and reads backward, from right to left." He began to interpret the symbols aloud.

Ted Henderson watched Robinson's brow furrow deeper with each phrase.

Chad Clark, concluding his interpretation, looked up at the colonel. "Unless I miss my guess, sir, this is some sort of a report on the strength of the Union forces in the Southwest."

The worried colonel clapped the lieutenant on the shoulder. "Your guess is correct, Clark. And the information on Union armies near the Rio Grande, northward from El Paso to Santa Fe, is surprisingly accurate. In fact, we have just heard a report more detailed than anyone outside the chain of command would have access to." Robinson scratched his chin for a moment, lost in thought. "It also predicts the number of troops and Union sympathizers along the Old Spanish Trail to Hastings Cutoff and on to the California Trail."

"Colonel," Ted said, still somewhat stunned by the developments of the last few moments, "this is not the sort of thing a Mescalero Apache would care about. No lone Indian would undertake such a project for his own amusement. The Apache that Yellow Crow killed at my ranch must have been a highly trained spy!"

"No question about that now, Ted," Abel said. "The big puzzle is why. I can see the military value in knowing the Union strength in the area north of Mesilla Valley, especially if I were the commander of a Confederate force there. But why all the way to near the California Trail?"

The silence held above the table for a long moment before Chad Clark suddenly snapped his fingers. He swept the deerskin aside, studied the map on the colonel's desk, then pulled a length of lanyard from a hip pocket.

"Sir," he said, "I have had no formal military training, and I'm sorry if this seems a bit far-fetched. But take a look at this."

Clark placed one end of the lanyard on the spot designated as El Paso del Norte. He wound the cord up along the Santa Fe Trail, paused to place a coin marker at the site of Fort Union northeast of Santa Fe, then stretched the cord all the way westward to the California coast.

Robinson and Henderson exchanged startled glances as the full impact of what they had just seen hit them.

"Get Frank Armbrister right away, Ted," Robinson said. "We're going to have an important meeting. And Lieutenant Clark—"

"Yes, sir?"

"Would you for God's sake stop apologizing all the time for being right?"

The lieutenant smiled weakly as he took one of the chairs by the colonel's desk. Ted, meanwhile, rushed coatless out of the office. Within minutes, Ted returned to the colonel's office with Frank Armbrister; they took their seats as Colonel

Robinson explained what they had to do. Part of the Third Cavalry would go south to New Mexico to aid the beleaguered Union forces there.

There was no sound from the assembled group until Ted's matter-of-fact voice broke the silence. "Gentlemen," he said, "this will be a painful and uncomfortable campaign. And it may be all for nothing. We don't know whether the confederates are ready to begin their drive. But we do know that General Murphy and his handful of troops cannot stop Roy Simon Humphries without reinforcements."

Colonel Wild Bill Robinson nodded, saying, "The stakes are worth the gamble, I believe." Abel Hubbard, Frank Armbrister, and Chad Clark all nodded silent agreement. "Ted knows this country from Canada to the Gulf Coast, and he knows the trail we must take in order to break through the mountain passes, avoid confrontations with the Indians, and still be effective as a fighting force when we toss our chips into the poker game down south."

Robinson rummaged in the desk drawer and produced his battered pipe. "We will travel light. We will take only such food and ammunition as needed to make the trip and engage the enemy if need be. We'll restock at Fort Union before heading home. We can spare no more than a few days' rations per man, and less than fifty rounds of rifle ammunition plus another fifty each for pistols. We're going to be cutting it thin, fellows."

"If I may say so, sir," Frank Armbrister chipped in, "if we choose the right men for the campaign, I think that will be sufficient."

Robinson fired the pipe and looked at the sergeant major. "Do you have someone in particular in mind, Frank?"

"Christian, sir. Bernie Christian, the galvanized Yankee. He's been working awfully hard to earn the respect of the other troopers, but whenever something goes wrong, they still suspect he had something to do with it."

"And?"

"Look at it this way, sir. It's a chance for him to prove his loyalty. And if I'm completely wrong on my judgment of Christian, what better opportunity than this campaign to find out whether he's still a Confederate?"

"Very well. We will take him along." Robinson turned to the young Chad Clark. "Lieutenant," he said, "since this will be a small-arms-only campaign, we will have no need for artillery. Anyway, we can't get the big guns through the passes because of the snow."

Clark jumped to his feet. "Sir," he said, a touch of excitement in his voice, "I think we're in luck. I mean, when I first arrived at the fort, I began tinkering with ways to carry cannon over the snow. I worked with the regimental farrier and wheelwright, and I think the answer to our problem is waiting in the shed behind the blacksmith's shop."

Robinson's eyebrows shot up. "Cannon through those passes in this weather? Son, either you are daydreaming or you are some kind of genius. I sincerely hope it's the latter."

Clark moved to the door. "If you'll be so kind as to follow me to the shed, gentlemen, I think I can demonstrate."

The officers pulled on greatcoats against the bitter wind and swirling snow. Clark summoned two husky artillerymen, and from the shed they brought a two-pound field cannon sitting upon a strange-looking carriage, with both overly wide wheels and sled runners mounted to the frame.

At Clark's nod, the two artillerymen stepped up to the hitch end of the cannon, took a firm hold, and lifted the carriage, cannon and all. Clark quickly lowered the runners. The entire assemblage was then set down so that the wheels rested on the skis. The episode had taken only seconds.

Robinson's low whistle was almost lost in the wind.

"It can be reversed almost as quickly, sir. We can go from sled runners to wheels and back in a hurry, if need be. And the two-pounders need only two strong horses each. If you think they would make a difference, sir, my men and I will certainly take a stab at it."

"Son," Robinson said, "I'd rather have you and those little popguns with me than any other artillery officer with a brace of twelve-pounders." The colonel turned to the other officers. "Now, gentlemen, let's return to my office. We still have more work to do." He turned on his heel and headed back to his office, the other men following him, glad to be getting out of the bitter wind.

They sat around drinking coffee late into the afternoon, putting the finishing touches on the plans for the coming campaign. With so many of Robinson's key men going out into the field, the safety of the women, children, and civilians was of paramount importance. No one, least of all Ted Henderson, forgot the fact that there was at least one Confederate agent in the area who was making life miserable at the fort, inciting the

Indians and committing acts of sabotage. Someone had also tried to have Ted killed on a number of occasions, and Wilma had almost died as a result. So the sooner the defenseless residents of the fort were taken to safety, the better.

Hubbard spoke up. "Our two infantry companies can accompany the women and children to Fort Laramie, where they will have better protection. Perhaps Mr. Dibley will be kind enough to furnish his wagons and teamsters for the trip." Ted thought he had detected a hint of bitterness in Abel's last statement; he could well understand the lieutenant's objections to having the impulsive and impressive Judy in close proximity to a man as handsome as Dibley.

"After the women and children and other civilians are safetly at Fort Laramie, our infantry companies should return here to protect whatever they can of this area," Hubbard continued. "We can also form a few loosely knit groups of volunteers—farmers and ranchers, mostly—to lend a hand. They have too much at stake to just completely pull out and turn their places over to the Indians. And I'm sure some of the ranchers will be willing to supply mounts for perhaps one company, so we'll be able to have more mobile troops in the field."

Robinson stood. "Well, gentlemen, I think we have covered everything. Now it's time to perform the duty we all dread: telling our wives that we'll be going off to fight a battle and they have two days to get ready to move to a new home!"

Wilma Henderson wondered if the sound of her heart beating rapidly inside her breast was actually audible. Ted's words seemed to hang in the air, leaving a double sear across her whirling mind. "There simply is no other choice, Wilma. If what we suspect is true, the Confederates are going to make a move against General Murphy, and soon. Without help, there is no way Murphy's undermanned force can stop them. We have to provide that help."

She felt the tears well up, and she wiped the corners of her eyes. Ted had talked to her at dinner and had just left the house to speak to some of the soldiers about the plans for the mounted companies of the Third Cavalry to begin the long, dangerous march through deep snow and roving bands of Indians, all the way from Fort Bridger to Santa Fe and possibly beyond.

With a determined effort of will, she choked back the

lump in her throat. Their separations since their marriage had been brief—only a few days at most while Ted was on patrol—but this was shaping up as an extended and difficult time to be apart.

Events, it seemed, never happened at the right time. And the worst part was that now she could not tell Ted her good news—that he was going to be a father. Not now. He was the one man who could succeed in getting a winter expedition through the mountains in time to help turn back any Confederate invasion of the West. If he knew about the child—their child—now growing in her womb, he would refuse to lead the expedition in order to stay by her side. He would resign his commission, and for the rest of his life he would be haunted by the memory that he had not heeded his country's call. She knew her husband well enough to know that each time he looked into his son's or daughter's eyes, he would remember. And it would tear him apart.

Wilma stood, walked to the window, and watched the swirling snow outside. She squared her shoulders. Perhaps it was a heavy load to bear, she thought, but she too had a duty to her country. If it meant losing the chance to see the excitement in his eyes, to share the magic moment of revelation, so be it.

Wilma made a silent vow: She would not even tell Vi Robinson about her pregnancy until the expedition was well under way. Upon his return, Ted would understand; and should her worst fears be realized and Ted not come riding home, at least he would have left her a part of himself. A legacy. It was something not all women had.

Viewed in that light, her decision to wait until she was sure before breaking the news to Ted pleased her.

It was a small sacrifice on her part, she knew, when seen against the possibility of winning or losing the Union. But still, it hurt a great deal.

Judy Hubbard stomped her foot; her eyes flashed anger and hurt through the tears.

"Abel Hubbard, you can't do this to me! If you loved me at all, you wouldn't even consider riding off to your precious war and leaving me alone, maybe even getting yourself killed!"

Abel reached for her, but she spun around to face the opposite wall. Even the set of her shoulders, Abel thought, was icy—like a high-country avalanche about to let loose. He checked his rising temper and tried once more to get his message across. "Honey, it's not that I don't love you—"

"Then why are you going?"

"Because I am a soldier." Abel felt his own voice tightening. "And I must—I *will*—serve my country. Would you rather be married to a coward, a man who puts his own selfish needs above those of his country?"

Finally she turned to face him. He noticed the set of her jaw, saw the tears running down her cheeks, and knew he might as well have been talking to a wall.

"I don't want just any man, Abel Hubbard! I want you. We've been married such a short time, and now you want to leave—"

He cut her off in midsentence. "You're using the wrong word, Judy. It isn't a 'want to' situation, it's a 'have to.' I'll prove my love for you almost any way you want, but not this way, not by ducking my duty!" He spun on a heel and stomped from their living quarters, welcoming the sting of snow against his heated face. *Why can't she understand?* he asked himself, and in the same moment, he answered his own question. "Because she loves me—and because she's young." Only when he noticed the quizzical look on a nearby sergeant's face did Abel realize he had spoken aloud.

Colonel Robinson held his wife long and tenderly, choking back the lump in his throat until he trusted himself to speak. "I'm sorry, Vi. I don't want to leave you not knowing when I'll be back."

"Bill," she said, stroking the back of his neck, "don't apologize for doing your duty—not to me. And I insist you not worry about me. You will need all your concentration for this campaign. I'll be just fine. And I'll be here to welcome you home when the job is done and done well, as I know it will be." Vi Robinson was somewhat surprised at the tone of strength in her own voice, when deep inside she wanted to break down and sob like a schoolgirl.

The colonel held his wife at arm's length, feeling the sting of tears in the corners of his eyes. "Vi, you don't know the void you've filled in my life, the strength you've supplied when I needed it most. How long has it been since an old worn-out cavalry colonel told you how much he loves you?"

"Too long," Vi said, pulling her husband to her breast. "I

wouldn't mind hearing it again. Surely you can spare an hour from your busy schedule?"

The next day was a terrible strain for Vi. Not only was she faced with the imminent departure of her husband and the packing of her things to take to Fort Laramie, but she, like Bill, was virtually besieged by the tearful Judy, who all day long badgered both her father and stepmother about leaving Abel Hubbard behind. Vi finally decided it was time to call on the one woman who might be able to help solve the problem. Vi put on her heavy coat and went to see Wilma Henderson.

Wilma was packing her things, trying hard not to weaken in her resolve to keep the news of her pregnancy from Ted. When Vi arrived, Wilma listened to her story and quickly decided to take action, glad for the opportunity to get her mind off her own problems. Throwing a coat over her shoulders, she and Vi rushed to the Hubbard quarters, where they found Judy, still fuming. They listened for a while as the younger woman complained bitterly. But finally Wilma lost all patience and broke in forcefully.

"Judy, think! Abel is one of the best officers in the territory. Your father is among the best—as is my Ted. It will take all their combined strength and knowledge to meet this challenge from the south. And the survival of the United States of America may very well ride with them."

"But we've been married such a short—"

Vi cut her off, her voice sharp. "And just how long, young lady, do you think your father and I have been married? About the same as you and Abel, am I correct? Do you think I love my husband less than you love yours? And do you think that being separated will be easier for me than for you?"

Judy's eyes flashed in defiance. "I don't care. I just know that Daddy is the commanding officer, and he could order Abel to stay with me."

Wilma sighed. "Vi, would you please ask that large corporal, Albert Jonas, to meet us here?"

Vi looked at her questioningly, then rose from her chair, picked up her coat, and left the house. When she reappeared a short time later with Albert Jonas, who had indeed been promoted to corporal by Colonel Robinson, Judy and Wilma were standing in the middle of the room.

"Corporal Jonas," Wilma said, "I wish to ask a favor of you."

"Certainly, Mrs. Henderson."

"Mrs. Hubbard seems to be reluctant to join the rest of us on our little trip to Fort Laramie." Wilma waved a hand around the room. "She has not yet started packing, even though all the other wives are almost ready to move out. Now we don't have much time left—you know that as well as I, Corporal Jonas, since you are going with Colonel Robinson. So, here is that favor I am asking: When it comes time for the women to leave, if Mrs. Hubbard is not prepared to go, I want you to bodily pick her up and place her aboard that wagon!"

Judy's gasp cut through the brief silence. "You—you can't be serious—you wouldn't—"

"Yes, ma'am," the huge black man said, "I certainly would. I'd hate to have to sling you onto that wagon like a sack of potatoes, Mrs. Hubbard. But whatever Mrs. Henderson asks me to do, I will."

Wilma saw the glint of amusement in the dark brown eyes and knew the corporal was having trouble controlling the grin that lurked just behind the solemn face.

"My daddy will break you back to private if you lay a hand on me!"

"I don't think so, Mrs. Hubbard. But anyhow, I been a private before. Not such a bad life. Now, if you ladies will excuse me . . ."

Judy glared at the back of the massive black man until the door had closed behind him. Then, ignoring the two women in the room with her, she yanked a trunk from a closet, banged the lid open noisily, and began to throw clothing into it.

Wilma winked at Vi Robinson, and the two quietly withdrew, each smiling at the sound of clanging and thumping as Judy packed.

"Would you have really gotten Albert Jonas to physically put her in the wagon?" Vi asked incredulously.

"Bet your last dime on it," Wilma answered.

The loading procedure went smoothly and efficiently, the hallmark of Colonel Wild Bill Robinson's command. And Wilma Henderson found herself wishing that, just this once, the colonel might overlook something, for every delay in his departure meant another precious moment with Ted.

She watched as the last of her trunks was loaded into the rear of the wagon she was to share with Vi on the move to Fort Laramie. She glanced toward the wagon nearby, where Judy Hubbard was calmly loading some of her valued trinkets, packing them carefully among protected spots in the load. Despite the heaviness in her heart and the dread of the upcoming separation from Ted, Wilma found herself wondering why Judy's complaining and whining had suddenly stopped. Wilma was sure her threat to have Albert Jonas bodily throw her into the wagon if necessary was not the reason for Judy's change in behavior. She frowned as she remembered seeing Judy and the tall, handsome Colin Dibley engaged in conversation only a few hours ago. Wilma was certain she had seen Judy's face brighten toward the end of the conversation. And after that, young Mrs. Hubbard had been not only industrious, but cordial, as preparations for the move began. Wilma knew full well that Judy's sudden change in demeanor was connected to that conversation. She decided to keep a close eye on Judy Hubbard, at least for a while.

At a touch on her arm, Wilma turned to face her husband.

"Something troubling you, dear?" Ted's voice reflected his concern, and again she offered up thanks that she had found such a man. Riding off into a snowstorm and possibly into battle, he worried about things that concerned her, no matter how trifling.

She shook her head, forcing a smile. "No, Ted, but thank you for asking. I suppose I was just dreading the fact that soon we will be separated." She swallowed the growing lump in her throat as she thought about the baby and how much she wanted to tell Ted. But she had made her decision, and for the welfare of the man standing before her now, she knew it was the correct path to follow.

"I'm not looking forward to it either, Wilma," Ted said, his voice tender. "I'm going to miss you more than I can say."

A call from the wagon master cut through Wilma like a knife. The time for parting had arrived. She glanced up and down the line of wagons, knowing her own feelings were shared by other women whose husbands or loved ones were making the dangerous trip south. Wilma welcomed Ted's assistance as he helped her onto the wagon seat, grateful for his final kiss and embrace.

"I must go now, darling," Ted said. "My scouts will be moving out in minutes, ahead of the main force." She placed her gloved hand over his.

"Take care of yourself, Ted. Come back to me soon." Then he was gone, and finally she felt safe in letting her tears flow. *At least Yellow Crow will be with him*, she thought.

Colonel Bill Robinson tucked his hand inside his wife's elbow. "Before you climb into the wagon, Vi, could we have a word in private?"

Alarmed at the note of concern in his voice, Vi merely nodded as she allowed the colonel to lead her into his small office. She noticed that he carefully closed the door. He reached into his tunic and handed her a parcel which bore a War Department seal.

"I hate to add to your troubles at such a time, Vi, but you must keep this for me. If there were any other way to handle it, I would save you the burden, but there is no other way. This envelope contains orders bearing the signature of Edwin M. Stanton, Secretary of War. It was delivered to me yesterday by special courier." She took the envelope in a trembling hand. "Those orders," the colonel said, "instruct me to report back East with my entire command."

Stunned, Vi instinctively tightened her grip on the envelope, placing a hand on her husband's forearm.

"I have chosen to ignore those orders," Colonel Robinson said. "I must. I believe a decisive battle in this war is going to be fought to the south of here, and the Third Cavalry Regiment can turn the tide in the Union's favor. You do understand the consequences of my action, don't you, Vi?"

She nodded, swallowing hard. "Disobeying a direct order in time of war is a court-martial offense. Bill, you are placing your career—perhaps even your life—in jeopardy!"

"I know. And believe me, Vi, if I were not convinced in my own mind of the importance of this mission, I would return east without hesitation. In the balance, my own career and even my life are expendable. I regret this for your sake, but not for mine. You may have to live out the rest of your days as the wife of a court-martialed colonel." Wild Bill sighed. "But what is more important, the War Department will know that I have received those orders.

"Now I want to ask you to carry a heavy burden. During this campaign, I want you to hold on to the orders. That way none of my men will know about them and therefore will not have to face any military punishment or have a blot on their records when the regiment returns. It was my decision and mine alone to disobey; no one else should have to pay for that decision."

Vi reached out, pulled her husband to her, and buried her face in his shoulder, painfully conscious of the terrible price he was paying in order to keep the West in Union hands. "Of course, I will do as you ask, Bill," she said, struggling to keep her voice from breaking. "I know you would do nothing like this unless it was the right thing to do."

They held each other for a long moment, then Vi pulled herself away and attempted a cheerful smile. "Well, I guess I'd better get going. The wagons might leave without me; then what would I do?" They laughed tenderly, holding hands briefly, and then Vi was out the door and on her way back to her wagon.

Meanwhile, at the side of Judy Hubbard's loaded and waiting wagon, Abel held his wife close, mildly surprised that she had not even so much as hinted that he remain behind. He was relieved she seemed to have finally accepted the inevitable. It made the difficult parting easier.

"I love you, Judy," he whispered into her ear.

"And I love you, Abel. Keep yourself from harm's way."

"I will be seeing you again soon," he said, noticing that his own voice was a bit tight.

Surprisingly, she smiled at him, dry-eyed. "I may be seeing you sooner than you think, Lieutenant," she said. "Now please be so kind as to help me aboard this lumbering hunk of wood, then you had best join Captain Henderson and the others. It appears the scouts are about to move out, and Ted has asked you to ride with them, you know."

Hiding his confusion at her cryptic remark, Abel helped his wife onto the wagon seat, then mounted his own sorrel. Halfway to the cluster of men that was Henderson's Scouts, he turned and waved. Her answering wave was bright, almost cheerful.

Judy watched her husband take his place between Ted and Yellow Crow. Yes, she would indeed be seeing Abel soon. She was going to join him in Santa Fe, thanks to the kind assistance of Mr. Colin Dibley. She imagined her husband's face when she would suddenly appear, dressed in the fine green gown that fit easily into a saddlebag. She knew that even if he should be angry with her, she had ways to assure that his anger would not last long. A smile tugged at the corners of her mouth.

The wagon train moved out, and at the crest of the hills south of Fort Bridger, Ted halted his gelding. He had left his stallion behind, to be sent to Fort Laramie with the mares.

There was no need to risk losing a good horse in a snow-covered mountain pass—or on the battlefield.

As Ted took one last look back, he saw the wagons carrying wives, families, and personal goods to the safety of Fort Laramie. They were already moving through the gate, the distance-diminished figures of infantrymen walking alongside. He glanced toward the gray sky. At least, he thought, the snow had stopped falling for the moment, and unless the weather worsened, their journey should not be an especially difficult one.

He sighed and kneed his mount forward, wishing he could say the same for his own journey.

V

General Kelly Murphy gnawed at the unlighted cigar between his teeth, pacing the floor of the office at Fort Union. A gust of chill wind momentarily fanned the small blaze in the fireplace as the last of his line officers arrived. The general glanced briefly at each face, reading concern and confusion in the expression of many of the officers, and he felt his own anxiety deepen. Few of the officers had any more battlefield experience than did their green troops. Only Kit Carson seemed relaxed and at ease. But Kelly Murphy noticed the dark eyes above the straight nose and high cheekbones were constantly on the alert, as Carson listened to the conversations that eddied among the assembled officers. Murphy knew that only three men in the room fully realized the magnitude of the job that faced them—himself; his adjutant, Major Keith Sanborne; and the slightly built Kit Carson, the former mountain man now wearing colonel's insignia.

The general rolled the cigar stub back to another corner of his mouth and sighed. *Might as well get on with it*, he thought. There was little enough time to spare as it was.

"Gentlemen," he said, "it seems that our worst fears have now become reality. It comes as no surprise to any of us that the Confederates at Mesilla are preparing to move. And it is up to us—and us alone—to stop them. Fort Union must not fall!" The general paused for a moment, letting the final declaration hang in the air.

"We cannot sit and wait for the Confederates to come to us. If they are able to lay siege to Fort Union, the issue will be decided in their favor. We must give them no opportunity to do so. Therefore, here is our plan of action." He turned to the map on the wall behind him. There was a smooth swish of steel on leather, and the point of the general's saber touched a spot on the map.

"We will attack the enemy here—at Valverde, a place of our own choosing. A victory there will send the Confederate column reeling back into Texas. But," Murphy said, turning to face the group, "should we not win a decisive victory, we will have to fight a defensive action—all the way back to the storerooms of Fort Union, if need be."

He slid the saber back into its sheath. "Do not for a moment think it is going to be easy, gentlemen. The commander of the Confederate force is a top-notch field leader. And don't underestimate the determination and fighting ability of the regular Rebel army and the Texas volunteers. I need not remind you that they have us outmanned and outgunned. Our only hope of defeating them, gentlemen, is if each officer and each soldier carries out his assignment to the fullest. A concentrated and coordinated strike must be made, and each unit will be like a link of a chain—the failure of one can have fatal consequences upon the creature as a whole."

General Murphy tossed the well-chewed cigar stub into a brass spittoon. "Report back here in one hour for battle plan details and your individual assignments, gentlemen. By this time tomorrow, we must be in the field." He waved toward the door, dismissing the officers, but his adjutant Sanborne remained behind as the others filed out.

"Any chance of our getting help—any help—from any direction, General?" the major asked.

Murphy shook his head. "I'm afraid not, Keith. I'd give a lot to have the assistance of Colonel Robinson's Third Cavalry at Fort Bridger, but there's no chance of it, not with the deep snows in the mountain passes blocking their way. And although General Carleton and his column of California volunteers are on patrol in the Navajo country, Carleton probably won't be able to reach us in time even if our messenger finds him. It's a big country between here and California. No, it looks as if we're going to have to go it alone."

A gusty north wind plucked small grains of desert sand from among the Saguaro cactus, whipping the miniature grapeshot into the faces of the men facing each other on the bank of the Salt River.

Lieutenant Kevin O'Reilly followed the example of his

commander, General James H. Carleton of the California Brigade, and ignored the sting of the sand against his stubbled cheeks. For a moment he wished he had been able to grow muttonchop whiskers like his commander's. But, the lieutenant thought to himself, he had not been able to do a very good job of it—just as he had not been completely able to mold himself in the general's image.

It seemed to O'Reilly that the silence had held for a long time, though his sweaty palms told him it was only his own nerves. He glanced at Carleton. The general stared from one set of dark eyes to another in the line across from him, letting the set of his jaw and the flash in his pale, piercing eyes set the tone. O'Reilly knew the general well enough to realize Carleton was about to deliver the California Column's ultimatum to the group of Navajo chiefs.

"Most of you," Carleton said, "I know personally, and many of you know me. We know each other as men of courage—and as men of honor." O'Reilly caught the heavy emphasis on the final word; it had the kind of tone his teachers had used when they caught him looking out the window and daydreaming instead of attending to his slate and books. "But among you," Carleton was saying, "are those who know nothing of the word honor. You have broken your promise. You have left your homelands, ridden far, killed the white man, stolen his stock and his grain, even his women. The Navajo are known and respected as a people who keep their promises. Yet, you continue to raid and burn."

Carleton fell silent for a moment, as though waiting for a challenge. None came. But in the corner of his field of vision, Kevin O'Reilly saw one chief's hand creep near the knife at his belt. O'Reilly caught the Indian's attention and made a show of putting his hand on the big army pistol at his hip. The message seemed to have been received; O'Reilly and the Indian both knew the Navajo would live no more than a few seconds should he raise a weapon against the whiskered general. Dark eyes flashed in anger, but the Indian's hand retreated from the haft of the knife.

"Now it has come to this," Carleton said. "I can no longer trust you as men of your word. Therefore, from this day forward, General James Carleton and his California Column will see to it that the Navajo keep the peace. It is your final word from me. And I keep my word. Go back to your own land. Leave our people alone, and we will leave yours alone. If you raid, we will answer you by raiding."

O'Reilly heard the determination in the level tone of the general, who feared no man, and whose well-trained and experienced troopers would follow him into the fires of hell if need be. The big lieutenant also noticed that the chief whose attention he had caught earlier was now stiffening, dark eyes flashing.

"No white man speaks the truth," the Indian called out.

Carleton turned his head slightly to face the muscular Navajo with the scarred cheek. "Is Gallegos the spokesman for the entire nation?"

"Chief Gallegos speaks for Gallegos. So long as the rivers flow and the wind blows, Gallegos and his warriors will not bend to the white man's will." The chief suddenly turned and strode away, leaving a ripple of murmurs among the remaining Navajo. One by one, the other chiefs rose and followed Gallegos toward the main Indian encampment a hundred yards away.

Carleton merely watched them leave, his face void of expression.

"Sir," Kevin O'Reilly said, "we can stop them if you wish."

The general shook his head, rippling the gray-streaked dark hair that fell almost to his earlobes. "No, Lieutenant. We came to talk and only to talk, and that promise will be honored. Even without my word, you will note that the Navajo camp includes women and children. Our quarrel is not with them, and I'll not see them hurt or killed. Incidentally, O'Reilly, thank you for preventing a possible incident. Had Gallegos pulled that knife, the situation could easily have gotten out of control. You handled that very well, Lieutenant."

O'Reilly felt a tinge of color rise in his cheeks. "I had a good teacher, sir—you."

"Some things are not taught, Lieutenant. They are in the man to begin with." Carleton glanced at the sun. "It is unlikely, though possible, that Gallegos will stir up any mischief for us, especially since our two camps are so close together. O'Reilly, I would like for you to keep a close eye on the Navajo camp, and particularly on that of Gallegos, for the remainder of the afternoon and into the night. If you spot anything suspicious, mount up and ride back, on the double. Above all, don't use your gun unless it's a life-or-death situation. A single shot could trigger a massacre of innocent Indians and possibly some soldiers as well."

"Yes, sir."

"Our scouts will contact you at regular intervals, and you will be relieved shortly after sunset."

"Yes, sir. I'll do my best, General Carleton."

"If I didn't think you would, Lieutenant, I would send someone else. And you'd better take an extra canteen along. The Navajo can drink this Salt River water, but an ordinary soldier who made that mistake might wind up spending more time in the bushes than in the saddle."

Lieutenant O'Reilly had little trouble locating the distinctively painted, animal-hide shelter of the Navajo chief, Gallegos. O'Reilly found a reasonably comfortable site on the riverbank where he could not be seen against the lowering sun and—hoping he did not stir up any tarantulas or scorpions—settled into the shallow depression to wait and watch. Of all the things he had learned in the army, he thought, being patient was the most difficult. Just waiting was tough enough, but when you had an Irish temper to begin with, it was worse.

The young Navajo woman pulled a final stitch through the leather and returned the freshly repaired moccasins to their proper place. She glanced at her father, sitting cross-legged, brooding and puffing on a pipe. Wind Flower stifled a sigh; she did not like the smell of tobacco, but she had learned to live with it. Of more immediate concern was the foreboding set of Gallegos's jaw, the way he stared unblinkingly at a spot on the wall of the hide shelter. Being the daughter of a powerful chief was more demanding than people might think, Wind Flower mused. When her father was in one of these moods, only two members of the tribe could break him free from the spirits that troubled his soul: herself and her grandfather, the shaman, whose wisdom was exceeded only by his mystical ability to read the sand paintings with such uncanny accuracy. And even then, she thought, there was a good time and a bad time to approach Gallegos. This was not a good time. When the dark spirits entered the chief, minor tribal disputes and family quarrels were brought to the daughter rather than to the father, and Wind Flower found some consolation in the fact that she generally could offer help.

She rose from tending the coals, which would soon feed the fire for the evening meal, and glanced again at her father.

Perhaps if she made some soothing herb tea for Gallegos, it might be easier to talk with him. Picking up a gourd container, she stepped into the late afternoon sunlight. Fresh water was needed for the herb drink, and she had seen a small spring, which should be salt-free, on the far bank of the river. It was a shallow river, carrying only a narrow band of brackish water, and it would be no trouble to cross. She felt sure she could locate the tiny spring in its small clearing among the scrub brush which lined the far bank.

She shook her waist-length black hair into place, letting it fall in its own freedom, and quickly crossed the river of mostly damp sand.

She knelt beside the small spring, lifted a cupped palm of the water to her mouth, and smiled at the taste. It was fresh and clean to the tongue. Taking care not to disturb the silt around the shallow spring basin, she lowered her gourd container and listened to the gurgle as the sweet water flowed into the opening.

Another sound, a footfall nearby, brought her to her feet, her senses alert. Disgust and anger rose in her stomach as Choshay, a junior warrior, stepped into the clearing.

Wind Flower did not speak but merely stared at the short, ugly Navajo with the overly large belly and twisted, broken teeth now laid bare in what passed for a smile.

"Wind Flower walks the evening," Choshay said. "It is not safe for a woman to walk alone." The tightly controlled voice had a thin edge of violence.

"Wind Flower walks alone because she chooses to walk alone," she said pointedly. Her discomfort grew as the dark eyes, one half-closed by a ragged scar, seemed to glitter. She drew herself to her full height of just over five feet, enduring the humiliation of knowing that Choshay was removing her clothing in his thoughts. Despite her rising anger, she held her tongue.

"The daughter of Gallegos need not walk alone," Choshay said. "There is in this camp a fine young warrior, one who has much to offer."

"Wind Flower does not know this man," she said, instantly realizing her mistake as anger flared in the half-closed eye. "If Choshay speaks of himself," she continued, "Wind Flower has twice refused his offerings. She will continue to do so."

Choshay stepped closer. Wind Flower stood her ground,

determined to show no sign of the fear that grew inside her. Choshay was close enough now that she could smell his foul breath, soured by decayed teeth, and braced herself; she would not step back from this man.

"Choshay has been marked many times in battle. It is not his fault that his face is no longer handsome. And now Choshay has more to offer a bride—many guns, pans, bolts of rich cloth, horses."

"And where did Choshay get these wonderful things? From the same man who gives him bad whiskey, which he then sells to others?"

In the low brush nearby, Lieutenant Kevin O'Reilly placed each foot with care. Drawn first by the sight of an attractive young woman crossing the river below and then by the sound of voices, he had worked his way to the edge of the small clearing around the stream. He took his first close look at the girl and felt the breath catch in his throat. Never had he seen so beautiful a woman, her finely shaped features framed in coal-black hair. Even the loose-fitting dress she wore could not conceal the woman's figure inside. But he sensed that her wide brown eyes, flashing now with anger, could be as tender as those of a doe nuzzling its new fawn.

The tone of the conversation pulled him back to the reality of the moment. Though he understood only a little Navajo, there was no mistaking the antipathy the young woman felt for the brave.

"It is not the ugliness of Choshay's face that Wind Flower does not like," the girl was saying. "It is the ugliness of the spirit. Now, go! Leave Wind Flower alone!"

O'Reilly saw the Indian straighten as though slapped, his powerful hand raised overhead, poised to strike the woman's uplifted face.

Without thinking, O'Reilly sprang from his hiding place, leaped the distance in a single stride, and grasped the Indian's wrist in a powerful grip. He hurled the fist and arm aside as Choshay spun to face the unexpected attacker. He heard the woman's gasp of surprise, then sidestepped quickly to avoid a blow by the Indian. O'Reilly's Irish temper suddenly flared, and he threw a short punch, which traveled only a matter of inches but stopped the squat, ugly Indian solidly as it thumped against the bone in the forehead.

Choshay staggered back a step, fumbling at his belt. O'Reilly knew instantly the Indian was reaching for a knife. He closed with the Navajo, driving a right hand to the ribs. He grasped the Indian's knife hand with his own left, trapping the fingers over the handle of the weapon, and squeezed with all the strength he could muster from his own two hundred pounds.

He felt bones crumple beneath his fist as he pounded another right into the Indian's midsection. The Indian staggered back two steps but remained on his feet. O'Reilly started to follow, then suddenly found his own arms pinned to his sides. A voice in his ear said, "Enough, Lieutenant! This ain't the place to start no Injun war!"

The voice of one of his comrades finally penetrated the fury in O'Reilly's brain. He stopped struggling, knowing the strength in the huge arms that held him was beyond even his own considerable power. Across the way, two Navajo suddenly materialized from the thicket; one spoke sharply in the Indian dialect. Choshay responded angrily and started to move toward the lieutenant, but the other brave stepped in front, placing a hand on Choshay's chest.

As quickly as it had begun, the confrontation ended. The two Navajo led Choshay and the woman away, but the expression in the ugly Indian's eyes would remain with Kevin O'Reilly—it was a look of pure hate, and the promise of a debt unpaid. Kevin returned the glare, just to let the Navajo know he had a ticket back at any time, any place.

After a few steps, the young woman turned to look at Kevin. The large brown eyes seemed to reflect relief. And, Kevin thought, a look of gratitude.

The powerful hand gripping O'Reilly's upper arm turned him in the direction of the California Column's camp. "Don't expect you've seen the last of the ugly one," Private Mike Connor said. "I speak a little Navajo, cusswords mostly, but I got the message. That one has plans to feed your private parts to the village dogs."

O'Reilly let his tension out with a hefty sigh. "Thanks, Mike. I guess I just lost control of myself."

The laugh at his ear was genuine. "Think nothin' of it, Lieutenant. We Irishmen gotta stick together. We'd best tell the general what happened though, just in case the Injuns decide to take it up with him."

But as they approached the general's tent, there was a commotion at the sentry lines. Two troopers stood with rifles aimed at a slender Indian, scarely more than a youth. Kevin recognized him as a Ute; the lathered, worn-out sorrel the young Indian led wore a U.S. Army brand.

At a wave of the lieutenant's hand, the troopers lowered their rifles. "He's one of the friendlies, boys," Kevin said. "The Ute have been among our best friends." He turned to the young Indian. "What brings you to the camp of General Carleton?" He hoped the boy understood English, for his own command of Indian dialects left much to be desired.

"The General Murphy send. Have writing for the General Carleton."

Kevin nodded, glancing at the growing number of California Column troopers gathering at the scene. "Al," he said to one of the soldiers, "take care of the horse. He looks to be in pretty bad shape, but see if you can save him." The Ute seemed reluctant to release the reins but surrendered the mount at the touch of Kevin's hand on his shoulder. "Come with me, please," Kevin said. "I'll take you to the general."

Carleton was just about to leave his tent to see what the commotion was all about when Kevin and the Ute reached the commanding officer's tent. The Indian youth silently handed a sweat-stained envelope to the general. Kevin, seeing the youth look longingly at the water keg in the corner, filled a dipper and handed it to the Indian. The youth sipped it slowly, the sign of a desertwise traveler too long with thirst and well aware that water downed too fast would not stay down long.

General Carleton looked up from the message. Kevin could read concern in his eyes.

"General Murphy is in big trouble, Lieutenant O'Reilly. He is outnumbered by a large force of Confederates, and by now the battle may already have begun. Alone, I don't think Murphy can stop them short of Fort Union. And I fear we can't reach him in time."

Carleton stood, stroking his full sideburns. "But we are going to make one hell of a try. And if we are too late to help Murphy, we can at least make life a bit less comfortable for the boys from the South."

"I go back with you," the young Indian said. "My people there. You give me horse?"

"Certainly, son. Any lone rider who can make the run you just made and find us in this wide-open desert is certainly worth a good army horse."

"Have more news," the youngster said. "Kit Carson there."

Kevin O'Reilly was surprised at the sudden grin that replaced the normally firm expression of the column commander. "Kit Carson!" the general said. "Why, I haven't seen him since the Jicarilla campaign. Yes, sir," Carleton went on, as much to himself as to anyone else, "if Murphy's got Kit, he's got at least one good hand." Carleton turned abruptly. "Please summon my officers, Lieutenant. I want all troops mounted at first light. I wouldn't miss this chase for all the gold in California."

The following morning, the troops rode out. In the chill desert wind of the fresh dawn, Kevin O'Reilly kept his fractious mount on a tight rein as he rode the left point of the California Column. He had asked for the assignment; the route would take him within yards of the spring where he had last seen the hauntingly expressive eyes in a fine-boned face. He might never see her again, but he did not believe he would ever forget her. On impulse, he reined his mount in the direction of the spring only a few yards distant.

He sat his horse for a long moment, looking across the Salt River, hoping for a glimpse of her in the now bustling Navajo camp.

He was not disappointed. He saw her on the far riverbank, accompanied by some of the other Navajo women, getting water to bring back for the morning campfires. She was escorting a few of the children, instructing them in their chores, and Kevin was struck anew by the woman's beauty, the warmth and gentleness of her spirit. She lifted her gaze and saw him sitting his mount, and she smiled and raised her hand in a gesture of thanks and farewell. Then she turned her attention back to the children, shepherding them as they went about their tasks.

Kevin would not forget this scene, nor would he allow it to be a permanent good-bye. He would see the young woman again sometime, perhaps when the army finished its work in New Mexico.

He rode away to join the other soldiers, his heart filled with gladness, when a glitter suddenly caught his eye. He dismounted for a closer look. There, half-buried in the sand where he had scuffled with the ugly Indian, was a small medallion. Kevin picked it up, blew the dirt from it, and stared for a moment at the unusual design. At first glance it seemed to be the French fleur-de-lis, yet somehow, it did not seem quite right. He stripped the broken cord from the medallion, tossed it aside, and dropped the medal in his pocket. The strange souvenir would remind him of the ugly Indian brave in the days to come. It also would remind him of another Navajo—a beautiful maiden.

He remounted and spurred his horse into a trot, quickly reaching his assigned position once more. With one quick look back, one last hope of again seeing the girl, Kevin O'Reilly finally gave up and turned his attention to the long, hard ride ahead.

General Kelly Murphy sat astride his big Morgan roan, surveyed the field below at Valverde, and turned to the grizzled major at his side. The crackle of small-arms fire faded before the frequent roar of cannon and blast of exploding shell.

"What do you make of it so far, Keith?"

Sanborne rolled the chew of tobacco to his other cheek, then spat an amber stream. "Don't like it much, General," he said. "So far we've turned back their advance units, but they really haven't come after us yet— Good God!"

"What is it, Major?"

Sanborne pointed downriver to the south. "They're going after our cannons! Lose those, General, and our right flank is in big trouble!"

General Murphy stifled a curse as a line of Confederate cavalry burst from the trees and swept toward the Union gun emplacement protecting the right flank. Even at such a distance Murphy heard the bloodcurdling war whoops from the long line of charging Texans. "Who's out there?"

"Johnson's unit, General. No chance— Wait!" The adjutant pointed an excited finger at a hard-running blue line dashing down a shallow gully toward the gun emplacement. "It's Carson's bunch, sir! The Texans can't see 'em—they're riding right into him!"

As the officers watched the distant drama unfold, a small blue-clad figure—Carson—dismounted and took cover in the rocks and shrub along the ridge, waving his men into position.

Murphy felt his jaw muscles tighten as the Texas cavalry charge neared Carson's thin line of defenders. The horsemen were only yards from the ridge when a solid volley ripped into their ranks, sending several Texans tumbling from their horses. The charge was momentarily stalled, horses milled in fear and confusion, and then a cannister shell from a hastily turned six-pounder at the gun emplacement raked the cavalry unit. The remaining horsemen wheeled their mounts and dashed back for the safety of the Confederate line in the trees across the valley. For the moment, the Union cannons were safe.

"How the devil did Carson know?" Murphy asked, awe in his voice.

Sanborne spat again. "No explainin' instinct, General. Kit Carson ain't your regular army man. Fights like an Injun mostly. But he turns up in the right place at the right time. Look now!"

Murphy's breath caught in his throat as a broad wave of mounted Texans launched a determined cavalry charge against the center of the Union lines. Foot soldiers followed, racing from boulder to brush, and though Murphy had heard it before, the piercing Rebel yells sent an involuntary shudder down his spine. The Texas war cries seemed even worse, the screech of the devil rising above the blast of rifles and double-barrel shotguns.

The blue line wavered before the onslaught. Murphy swallowed another curse as first one, then scores of volunteers bolted, flinging down their weapons; others merely cowered in whatever cover they could find. Only a scattered number of defenders stood their ground.

Murphy and Sanborne exchanged glances; their worst fears had been confirmed. As one, they spurred their mounts toward the thick of the battle below, pistols drawn.

Murphy's big horse raced into a group of fleeing volunteers. "Stand fast, damn you!" he yelled. "Stand and fight!" The terrified soldiers merely veered past Murphy's horse, their legs pumping in full flight. A hundred yards away, the first of the yelling Confederate horsemen breached the forward Union line, firing double-barreled shotguns into blue bodies.

Murphy spurred his mount toward the approaching Texans and felt a rifle ball tear at his sleeve. The sight of the general charging the assault line inspired the trained soldiers in blue, and they began to lay down a withering fire. The general emptied his handgun at close range, saw one rider tumble from the saddle, and by then, his charge had carried him through the first wave and into the Confederate infantry. He holstered the now useless pistol and whipped the saber from its sheath. He felt the big horse shudder and stumble and knew the animal had been hit.

In the swirling dust and heavy cloud of gun smoke,

Murphy's heart sank. He knocked aside the barrel of a shotgun with his saber, slicing the shoulder of a wild-eyed, bearded man, and battled his way toward the edge of the field of fire, knowing the battle for Valverde was lost. Ignoring the buzz of rifle balls about his ears, Murphy reached the safety of a clump of boulders just as his horse went down heavily. The general rolled free of the dying animal's body and scrambled to the rocks.

The Texans' charge had overwhelmed the ranks of the desertion-weakened defenders, leaving behind the bodies of dead from both sides, the moans of the wounded. Trapped in the rocks and now on foot, General Kelly Murphy could only watch and wonder how this rout of Union forces could be turned into an orderly retreat.

Murphy became aware of the sound of pounding hooves bearing down. He turned and lifted his saber, then tossed it aside and swung aboard the riderless horse led by Kit Carson.

The wiry mountain man shouted above the din of battle. "Get out of here, General! We've got too much work to do to be burying the commanding officer!" Carson slapped the horse on the rump, and the animal leveled its ears in a dead run toward the safety of the nearest Union line.

The Union guns, undermanned by units suffering heavy casualties, could not be aimed at the battlefield proper because the shells would fall among friend and foe alike, and so the gunners settled into a long-range duel with the Confederate artillery. Murphy watched as one gun emplacement was overrun; then, from the corner of his vision, he saw two dozen mounted men in blue charge directly across the battlefield and disappear into the trees on the opposite side.

For a long moment, only the occasional bark of sidearms could be heard over the distant thunder of the artillery duel. The Texans had wheeled their horses and were headed in a flanking maneuver to trap and destroy three regular army infantry companies. But suddenly, a volley of accurate rifle fire from the trees across the field broke the back of the attack, allowing the men who would have been trapped to retreat to relative safety. Kelly Murphy suddenly realized who had led those mounted men into the trees and saved the lives of perhaps two hundred Union soldiers. Murphy idly wondered where Kit Carson had managed to find more than twenty men who not only knew how to ride but also how to shoot.

* * *

From his observation point atop a rocky knoll, Lieutenant Colonel Roy Simon Humphries turned from the field of battle, fighting back a wave of nausea.

"Send out a flag of truce," he said to his second-in-command. "We must bury the dead, tend the wounded."

"But, sir! We have them on the run! We can wipe out the entire command!"

Humphries's eyes flashed anger. "You think so, do you? We're short of ammunition, medicine, supplies, and we've taken heavy casualties. Our men are exhausted. They need to rest. Only then will we be able to accomplish our objective."

Humphries's sigh was heavy. "Murphy was obviously gambling on stopping us dead in our tracks here—and he nearly did. You saw how many of his troops broke and ran. He gambled and lost. But we can't spare the time to dig each and every one of his soldiers out of the hills. Fort Union is our objective. We will not press our luck or our overextended supply lines. Now, get me that white flag! And do it now!"

The Union casualties had been heavy. None was more painful to General Kelly Murphy than the death of his second-in-command and longtime friend, Major Keith Sanborne. But there was no time for mourning. A trooper came up to the general and announced that a white flag was approaching.

Murphy stood, looking onto the battlefield. He recognized the figure standing there alone, bearing the white banner—Roy Simon Humphries.

The general went immediately to hear what the other officer had to say. The two men met in the center of the open, cannon-shell pitted battleground. Each touched hat brims in salutes.

"Hello, Kelly."

"Roy."

"It has been a long day, General," Humphries said. "We have both suffered numerous casualties. I propose a truce to allow for the treatment of the wounded, an exchange of prisoners perhaps, and the burial of the dead."

"On what terms?"

"None, sir, other than each side lay down its arms and lick its wounds."

"Agreed."

"And General Murphy, there will be more fighting, you know. We will meet again. We must."

"I am aware of that, Colonel Humphries. And I must admit I do not look forward to those encounters. But if we must each choose to battle on the field of honor to save our countries, there is no alternative. We can only do our best to limit any needless bloodshed."

A handshake sealed the truce, and within moments blue-coated army surgeons worked alongside their counterparts in butternut uniforms, frequently working together on the same patient. Kit Carson moved among the wounded as well, applying his frontier mountain medicine to the lesser injuries, helping privates and officers alike, regardless of uniform color.

At length, Carson located both General Murphy and Lieutenant Humphries.

"My wife, Josefa, has established a military hospital at Taos," he told the two leaders. "Those who need extended care from either wound or sickness are welcome there. She has trained many women in the area as nurses and secured the support of physicians in both Taos and Santa Fe."

Carson's sharp eyes moved from officer to officer. "It is a long way from here to Taos," he said, "and the more seriously wounded would not survive. But if I might be so bold as to make a suggestion, perhaps each force could supply some men and two or three wagons for a joint escort of the wounded to the Taos hospital. You have my word that any men I select will cause no problem on the journey."

"An excellent suggestion, sir," Humphries said. "You also have my word as to the conduct of my men." General Murphy quickly agreed, then began issuing orders for the procurement of the wagons and selection of troopers to accompany the cavalcade.

"General Murphy," Kit Carson said, "I would very much like to accompany the wagons to Taos. Josefa—" He left the sentence unfinished as a look of despair crossed Murphy's face. Carson knew there was no way he could leave now. Even with his help, the prospect of saving Fort Union from falling to the Confederacy was very slim indeed.

Captain Ted Henderson tucked his chin down into the partial protection of the collar of his greatcoat trying to ignore the howling wind that screamed through Green River Pass. The wind turned simple snowflakes into tiny spearpoints, driving them into exposed skin. But despite his own suffering and fingers so stiff they would scarcely flex, Ted knew he was in better condition than many of the soldiers in the Third Cavalry Regiment. Many years in the mountains had toughened his tolerance to cold and discomfort, but not all of the men had experienced a February blizzard in the high mountains. From the comfort of a warm cabin, he thought to himself, a blizzard could be a thing of beauty. Outside, it was a different experience entirely.

He turned his attention back to the front of the column, where the black giant Albert Jonas labored shoulder to shoulder with Yellow Crow, breaking a path for the horses and mules, reducing drifts that in spots had been waist-deep to more manageable levels. Skidding and lunging, the horses and pack mules were able to break through, nostrils flaring from the effort of tremendous exertion and from the panic of unsure footing beneath their hooves.

Ted led his own mount forward, tapped Jonas on the shoulder, and raised his voice to a shout to be heard above the wail of the wind.

"I'll take over for a while, Corporal! You've been at this for almost an hour already!"

Jonas shook his head from side to side, leaving Ted with the impression of a black grizzly bear sprouting frozen whiskers.

"No need, Cap'n!" Jonas yelled back. "I still got some work left in me! And I done worked up a sweat—quit now and I'll freeze for sure!" A grin split the black face, breaking a few particles of ice from the beard. "Besides, Cap'n, it gets cold in Pennsylvania in the winter, too! I'll holler when I can't take no more!"

Ted merely put a gloved hand on the heavily muscled shoulder. He glanced at the wiry Cheyenne working alongside. Yellow Crow, shaking his head, continued to wield a pickax against a particularly stubborn ice-packed snowbank. Ted marveled at the strength and stamina of the Indian. Though the Cheyenne were accustomed to hard winters, the cold had to be hurting even Yellow Crow. Yet he gave no outward sign of discomfort.

"Just a few more yards and the worst will be passed!" Ted yelled, then began working his way back down the long line of troopers, most hunched against the wind, some shivering, but all still gamely plodding forward. Even Wild Bill Robinson pitched in to help control the frightened horses, moving from one point in the line to another, coaxing a packhorse here, stopping there to offer a word of encouragement to an exhausted, half-frozen trooper.

Ted felt a surge of pride in these men and wondered if any other officer in the entire United States Army had the privilege of serving with such dedicated and tough soldiers. He fell into step alongside little Bernie Christian.

"How are you doing, Private?"

The pain was obvious in the dull eyes beneath ice-coated brows. Ted noticed a slight shuffling in Christian's step; frostbite was probably beginning to take hold. Time was of the essence for many of the men. The sooner they broke through the crest of Green River Pass and found shelter, the fewer toes and fingers would be lost.

"I'll make it, Captain," Christian said through chattering teeth, "and if this war ever ends, I'm haulin' my tail back to Georgia and never lookin' at no mountain again!"

Ted smiled as he watched the galvanized Yankee plod alongside the two-pounder cannon, pickax over a slender shoulder, laboriously swinging it from time to time to break ice off the sled runners improvised by Chad Clark.

The smile faded as he wondered how Frank Armbrister and the other four scouts now on patrol were faring. At least the men with the main column could walk. And swinging a pickax and wrestling with a balky mule kept the blood flowing through the muscles, staving off frostbite until the cold sapped the final bit of strength. But Frank and his group were out on horseback in the storm, scouting for potential danger and checking the condition of the trail ahead. If a horse should happen to slip and fall, a man alone would quickly freeze to death in this weather. And, Ted thought, there is no colder place than on horseback in a howling blizzard.

It took a few minutes in the nearly blinding snowstorm to locate Lieutenant Chad Clark. The artillery officer was fretting over his ammunition sled, checking the bindings to make sure the load remained stable in spite of the jerky lunges of the workhorses harnessed to the rig.

"My compliments on your invention, Lieutenant!" Ted yelled, his mouth close to the officer's ear. "The sled runners seem to be the answer to mountain country!"

"So far, so good, sir!" came the answering shout. "We'll know soon enough if they'll hold up! I'm concerned about the hinges breaking in this bitter cold—iron just isn't tough enough for these conditions!"

Ted nodded, clapped the lieutenant on the shoulder, and was pleased at the sting of pain in his hand. At least his fingers had not gone absent without leave in the cold.

A shout from the front, passed from man to man down the column, sent him hurrying toward the lead animals in the column.

"We broke through, Cap'n!" Albert Jonas yelled. "But it don't look like Sattidy night up there!"

One glance at the trail ahead was enough to confirm the black corporal's fears. They had come to the most dangerous point of the entire route.

Fifteen yards ahead, the trail narrowed and fell away to a thousand-foot drop down the boulder-strewn mountain. And for the next two hundred feet, a solid sheet of ice glistened on the windswept ledge.

Yellow Crow went first, cautiously testing the footing as he led his big palomino. The horse slipped once and almost went over the side, and the Cheyenne had his hands full for a few seconds quieting the frightened animal.

Ted shuddered. But they had no choice; they must make the crossing. He could barely make out the form of Yellow Crow as the Indian retraced his steps and neared the front of the column once more, without his horse.

"Leave horse other side," Yellow Crow said. "No need take chance, lose good mount. Hard to find."

Ted took a deep breath. "All right, let's go!" he called out. He lifted an arm that suddenly seemed to weigh twice as much as normal and waved the column on toward the treacherous ice field. One by one, the men and animals crossed, choosing footholds with care and sticking as close as possible to the mountainside—and away from the yawning canyon.

The long string of pack mules, more sure-footed than the cavalry horses, crossed grudgingly but without incident. Then the first cannon was eased onto the ice, the draft animals snorting, their nostrils flared and eyes wide. Chad Clark led the way, a few steps in front of the team pulling his precious cannon, while Bernie Christian eased his way along at the rear of the carriage, pickax over his shoulder.

Two-thirds of the way across, Ted's heart leaped as he saw the horse in the left trace slip and go down on the ice. The other animal panicked, lunging against the harness. The twisting motion of the team sent the cannon carriage into a slow but relentless skid toward the precipice. In a matter of seconds the cannon would slide over the edge and pull the team of horses after it to certain destruction on the rocks below.

Ted heard his own voice cry out, the words useless in the howling wind: "No, Christian!" But the little soldier from Georgia was already on the move, flinging himself between the sliding cannon and the sheer drop down the mountain. Ted caught a glimpse of a pickax raised high, then slammed down, and Christian disappeared from view. Chad Clark struggled to regain control of the team, and the wagon-sled slowed, then stopped—less than four feet from the edge of the cliff.

"Christian!" Ted cried, as he stepped onto the ice field. He almost went down as a boot slipped, but he threw himself onto his belly, distributing his weight on the ice, and crawled the few yards to the cannon as quickly as he could move. He reached the rear of the wagon-sled, glanced around the side, and there, clinging tenaciously to the handle of a pickax half-buried in the frozen path, one foot braced against a small rock and the other dangling in space, Bernie Christian strained against the weight of the cannon pushing against the pickax.

Ted squirmed around the carriage and found a rock to brace himself, then added his own strength to that of the smaller soldier. Chad Clark, with help from the quick, sure hands of Yellow Crow, regained control of the panicked horse. After a couple of unsuccessful tries, its downed teammate regained its footing and struggled upright.

Ted felt the pressure against the side of the wagon carriage lessen. He glanced up into a massive face straining above the muzzle of the two-pounder. Albert Jonas's greatcoat tightened across his broad shoulders as he slowly pulled the cannon back onto the center of the path.

Ted sighed with relief, then turned to the white-faced Christian beside him. The slightly built soldier's face was almost the color of the surrounding snow. Ted clapped him on the shoulder and yelled above the wail of the wind, "You did it, Christian! You saved the cannon!"

Frightened eyes glanced over a small shoulder toward the yawning chasm beneath a boot, then moved to Ted's face.

"Maybe so, sir!" Christian yelled back. "But now who's gonna save me? I'm too scared to move!"

Ted grabbed a handful of cloth on Christian's greatcoat and gave a tentative tug. The material held, and soon he had eased the former Confederate soldier away from the edge of the cliff.

Side by side, they crept across the ice on their bellies, finally reaching the relative safety of the side of the mountain.

Despite the bitter cold, Ted felt the perspiration trickle down the small of his back.

"Captain!" Bernie Christian nodded back toward the edge of the cliff. "I left my pickax!"

Ted stifled a small smile. "Don't worry about it, Bernie! The army can afford to buy you another!"

Hugging the protective mountain wall, the two men inched their way over the last few feet of the ice and at last were able to take a step on solid, if snow-covered, ground.

Christian sank to his knees. Seeing shudders wrack the small body, Ted knelt beside him.

"Are you hurt, Bernie?"

"No, sir." Christian swallowed. "It's just—well, high places plumb scare hell out of me."

The two were quickly surrounded by troopers, some talking excitedly, others gazing solemnly at the young galvanized Yankee kneeling in the snow.

Christian tried to rise as Colonel Robinson shouldered his way through the gathering. "Stay down, son," the commanding officer said. "Rest a few minutes. God knows you earned it. I've seen some brave men under fire, but that took more pure guts than I can imagine."

"I didn't think, sir. It just sorta happened, quick-like."

Robinson rose and turned to face the assembled soldiers. "If any of you here now doubt this young man's courage and loyalty," he yelled, "you have my invitation to leave my command at once!"

A burly trooper stepped from the circle and knelt by Christian. Ted recognized him. It was Langston, the one who had wanted to lynch Bernie Christian when the storehouse at Fort Bridger had caught fire. Ted felt his muscles tense, ready to lash out if Langston so much as looked cross-eyed at the smaller trooper.

Langston extended a hand. "Reckon I owe you an apology or two, Christian," he said. "Too late to make friends?"

Bernie Christian merely reached out, taking the hand that almost swallowed his own. "Never too late to have a friend," he said, then allowed the bigger man to assist him to his feet. One by one, troopers filed past, most offering a hand, the rest a word or a nod, to the man the majority of them once had wanted to hang.

"We'd best get on the move, Bernie," Ted said. "Stand here too long, we'll pick up a touch of frostbite. And there's still a lot of stuff to move across that ice." It was the ultimate test. After the briefest of hesitations, the one-time prisoner of war turned his small frame into the wind and stepped back onto the ice.

The remainder of the passage was not without its mishaps; two pack mules and a cavalry horse died of exposure, and a trooper broke a collarbone in a nasty fall on the ice. But eventually the final piece of equipment safely crossed to the eastern side of the pass.

Ted turned to Colonel Robinson. "About a half-mile down, there's a flat ledge big enough for a campsite," he said. "We'll have some protection from the wind, and I think it would be safe enough to let the men build small fires for a hot meal and to thaw out a little, Colonel. The rest of the way isn't going to be nearly so difficult. We have only one more obstacle to contend with—the narrow pass that will lead us to Santa Fe."

Josefa Carson pushed a strand of hair back under her bandanna, aware of the unladylike beads of sweat on her forehead and upper lip. But she had a job to do, and she could not worry about her appearance at a time like this.

She turned back to the young soldier on the makeshift pallet. "Time to change your bandage," she said. "Your name is Andy, isn't it?"

"Yes, ma'am." The easy Texas drawl gave lie to the pain in the wounded shoulder. "Andy Holliman, Seventh Texas Volunteers."

Josefa loosened the strips of cloth holding the blood-soaked pad in place. She knew at a glance the bandage would be stuck to the wound. She reached for a pan of water and a soft cloth.

"You were hit at Valverde?"

"Yes, ma'am. Nasty little scrap, that was—" The young soldier winced as Josefa began alternately to soak and then peel small areas of the bandage adhering to the wound. "Reckon both sides are still tryin' to figger who got hit hardest. First time I ever been shot. Skeered me some; thought I was gonna flat-out die in that wagon. Warn't exactly the way I'd planned to ride into Taos."

Josefa tugged the final bit of bandage away and peered at

the wound. "Coming along nicely," she said. "No sign of any blood poisoning. Does it hurt much?"

"Sometimes, ma'am."

Josefa sprinkled a bit of yellowish medicinal powder around the wound, applied a fresh bandage, and started tying it into place.

"Ma'am?"

"Yes, Andy?"

"How come you're doin' this? I mean, takin' care of a Texan an' all? And 'specially since my daddy, back when he was a kid, fought your people in the Mexican War."

"Andy," Josefa said, "in case you haven't noticed, all blood is red, whether it's from a Texan, a New Mexican, a Yankee, a red man, a black man, or any other color of skin. People hurt; I help. It's that simple." She tugged the last knot into place. "Besides," she said, "there were some Mexican names among the Texans who died at the Alamo and at Goliad. I don't consider myself Mexican, though you obviously can see that I am. In fact, I have two countries and two cultures. And that isn't counting the Indian influence. Now, you settle back and rest if you can, Andy."

"Ma'am?"

"Yes?"

"I know it ain't polite to ask, but I gotta know. Is it true? Are you Kit Carson's wife?"

"It's true, Andy." She smiled at the young face looking up at her in awe. "Have you met my husband?"

"In a way of speakin', I reckon I have. Ain't sure, but I think maybe he was the one who shot me—and from a couple hundred yards out, too. Is Mr. Carson all right? I know they's been some fightin' since Valverde."

"Thanks for asking, Andy. The last time I saw him, he was well and healthy. Now if you will excuse me, there are others who need attention."

"Sorry, ma'am—and Mrs. Carson, when I get where I can move around some, I'd be pleasured to fetch and carry for you."

Josefa laid a hand against the pale, barely whiskered cheek. "Thank you, Andrew—and rest assured, your offer will be accepted."

Josefa moved to the next bed, placed a hand on a neck, then swallowed the lump in her throat as she pulled the bedsheet over the still face. The excessive heat generated by the fireplaces in the Taos mansion, now converted to a hospital, compounded by the warmth of too many feverish bodies in too small an area, brought a brief sense of nausea.

Josefa Carson fought back the burning sensation in the upper part of her stomach, feeling the exhaustion of working among the sick and wounded for sixteen straight hours. She glanced out the window, longing for a breath of the fresh, crisp air. Then she sighed, turned to the next cot, wondering when it would end, when Kit would come home.

Vi Robinson ran a clean dust cloth across the spotless counter top of the small kitchen in her new quarters at Fort Laramie, aware it was little more than an unsuccessful attempt to check her growing concern by giving her hands something to do. With a sigh, she folded the cloth, carefully stored it in its proper place, and strolled to the single small window facing the parade ground.

The compound bustled with activity as a patrol prepared to move out in what she fully expected to be another futile attempt to thwart the Indians in their increasingly violent attacks on settlers in the area. A premature warm spell had turned the ground into mud almost up to the fetlocks of the horses, but she knew more bad weather was on the way. And in the higher elevations of the mountains, snow continued to fall; there would be no early spring this year.

The oft-folded note seemed heavy in her apron pocket. She opened it once more and read the short message in Judy's handwriting:

> Vi: *Going to spend a few days with friends outside the fort. Will be perfectly safe. Love, Judy*

Vi refolded the note, then put it back in her pocket. It had been more than a week since she had found the note pinned to Judy's pillow in the small house where she was living while at Fort Laramie, awaiting, she had said at the time, Abel Hubbard's return. And in the days that followed, all the friends and acquaintances who drifted into the fort said they knew nothing of Judy's whereabouts. Vi now realized that Judy was not visiting anyone she knew. Only a small carpetbag was missing from Judy's belongings, and Vi knew it was unlike the young woman who put so much stock in her physical appearance to pack so little for a stay of this length.

But what concerned Vi more at the moment was that she had not seen Colin Dibley for the last few days. She tried to tell herself that the disappearance of both Judy and Dibley was a coincidence. Her instinct did not listen. If the girl had done something foolish, it would destroy the two men who had such love for Judy Hubbard: Abel Hubbard and Bill Robinson.

Vi was sure in her own mind that Judy would not be unfaithful to her husband; there was too much love between them. Yet a young woman unaccustomed to being alone might be sorely tempted with the handsome, charming, and articulate Colin Dibley around. And Vi had to admit she did not know Judy well enough to do more than speculate about what might happen.

Snowflakes swirled about the abandoned trapper's cabin in the mountains near the pass where the Old Spanish Trail crossed the Continental Divide near Santa Fe. Judy Hubbard, sitting on a blanket on the floor, huddled closer to the blaze in the fireplace, letting its warmth chase from her body the chill of hours in the saddle.

Several times on the long, hard ride through little-known and seldom-used trails, she had almost cried out for a halt. But she had drawn on her inner reserves and her excitement at the promise of the surprise reunion with Abel to keep going, to follow Colin Dibley as he led her on the grueling trip south. She knew she would be forever grateful for Colin Dibley, the only person in Fort Bridger or Fort Laramie who could see how much she needed Abel. She had jumped at his offer to serve as a guide, to take her to her husband's waiting arms.

The door swung open, letting in a chill breath of the mountain air. Dibley stepped into the cabin, brushed the snow from his hat, and smiled at Judy.

"You will be delighted to know, Judy, that we are within only a few hours' ride of Santa Fe—and we will get there before your husband," the handsome blond man said. "The shortcuts plus the fact we had few pack animals and no wagons to slow us down will put us there a couple of days ahead of the Third Cavalry. You will have time to rest from the trip, don the finest gown you can find, and greet your husband in the style which he deserves.

"And," Dibley added, "I must say I envy Abel Hubbard. To have a woman go to such extremes merely to be with him— well, he is a lucky, lucky man."

Judy placed a hand on Dibley's forearm. "And I have you to thank for it, Colin. To find a gentleman in this awful wilderness is an unexpected blessing."

He patted the back of her hand. "I think that this calls for a small celebration," Dibley said, a wink closing one sparkling blue eye. He walked to the saddlebag piled in the corner of the cabin, rummaged around, produced a bottle, and held it high.

"The horses are bedded down and comfortable for the night, and we have the prospect of a hot meal and a warm fire until dawn," he said. "I propose a toast to the most beautiful woman in the country, Judy Hubbard, and to her fortunate husband, Abel. Even from tin cups, this should be the finest brandy you have ever tasted. And although you deserve the finest of crystal and elegant settings, the circumstances do not detract from the sincerity of the host."

Judy watched him pour generous amounts of brandy into cups, accepted one of them, and lifted it to her nose for a gentle sniff. "It smells wonderful, Colin."

He raised his cup, she followed suit, and they each took a swallow. Judy was mildly surprised at the delicate flavor of the brandy and soon became aware of its potency as warmth began to flow from her stomach.

"Another toast before dinner," she said, raising her cup. "To Colin Dibley, an understanding man, with gratitude." Again they drank. Dibley refilled their cups and sat beside her.

"I really shouldn't drink until after supper," Judy said. "We haven't eaten all day, you know."

Dibley laughed, eyes dancing from reflected firelight. "It's been a long trip, Judy. Now we are safe and near the end of the journey, so let's have a small, quiet party. I think we deserve it."

Judy nodded and raised her cup. The warmth spread from her stomach to her cheeks as the brandy began to take hold. A cup later, her spirits were soaring despite the heat in her neck, a slight numbing sensation in her cheeks, and just a touch of dizziness. She wondered how Dibley could consume as much of the potent brandy as had she and still show no outward effects of the drink.

She became aware that Dibley's face had drawn closer to her own. "Someday, Colin," she said, noticing that her words were slightly slurred, "I will repay this favor."

"You could repay it now, Judy," Dibley said. Slowly she

became aware of the touch of his hand on her thigh, felt his lips caress the side of her neck.

"No, Colin," she said, her voice soft as she lifted the hand from her leg and shifted her position to move a few inches away from him. "I must repay—in another manner." His features seemed to waver slightly in her brandy-glazed eyes. Wanting to soften the rejection, she added, "But if I were not so much in love with my husband and determined to remain faithful—" She suddenly stopped in midsentence, a flicker of alarm flashing through her brain. His hand was back on her thigh, higher up. She grasped his hand with the intention of removing it gently, then winced as his fingertips dug bruisingly into her flesh.

She looked into Dibley's eyes and her fear grew. The gentleness was no longer there; his eyes were hard, cold, and ruthless.

As she attempted to move away, she felt a hand rip at her shirt and stroke a breast. "You'll pay now, Miss Tease," Dibley said. "I have a right to my fee."

"Stop it, Dibley!" Judy's brain was now fighting the effects of the brandy. "Stop it now, and I won't tell Abel of this—I'll forget it as just the result of the brandy. Now move your hand!"

She felt Dibley's heavy breathing in her ear. His hand moved, and Judy felt a sudden sting of pain as his fingers closed cruelly on her breast. She forced herself to ignore the piercing pain, slipped her left hand down her leg into the boot top, and gripped the handle of the small hunting knife Abel had instructed her to carry at all times.

She forced herself to relax, to lean into Dibley's body, to give the outward indication of weakening to his advances. Then with one swift stroke, she slashed with the knife.

Dibley's cry of pain from the unexpected wound seemed to hang in the cabin for a split second, and Judy took advantage of the moment to roll away from him and crouch, knife at the ready. Beads of cold sweat formed on her brow as she stared into the cold blue eyes, now touched with madness. She could see blood flowing down Dibley's forearm where the knife had cut him. Judy waited, her heart racing, as he rose to his feet. She realized that he was between her and the door. Her escape was blocked.

Dibley continued to stare at her for a long moment, then glanced down at his bleeding forearm. The eyes flashed hate when he looked back at her.

"You'll pay for this, Judy Hubbard! Perhaps with your life." Dibley's voice was dangerously tight, and Judy finally realized the true desperation of her plight. She was trapped in a remote cabin, her whereabouts unknown, armed with only a small knife, and facing a man who outweighed her by a hundred pounds.

"Do you think for a minute all I wanted to do was help you, you whining, spoiled little slut?" The tone of Dibley's voice washed the last trace of brandy from Judy's whirling brain. "It wasn't you I wanted, Judy Hubbard. You're only a tool. That is the only thing saving your life at the moment, for I could pull this pistol from my belt and shoot you between the eyes with no qualms."

Dibley took a step toward her. Judy involuntarily retreated until she felt the heat from the fireplace against the backs of her legs. The handle of the small knife became slippery with the perspiration in her palm.

"You see, Judy, you aren't a simple favor. You are the reason the Confederacy will win the war. Ah—I see you look a bit confused. I will explain, because no one should die without knowing the reason.

"I am a spy for the Confederacy." Judy froze with a sharp intake of breath. "Who do you think supplied the Indians with guns and started them on the warpath? And who is in a better position than I to know the Union strength in the Southwest?"

Dibley's smile was a twisted, evil grin now, and Judy felt her fear turn to panic.

"You are a hostage, Judy! Your father's cavalry company must not reach Fort Union—and you are the one thing that will keep Colonel Wild Bill Robinson and his troops at bay. He will stop his drive toward Santa Fe, or you will be delivered to him a piece at a time—first an ear, then a finger, another finger, a hand, until there is nothing left of you except flesh for the coyotes!"

The enormity of the scheme was staggering. Judy knew now that far more than her own life was at stake in this small cabin in the mountains. Colin Dibley must be stopped. She suddenly crouched, reached back, and snatched an unused piece of kindling from the hearth. She hurled it at Dibley's head. With a curse, Dibley parried the wood with his injured forearm and hurled himself toward Judy.

She raised the knife to strike, only to find her wrist

trapped in a crushing grip. Then something slammed into the side of her head and she felt herself spinning through a pinwheel circle of light toward the dark center of unconsciousness.

Captain Ted Henderson let his horse pick its own way along the well-defined and much-traveled route marking the pass where the Old Spanish Trail crossed the Continental Divide and headed on to Santa Fe. The narrow passage, lined with trees and boulders, represented a considerable danger of ambush, and as usual when potential hazards lay ahead, Ted rode the point.

The March wind still bit sharply into exposed skin, but after the blizzard-swept and bone-chilling traverse of the Green River Pass, Ted was comfortable in abandoning the cumbersome greatcoat for a snug buckskin jacket.

There had been no sign of Indians yet, and the scouts who ranged far ahead of the main column each day had reported back that the Confederacy apparently had not yet penetrated General Murphy's defenses. Perhaps, Ted thought, their luck would hold for just a short time longer. Then this difficult ride and considerable sacrifice by men and animals would not have been in vain. All they needed now was a couple of days—

He reined his horse to an abrupt stop, his eyes riveted to a movement at the highest point of the narrow opening of the pass. It seemed to Ted that his heart stopped beating for a moment. Fluttering from a piñon tree ahead was a thin strip of green cloth. He recognized it immediately. The green gown that Judy Hubbard often wore!

Momentarily confused by the unexpected sight so far from home, Ted only sat the saddle and stared. Then he braced himself for whatever he might find, slipped the carbine from its scabbard, and kneed the horse toward the piñon, every sense alert. The dread building, Ted leaned forward and plucked the green cloth from the branch. Already it had begun to fray at the edges, whipped by the gusting north winds.

A piece of paper had been affixed to the material with a thin, sharp stake. Ted felt his heart sink as he read the brief, ruthless message addressed to Colonel Robinson.

Ted fought back the impulse to plunge ahead, find a trail, and bring the matter to an end. But the life of the daughter of his commanding officer, the wife of one of his best friends lay in the balance. Reluctantly, he turned his horse back toward the approaching column of blue-clad soldiers. He sought out Colonel Robinson at once and showed him the message.

An expression of stunned disbelief was on the colonel's face as he looked up from the note. "Judy? Colin Dibley?" Robinson was struggling with the implications of the message and the green gown. "So it was Dibley who was causing all the havoc up at the fort! It was Dibley who was inciting the Indians, killing our dispatch riders—and trying to get you out of the way, too!"

Ted was about to reply when Abel Hubbard skidded his mount to a sliding stop and dismounted in one motion. In two strides, he stood looking from scout to colonel.

"What happened?"

Ted glanced at Robinson, decided the colonel was in no shape to relate any details, so spoke himself. "Colin Dibley has taken Judy hostage," Ted said, trying to keep his voice as even as possible. He handed the green cloth to Abel who reached for it slowly, uncomprehendingly.

"I don't know how he managed to take her hostage," Ted said, "but I don't for a moment doubt that we must do as he says. His instructions are for us to withdraw, turn back to Fort Laramie—or Judy will die." Ted took a deep breath. "If we do not do as he says, Abel, Colin Dibley threatens to do her great harm." He handed the message to the lieutenant.

"Judy . . ." The name sounded almost strangled in Abel's throat. Ted saw the murderous flash of fury in his friend's eyes; Abel started back toward his horse.

"No, Abel! Don't do anything foolish!" Ted grasped at a muscular arm, felt Abel yank free, then threw both arms about the lieutenant and wrestled him to the ground.

"Get hold of yourself, man! Let's think this through."

"That's my wife out there! I'll skin that bastard Dibley alive!"

"And get Judy killed in the process? Abel, get some sense back in your head!" After a long moment, Abel finally relaxed. But when Ted loosened his grip, Abel turned, and the captain could read the hard, cold fury in his friend's eyes. He led the lieutenant back to the still-dazed Robinson. The colonel sagged against the side of his horse, as though his knees could no longer bear his weight.

Robinson looked up, eyes pleading. "What do we do now, Ted?"

"We stop for a while and try to do some rational thinking,

Colonel. And if I were you, I think I would have the troops retreat a quarter of a mile or so. Dibley is out there somewhere, watching us. He knows we have the message. If we don't do something immediately to let him think we intend to comply with his terms—" He left the remainder of the thought unspoken.

White-faced, Robinson nodded a numb assent.

Ted glanced around the circle of soldiers who had gathered about the officers, drawn by the ripple of excitement that had spread throughout the column. Ted nodded toward Chad Clark. The young lieutenant stepped forward.

"Chad, have the men withdraw to the little valley we passed about a quarter of a mile back. There's water there and some shelter from the wind. We'll make camp there for the night," Ted said.

"Frank!" Sergeant Major Frank Armbrister stepped from the circle. "Find Yellow Crow. He's riding right point somewhere. You know our signal. Three calls of the prairie owl." Ted lowered his voice so that only Frank could make out the words. "That Cheyenne may be the most important man in the army right now, at least as far as Judy is concerned."

Armbrister merely nodded and swung aboard his huge bay gelding. Ted watched as the wiry man on the big horse reached the edge of the timbered slope, then both man and mount seemed to simply disappear. If anyone could find Yellow Crow, Ted thought, Frank Armbrister could.

Ted turned to the black corporal at his side. "Albert," he said, keeping his voice low, "I want you to keep an eye on Abel Hubbard until this is settled—one way or the other. I know Abel's temper. If he tries to ride out or sneak out, hit him with your best punch and sit on his chest until I tell you to get up."

Jonas's eyes reflected the concern in the massive black chest, and Ted was sure he saw a quick flash of anger there as well. "Captain, what do you think of Mrs. Hubbard's chances?"

Ted's mind had been feverishly working in that direction even as he was issuing orders. "I can't say for sure, Albert. It's mostly in Colonel Robinson's hands now. And I can't think of a heavier burden for any man to bear."

The colonel had already ridden to the new camp, where his tent had been put up. When Ted arrived on the scene, Wild Bill Robinson was sitting in the folding chair behind his field command table, an untouched dinner cooling before him. He looked across the tent at Ted.

"Thanks for taking control out there this afternoon, Captain," the colonel said. Ted noticed with relief that Robinson's voice had returned to normal. His eyes still held pain and worry, but Ted knew the commander had regained control of his emotions, turning his keen analytical mind into a search for a way to steal the bait without tripping the bear trap. "I'm afraid I didn't react the way a field commander should under stress."

"Don't apologize, sir. I know how much Judy means to you. If it were Wilma out there, I would respond the same way."

Robinson pushed his chair away from the folding table and stuffed his battered pipe with tobacco from a soft leather pouch. He struck a match, then looked across the flame at Ted.

"I have reached a decision, Captain," Robinson said, touching match to pipe and puffing until the blue smoke curled up under his hat brim. He shook the match out, snapped it in half, and wetting the ends of his thumb and forefinger, pinched the burnt end. It was the ingrained reflex of a man who lived outdoors and knew that a carelessly tossed hot match could ignite a prairie fire that might destroy hundreds of acres and many human lives.

"As much as I love Judy," Robinson said, and Ted noticed the slight quaver in his voice, "her life will not stand in the way of this mission."

Ted started to object. The colonel cut him off with a wave of his hand. "If it comes to a choice between one life—even that of my own daughter—and the fall of the West to the Confederacy, I will choose my country. But I won't sacrifice Judy's life, or anyone else's, lightly."

Robinson began to pace the dirt floor of the tent, puffing on his pipe.

"Every man has his price, Ted. Maybe there is some way we can buy off Colin Dibley. I'm riding out under a white flag for a parley with him at first light. If he has a price, I'll find it. If he doesn't, I will violate my own code of honor and shoot him on the spot."

"Colonel," Ted said, alarm in his voice, "I'm not sure that is a good idea. Suppose Dibley doesn't honor the white flag?"

"I've thought of that, Ted. But I see no other approach. I have to give it a try."

"In that case, sir, if you are determined, I will accompany

you. Yellow Crow should be here by then, and I believe he should go as well."

"I can't ask you to do that, Ted."

"You didn't ask. I volunteered," Ted pointed out.

"And Yellow Crow?"

Ted raised an eyebrow. "We have no guarantee that Dibley is alone. He may have some of his Confederate spies with him. Whether he does or not, should the opportunity to rescue Judy arise, can you think of any other man you would rather have along?"

Robinson tapped the pipe against a boot heel, then ground the ashes into the dirt. "I suppose I might as well agree," he said, sighing, "because the two of you will go along anyway unless I have you put in irons."

"We will be in the saddle at dawn, Colonel."

The wind had shifted during the night, carrying with it the sharp bite of the snowfields to the north, and Ted shivered momentarily as he stepped into the saddle. But he still disdained the greatcoat, which tended to hinder movement, in favor of the better designed buckskin jacket. He glanced at the morning star, fading now in the growing light of dawn, then kneed his horse alongside Colonel Robinson. At the colonel's right, a grim-faced Yellow Crow sat astride a powerful palomino, the Spencer .56 resting across his arm. The trio moved out as clusters of silent troopers and scouts stood and watched.

In the corner of his vision, Ted saw Abel Hubbard step forward, only to be stopped by the pressure of a big black hand on his shoulder.

The ride was only slightly more than a quarter of a mile, but to Ted it seemed half the day had passed before they reached the approach to the narrow pass. One more turn in the trail and they would be in full view of the crest.

Ted kneed his mount a few feet to the left of the colonel, whose right hand gripped a standard staff from which a white flag crackled in the wind. At the colonel's right, Yellow Crow also drifted his palomino a few steps away, as agreed upon. Should something turn sour, at least they would not be lined up like ducks in a pond.

Ted glanced at his commanding officer. Wild Bill Robinson's jaw was set, eyes fixed straight ahead. Ted could see no sign of the almost unbearable tension that must be building inside the veteran soldier's mind and body.

As they negotiated the final turn, Robinson suddenly yanked his mount to a stop. At almost the same instant, Ted saw it, too. There, at the very top of the highest point in the pass, a slim figure sagged, head down. Judy Hubbard was tied to a dead cedar trunk, only a thin camisole between her body and the piercing north wind.

Ted heard the sudden, strangled cry to his right, a sound of outrage and pain. But before he could react, Wild Bill Robinson had thrown the white flag to the ground and slammed spurs to his horse, driving the animal up the trail toward his daughter.

Over the sound of pounding hooves Ted heard the sickening slap of a slug against flesh, then saw the colonel tumble from the saddle. Ted whipped his own carbine from its boot, barrel aimed in the direction of a cluster of boulders a hundred yards away.

Then he eased the pressure already beginning to build on the trigger and lowered the weapon as the voice reached his ears.

"She's still alive, Henderson! But the next one's going through her head if you move one more step!"

Distance and angles and wind drift flashed through Ted's brain, and he felt his heart sink, the last spark of hope draining from his body. Even if he could get a slug into Colin Dibley, Judy would likely be dead before the lead made contact. There was no doubt in Ted Henderson's mind that Dibley would shoot Judy. At the moment, her life hung by a thread.

"Dibley!" Ted heard the tight fury in his own shout. "If you've harmed her, I'll kill you!"

"Maybe, maybe not!" The derisive call came back. "If you do, it will be over Judy Hubbard's dead body!" There was a moment's silence. Ted studied the standoff. Dibley no doubt knew he was a dead man if he killed Judy. Yet Ted and Yellow Crow could make no move without insuring the woman's death.

"Deal still stands, Henderson! Call off the troops and she lives! Make one wrong move and she dies!"

At the edge of his field of vision, Ted saw movement from the crumpled form of the colonel; at least Robinson was not dead yet. But from the way he had been thrown from the saddle, Ted knew Robinson had been hit hard.

"All right, Dibley! You still hold the cards!" Ted shucked the carbine back into its boot and turned his horse toward the downed officer. Yellow Crow reached Robinson first, placed an ear against the colonel's chest, and nodded toward Ted. Then the Cheyenne lifted the big colonel gently and with a surprising lack of effort onto the back of the palomino.

Yellow Crow held the injured officer upright, with Ted lending a hand alongside, as the trio turned back toward camp.

"What are his chances, Yellow Crow?"

The Indian shook his head. "Not good. Miss Judy's not good either. She not last another night in cold." Yellow Crow glanced at Ted, his dark eyes narrow. "When we go after snake in rocks?"

"Soon," Ted said, his voice falling with a strange calmness on his own ears. "Very soon. Just you and I, Yellow Crow."

"Is good. Like old times again."

They rode into camp and immediately brought the colonel to the surgeon's tent. The doctor, working frantically, only had time for a quick glance and a shake of the head in Ted's direction. Ted stepped outside the tent, swallowing hard against the lump in his throat. Then he turned at the sound of a footstep.

Abel Hubbard stood before him, eyes defiant, shoulders squared. "I'm going out there, Ted, and nothing you can say is going to stop me! The man on that cot is more than a commanding officer—he's my father-in-law. And that scheming Rebel son of a bitch still has Judy! She's my wife, Ted! I've got to do something!"

"Abel, we've ridden together a long time. I know how you feel—how I would feel if that were Wilma out there." He forced his body to relax, his face to reflect resignation. "But, Abel, we can't just mount up and charge, or Colin Dibley will kill Judy. We've got to work out a plan."

Ted moved alongside Abel, took the lieutenant's upper arm in his left hand, and led him out of the sight of the rest of the camp into a cluster of empty tents. He turned to face Abel. "What we need," Ted said, "is a diversion—" He slammed his right fist into Abel's temple, caught the lieutenant before the unconscious man could crumple to the ground, and held him upright. "Sorry, Abel," he whispered to the slack face only inches from his own, "but we can't take the chance. Emotion gets in the way at dangerous times. Jonas!" Ted's call was soft in the late morning air.

The black soldier materialized from between two tents. "Yes, sir?"

"The lieutenant seems to have taken ill, Corporal. Would you see to it that he gets plenty of bed rest over the next few hours?"

"Sure will, Captain. I heard the lieutenant get sick. Musta hit him awful hard, that illness. Sounded like slappin' a side of beef." The corporal slid a bulky forearm beneath Abel's armpit. "I'll take good care of him, Captain. Maybe when he starts to get better, he'll listen some."

"By that time, Jonas, I'm hoping this whole thing will be settled."

Jonas watched Ted stride purposefully away. "Yes, sir," he said to himself, a note of pride in the accented voice, "I reckon it will be settled pretty quick, and I wouldn't give a jug of bad whiskey for that Dibley feller's chances."

In the quiet, grim bustle of the camp, only one man noticed the two figures quietly slip away on foot. And Albert Jonas knew he was not going to tell a soul. Especially after he had seen the Cheyenne stop, dip a finger into a small tin, then streak his bronzed face with war paint.

It was a long, circular walk and steep climb around the narrow mountain pass, followed by a hundred-yard crawl through rock, thorn, and brush. But Ted's breathing was even and unlabored, as he eased forward, inching his way along on his belly, pistol cocked and ready in his right hand. Finally he almost had the position he wanted—above and beyond the clump of boulders where Colin Dibley watched and waited. But Dibley would be looking in the wrong direction. Back toward camp.

Ted caught a quick glimpse of a fine beaver coat moving across an open space in the boulders now only a few quick steps away. Just another few minutes . . . He chanced a quick glance at the slim figure staked to the cedar off to his right. The woman's head still drooped forward on her chest. Ted breathed a silent prayer with a double message: that she would still be alive, and that she would not look up at the wrong moment. He cupped his free hand over his mouth and sounded the chatter of the ground squirrel. A moment later, the answering call reached his ears, the sharp *chinng* of the blue quail. The trap, he thought, was about to spring.

Ted came to his knees, crouched, ready to dash the final

few feet between himself and his quarry as soon as Yellow Crow made his move.

It was a short wait.

He heard Colin Dibley's sudden, surprised intake of breath, a muttered curse, and then a blast of a heavy rifle. Ted sprang to his feet, the noise of the rifle shot covering his approach, and slipped between two boulders.

In a small clearing in the center of the rocks, Colin Dibley stared downhill as he levered another round into the rifle. Ted saw a flash of brown skin in the brush below, and Dibley's rifle muzzle jerked in the direction of the movement. Ted stepped into the clearing, only a dozen feet separating him from the man with the rifle.

Ted gripped the big army pistol snugly in his right hand, placed his left hand over his right wrist to further steady the weapon, and set the blade of the front sight on the center of Dibley's back.

"Drop it, Dibley!" Ted's voice cracked across the clearing.

The big man tensed for a split second, then Dibley dove to the side, rolled, and attempted to bring the rifle into play. Ted took his time, made sure of his aim, and squeezed. The recoil of the heavy pistol carried his hands upward, and through the smoke he saw the small round hole appear at the bridge of Colin Dibley's nose. The big man's head snapped back, then fell forward into the dust.

The muzzle blast of the pistol left his ears ringing. For an instant he felt his own knees try to buckle as the tension rushed out of his body.

"Yellow Crow! Are you hurt?"

"Snake with yellow hair miss. But too close to make happy."

The Cheyenne suddenly appeared at the edge of the clearing, took one glance at the body, then nodded at Ted.

"Now," Ted said, "let's go cut Judy loose and get her back to camp."

Yellow Crow raised an eyebrow in the direction of what had once been Colin Dibley.

"Leave him," Ted said. "I only hope his carcass doesn't make the coyotes and buzzards sick."

Yellow Crow shrugged, plucked the dead man's rifle from the dirt, and followed Ted in the direction of Judy Hubbard.

As Ted cut the final bonds holding her to the cedar trunk,

Judy staggered and would have fallen had he not caught her. He took her gently in his arms.

"It's all right now, Judy. You're safe. It's Ted."

The eyes that met his were blank, uncomprehending. Ted had seen the expression before on the faces of tired, stunned, young soldiers emerging from the terror of their first battle. It was as though her mind had simply had enough and had switched itself off. He slipped out of his jacket and draped it across Judy's shoulders.

"How Miss Judy?" Yellow Crow added his own buckskin to the one Ted had tossed over the woman.

"She seems cold—maybe some light frostbite—but generally, she's unhurt. On the surface, at least. What damage was done to her mind, only time can tell."

He slipped an arm around the slender young waist, and Yellow Crow did the same from the other side.

"Come on, Judy," Ted said, his voice soft, "let's go home."

Ted knelt beside Colonel Robinson's cot. It seemed he could feel the fever from the officer's body a full two feet from the sickbed. The colonel's eyes were bright with fever and pain, yet Ted could sense an alert mind at work behind the bushy eyebrows.

"How—how is Judy?" The hesitancy and weakness in the normally direct, firm voice took Ted somewhat by surprise.

"I can't say for sure, Colonel. Abel and the surgeon are with her now. She may be suffering from exposure, and she has some nasty bruises. But she's young and strong, and physically she seems to be in pretty good condition, considering what she has been through in the last few days." Ted did not tell his commanding officer that Judy had failed to recognize anyone, even Abel, since she had been freed from her ordeal. But it had only been a matter of hours, and the colonel had enough problems as it was.

"Surgeon—told me—what you did, Ted. I'm grateful. For Judy's life. I—almost got her killed. Just—went crazy for moment."

"Any father would have done the same, sir."

Robinson shook his head weakly. "What's done is done," he said. "We must—get on with—campaign."

The tent flap swung open, and Abel Hubbard, face drawn and tight, entered with Chad Clark in tow. Robinson turned his head in Abel's direction.

"Judy?"

"She's resting, sir," Abel said. "The surgeon gave her something to make her sleep. She—doesn't fully understand yet what has happened. But she hasn't been injured."

Robinson nodded. "That's good news." The weathered face grimaced involuntarily at a sudden stab of pain. "Abel, in my dispatch case you will find a small packet. Please bring it to me."

It seemed to Ted that the colonel's voice was growing a bit stronger, despite the ravaged body. Robinson took the package from Abel's hand and opened a flap with difficulty. "I had hoped," he said, "to do this in a more formal setting—with parades and color guard. Captain Henderson, please remove your insignia of rank." Puzzled, Ted did as he was told. "You are no longer a captain, Ted. As of now, your rank is major. Abel, you are now Captain Hubbard. You will have to—do the pinning honors yourselves."

The colonel turned to Chad Clark. "Lieutenant Clark, I have recommended you for—individual citation and next available promotion. Tell Bernie Christian he also may expect a citation from the War Department."

Ted self-consciously pinned the major's insignia on his uniform tunic, and Abel blinked rapidly a few times as he attached his own captain's bars.

"I won't say congratulations, gentlemen, because you've earned it. And more." The colonel coughed lightly, and Ted almost felt the stab of agony in his own body.

"Major Henderson, you are now in command. Your only orders are to complete this mission."

"Yes, sir. We will prepare to move out at once. I'll leave two squads of experienced riflemen here to protect you and Judy."

"One squad should do the job, Ted. I do ask that Abel remain here—" Robinson waved a hand to cut off Hubbard's protest "—because Judy and I will need him."

"Yes, Colonel. I will report back to you at the end of the campaign." Ted felt the touch of the colonel's hand on his forearm, the slight squeeze of the fingers, and he realized they both knew that he would never see Colonel Robinson again. It was a silent farewell.

"You had better get moving, Major Henderson," the colonel said. "There is a war waiting for you, and you don't have much time to get to it."

VI

General Kelly Murphy had withdrawn his troops a few miles outside of Santa Fe at Glorieta Pass. Here they were dug in to make their last stand against the Confederates, who, if they broke through the Union lines, would go on to take Fort Union and perhaps the entire West as well. True, the Confederates were working on short rations, and they had managed to capture very few supplies on their drive north. But the Union forces were also greatly weakened, and it was now certain that General Carleton and his California Column would not arrive in time to come to their aid. The New Mexican regulars and volunteers would have to go it alone.

The general fought back the urge to mount his horse and once more inspect the forward lines. He silently surveyed the position of his forces, satisfied that little more could be done. The terrain worked in favor of the Union defenders by limiting somewhat the ability of the Confederates to launch a massive frontal assault without sustaining heavy losses.

Murphy also knew that Lieutenant Colonel Humphries's situation was almost as desperate as his own. The hit-and-run raids by Kit Carson's elite group of frontiersmen had weakened the invading forces, chipping away at supply wagons and foraging parties. And a desperate enemy was a dangerous enemy. If the Confederates broached his forward lines, Murphy knew his troubles would be compounded. In a tree-to-tree, hand-to-hand struggle, there were no more efficient soldiers in the country than those Texans.

Murphy sighed, hoping it would release some of the tension building in his own body. He watched as the approaching Confederate force raised an impressive cloud of dust. The day was barely an hour old. Soon enough, Murphy mused to himself, the artillery duel would begin, then the small-arms clashes. Idly, he wondered if history would ever take note of the battle of Glorieta Pass. Two small armies, a remote mountainous region far from the thousands of troops in the East, and yet so much at stake. . . .

He settled back, spat out a cigar stub, and waited. There was not much else to do at the moment except admire the mountains, the leaves of the trees, even the ants, already beginning to prepare for next winter at the dawn of a new spring.

Only when a man faces the possibility of death, the general thought, does the intricacy and beauty of life take on such sharp detail. He found himself wondering what would be the last thing he saw on this earth? The veins of a leaf? The track of a night beetle? Stars? A sunrise? His own home with his grandchildren standing around the bed? Silently, he prayed it would be the latter.

"Something bothering you, General?"

Murphy started at the sound of the unexpected and nearby voice. He glanced at young Lieutenant Davis of volunteers, who, when he was not manning one of the cannons, served as unofficial chaplain of the Union contingent in the New Mexico mountains. He shook his head.

"Just woolgathering, Lieutenant," Murphy said. "Wondering what tomorrow will bring."

"No need to worry, sir. God is on our side."

Murphy raised an eyebrow. "Is that so? I will bet that Roy Simon Humphries and his army of Texans and Confederates think the same thing. And, of course, the Indians have their own spirits and magic on their side." The general plucked a cigar from his tunic, stuck it in his mouth, and began worrying the unlighted tobacco between his teeth.

"Son," he finally said, "I don't think the Deity can be on any one side when armed men meet in battle. I rather doubt that the Creator has chosen sides when one of His most sincere commandments has been broken by both and will be broken many times over within the next few hours." The general shook his head. "Lieutenant, any prayers for victory from this camp will not be spoken by me. I expect it is enough of a strain on the Almighty just wondering what madness has invaded that which He made in His own image—without having some character waving a saber and asking for His help. Don't get me started, Davis. I've enough on my mind without arguing about theology on the battlefield."

General Murphy plucked the cigar from his mouth and pointed it toward the south. "I suggest that you rejoin your gun crew rather quickly. It seems that the dust from Humphries's troop movements has settled. For now."

Lieutenant Colonel Roy Simon Humphries shifted his weight in the saddle and stared through his field glasses at the terrain ahead. At his command, Confederate troops and the Texas volunteers would be committed to the battle. And, he thought, from the looks of things up ahead, a lot of them would not return.

He twisted in his saddle, surveying the troops deployed on either side, sensing the growing excitement and tension along the lines that seemed entirely too thin for the job at hand, worn down by Valverde, by constant harassment of patrols, and by disease and illness. He felt a surge of dismay as he realized many of these men were anxious to engage the Union forces. He wondered how any man could enjoy the prospect of killing—or being killed.

Murphy had done his job well, Humphries thought. It was not going to be any Sunday afternoon buggy ride out there.

Reports swirled constantly about his ears:

"Gun emplacements ready, sir."

"Infantry in place and eager, sir."

"Cavalry in position, Colonel."

Humphries felt the beginnings of the strange sensation that swept over him before each battle, a feeling that someone else was in command—not the Roy Simon Humphries who liked soft women and honeysuckle smells and good cigars and smooth bourbon. He looked at the weather-cracked hand holding the reins, knowing it was attached to his arm, yet not recognizing it.

Humphries was not conscious of moving his own lips. Yet he heard the words in his own voice:

"Inform the officers of the gun crews they may open fire when ready. . . ."

Major Ted Henderson raised a hand, waving the column of saddle-weary men and horses stumbling from exhaustion to a ragged halt. The forced march from the Old Spanish Trail

Pass had taken its toll on men and beasts. Even Ted, former Pony Express rider, long accustomed to hard work and seemingly endless hours on horseback, felt the strain.

He turned to the wiry noncom at his side. Sergeant Major Frank Armbrister sat his oversized horse in a seemingly relaxed manner, appearing little the worse for wear.

"Frank," Ted said, "spread the word. We will camp here for a few hours to let the men and horses rest. By my guess we still have four or five miles to reach Glorieta Pass—and unless I've severely underestimated the tactical ability of General Kelly Murphy, that will be one of the places he has chosen to do battle. Stretch our supplies with a double grain ration for the horses and a full, hot meal for the men."

"Yes, sir, Major Henderson," the smaller man said with a snappy military salute.

"And, Frank . . ."

"Yes, sir?"

"Knock off the 'Major Henderson' and 'sir,' will you? I'm Ted. Save the titles for the parade ground."

Armbrister's only reply was a wide, toothy grin, then he wheeled his mount and made his way along the line of blue-clad soldiers and buckskinned scouts.

Ted waved off the offer by a trooper and tended to his own horse, a rangy, rawboned bay that still had enough energy left to try to bite the major. A swift kick in the belly promptly reminded the horse to keep his place. Throughout the camp, other troopers tended their animals, and Bernie Christian herded the spare mounts toward a trickle of water in a nearby creek.

Ted grunted in satisfaction. Christian, who had walked most of the distance until the incident with the cannon at the high pass called attention to his frostbitten toes, was proving adept as a horse wrangler. And, Ted thought wryly, the Third Cavalry's mounts were not exactly pets, either.

Lieutenant Chad Clark had disdained the instructions to rest; and with the aid of the burly Albert Jonas, was personally pulling a wheel from one of the two-pounders, preparing to repack it with grease. Ted felt he now fully understood Wild Bill Robinson's pride in this unit. They got the job done.

With a start, Ted strained his ears toward the southeast. A moment later, his suspicions were confirmed; a distant rumble like thunder in a faraway storm floated through the still, thin mountain air. Ted had heard that sound before.

Cannon fire.

He glanced in the direction of Glorieta Pass. There was no sense sending a scout ahead to tell General Murphy that the Third Cavalry had arrived in the vicinity; Ted would need every one of his men to successfully strike a devastating blow at the Confederates. He had some important strategic planning to do, and as he heard the sound of cannon fire once again, Ted muttered aloud, "Hang on until daylight, General Murphy. Help is on the way!"

General Kelly Murphy watched the battlefield below as if observing a play on a St. Louis stage. The rolling thunder and smoke of the cannonade belched from first one side, then the other. The initial artillery exchange had proven somewhat less than satisfactory as batteries dueled at long range. From his own quick count of smoke-roiled emplacements, neither side had suffered much damage among the artillery units.

Then came the sight Murphy had been dreading. A brief silence from the Confederate guns brought a vision in his mind, the scene of artillerymen frantically changing the elevation of cannon muzzles. The image turned to reality as the first salvo from the Rebel lines landed just short of his own forward infantry defenders. Then shot after shot marched along the open field, reaching his front lines, shells bursting among the defenders on the perimeter, clearing the way for the infantry assault that was sure to follow, possibly reinforced by cavalry units.

Murphy cursed as his own artillery emplacements continued to pound ineffectively at the Confederate cannon. The inexperienced volunteers, not knowing what was coming, had not yet adjusted the range of their cannon to rake the attackers who soon would be pouring toward them.

Through the bellowing of cannon and the increasing staccato bark of small-arms fire, Murphy heard the shrill Rebel yells and the whoops of the Texans as the charging Confederate forces stormed toward the forward perimeter of the entrenched Union troops. Then suddenly the attackers wavered and began to fall back under the deadly fire of the forward line—the few seasoned, regular soldiers he could spare after reinforcing Carson's unit. Through his field glass, he could see crumpled figures on the field below, some in Confederate gray and butternut, others in no particular uniform—and several in the Union blue.

Murphy felt a momentary satisfaction. The first assault wave had been turned back after all. But he was painfully aware of the thin ranks in his forward perimeter, and through the glasses, he saw that Humphries had begun to organize the horse soldiers. He dispatched a runner to his front lines with a message to fall back to the second perimeter. If his men were caught in the open, they would be run down and massacred like sheep. Within a few minutes a blue-clad figure scurried from a shell hole, moved back, then was followed by another, and another.

The general felt his heart leap as he realized two of his squads had failed either to hear or to heed the message to retreat. Sixteen men were grimly digging in against the charge that was sure to come.

With great sadness, General Kelly Murphy prepared to give the signal that would surely doom these men. When the Confederate cavalry charge neared, Murphy would order a concealed battery of Union six-pounders to unleash a rain of grapeshot across the field below. There was no turning back. And the two squads were lost anyway; they would go down beneath pounding hooves and shotgun blasts when the charge did come.

Roy Simon Humphries could not shake the feeling that something was wrong. He was not surprised that his first wave had been thrown back; in massed battles, the first poor devils in the charge were cannon fodder, probes into the enemy lines. From the ridge to the east, where his scouts had told him the ex-frontiersman Kit Carson and his troops were dug in, the Confederate charge had been hit hard. Yet, Humphries mused, the center of the defensive line seemed unreasonably soft. A breakthrough there by his mounted Texas units could flank Carson, pin down the mountain man and his soldiers, then drive straight to Fort Union.

Perhaps, he thought, General Kelly Murphy had finally made an error in judgment. Maybe he had counted too heavily on holding the eastern ridge and had overcommitted his troops there. Humphries glanced at the sun, now well past its zenith and descending toward the western mountain range. He knew he had to make his move soon. It was time to pit his pawns of war against those of General Murphy in a bloody chess game, where the entire West was the prize. He tried to shake off the worm of worry in his belly and rely on his training from West

Point—find a weakness and exploit it. That meant a cavalry charge, infantry close behind, straight into the center of Murphy's line. Despite his misgivings, he raised his sword high, then dropped the point in a forward and down sweep.

The wild yells of the cavalrymen echoed in his ears as spurs slammed into horsehide.

From his vantage point on the mountainside, General Kelly Murphy watched the three-deep line of horsemen race across the battlefield. As the first rider passed a jagged rockfall, he heard himself mutter, "Now!"

A split second later, smoke puffed from the concealed Union batteries on the western side of the valley. Grapeshot raked the charging cavalry, ripping through ranks of foot soldiers racing in the horses' dust. Murphy winced as he saw his two squads swept away in the maelstrom, the Texans hardly checking their mounts as they spurred past, firing shotguns and handguns at the small cluster of blue-clad bodies.

Murphy shook his head with the never-ending disbelief of war. Despite the pounding from the artillery, the Confederate cavalry spurred on. He saw a horse go down, but the rider rolled clear, and with rifle in hand, he charged forward on foot.

The cannon barrage had slowed but not checked the cavalry charge. The horsemen neared the Union lines, and a withering volley of rifle fire emptied several saddles. Still the riders came. The Union line wavered, and Murphy played his final hole card, throwing his two reserve companies of riflemen into the front-line fray. The battle raged from tree to tree and rock to rock, and several times Murphy saw individual soldiers clash in hand-to-hand combat. But the Union lines held, regaining lost ground, rock by smoke-stained rock, and finally the Texans were forced back into the open, under the muzzles of the concealed six-pounders.

Murphy glanced at the sun. The battle had gone on for almost three hours. There would not be another tonight. Humphries was too good a field commander to try to take the offensive with only a half-moon for illumination over broken, shell-pitted ground. He sighed, issued the command for cease-fire, and the guns gradually quieted as the word spread.

The general left his command post, walked among the wounded, and realized that he had paid heavily to buy another day in the life of Fort Union. The Union ranks had been so thinned he knew they could not withstand another assault like this one today. And there was no question that the new day would bring a fresh assault.

He stopped short, suddenly realizing his hands were bloody from helping attend the wounded, for he had wandered far out onto the battlefield.

A hundred yards away he saw a familiar figure. The ramrod-straight Roy Simon Humphries was directing the recovery of the dead and wounded, occasionally kneeling to lend a hand with a bullet-pierced body. Like Murphy, Humphries too was comforting his troops during the unofficial but customary truce allocated to retrieval of casualties who already had paid a high enough price without the pain of extended suffering.

Murphy, straightening, found himself staring at his counterpart only a short distance away. Slowly, General Kelly Murphy raised a hand in a salute of respect. Roy Simon Humphries returned the gesture.

Murphy turned, making his way back to his own lines. Josefa Carson, he realized, was going to face another busy night at the makeshift hospital in Taos.

Major Ted Henderson gathered his company commanders about him in the fading dusk.

"We're going to have to range pretty far out to the east in order to skirt the flanks of the Union troops and hit the Confederates from behind," he said. "While I dislike the idea of splitting the command, we must get help to General Murphy as quickly as possible and in the right place. Thus, Company C and my scouts will move out at first moonlight. It will be a difficult and fast ride over rough terrain, so catch your best horses. Travel light—water, weapons, and ammunition only. Yellow Crow already has ridden out to assess the situation. We will meet an hour before daybreak at a spot each of us knows well."

"Major?"

"Yes, Albert?"

"I'd sure like to ride along with you. And I can see darn good at night—almost as good as Yellow Crow," Albert Jonas said.

Ted turned to Chad Clark. "Lieutenant, if you have no objections and can spare the manpower, I'll take Corporal Jonas with me."

"I have no objections, sir. Just leave me Bernie Christian.

He's a natural-born artilleryman, Major, and when we put your plan into action, I'll need all the talent with guns and horses I can get."

"You'll have the horse talent. Christian's good, but Sergeant Major Armbrister can do things with animals you have to see to believe. Blucher?"

A short, slightly built scout stepped forward. "Yes, sir?"

"You know this country as well as I do. Bring the rest of the troops along as fast as you can, but save the horses and men as much wear and tear as possible. If my bunch gets there in time to help, we're going to need reinforcements in a hurry."

"Sure enough, sir. I'll get 'em through with powder and lead to spare."

"Well, let's get things moving," Ted said. "Chad, would you mind staying for just a moment?" Ted waited until the rest of the company had moved away, then said in a quiet voice, "By rank, you will be commanding officer of the column, Lieutenant, but if I might offer a suggestion?"

"By all means."

"Listen very carefully to what Frank Armbrister has to say. And if you are ever in doubt, ask him."

Chad Clark's chuckle was soft in the chill night air. "Sir, no one knows better than I do who actually runs the army. One sergeant major is, with all due respect to your rank, worth a pile of brass insignia big enough to load a cannon. Besides, I'm an artilleryman, not a scout. If he won't take over, I'll pull rank and order him to."

Ted slapped the lieutenant's shoulder. "Good. And good luck, Chad."

"You too, sir."

Ted turned into the night, wondering what the dawn might bring, wondering if General Murphy could hold out long enough for the Third to pitch in. The Third might be short on numbers, he thought, but they sure were long on fighting savvy and courage.

Josefa Carson stepped onto the porch of the makeshift hospital and inhaled deeply the crisp, clean mountain air. Exhaustion weighed heavily on her muscles, and her mind protested the twenty straight hours in the cramped and crowded Taos building.

The moans from the sick and wounded inside, Confederate and Texan and Union alike, reached her ears through the thick walls. She sighed. There was never, it seemed, enough help to go around.

"Mrs. Carson!"

The call snapped her head around. She felt the alarm rise in her breast, and a leaden lump of fear began to form in her stomach as the horseman appeared in the light of the half-moon just over the eastern horizon. *Dear Lord*, she prayed, tracing the sign of the cross over her breasts, *please don't let this be the message I have feared*. Her anxiety doubled as she recognized the young man in the saddle. It was the corporal who had delivered the message to their home in Taos. Despite her inner turmoil, she forced herself to remain outwardly composed as the corporal tipped his hat.

"Mrs. Carson, I hope I didn't startle you," the young rider said, "but I thought you might want to know—Colonel Carson is hale and hearty."

Josefa heard her own sigh of relief. A weight seemed to lift from her shoulders.

"Thank you, Corporal. I've not had such welcome news in a long time." She stepped from the porch and placed a hand on the rider's forearm. "You must be tired," she said. "Please dismount; we will find a place for you to sleep tonight."

"Thank you, ma'am, but I can't stay. Colonel Carson would likely skin my hide if he knew I was here. But I knew you would be worried, so I borrowed a horse. And I have to get back. It's kind of a scary ride at night, and you have to go slow—"

Josefa felt the sting of tears, relief, and gratitude tugging at her heart. This young man had ridden all this distance, just to let her know Kit was alive and well. She watched the corporal ride away in the direction from which he had come.

"God go with you, my son," she said to the retreating figure, her voice quiet in the partial darkness. Then, her spirits buoyed by the short visit, she turned and went back into the hospital. There was much work to be done and probably more to come with the dawning of a new day.

The surgeon stepped from the small tent along the Old Spanish Trail, sighed, and shook his head at Captain Abel Hubbard.

"I'm sorry, sir," the surgeon said. "There is nothing more I can do for Colonel Robinson. He's dying. The end will come soon, I fear." He shook his head again, this time in amazement.

"Only a bull of a man could have lived this long with those injuries, Captain. And although he must be in pure agony, he refused laudanum for the moment. He has asked to see you, first alone, and then with Judy." The surgeon's eyes were sincere as he said, "I'm truly sorry, Captain Hubbard."

Abel felt the tears in his eyes. He placed a hand on the surgeon's shoulders. "You did your best," he said, "and no man can do more."

Abel stepped inside the tent, illuminated by candles on each side of the cot. The familiar face, pale and drawn with pain, brought an additional stab to Abel's heart. He sat beside the cot, waiting until Robinson's feverish eyes had blinked themselves clear.

"You wanted to see me, Colonel?"

"Yes, Abel." The weak voice was shaky. "I have something to ask of you—several things, in fact. First, would you please call me Dad for these last few hours? You never have, you know, although you've been as fine a son as a man could hope for."

"Thank you—Dad." Abel heard the crack in his own voice. "I couldn't have had a better man to set my own standards by."

"What have you found out about Dibley?"

Abel swallowed hard. "We located his hideout and his saddlebags, along with a small courier pouch. There is no doubt now. The man was our Confederate spy." Abel fumbled in a pocket and produced a small silver medal. "He was carrying this." Abel held the medal close to the colonel's face and watched the slightly filmed eyes struggle to focus. "It's an engraving of a cotton boll," Abel said, "identical to the one Ted found on the body of the Indian at his ranch. The camp surgeon, who is from Alabama, identified it. It is the seal of a powerful consortium of cotton growers. Dibley was working for them, not for the Confederacy itself. We found papers detailing his work in the West and elsewhere on behalf of the cotton growers. It also explains where he got the money for the mass purchases of rifles and goods for the Indians."

Abel waited for a moment as the body of the man on the cot convulsed in an apparent jolt of pain. Wild Bill Robinson tensed, then gradually relaxed. His eyes opened again.

"What else did you find?" he asked.

"Dibley was a master forger. In his cabin we found copies of documents he had made. He had forged my signature on that fouled-up shipment we got by wagon train just before he arrived on the scene in Fort Bridger. And it was his signature, not that of the secretary of war, on the orders which would have sent you back East."

"The orders were fake?" The colonel closed his eyes for a moment, then looked up and sighed. "So now you know—your commanding officer disobeyed what ostensibly were orders from Washington. But at least," he went on, as a tinge of relief and excitement touched his fading voice, "Vi will be spared the torment of knowing I might have been court-martialed. You must tell her, Abel. For her sake, not mine . . ." The voice trailed off.

Startled, Abel reached out, touched a weathered hand, and felt Robinson's fingers close around his own. The grip was weak, and Abel was painfully aware of how much the simple act of squeezing a hand was draining his father-in-law's strength. The eyes flickered open once more.

"Abel, my son—"

"Yes, Dad?"

"On the ridge to the east is a piñon tree. I wish to be buried there. A soldier should stay where he falls. Fire no salutes over my grave. The sound of shots might invite trouble, and we don't have the spare ammunition anyway. I would like to be draped in the American flag; I've a spare in my trunk." A feeble wave cut off Abel's protest. "Also, son, I want you to carry the message to Vi personally." Abel thought he caught a glint of moisture at the corner of the colonel's eyes. "She deserves a better fate, son. But for a time we had each other, and still, a love that lasts beyond the grave. Finally, I want you to take command at Fort Laramie; they desperately need a skilled Indian fighter there. And you must escort Judy to safety, nurture her and Vi to the best of your ability. Will you do this for me?"

"Of course." Abel felt the tears run down his cheek, and he was not ashamed.

"Now I would like to say my farewells to Judy."

"Sir—Dad—I'm not sure she would recognize you. Since she was—brought back from Dibley, she has done nothing but stare into space."

"All the more reason I should see her, Abel. Perhaps it will jar her back to reality. And even if she doesn't recognize me, I will know her. I must see her once more before I die. And Abel—"

"Yes?"

"Help her. Stand by her. Support her. And do what you can to convince her my death was not her fault. Now bring her to me, and leave us alone together for a few minutes. Maybe she will not hear; perhaps someday she will remember. I have to tell her how much I love her." The colonel waved weakly toward a thick packet on the small campaign table by the cot. "Take this to Vi. It is my last will and testament and my final message to her. Perhaps it will ease her pain."

Judy, in a trancelike state, was ushered into the colonel's tent, and as Abel had predicted, she did not appear to know her father. But if the dying Bill Robinson was distressed at her inability to recognize him, he did not show it. He took his daughter's hand in his own and in a weak, gravelly voice told her he loved her very much. Then Abel came and led Judy away and closed the flap of the tent.

Colonel Robinson died during the night. As he had requested, he was buried beneath the piñon tree. In the dim light of early dawn, Abel forced himself to sit straight in the saddle, to show the strength that was expected of him. At his side, Judy sat her sorrel mare, her expressionless face staring straight ahead. Abel found himself wondering how and when this spell would be broken. And would he himself be strong enough to cope if it did not?

Wilma Henderson came awake with a start. In her bed, she lay still for a moment, wondering what had brought her awake a full half hour before her usual time to rise. Could it have been the baby moving? Even as the thought formed in her mind, she smiled. It was not likely, not after just three months. But still, she could savor the possibility. She was almost constantly aware of the new growth inside her body and eagerly awaited the day when the baby would take her breath away with a solid kick.

She tossed back the covers, knowing in her wide-awake state she could not return to sleep. Always an early riser, she enjoyed the quiet hour before the rest of Fort Laramie began the bustle of a new day. Shivering slightly in the early-morning chill, she snuggled into her heavy housecoat, lit a candle against the dim light, and put the coffeepot on the stove. She poked a few embers to life, added small shavings and then a few larger sticks of firewood.

Awaiting the growing warmth from the stove and the

delicious smell of brewing coffee, she reached for her ledger and dipped a pen in an inkwell. Wilma had found that recording her thoughts and feelings lifted her spirits and cleared her mind. Later, she would read through the journal, select the more happily phrased passages, and compose a letter to Ted. Even if she knew for sure where the Third was, correspondence had been forbidden by Colonel Robinson for a period of six weeks, to avoid the possibility of enemy agents intercepting a letter and learning the location and intent of Robinson's troops.

> *March 28. Cool morning, but feel of spring in the air. Baby may have moved this morning, could not tell for sure. Appears Ted has found himself a good brood mare. I have very little morning sickness, and the post surgeon tells me I'm healthy as a horse.*
>
> *Gray mare is in foal to Ted's stallion, so it looks as if we may have two new additions to the family within a few weeks of each other. So now I have two pleasant surprises for Ted.*

She paused, chewed at the end of the pen for a moment, then applied the nib to paper once more.

> *Still worried about Vi Robinson and Judy. No word as to Judy's whereabouts or Colin Dibley's. I just hope Judy hasn't done something foolish—or worse, been captured by Indians. Vi tries to put up a brave front, but it is obvious from the look in her eyes that she is deeply concerned. I admire her courage; I am not sure I could cope with the worry and the inner struggle Vi has had.*

The smell of aromatic coffee began to penetrate the room, the growing heat from the stove taking the bite from the morning air.

> *A curious and frightening thing happened just the other day. Vi and I were busy doing the wash when all at once she stiffened and seemed to shiver. She cried out, "Bill!" Later, she told me she did not remember the incident. But she has seemed more deeply troubled since.*

But enough of this gloom. On a lighter note, all of us are eagerly awaiting springtime, though yesterday one of the veteran soldiers here said, "Wyoming has just two seasons—winter and August." But you could tell from the look in his eyes that he, like the rest of us, loves this wide-open and beautiful country. It is a perfect place to raise colts—and children.

This one final note will conclude this morning's entry. Ted, wherever you are, may the Lord keep you from harm's way—for I love you more, it seems, with each passing day.

Wilma blew gently on the last paragraph, drying the ink, then closed the ledger. A cup of fresh, hot coffee in hand, she stepped to a small window and opened it. It was going to be a pleasant day, she thought, as she inhaled the fresh, moist air that had the smell of springtime in it.

Major Ted Henderson brought Company C and the scouts to a sudden stop, halting when he heard the call of the prairie owl.

"Wait here," he said to the trooper at his side. "Have the men dismount and rest the horses a moment. It seems our scout has returned."

He stepped from the saddle, handed the reins of his mount to the trooper, and walked briskly into the night.

Yellow Crow waited in the inky shadows of a cluster of boulders. Ted could hear the palomino's heavy breathing and soon saw the wisps of steam drifting from the sweating animal's flanks into the chill dawn air. Ted knew instantly that Yellow Crow had found something of major importance, or the horse would not have been ridden so hard.

"Greetings, brother," Ted said.

"Yellow Crow find supply wagons," the Cheyenne said without returning the traditional greeting. "Follow pack train led by man in light uniform."

"Confederates?"

Yellow Crow grunted an affirmative answer.

"How many wagons and soldiers?"

Yellow Crow shrugged. "Not take time to count. Many weapons. Maybe fifty, sixty soldiers."

Ted felt his spirits soar. The Cheyenne had stumbled on the one thing that Lieutenant Colonel Roy Simon Humphries could ill afford to lose. Without their supply wagons, the Confederates could not continue to fight.

"How far?"

"Ride hard, there by time sun rise."

"Then we ride hard. Can your horse make the return trip?"

"Corn-color horse tougher than hungry squaw with toothache. Run all way to Mexico, get drink, run back. You keep up?"

Ted clapped the Cheyenne on the shoulder. "You can bet two rifles and a blanket on that."

Ted quickly reported back to his men, then all remounted, and Yellow Crow led them at a gallop for almost an hour. As the sun was about to rise above the tops of the distant mountains, they came to the supply train located within the protective walls of a canyon, just as Yellow Crow had said. Henderson's Scouts, led by the Cheyenne, made quick work of rounding up the wagon train sentries, slipping up on them from behind and giving them the choice of being killed or taken prisoner. To a man, the sentries chose capture by the scouts.

With the last of the Confederate wagon train sentries safely in tow, Ted deployed his scouts and Company C in a skirmish line along the crest of the canyon cradling the Rebel supply train. He admitted to himself that after the fear of the unseen badger hole waiting to trap a horse's leg during the pell-mell race through the night, he would welcome the approaching action. At least it would give his muscles something to do besides ache.

The stage was set. At the first sound of cannon fire from Glorieta Pass, Company C and Henderson's Scouts would take the wagon train. By the time the sun was an hour high, Chad Clark and Frank Armbrister would be in position to enter the battle. Yellow Crow, having sketched the positions of the Confederates' major concentrations and gun emplacements, indicated where Union reinforcements would be needed most, and Ted had dispatched a scout to inform the others. By now, the remainder of the Third column would be within a couple of miles of the point of attack.

Ted glanced toward the northwest, where General Kelly Murphy would have his troops dug in, each squad, company, and platoon placed for maximum defensive strength and effectiveness. "Wish we could have gotten word to you that help was on the way, General," Ted whispered into the growing dawn, "but there just wasn't a way to do it. Hang on for that first charge, and there will be a little surprise in store for both you and Colonel Humphries."

Lieutenant Colonel Roy Simon Humphries, leader of the New Mexico force for the Confederate States of America, felt the sense of detachment work its way through his body. It was time. He had work to do.

He turned to the Texan at his side. The stocky man's forehead was wrapped in a bandanna bandage, his sole concession to the wound suffered the day before.

"Kilgallen," Humphries said, "much of our success today depends upon you and your men. You must give the impression that you're going to storm the east ridge and keep Carson there. Apply enough pressure to make him stand until our soldiers break through and circle the ridge to close the trap."

"You bet, Colonel."

"Kilgallen?"

"Yeah?"

"Take no unnecessary casualties. We don't need heroes or dead or wounded soldiers. What we do need, and desperately, is Fort Union. Keep Carson on that ridge for a few hours, and Fort Union will be flying the Confederate flag before nightfall."

The Texan merely nodded and walked away in the growing light of dawn. Humphries, watching the retreating figure, found himself thinking that while the Texans might be disorganized and untrained in military maneuvers, when it came to raw courage and individual fighting skills, there were few units anywhere to match them. For the first time, Humphries began to understand how an undermanned, undersupplied, impoverished army defeated Santa Anna's hordes and created a nation from a vast, wild chunk of the South. He raised his sword, hesitated for a moment, then swept the point downward.

The sharp, clear notes of the bugle started a chorus of Rebel yells. The sun, Humphries noticed, had bathed the upper third of the western mountains. By the time the east ridge was in full sun, he thought, the Confederacy will have won or lost the West.

* * *

General Kelly Murphy cursed as the first artillery shell fired by the normally inaccurate Confederate gun crews landed squarely on one of his six-pounders. That cannon had controlled the field of fire on the northeast point, the most critical spot in the artillery defense. He shouted an order to his new adjutant to shift a replacement battery to the spot, but he sensed, even as he gave the order, that there would be no time to refill the position should the first assault wave break through.

He turned his attention back to the main battlefield. Grapeshot and ball from his own cannon landed amid the approaching Confederate infantry and cavalry, but the Union fire was insufficient to halt the forward thrust. This, he thought, was going to be a dog-eat-dog, eyeball-to-eyeball battle before it ended. And Murphy knew his troops were no equal for the yelling Texans, experts at man-to-man fighting.

He glanced at the east ridge. Alarm rose in his chest as an assault wave of rough-clad Texans advanced on Carson's position—yet there seemed to be something wrong. The realization hit Murphy hard. The Confederate commander had no intention of launching a full-scale attack against Carson; instead Humphries intended to throw the majority of his numerically superior force at the center of the Union lines, while the fighting unit under Carson was effectively cut off from the action. "God help the boys in blue in the front lines," Murphy said aloud.

Through the dust and smoke, Murphy watched as the first Confederate wave neared the Union forward line, the almost constant crackle of small arms fire underscoring the heavier cough of the big guns. The first assault wave faltered before the accurate rifle fire of the Union soldiers, then dug in. A second wave swept past, gained a few more yards, and still the Union line held.

"So far, so good, boys," Murphy shouted to his distant troops. "Hang in there as long as you can!"

The rolling thunder of distant cannon reached Ted's ears, sending a jolt of excitement along his spine. Below, the soldiers guarding the wagon train had all turned to look in the direction of Glorieta Pass, unaware that Henderson's Scouts had crept to within yards of their position just before sunrise. Behind the ridge, Company C waited. Yellow Crow turned from his forward position toward his brother, and at Ted's hand signal, the scouts raked the wagon train with a volley of rifle fire. Then, pistols in hand, the scouts mounted their attack. Ted drew his own saber, waved it overhead, and Company C spurred over the crest and down the steep canyon wall, the troopers yelling and whooping, a grim-faced Ted in front. The soldiers guarding the wagon train panicked at the sudden, unexpected assault, many of them throwing down weapons and diving under wagons for protection. Only a few desultory shots were fired by the defenders and those went wide of the mark.

Company C swept through the wagon train, a prairie fire of blue and buckskin. Ted, his mount on a flat-out run, closed on one defender who seemed determined to make a stand. The Texan fumbled with his rifle, trying to reload; Ted's saber was extended, his wrist stiff, ready for the fatal swing. But he suddenly yanked his horse to a sliding halt within a saber's length of the Texan. Frightened eyes stared from a teenage face into Ted's.

"Put the rifle down, boy. You're too young to die," Ted said.

The rifle thumped into the dirt, and small, trembling hands raised high. Ted gestured with the tip of his sword toward a cluster of captives already being herded away from the wagon train.

It was over in a matter of minutes.

And there are no casualties among my own troops and only a few injured among the defenders, Ted thought with gratitude. To his right he saw a huge black figure fire a torch and, kneeing his horse along the lines of wagons, set fire first to one, then another, until the entire column was in flames. Now and then the inferno erupted with a blast as a powder wagon blew, sending black smoke roiling into the sky.

Albert Jonas kneed his lathered sorrel alongside Ted's mount, his teeth flashing in a wide grin.

"Guess that'll take some of the sting out of the southern scorpion," Jonas said.

Ted glanced over the long line of burning wagons. "It sure couldn't hurt, Albert," he said. "Now, let's go see if we can lend a hand to Murphy. Sounds as if he may be in big trouble."

Ted quickly assigned a guard detail to watch the prisoners, then rode to the highest point on the ridge, letting his ears tell him where the heaviest fighting was going on at Glorieta Pass. Then he raised a hand and waved his men forward.

* * *

Colonel Kit Carson took in the situation at a glance, the Confederate strategy snapping into sharp focus in his mind.

"Major!"

A lean, angular officer stepped to Carson's side. "Sir?"

"Take every third mounted man from the line!" A rifle ball pinged at a rock only inches from Carson's head, but the veteran frontiersman never flinched. "Flank along the back side of the ridge"—he pointed a gloved finger—"until you reach that opening in the canyon wall. Then hit the Confederate lines; we've got to take some pressure off Murphy's front!"

The major immediately turned, vaulted into the saddle, and began barking orders along the line.

"Lieutenant!"

"Sir!"

"You're in command of this ridge! Dig in and hold. Don't try a counterattack, but burn lots of powder! Make them think we're still here in full force!"

"Yes, sir."

"Sergeant Phillips!"

The swarthy man dashed the few yards to Carson's side, ignoring the rifle balls kicking dirt over his boots.

"Phillips, you and I are going to take two squads of crack riflemen. A big howitzer within a hundred yards of this canyon ridge is giving Murphy's people fits. We're going to take it."

"It's as good as took, sir. Let's go! I know just which men we want!"

The colonel and the noncom sprinted down the line, stride for stride. Soon sixteen chosen men were cautiously working their way along the ridge behind Carson and the sergeant.

At the end of the ridge, Carson waved his men to a stop, motioned for them to gather around. "Any of you men ever fight Indians?"

Several in the group nodded.

"Good. That cannon is our Indian camp, only they have some rifles to protect it. None of the men around the howitzer will be looking for an attack from behind. We hit them by surprise, take the howitzer, spike it, and blow it to kingdom come! Now, let's move out, slow and easy. We have more time than it appears, but we're going to get only one good crack at it."

* * *

General Kelly Murphy felt pain in his midsection as the Confederate force breached his forward wall, the screams of injured mingling with the clash of saber against saber. A horseman broke through the Union line, then another, and it seemed that dozens of mounted men were pouring through. Murphy hung his head; there was a leaden weight heavy in the pit of his stomach; the battle for Glorieta Pass was lost for the Union.

He opened his mouth to issue the order he hated, the order to put the torch to Fort Union—but suddenly his frown turned into a smile.

Lieutenant Colonel Roy Simon Humphries felt the elation surge as he wheeled his mount toward the thickest fighting. "We've got them, men! The line has been breached! The battle is ours!"

From the rear, he heard a monumental blast, a crackle of rifle fire, and the big howitzer at the rear fell silent. Not comprehending, Humphries turned his horse in that direction; in the distance, blue-clad figures retreated from the wrecked cannon, rock by rock, a blistering rifle fire covering their escape.

Humphries mouthed a silent curse; one of his most effective field pieces had been spiked! The elation sank further as horsemen in blue suddenly wheeled through a break in the east canyon wall and cut through one of the Confederate forward units like a scythe, hammering at another, forcing a Texas unit to dive for cover.

Then, from the northeast quadrant of the fighting, the spiteful bark of a little two-pounder sounded, and Humphries saw one of his remaining artillery pieces shatter, its carriage pummeled and useless from the small shell. Seconds later the two-pounder spat again, and another Confederate gun fell silent, raked by grapeshot.

Humphries watched, stunned, as the forward Confederate lines sagged, then shattered, under a withering barrage of rifle fire. Texan and Confederate cavalrymen went down, and a wave of blue-clad riders suddenly swept from either side of the canyon. Humphries's heart sank as he saw the blue-and-gold standard of the Third Cavalry Regiment whipping in the smoke-laden breeze.

Humphries became aware of an urgent voice at his ear: "Sir—look! The supply train!"

A solid wall of smoke billowed from the canyon where the precious Confederate supplies had been concealed. Ahead, his troops were taking a pounding from the fresh, efficient Third Cavalry. Only two of his guns remained operative, and now his supply train was in flames.

He felt a sting against his cheek, then barely broken skin trickled blood down his jawline. Ignoring the ache in his chest, he turned to the officer at his side.

"The battle is lost!" Humphries shouted over the din. "We've been whipped! Get me a bugler!"

Lieutenant Colonel Humphries had tasted defeat before, but never had it been so bitter. Swallowing bile in his throat, he issued an order to the young bugler who appeared at his side.

The crisp, clean notes of the bugle cut through Roy Simon Humphries's heart like a keen blade. The great Confederate plan for the conquest of the West had failed.

One by one, the guns fell silent. Dazed, bleeding men in gray and tattered, ill-clothed Texas Volunteers silently filed by Humphries's stirrup.

"Does anyone here"—Humphries's voice cracked with emotion—"have a white flag?"

General Kelly Murphy rode alone across the shell-pocked battleground toward the Confederate officer flanked by a bandaged Texan and a dazed major in a Confederate uniform. Murphy, reining his horse to a stop, raised hand to hat brim in salute.

He watched as Humphries unsheathed his saber and, holding the haft in one hand and the blade in the other, offered the weapon to Murphy in the universal gesture of surrender.

"Keep your sword, Colonel Humphries," Murphy said in a level voice. "There shall be neither captives nor reprisals. The terms are simple and honorable. Your men will keep their weapons, since the danger of hostile Indian raids and need for game will be great on your trip back to Texas. I will offer you such supplies as you need in the way of staple goods and enough ammunition for hunting and protection.

"In addition," Murphy said, "I will supply an armed and mounted escort to see you safely back to the Texas border. Please explain to your men that the Union soldiers are not accompanying them as victors or guards, but merely to assist in the event of hostile raids. All that is asked in return is your word of honor that never again will you or any of these men invade the territory of New Mexico."

Lieutenant Colonel Humphries bowed slightly in the saddle. "Your terms are most generous, General."

"I am sure, Colonel, that had the battle turned out differently, you would have offered the same terms."

Humphries nodded. "Once the military objective is won or lost, there is no need for further animosity or bloodshed," he said. "Your terms are accepted with my personal gratitude, my word of honor that they will be observed, and with my admiration for an officer and a gentleman." Humphries raised a hand in salute.

"One officer and gentleman to another," Murphy said, returning the gesture. "We will work out the details later, Colonel. But now we each have wounded to tend, dead to bury. Should you need additional surgeons or medical supplies, they are yours for the asking."

"Thank you, General. My compliments to your troops."

"And mine to yours. A great deal of courage and dedication was exhibited by both sides. I will now take my leave, with your permission."

General Kelly Murphy reined his horse back toward his own headquarters. He watched as surgeons and medical aides moved among the wounded, and sighed. "You have just won a major victory, General Murphy," he said aloud to himself, "so why don't you feel better about it?"

Just then, the corporal of the guard rode up to announce that the sentries had stopped a lone rider coming in from the west. General Murphy, looking very tired, followed the corporal to where the man was being detained.

Lieutenant Kevin O'Reilly, exhausted from the long, hard ride from outside Tucson, had dismounted and was drinking from a water barrel when General Murphy approached. He straightened, quickly put on his hat, and saluted.

"Greetings from General Carleton of the California Column, sir," the big lieutenant said. "I have been instructed to ride ahead of the troops and tell you help is on the way."

General Murphy returned the salute, but there was no need for any words. Lieutenant O'Reilly could already see that the critical battle had been fought and that the Union forces in New Mexico had emerged the victors.

"You probably wouldn't mind a good, long rest after the ride you just took, Lieutenant," Murphy said. "My men will look after your horse and will show you to a tent where you can sleep undisturbed until the other Californians get here."

"Thank you, sir," Kevin said. "And, sir, I just want to say I'm sorry we weren't here earlier to help out. I would have liked the chance to show those Confederate boys that they weren't welcome in California, either."

VII

Major Ted Henderson pushed aside the flap and stepped into the tent which served as General Kelly Murphy's field command post.

A single lantern set shadows dancing on the canvas walls, illuminating the square-jawed face of the stocky man behind a battered table, unlighted cigar clamped between firmly set lips.

"General Murphy?"

At Ted's question the commander glanced up, then came to his feet and extended a hand to Ted.

"Ted Henderson, sir, Third Cavalry. At your service. I apologize for not getting word to you that we were on the way, sir, but there just didn't seem to be an opportunity."

Murphy's eyes glittered in the lantern light. "Major Henderson," he said, "you have my permission to drop in unannounced any time I happen to be in trouble." The general released Ted's hand and waved toward a folding chair at the end of the table. "Sit, Major, sit."

Ted eased himself into the canvas chair, letting the weariness of the past few days begin to surface.

"I must tell you, Major Henderson, I have never seen a more welcome sight in my life than the smoke from that Confederate supply train and the Third Cavalry banner. They had us between a rock and a hard place, and we were standing on the rock."

"Just glad we could get here in time to help, sir."

"Not half as glad as my men are, Major Henderson. You and your people saved a lot of lives out there today, not to mention stopping a bold military stroke which could have turned the balance of the war in the Confederacy's favor. I am recommending a unit citation for the entire Third."

"Thank you, sir. We were just doing a job. If citations are to be recommended, sir, Colonel Robinson should be first on the list." He now told the senior officer about the turn of events at the pass near the Old Spanish Trail.

Kelly Murphy shook his head, a touch of sadness in the expressive eyes. "Please give my personal condolences to Mrs. Robinson," the general said. "Wild Bill and I knew each other for many years. I have lost friends on the battlefield, from Indian arrows, snakebite, freezing, and heat, and it never gets any easier. But enough of this personal chatter. Tell me, how in the green-grassed world did you ever get through those mountain passes? And how did you know we were in trouble in the first place?"

As succinctly as he could, Ted filled in the story for the general. Murphy listened silently, shaking his head from time to time in admiration. He tossed away the cigar stub, plucked a fresh one from a pocket, and offered it to Ted, who declined. "The men in your unit are an outstanding bunch," Murphy said. "This Clark fellow—he would have been the man on the little pipsqueak two-pounder that performed like a howitzer?"

"Yes, sir. Top-flight gunnery officer, General."

"I would have liked the chance to meet him."

Ted almost came out of his seat. "Clark's dead?"

"Yes, Major. He was killed by a stray bullet. You didn't know?"

Ted collapsed back into the chair, his face registering his distress. "No, sir. My men were somewhat scattered in the fighting, and I haven't yet had time to check on any casualties."

"Then we'll find some time—and if you don't mind, Major, I would like to accompany you. I want to thank each of your men personally. I also want to see that Clark is given a proper burial with full honors."

A rustle of canvas drew both men's attention to the front of the tent. A slightly built officer in colonel's uniform, blond hair showing streaks of gray, stepped inside.

"Ah," Murphy said. "Colonel Carson, meet Major Ted Henderson, Third Cavalry."

Kit Carson extended a hand. "Ted Henderson. I feel as if we've already met. You've quite a reputation out here, you know."

Ted found the handshake firm and sincere, and in the rather close-set eyes he detected a genuine warmth.

"Colonel Carson, it's a pleasure to meet you in person. From the tales I've heard, I expected you to be nine feet tall and chewing on a horseshoe."

Carson laughed. "I haven't eaten a horseshoe since daybreak," he said, "but right now I think I could eat the horse it came from." Ted noticed the twinkle in his eyes. "So. Famous Pony Express rider and worn-out scout and Indian fighter finally meet. And at the right time, too, I might add. When things settle down a bit, let's get together and trade some tales. I'll bet we have a lot of common acquaintances, including a few of less than savory reputation."

"I would be delighted, Colonel Carson."

Carson turned to the general. "Kelly," he said, "what are my chances of getting the major here assigned to my command for a few days until we get this mess cleaned up?"

Kelly's eyebrows arched toward Ted.

"With your permission, General," Ted said, "I would like to place myself and my men at Colonel Carson's disposal until such time as we return to Fort Laramie."

"Granted," Kelly said. "Just invite me in from time to time to listen in on the conversation. I've never heard two legends spinning tales at the same time."

The sound of a single rifle shot carried from the ridge above Fort Laramie to the ears of the sentry at the gate. The guard studied the distant horsemen for some time through his field glass and recognized the former lieutenant of the Third Cavalry.

"Patrol coming!" he called. "Looks like Abel Hubbard! Got a woman with him!"

The corporal of the guard turned and walked rapidly toward the officer's quarters. Vi Robinson and Wilma Henderson had as much right as anyone did to welcome the approaching group home.

Vi swallowed hard when she learned Abel had returned. It could mean any number of things, none of them very promising. She and Wilma went running out into the compound just as the small procession made its way into the fort. The square set of Abel's shoulders and the pinched look of pain in his eyes alarmed her, and when she saw Judy's blank, expressionless stare, Vi's heart went skidding. Her knees began to buckle, and she forced herself to stand straight, to meet the dread truth head-on.

Abel Hubbard reined his horse to a halt in front of his mother-in-law. He made no attempt to dismount. Vi saw the Adam's apple in his throat move, the lips twitch as though to form the words.

"Bill's dead, isn't he, Abel?" Vi's voice was quiet against the afternoon breeze.

At Abel's nod, she felt the tears well at the corners of her eyes, and the overwhelming sense of loss and pain slammed against her resolve to maintain her composure.

Then Abel was on the ground, his arms wrapped about his mother-in-law, and Wilma saw the tear-tracks through the trail dust on Abel's tanned face.

Wilma swallowed the lump in her throat, feeling her own emptiness inside. She knew she would break into tears on the spot if she did not do something. Her eyes fell on Judy's face. The once beautiful contours had turned slack, the formerly bright and alert eyes were dead and lifeless, the hair tousled and left untended, so unlike the proud and vain young woman she had known before.

Wilma moved to Judy's side and reached up for her. Judy, turning her head, looked down at Wilma with no sign of recognition in the expressionless eyes.

"Judy," Wilma said softly, "please come down."

The slender young woman dropped the reins, dismounted, and stood, arms hanging at her sides, unresponsive as Wilma embraced her. Wilma became conscious of a presence, felt another set of arms around the hapless Judy, and realized Vi had joined her.

"How long has she—been like this?" Vi asked.

"Since before Colonel—before Dad died," Abel answered.

"Come," Wilma said, "let's get the poor girl inside."

Together, they led the once vibrant girl into Abel's quarters. Like an obedient doll, Judy stretched out on the bed, eyes staring at the ceiling. Abel sat on the side of the bed, a hand placed over the motionless fingers of his wife. "I don't understand," he said again and again. Wilma heard the pleading note in his voice.

Wilma placed an arm over Vi's shoulders.

"I'm so sorry, Vi."

Vi merely nodded. Abel reached into his tunic, produced a packet, and without speaking, handed it to his mother-in-law.

Vi took the packet in a trembling hand, holding it close to her breast for a moment. Then she turned her face away. "If you will excuse me, I would—like to be alone for a while." Vi squared her shoulders with an obvious effort and walked out of the room. Wilma watched her friend go, then dabbed at the corners of her own eyes with the sleeve of her dress. She took a deep breath and turned back to Abel.

"What happened, Abel?"

"It's a long story, Wilma," the young officer said. "Could we discuss it later?"

"Of course." Wilma placed a gentle hand on his shoulder. "I hate to sound selfish at such a time, but I must ask. What do you know of Ted?"

Abel shook his head. "He led the column south after Colonel Robinson was shot. I have had no word since we parted."

Wilma patted his brawny hand. "I'm sorry, Abel. I know the colonel meant as much to you as he did to anyone." Aware that she was near the point of losing control, Wilma suddenly turned and left the room, seeking the comfort of her own quarters, a private corner where she could grieve alone.

The memorial service at the Fort Laramie chapel was mercifully brief, and afterward Wilma made it a point to thank the post chaplain for keeping the service a glorification of God, not an emotional tribute to the memory of Bill Robinson. Vi and Abel had been among the first to leave, both dry-eyed and standing straight, and Wilma hoped they had found some comfort in the chaplain's well-chosen words.

Judy had not attended. She had remained in her quarters, rocking back and forth in a chair Abel had made for her when they were still at Fort Bridger, staring straight ahead, oblivious to the occasional comment from Anna, the robust wife of one of Ted's scouts. The woman had volunteered to stay with Judy during the service, and Wilma fell into step with her as she made her way back to her own quarters.

"What do you think, Anna?" Wilma asked the woman who had recently arrived from Germany.

The scout's wife shook her head. "Don't rightly know, Mrs. Henderson. Seen cases like this before, back in the old country. Our town used to get sacked regular by one army or another; seemed as if we were always in the way of something somebody wanted. Anyway, every time an army came through, one or two like poor Judy were left behind. Sometimes they came around, sometimes they didn't. It was as though they had been handed something they couldn't carry, so they just sat down and didn't try."

"Is there anything we can do?"

'Just be patient and kind, Wilma. That's about all a body can do." Anna sighed. "The mind's a strange thing. It's like a tap on a water keg. It can turn itself on or off, but sometimes it gets stuck. Like when it leaves itself open and drips all night and you can't sleep. Judy's tap seems to be stuck shut, but it isn't like a broken bone. You can't fix it. It has to fix itself."

"Thank you, Anna. I believe I understand now."

"So how are you feeling?" Anna had been the first to notice the swelling in Wilma's abdomen, and thus the first in the fort to know of her pregnancy.

"Fine. No problems at all."

"Well, when your time comes, you just sing out if you need help. I've been to nearly as many birthin's as the post surgeon, maybe more. And my Carl—you'll have trouble keeping him away from the youngster. We always wanted some kids ourselves but the Lord didn't see fit to bless us so. But my, how Carl loves babies—I'd best drop off here, Wilma. You take care now, you hear?"

"I will, Anna. And if I need anything, I'll ask for you."

Anna's ample brow furrowed in thought. "Is your husband going to be back home when the baby is born?"

"I honestly don't know, Anna. As a matter of fact, he doesn't even know about the baby yet."

"Then I reckon you'd better write and tell him, as soon as you find out for sure where he is; man has a right to know something like that. And you know how long it takes for a letter to get anywhere these days."

The Mescalero subchief, Tanaya, sat cross-legged and watched as the medicine man raised the pipe to the four winds and murmured the ancient chants which would bring strong medicine to the tribe. A wisp of steam rose from the pot above the small fire in the center of Tanaya's oversized lodge. The Apache savored the mule-meat stew, the aroma of woodsmoke, and the incantations of the shaman.

Finally the medicine man had called upon all the spirits,

then took his seat as one of the more prominent tribal leaders. Tanaya waited until the pipe had made its full circle, then took a deep drag of the strong tobacco. He exhaled slowly, letting the smoke filter through flattened nostrils. After a time, he rose.

"These have been days of good hunting for the Apache," Tanaya said. He waved a powerful arm about the lodge. "Many new scalps hang in Apache tipis. New ponies in Apache herds, young ones with bellies full of meat. It is the same with the Kiowa, the Comanche, the Navajo.

"When the gray soldier came with the general named Humphries," he continued, "the Apache had new guns, new blankets; the Apache was free to follow the ways of his ancestors, to raid deep into Mexico. The Apache were strong again!"

Tanaya paused as solemn nods of agreement rippled around the council fire.

"And," he went on, "the strongest Apache tribes of all were the Mescalero." Murmurs of agreement whispered through the lodge. "However, some weaker brothers told the white man, 'Apache are hungry. Apache ask for peace. Apache will be tame.'" Tanaya raised a clenched fist.

"The Mescalero will never be tame Indians! The sacred mountains will be regained, the streams, the forests! Never again will the white men shoot the Mescalero deer, tear up the earth with pointed sticks! This Tanaya, whose medicine is stronger than the mightiest of the Apache, swears!"

Tanaya paused again, enjoying the mutters of approval and agreement from the circle.

"But now," he said, dropping his voice, "the way will not be so easy. The blue soldiers have driven out the gray soldiers and may try to take the land of the Mescalero. Yet what Long Knife can ride with the skill of the Apache? Stalk the night with such stealth? Take the wife of a man asleep and never wake him?"

He waited until the scattered chuckles from his small joke had died.

"Now, brothers, is the time! Who rides with Tanaya? Who will join with Tanaya and fling the white-skinned ones beyond the far mountains, as buffalo chips in a high wind?"

Tanaya half smiled at the high-pitched yelps of allegiance. With a grace that belied the heavy bulk of his upper body and massive thighs, Tanaya strode to the front of the lodge, threw back the flap, and called:

"Let the Long Knives come! Then the wolves shall feel no hunger!"

"Sentries report column approaching from the west, sir," the corporal of the guard said.

General Murphy made no attempt to hide his grin. "That must be General Carleton with his California bunch."

A few minutes later the California Column, a bewhiskered general in the lead, came into the Union camp at a fast trot.

Carleton stepped lightly from the saddle, snapped a soldierly salute, then took the hand of General Kelly Murphy in a warm grip.

"Ah, General Carleton, your lieutenant told us you were on the way. Good to see you again."

"Sorry we weren't here sooner," Carleton said. "I was afraid there for a while we might find you taking in Confederate laundry."

Murphy grinned. "Except for a stroke of fortune in the form of some unexpected and highly efficient reinforcements, and no small amount of help from an old friend of yours, I might very well have been."

"Is Kit all right?"

"Hale and hearty." Murphy slapped his slight paunch. "I don't understand the man, General," he said. "Kit Carson is older than I am, and he still looks as if he could run from here to Salt Lake and back without breaking into a sweat. Any problems on the ride in?"

"Aside from missing the party here, only one to speak of." General Carleton adjusted his long stride to the shorter steps of the stocky Murphy as the two officers made their way to the command tent. "We had a little conversation with a Navajo named Gallegos. I think we are going to have some problems with that one."

"Lieutenant O'Reilly told us about your meeting with the Navajo chiefs," Murphy said. "It comes as no surprise. There have been problems with just about every tribe you might want to mention—Navajo, Apache, Kiowa, even Comanche."

Murphy stopped outside the command tent and held the flap open for Carleton. He smiled at the Californian's whoop.

"Kit! You misbegotten excuse for a mountain man. How've you been?"

"Just fine, General," Carson said, turning a brief handshake into a short bear-hug of greeting.

Kelly Murphy decided to leave the two friends alone for a few minutes to rehash old times, before bringing up military matters. He dispatched a sergeant to locate Ted Henderson.

Within minutes, Ted seemed to materialize at the general's side. "You sent for me, sir?"

"Yes, Major. Come inside, please. There are some new developments we need to discuss."

Murphy again held the tent flap open, and Ted found himself wondering how many generals would do that for a junior officer.

"General James Carleton, meet Major Ted Henderson of the Third Cavalry. His group is the primary reason we are still in control of the West today."

Ted took the extended hand, sized up the man behind it, and decided he liked what he saw—muttonchop whiskers, a determined jawline, light-colored eyes, weather-bronzed skin. A man, Ted thought, who not only demanded results but also got them. And he was not unfamiliar with the name; Kit Carson had mentioned Carleton's name several times over the past few days.

General Murphy summarized the expedition from Fort Bridger, its timely arrival despite seemingly impossible odds.

General Carleton's brows lifted as the story unfolded. "My compliments, Major," Carleton said at the conclusion of Murphy's account. "That ride should go down in military history."

Ted shrugged off the praise. "The men made it possible, sir. All I did was point them in the right direction."

"Then," Carleton said, "I'm glad your men are on our side." He turned to the square-jawed Murphy. "So now what, General? The West seems to be secure from any Confederate danger at the moment."

Murphy rolled a soggy cigar stub between blunt fingers, casually tossing it into a cuspidor. "Latest instruction from Washington is that we are to establish headquarters in Santa Fe and await further orders. According to the War Department's wishful thinking, our combined forces are to put an end to what the desk generals call the 'Indian problem.' I already have patrols out, but it's like chasing a dust devil. But I don't have to tell you that, General, or you either, Major. Both of you have been there before, and the Lord knows Colonel Carson here has seen more than his share of Indians."

Murphy sighed. "For the moment, we do the best we can. We hunt; we hope. And we wait."

General Murphy had scarcely reorganized his command in Santa Fe when new orders arrived from Washington, recalling him and his troops to the eastern front. He was replaced by General Carleton, who arranged a special farewell dinner on the eve of Murphy's departure. It was a solemn occasion, not only because General Murphy was going to eastern battlefields, but also because he was taking his leave from a group of men who had come to mean so much to him.

On the day after General Murphy's departure, Kit Carson went to see his new commanding officer. Entering the general's office in the newly occupied Santa Fe headquarters, Carson leaned against General Carleton's desk, jaws clenched in defiance.

"This is one bitter pill you've handed me, General," Carson said.

"Now, calm down, Kit. I know the agreement you had with General Murphy was that your commission would expire as soon as the war with the Confederates in the Southwest had ended. And I'm not refusing your resignation, Colonel; I'm merely holding it in abeyance." Carleton leaned back in his chair and sighed. "With General Murphy and his troops transferred East, our forces in the West have been further weakened. But these Indian depredations have to be stopped. You are obviously the best man for the job. With you and Major Henderson and his scouts, the Indians can be brought under control with a minimum loss of life to both sides.

"What I propose is this, Kit. Go to Josefa. Talk it over with her. Then, if your decision still is to resign, simply get word to me and I will put my signature on the papers. Should you decide to stay, just ride back in."

Carleton rose from behind the desk and put an arm across Carson's shoulders. "Kit, I know what I'm asking, and I wouldn't ask it of a lesser man. We've been through a lot together, and Lord knows you've contributed more than your share to the West and to your flag. I need you, Kit. You know that. You should also know that, should you decide to resign, I will certainly think none the less of you for it and will hold no animosity. I'm merely asking that you talk it over with your wife. Your decision, whatever it may be, will be honored."

Carson sighed. "James, I'm not getting any younger. On damp mornings I ache in the joints. I have a wife and a family and a ranch. But I also see your need. I'll talk it over with Josefa."

"That's all I ask, Kit. And give my love to Josefa. She's a rather remarkable woman in my eyes as well as yours."

Ted leaned against the trunk of a pine high above the cluster of lights called Santa Fe. Wilma's letter lay heavy against his heart inside his tunic. He stared toward the northwest, the need and longing for her as sharp as the brilliant pinpoints of light in the clear spring sky above.

He had just learned that Wilma was going to have their baby. This news came on the same day General Carleton had made a fervent request of him and his scouts to remain in the Southwest and help subdue the belligerent Indians. The situation was indeed critical. In the last few days the Apache Tanaya had led his warriors in brutal raids against the settlers of the area, and Ted knew that serious measures had to be taken to put a stop to the bloodshed. But why did it have to be he who was called upon, when all he now wanted to do was leave the area and go home?

"My brother is troubled?"

Ted started at the unexpected comment. He had not heard Yellow Crow approach. The Cheyenne squatted on the other side of the pine tree, silently waiting a reply.

"Yes, brother," Ted replied at length, speaking in the Cheyenne tongue as Yellow Crow had done. His hand drifted to the three-page letter. "He finds himself torn between two worlds."

Yellow Crow snorted, but Ted's ears caught no derision in the sound. "It is a feeling Yellow Crow knows well, brother. It makes the heart ache. What is it that has brought my brother to a solitary place alone to think?"

"A letter from Wilma. It arrived this week. Before the leaves turn, your brother will be a father."

"It is good. Each man should have sons to teach and to learn from. This should bring joy to your soul, not darkness."

Ted sighed. "In the middle of an army is only loneliness. Wyoming calls. In the night, your brother dreams of Wilma, smells the pot roast she cooks so well, touches her skin—and then he wakes up alone. He is homesick, Yellow Crow."

"It is the lot of the man who fights," the Cheyenne replied. "My brother feels the need to be with Wilma when the baby comes?"

"Desperately."

Surprisingly, the Cheyenne chuckled softly in the near-darkness. "It is another of the strange ways of the white man. He has not yet come to know that he is needed to plant the seed, but nature and the woman shall produce the harvest. But if the heart says go, then return to your squaw."

Ted plucked a blade of grass and chewed thoughtfully on the stem for a long moment. "It is not that simple, Yellow Crow. Your brother has been asked to stay, to join in the campaign against the red man who will not live in peace with the whites. It is a duty. He has a duty to his wife. Which one outweighs the other?"

"That is why the spirits made places like this, where a man asks the darkness and himself for answers," Yellow Crow said. "Yellow Crow also has faced the inner battle. But in a spot not far from here, the spirits led him to the answers.

"To his friend Ted, and to no other, will he admit that Yellow Crow was very near to mounting his horse and riding north just two suns ago. But the spirits spoke to him. Yellow Crow was troubled, for if he helped the white man fight the Apache, the Kiowa, the Navajo, what tribe would be next? His own people, the Cheyenne? But the spirits held the answer. First, there is the matter of Tanaya"—Yellow Crow spat in disgust at the name—"whose people killed his parents when he was very small. But the spirits said, 'He is but a speck of dust, and Yellow Crow has the blood right. Yellow Crow will someday defeat him and will find peace.' And then they said, 'Yellow Crow, is it possible that by helping the white man the Cheyenne are also being helped? Is it not true that should the war tribes be punished, then the hotheads among the Cheyenne will listen to reason? Then talk, not war parties, will bring red and white man together in peace on the great plains from Montana to Texas.'

"But, Yellow Crow argued, will the white man talk and live in peace? And the spirits answered, 'Does Yellow Crow believe his own red brothers are not also at fault? The future is the hunting ground of the medicine man.' With that, Yellow

Crow cast the medicine bones upon the earth. They told him to stay. So, he stayed."

Ted let the silence linger, pondering what Yellow Crow had said. It was the longest speech the Cheyenne had ever uttered in his presence. Then he reached out and placed a hand on the Cheyenne's shoulder.

"Thank you, brother, for sharing the talk with the spirits. They spoke the truth to you. Perhaps they will do the same for your brother."

Yellow Crow rose to leave. "Yellow Crow hopes they will. By the time the sun appears, peace will be within my brother."

As quietly as he had appeared, Yellow Crow vanished into the night.

Josefa Carson snuggled closer against her husband's side. She stroked the side of his chest. "You are going back, aren't you, Kit?"

"Yes, Josefa. You know my compassion for the Indians. James Carleton feels the same, and I sense that Ted Henderson does as well. A majority of the tribes are anxious for peace, and the sooner we run down the troublemakers, the better. And it can be done with a minimum loss of life on both sides."

Josefa sighed. "No woman wants to send her man back into war. But if you do not go, Kit Carson, the job might fall to some Indian-hater who could fan the flames into a forest fire and cause much blood to flow. There is too much human life at stake for a lesser man to be guiding the team."

Kit Carson sighed. "At times," he said, "I wish you did not have this ability to cut right to the core of the apple. A logical mind in a beautiful woman is a frightening thing."

She felt a callused hand stroke her body, as he nuzzled closer into the hollow where her neck and shoulder joined, nibbling playfully at her ear.

"Ah," she said, moving her own hand, "it appears that the old, tired mountain man still has a bit of life left." She pulled her husband closer in the soft, spring night.

Wilma struggled from the bed, her ribs still ringing from a solid kick. She patted her swollen abdomen. She stretched as best she could, massaged the small of her back, and wondered idly what it would be like to be able to walk on her toes instead of her heels once more, or for that matter, even to see her toes. She reached for a bottle on the bed table, dribbled some oil into a palm, and massaged it into her breasts and stomach. Anna had said it would cut down on the stretch marks.

She put the coffeepot on, patting her stomach again. "Time to wake up, youngster. Morning coffee call." While she waited for the coffee to brew, she lumbered to the window, parted the shutters, and breathed in deep whiffs of the fragrant, predawn spring air. A light glowed between the slats of the shutters at Vi's window, and Wilma wondered if her friend was still troubled by nightmares. There would be time for a visit later with Vi and poor Judy. She turned and, picking up Ted's letter from the table, reread it, savoring each word, until the coffeepot signaled the real start of the new day. She poured a cup, returned to the table, and took out pen and paper. She thought for a moment, then dipped pen in ink and began to write.

> *My dearest:*
>
> *Your letter reached me yesterday, and just by touching the paper that had been in your hands I felt we were physically together again. Distance may lie between our physical beings, but our spirits and hearts remain as one.*
>
> *Your decision to stay and do what you can to bring peace between the Indians and the white man was not only noble, but, I believe, correct. I also think I know how much it hurt you to write those words; but you are needed there. It is a time for a firm but gentle hand on the reins, and from what your letters have told me of General Carleton and Colonel Carson, I believe the future of both red man and white are in the best of hands. I am proud of you, Ted.*
>
> *And perhaps it is just as well that you can't see me at the moment. Remember that lifelong battle I've had against putting on weight? Well, I'm losing this skirmish. Instead of eating my bread, it seems I should just pack it directly onto the hips. I'm also waddling like a duck. Ever try walking on your heels for weeks on end? But I'm healthy and content—and your son packs a strong kick! He really rattled my traces this morning. I say son because Anna says it will be a boy, and she has been right so often in her*

forecasts about the sex of an unborn child it's absolutely uncanny.

Speaking of Anna, on her behalf I say thank you for sending Carl and the other two scouts back home. Abel has welcomed the help, too; he has so much territory to cover and so few people to do it with. The new commander of Fort Bridger, a captain with only one company of cavalry and the remainder in infantry, is not mobile enough to be much help, but Abel's name already brings fear to renegade Indians. By the way, the War Department has given Abel a temporary promotion. He's now Major Hubbard.

Poor Judy is unchanged, and I think it's tearing Abel apart. I don't know how much longer he can cope. All we can do, I suppose, is hope that time or possibly a miracle will bring Judy back to us.

But back for a moment to Anna and Carl. Since his return, they finally have that child they've wanted so desperately all these years. They adopted an Arapaho orphan, a beautiful little girl with the longest lashes you've ever seen. Her Indian name is all but unpronounceable, so they call her Ellen. Perhaps by the time Ellen and our son are grown, the color of a person's skin will no longer matter. In fact, I firmly believe that it is necessary, even crucial, or I fear the Indian will vanish forever from the Americas. And that would be a loss history could ill afford.

On more personal matters, would you object to naming our son after Colonel Robinson? With Vi as a godmother, and Yellow Crow as godfather? They are the people who have been closest to us during this wonderful time of our lives.

There is so much to say that it would take all the paper in Wyoming Territory to write it down and a twenty-mule-team hitch to deliver it. So I shall be content to parcel it out in little dribbles of two or three pages.

Ted, you know there aren't enough words in the English or Arapaho or Cheyenne languages to tell you how much I love you and miss you. So take care of yourself, may the Lord ride with you, and come

home to your wife and son when—and only when—
your duties are done.

                                                    With love forever,
                                                              Wilma

Wilma carefully cleaned the pen, returned it to its resting place, and finished getting dressed. She made her way to Vi Robinson's quarters just as the sun was rising. Her tap on the door brought a soft call from within.

Wilma stepped into the room and felt her heart sink as she stared briefly at her good friend. Dark circles lay beneath the normally expressive eyes, emphasized by the guttering of an oil lamp on a table nearby. Vi still wore the same dress she had donned the previous day, and Wilma sensed she had not even attempted to sleep. The room was in disarray, a stark contrast to the character of the ordinarily immaculate Vi Robinson.

"It's worse, isn't it, Vi?" Wilma said.

Her eyes tearing, Vi lowered her head into her hands. Her words were partially muffled through her fingers.

"Yes, Wilma. I'm ashamed of my weakness, but I don't know how much longer I can stand this. I can't sleep, I can't eat—I can't even think straight anymore."

Wilma rounded the table where Vi sat hunched over a cup of cold, forgotten coffee and placed an arm around her friend's shoulders.

"Vi, listen to me," Wilma said in her most reassuring tone, "what you are going through isn't a sign of weakness. It is grief over the loss of a loved one. I know how much Bill meant to you."

"It isn't just Bill," Vi said. "As a soldier's wife I conditioned myself for that moment, though the pain will always be there, of course. But it's Judy, poor Judy—she just sits and stares and rocks, and nothing I say seems to reach her ears." Vi reached up, gripping Wilma's forearm in her hand. "She and Abel are all I have left, Wilma. I can't bear to see her like that and to see Abel suffer so—"

Wilma placed her own hand over Vi's. "Vi, I've been talking to Anna. She has seen similar conditions in the old country. She has an idea that might or might not work. Sudden shock or confusion sometimes helps people like Judy break free of the walls they have built around their minds. Are you strong enough to try and help her break through? It won't be easy for you, for me, or for Judy."

Vi sighed, exhaustion weighing heavily in the sound. "I'm desperate, Wilma. At this stage, I'll try anything. What do you have in mind?"

As Wilma explained, Vi nodded slowly, realizing she would need a great deal of courage and strength to go through with the plan. She rose wearily, took the coat Wilma held out for her, and together the two women left the house to go to the Hubbard quarters next door.

Abel had already gone to his office, which adjoined the living quarters, and as Wilma and Vi entered the room, Judy sat motionlessly, staring at a far wall. Wilma gathered her courage for the scene that was to come, then ponderously made her way to the frail figure in the rocking chair beside the dying coals of the fire.

"Good morning, Judy," Wilma said, her tone soothing as she adjusted the shawl about the young woman's shoulders. Then she gently embraced Judy. "You must be hungry, dear. I'll fix you something to eat—"

"You'll do no such thing, Wilma Henderson!" Vi called out, her voice shrill and angry. She quickly stomped across the room, grasped Wilma's arm, and tore it from Judy's shoulders. "Let her get her own breakfast! She will learn to do for herself, or she will starve!"

Wilma raised a hand. "Now, Vi! Calm down. You know what the poor girl's been through. Let's not add to her troubles—"

"Troubles? Hah! What about my troubles? I have nobody now—Bill's dead and it's all Judy's fault!" Wilma watched for reactions in Judy's face but found none.

"Leave her alone, Vi!" Wilma yelled, and turned back to Judy. "Forgive her, Judy. Poor Vi's not been herself of late. She doesn't know what she's saying—"

"You stay out of this, Wilma Henderson! Step aside!" Vi thrust her face close to Judy's. Wilma could see the pain in Vi's eyes and realized how much the charade was hurting her friend.

"It's you who caused all the trouble!" Vi's voice was strident, almost hysterical. "It's all your fault! It's you who's to blame!" Vi's work-hardened hands gripped bruisingly into Judy's slender shoulders. "You're irresponsible, foolish, stupid—"

Suddenly Vi felt her hand trapped in a solid grip. Judy slowly lifted the older woman's hand from her shoulder and in one quick motion tossed it aside. Watching Judy's eyes, Vi saw the sudden flash of panic. And then the curtain fell once more. Her body rigid, Judy continued to stare straight ahead. The jaw muscles that had momentarily tensed again fell slack.

It was more than Vi could stand. With a sob, she threw her arms around Judy's neck and buried her face in the girl's hair.

"God, Judy—I'm sorry—please forgive me," she said between sobs. "But we—had to try—to reach you some way—"

Wilma, moving closer, pulled Judy's head against her swollen abdomen as though comforting a child. She felt the sting of tears at the corners of her eyes. "Don't hate us, Judy," she said, her voice quiet. "It's just that we love you, and we want you back so badly—" Her voice trailed off in surprise as she felt a gentle touch on her belly; at the same moment the unborn baby moved. After the briefest of hesitations, Judy's hand fell away, dropping back lifelessly into the young woman's lap.

"We—we'll be back in a moment, Judy," Vi said. "We'll fix you a nice breakfast and a bath."

Outside the door, Vi almost collapsed into Wilma's arms.

"Wilma, how can I live with myself after this? I feel—completely despicable."

Wilma stroked Vi's shoulder. "No, Vi. What you did was done from love. Miracles aren't made in one encounter, but small victories add up to a larger sum. For the first time, I sensed Judy reacting to something from outside herself. Just for a moment, she was struggling to break free, I believe. One day she will breach that wall.

"But we will not try this approach again," Wilma added. "It cost us all too much. Patience and love and caring are the road to travel now."

Ted glanced across the rough pine table at Kit Carson. He saw his own concern reflected in the former mountain man's eyes. General Carleton had just finished describing his plans to subdue the rebellious Indians of the Southwest and had asked if there were questions.

"Sir," Carson finally said, "aren't those terms pretty stiff? Unconditional surrender is a hard thing to sell to an Indian with a free heritage dating back centuries."

"Perhaps the terms are stiff, Kit," Carleton said, "but

remember, the Apache and Navajo signed a treaty of peace. They broke that pact of their own free will, looting and burning and stealing. They have made their own bed; now they must lie in it."

The general stroked his muttonchop whiskers. "You know as well as I that leadership of the Indian tribes is fragmented to the point that no one chief commands more than a small portion of the tribe as a whole." Carleton sighed. "In a way, that is a blessing for us. If all the tribes ever should unite into a single army under the leadership shown by some of the better war chiefs, they would sweep the West clean of white faces.

"At any rate, you are to take the following message to the Apache to the east; Major Emery Church will do the same with the Navajo to the north and west: Surrender and be relocated to the Bosque Redondo, or be annihilated! The message is direct, to the point, and cannot be misunderstood by accident or design. I see no other prompt solution unless we settle in for a long and bloody war.

"The major chiefs are to be informed and instructed to spread the word among their people. At the Bosque Redondo, the Indians will be fed, housed, clothed, taught to farm, and supplied with sheep, cattle, and such tools as they need to become self-sufficient. They will each receive a specified amount of land as their own."

"Perhaps this is best, General," Carson said. "These are harsh times. A quick end to hostilities will, in the long run, save lives."

"That's why you're here, Kit. The Indians know you as a man of his word. They know you sympathize with the red man's plight. If they will listen to any white man, they will listen to you.

"Kit, the Apache—and particularly the Mescalero—have been causing the most havoc. That is why I have assigned you and Major Henderson to put an end to it. Once the Apache are controlled, all our forces will be turned toward the Navajo."

Carleton paced along the table, back again, then stared at first one face, then another. "Gentlemen, I will not have these standing orders breached! Follow them to the letter, or face the consequences. Treat the captives with kindness, and slaughter those who resist until the back of the Indian nations breaks from constant pressure. That is all. Good luck and Godspeed."

Kit Carson cleared his throat. "A word with you in private, General?"

"Certainly, Colonel."

The two officers waited patiently until the others had left.

"What's on your mind, Kit?"

"James, you said you're sending this Major Emery Church to the Navajo. There's something about the man that gets my hackles up. What do you know about him?"

"From a personal standpoint, not much," Carleton said, scratching a sideburn. "He's been with the California Column only a short time. But he speaks Navajo and has come to me with letters of praise from the territorial governor's office."

"But will he follow orders to the letter? The entire campaign is based on the premise of fair treatment of prisoners and severe punishment of renegades. One show of weakness in either area could jeopardize the whole campaign."

"That remains to be seen, Kit. But if he doesn't follow orders, Major Emery Church is going to find his backside in a cactus patch with me standing on his belt buckle!"

Ted Henderson and Kit Carson rode stirrup-to-stirrup into the remains of the buildings that had been Fort Stanton in New Mexico Territory. Union forces, under pressure of the recent Confederate invasion, had pulled out of the fort and put it to the torch before joining General Murphy's consolidated command to meet the Rebel thrust. Many of the buildings were heavily damaged, but others still seemed serviceable as headquarters for the Mescalero campaign.

A few gaunt, weary Indians watched as the long column of blue-clad soldiers, flanked by the buckskins of perhaps twenty of Henderson's Scouts, filed past and occupied the fort.

By nightfall of the first day, a half-dozen Indians had petitioned to meet with Carson. The colonel saw that they were fed. The strongest of them were issued cavalry mounts to spread the word to other tribes about the new rules issued by the Great White Father in Washington through General Carleton to the Apache.

Kit Carson sighed as he watched the last of the Indian messengers depart. "They will probably eat their horses," he said to Ted, "but at least the Mescalero, some of them, will get the message. Seems a shame, though. Soldiers get all the letters of praise, promotions, and a place in history. And the poor horse goes on short rations, burns himself out, and never a word is written about his contribution to the taming of the West."

The two officers made their way back to the single room Carson had chosen as his billet and office. Carson said, "We can't just sit here waiting for the Indians to come to us, Major. How soon can we have patrols in the field?"

Ted glanced through a hole in a charred wall at the lowering sun. "Daybreak tomorrow, Colonel."

"How are we fixed for experienced Indian patrol leaders?"

"Yellow Crow is the best of the lot, including the two of us," Ted replied. "Frank Armbrister is no stranger to Indians. The newly promoted Sergeant Jonas may be short on experience, but he's long on common sense. We can draw on my scout company for maybe seven or eight more, all top horsemen who think like Indians."

"Fine. By the time this is over, Ted, we will have an oversupply of experienced Indian fighters. Firm up four patrols for Boots and Saddles at first light; we can't waste any time getting a show of strength out in the field. I want to see artillery covering all fields of fire from this post by sundown. The cannon won't be much use in the field, but they will make an impression on any Indians riding in. The Apache have been known to attack a fort, and I want to be in a position to thoroughly discourage any such attempt on Fort Stanton."

"Yes, sir. I'll get on it right away."

"And, Ted, one more thing. When you've finished, would you do a personal favor for me? Make out a report of the day's activities for my signature. General Carleton is setting up a courier system, and if he doesn't hear from me on every run, he will be on my tail like a squirrel on a hickory nut."

The first patrol had not yet returned when a small band of Indians—the first to surrender willingly—approached Fort Stanton on foot. Kit Carson stepped forward, spoke in the Apache tongue with an aging, stooped Indian who seemed to be the leader of the group, then turned to Ted.

"See that they are fed, Major. I want the Indians in my custody to receive the best care." Carson wheeled and stalked back toward his office, but not before Ted glimpsed in the colonel's eyes the determination to see this job through to the end.

Frank Armbrister, fully recovered from a wound he had received during the battle at Glorieta Pass, had ridden in with his patrol, escorting a group of twenty women, children, and old men. The young sergeant was among the first to mingle with the Indians who had surrendered. Ted could not suppress a smile as he watched the tough, no-nonsense Armbrister prop a toddler on his lap and carefully feed it from his own mess kit. The anxious mother sitting at his side soon relaxed, and Ted could guess at the conversation as Armbrister pointed first to one object, then another, nodding at the woman's words, repeating them. Frank Armbrister, it seemed, was learning the Apache tongue.

Yellow Crow's patrol returned with a dozen braves in tow, a hunting party that had surrendered without a shot having been fired. In a matter of hours the other patrols also rode in, bringing the total number of Indians who had surrendered to seventy-five. Ted noted with satisfaction that one of the old men who had just come in was a shaman. It was, he thought, a good omen for the Mescalero campaign. Now the captured Apache could call on their own medicine man as well as the regimental surgeons to treat the sick and wounded.

Colonel Carson instructed the cavalry physicians to observe the medicine man, for the Apache shaman was a wealth of information on medical treatments using the roots and leaves of desert and forest.

By the end of the second week, more than a hundred Apache had surrendered and were camped beneath the shadows of the Fort Stanton buildings.

But Tanaya was not among them.

The rays from the lowering sun fell through storm-washed air and tumbled into the mouth of the cave high up on the side of the canyon wall. The hot, early summer sunlight bathed the crumpled body in blue at the cave entrance, a dead hand still grasping one of three feathered shafts protruding from the chest.

Corporal Bennett cursed long and fluently, then ducked his head as a rifle ball struck a cave wall, ricocheted past his ear, and plowed into the hard-packed dirt of the cavern floor. They had been on patrol when they were ambushed by Tanaya's Apache, and the sergeant had told them to take cover in this cave, thus leading them into a trap.

"Told Sarge not to walk into this cave," Bennett muttered, "better to take our chances out there." He winced as an arrow arched through the opening and buried itself between two troopers crouched on the cave floor.

The corporal, becoming aware of movement beside him, turned his head to stare into the wide eyes of Bernie Christian.

"What's our status, Corporal?"

"Not good," Bennett said. "There must be twenty, thirty Indians out there. We can't get out, but they can come in just about anytime they want. Best we can do is hope to take a few of 'em along."

"Let's not give up too soon, Corporal," Christian said, the deep southern drawl reflecting little concern. "I might have found us an answer."

"Let's hear it, Christian. I ain't overly anxious to get my brisket slit by no Apache."

"Back about twenty yards from here, there's a small opening in the roof of the cave about ten feet up. If somebody could give me a boost, I can maybe squeeze through it. Been teased all my life about being little, but this time it just might pay off."

The corporal glanced over his shoulder toward the back of the cave. "And if you can get out?"

Christian shrugged. "I can try to set up a little surprise. Or maybe get hold of a horse, make a run for the fort, and get some help."

Bennett snorted. "Christian, they'd cut you to pieces out there. We ain't got the time to spare for help to get here. Them redskins will be all over us come sundown."

"So what do you have to lose, Corporal? It's my skin."

The corporal sighed. "You want to get yourself killed, might as well do it on your own terms. What do you need?"

"A boost up the wall and three pistols."

"Well, let's get to it."

With an assist from the corporal, Bernie Christian worked his way up the final few inches of the cave wall, eased his head above ground level, and slowly looked around. There was no movement, but that was not reassuring. It was said among the troopers that you never saw an Apache until he wanted you to see him.

Even with his slight build, it was a tight squeeze. Half-expecting an Indian cry or an arrow at any second, Christian flattened himself on the top of the hill beside the hole, then pulled up the pistols, roped together. Keeping on his belly, he wormed his way to the edge of the canyon several yards from the cave entrance.

Across the way, he spotted first one, then another brown body among the rocks and scrub brush. A short, powerfully built Indian in full war paint moved from one post to another. Well, better to die in the open, Christian thought, than be hemmed in on three sides. Suddenly a movement off to his right caught his attention. The Indian horses, guarded by a single brave, waited behind the ridge, down-canyon from the main Apache force.

Below, the braves appeared to be gathering for an assault on the cave. Bernie Christian took a deep breath and then began to move, slipping from rock to rock, scrub brush to tall grass, until he was below and behind the Apache horse herd. He paused to catch his breath and let his heart calm down while he checked the loads in the three pistols. He slipped off his cavalry boots and glanced at the sun. His fellow soldiers in the cave, he knew, were running out of time. He tucked the pistols firmly into the waistband of his trousers, slipped the knife from its sheath, and began working his way toward the horses.

The lone Indian had left the tethered mounts and had climbed the few steps to the crest of the ridge, apparently to watch the attack unfold. Christian held the knife, cutting edge up, in his right hand, praying silently that the Apache would not suddenly turn, that a noise from the horses would not draw the Indian's attention.

He felt the beads of sweat break out along his forehead and on his lip; the haft of the knife seemed slippery in his hand. He was within two strides of the horse guard now, preparing to spring, when the Indian suddenly turned. Christian launched himself through the air, felt the impact as his shoulder struck the Indian's chest, and swept the knife upward with all his strength. The Apache's muscles went limp, and the Indian fell heavily, dragging the smaller man down in a heap.

Christian, struggling free of the body, felt his stomach churn at the gory mess the knife had made. He ground his teeth and tugged at the handle until the weapon came free. Christian waited until his chest stopped heaving, then made his way to the horses. The animals snorted nervously at his approach but made no attempt to strike out with hooves as he quietly sliced through the picket ropes. At the first sound of gunfire, the animals would spook.

Now Christian worked his way to the top of the ridge. Less than a hundred feet below, a line of brown bodies crouched behind boulders, eyes on the cave above. Christian pulled the first of the three revolvers, braced his wrists against the bole of a small cedar tree, brought the sights into line, and squeezed. Through the muzzle smoke and the upward buck of the handgun's recoil, he saw the brave that had been in his sights crumple. He swung the muzzle toward another Apache, squeezed the trigger, and saw the man spin and fall heavily. Christian stopped aiming then, merely emptying the handgun in the general direction of the other Indians. Then he flung himself from the tree and behind a cluster of boulders.

Caught by surprise in the attack from the rear, the confused Apache below glanced first in one direction and then in another. Two went down under a volley of concentrated rifle fire from the cave above; a third ran straight toward Christian, apparently bolting for the horses. Christian's slug caught the brave squarely in the chest and sent him tumbling into the dust. Then something slammed into Christian's shoulder, knocking him backward, and the sunlight winked out from the sky above.

Private Bernie Christian sensed rather than saw the light above. He fought his way back into consciousness and found himself looking at a trio of faces smiling down.

"Welcome home, Private Christian," Kit Carson said.

Christian made a move as though to salute, then gasped at the sudden agony that flared in his arm.

"Easy, Bernie—don't move," Ted Henderson said. "The surgeon patched up your shoulder. Nothing too serious, he said, but you can expect to be hurting some for a spell."

"Corporal Bennett told us what happened out there, Christian," Carson said. "You saved the lives of eleven men. And picked up a few scalps of your own in the process. As soon as you're well enough, I think we should stage a little parade-ground salute for an unlikely hero."

Christian shuddered as the memories flooded back. "Didn't want—to kill anybody, sir."

"None of us do, Christian," Colonel Carson said. "The difference is in knowing when it is necessary and when it is not."

"My shoulder?"

"You collected a souvenir, Bernie," Ted Henderson said.

"An Apache arrow. Yellow Crow identified the markings. It came from the bow of none other than Tanaya himself."

"Is there anything you need, Christian? Anything at all?" Carson's question was quiet, sincere.

"Maybe a cup of coffee, sir. And someone to tell me how I'm going to live for the rest of my life in the body of a killer."

Bernie felt Carson's hand on his good shoulder. "You'll learn to cope with the idea, Bernie. It's a soldier's lot. And his cross to bear once the shooting stops."

Bernie felt an arm slide behind his back and help him to a sitting position. He accepted the fresh, hot coffee with thanks. He sipped, then noticed that Ted had slipped out of the room.

"Where has Major Henderson gone?"

"He's going to try to catch up with Yellow Crow's patrol. They're chasing what's left of Tanaya's bunch," Kit Carson said with a half-smile. "I have an idea that we will be seeing an end to the Mescalero campaign when that renegade Tanaya is brought in. And if Ted Henderson and Yellow Crow together can't do it, Bernie, it can't be done."

Ted caught up with Yellow Crow's patrol after a long hard ride that carried him almost to Laguna. He raised a hand in greeting as he rode into the patrol's camp, then felt a shock go through him as Yellow Crow returned the salute.

The grim-faced Cheyenne was in full war paint, stripped to breechcloth and moccasins.

"You take command, brother?"

Ted shook his head. "It's your mission, Yellow Crow. I'm just along to help if need be." Ted had learned over the years that there were times to stay out of Yellow Crow's way; this was one of them.

The Cheyenne gathered the members of the patrol around him and drew a rough map in the dirt.

"Tanaya lose time catching horses, not fear pursuit so soon. His camp at Laguna. We rest horses, strike at first sun. No hurt women and children. Kill braves. Save Tanaya for Yellow Crow."

The men of the patrol, all seasoned veterans, nodded, exchanging glances.

The war whoop of the Cheyenne shattered the dawn, sending the column of horsemen in blue racing through the sleepy camp of the Mescalero subchief Tanaya. The veterans needed but one pass to break the back of any potential resistance, leaving bodies of braves strewn about the smoldering campfires and overturned tipis.

Squaws and crying children huddled among the old men who stood, beaten but defiant, as Ted completed his report entries: "Forty-three women, children, and elderly Indian men captured. Eighteen fighting braves dead, six wounded. Yellow Crow in personal pursuit of Tanaya. Both men on foot." He tucked the small tablet back into a shirt pocket along with the stub of a pencil, then turned to the bearded scout at his stirrup.

"Take over here, will you, Alex? I want to see what happens when Tanaya and Yellow Crow finally meet." He swung down from his horse, slipped the carbine from its scabbard, and set off in the direction the two Indians had gone.

Yellow Crow had made no attempt to cover the signs of his passing, and Ted was able to follow the tracks at a fast trot. The sound of voices from a tangle of wild plum thicket ahead brought him to a stop for a moment. Then, moving silently with care, he crept to the edge of a small clearing.

Yellow Crow's face was turned away from Ted, the Cheyenne facing the stocky, powerful Tanaya across the twenty-foot-wide clearing.

Yellow Crow spoke in the Apache tongue. "So, at last Yellow Crow meets the killer of squaws and old men. Does the great Apache chief Tanaya fight as well against a man, or does he slay only squaws and children?" Yellow Crow was on the balls of his feet, poised, war ax in one hand, knife in the other.

Tanaya spat in contempt. "The Cheyenne makes much talk. Words are as the yapping of dogs in the night." The Apache suddenly charged, tomahawk raised high. Yellow Crow seemed to be calmly awaiting his doom, and Ted was tempted to cry out; yet at the last moment the Cheyenne sidestepped the Apache's charge, went down on his side, and scissored the heavier man's legs with his own. Tanaya fell heavily but rolled to the side as Yellow Crow's war ax split the sand where the Apache's head had been.

Despite his concern for Yellow Crow, Ted found himself admiring the movements of the two men. Tanaya feinted a knife thrust, then swung his tomahawk. Yellow Crow parried the blow and slashed upward with his own knife, just missing as the Apache leaped back, surprising Ted with the agility in the strong, blocky body.

The adversaries circled in silence, each waiting for the

proper opening. Abruptly, Tanaya hurled his tomahawk. Yellow Crow turned sideways, the weapon missing his body by inches. Then, contemptuously, he tossed aside his own war ax. Crouched and with knife at the ready, he waited for the Apache to strike again.

Suddenly, Tanaya charged, sweeping the keen edge of his knife, and Ted felt his breath catch in his throat as Yellow Crow's pivot foot slipped. The Apache's knife traced a line across the Cheyenne's chest as Yellow Crow went down. Tanaya hurled himself on Yellow Crow, knife raised for the final strike. The descending blade jolted to a stop inches from Yellow Crow's neck as Tanaya's wrist was trapped in the powerful grip of the Cheyenne's left hand.

Slowly, incredibly, the knife was pushed upward, despite the bulging muscles across the arm and upper torso of the Apache. Ted saw Tanaya's eyes widen in surprise, and then in fear, at the strength in the Cheyenne body beneath him. The contest of power ended abruptly as Yellow Crow adeptly twisted his own knife hand free and slammed the blade home at an upward angle just below Tanaya's ribs.

Ted saw the Apache stiffen in shock and pain, and then Yellow Crow placed a moccasined foot against a hip and tossed the mortally wounded Tanaya aside. Tanaya attempted to rise but sank back into the sand. He pitched forward on his face, shuddered, and was still.

The Cheyenne's victory cry pierced the early morning quiet. Then Yellow Crow bent, slashed with the knife, and raised the bloody scalp high overhead.

"Now, my father! The blood right is avenged! Your spirit is free of the darkness! My mother! Join your husband in the Land Beyond! Be free of the Dark World! The butcher now walks the night in your place!"

Yellow Crow stood so for a long moment, eyes closed. Then he slowly wiped the blood from his blade on the back of the dead Apache. Ted watched as Yellow Crow tucked the gory scalp into his breechcloth, and only then did Ted step into the clearing.

"My brother is now at peace within himself?"

Yellow Crow looked up, and Ted saw the flinty hatred slowly drain from the dark eyes.

"Yellow Crow is at peace because his parents now walk in sunshine. The blood right has been taken."

Ted examined the cut across Yellow Crow's chest. It was shallow and clean and would knit well.

"Tanaya was a bad Indian," Yellow Crow said in Cheyenne. "He made life hard for good Indians. Let us go now."

Ted fell into step behind the lanky form of his blood brother, listening to the calls of the morning birds, the rustlings of small animals in the brush. It had been, he thought, a good morning's work. With the death of Tanaya, the war against the Mescalero Apache had come to an end, and the soldiers could devote all their attention now to subduing the most hostile of the Southwest Indians: the Navajo.

Wilma Henderson gritted her teeth and clamped her hands hard on the bedpost, as the slash of pain cut across her body. "Remember to breathe, little mother," a voice in her ear said. "It won't be much longer now."

Wilma welcomed the touch of a damp cloth held against her forehead by the square-faced woman sitting beside the bed. "You're doing just fine, Wilma. Dr. Mason is on his way."

"Anna—" Wilma's breath came in short, panting gasps. "I'm trying to—be brave and—strong. But it—hurts."

"Sure it does, Wilma. But you will find it is a pain soon forgotten when you hold your little one in your arms. And the next one will be easier."

Wilma felt the next contraction building, steeled herself against the pain she knew was to come, and heard the door swing open.

"About time you got here, Doc," she heard Anna scold. "Another three minutes and I would have had to usher this young'un in myself."

The pain subsided, but Wilma felt another wave building. "Now, Wilma," she heard the physician say, "it is time to stop fighting it. Give us a push."

William Ted Henderson quickly became the chief attraction at Fort Laramie. Well-wishers came to see the new mother and her son, and Vi Robinson was deeply touched that the child had been named after Bill and that she herself was godmother.

In addition to the baby's birth, there was another happy change at Fort Laramie. Abel Hubbard's patrols had been going out regularly, and they were able to report that there was slow but sure progress with the Indians of the area. Fewer and fewer braves were willing to engage in hostilities, and more and more Indians seemed content to live in peace. Indeed, the residents of Fort Laramie were sometimes permitted to leave the confines of the compound—with an escort of soldiers, of course—and there were even occasional picnics and outings to pick berries and gather nuts.

The only thing that did not improve was Judy Hubbard. She was still withdrawn and spoke to no one, not even her husband, and her uncommunicativeness was getting to the point that Abel was fearful he could stand it no longer.

Sitting at the battered desk that had been his father-in-law's, he threw down his pen in disgust, unable to concentrate. He pushed his chair back, massaged his saddle-wearied backside, and glanced across the compound. A light still burned in Vi Robinson's window.

Abel sighed. Before he knew it, he found himself crossing the compound, knocking on Vi's door.

"Please come in, Abel. I have some fresh hot tea." Abel stepped into the spotless room, inhaling the aroma of steeping tea.

"I know it's late, Vi," he said, kissing her lightly on the cheek. "If you would rather I come back another time—"

"Nonsense, Abel. My house is your house, no matter the time." She poured tea into a pair of fine china cups, and Abel noticed the hands were steady, even though Vi's face reflected the lines of strain and worry. For a moment he felt a pang of guilt at adding his own problems to her burden, but, he thought, a man must have someone to talk to. "Sit, Abel. You look tired."

"Thank you. I guess I am feeling the miles."

"Abel, I don't mean to pry, but I don't think it is the miles you spend on patrol that has brought you to this state of near-exhaustion."

Abel sipped at the tea and savored the crisp warm flavor. He looked deeply into Vi's eyes, found a gentleness and patience there, and hoped she had enough to lend to a troubled major.

Abel took a deep breath. "It's—difficult to express."

"So try."

"It's Judy." Abel noticed the flash of pain in Vi's expression. "It's just—well, I feel angry and helpless. She still doesn't respond to my voice, my touch. She just sits, rocking and staring straight ahead. She eats, but mechanically, even foods she normally hates. I've caught myself losing patience with her, Vi, and I feel guilty about that, too. I can't reach her, and it's tearing me apart."

"I know, Abel. I've seen it in your face, and I have felt the same emotions when I've tried to reach her. It's as though I have lost my daughter as well as my husband." She raised a hand. "Please don't interrupt; I need no more condolences. I have learned to accept Bill's death, and I prefer to do my crying alone." Vi sipped at her cup, and Abel found himself marveling at her composure. "Abel, I need to ask you a highly personal question. Don't answer if you don't want to. Have you and Judy made love since—the incident?"

Abel shook his head. "No. Each time I've touched her in any way suggesting intimacy, she goes rigid—stiff as a chunk of rawhide three years in the sun. She sleeps in a separate room, and she even dresses and undresses behind a bolted door."

Vi nodded. "I suspected as much," she said, reaching out to touch Abel's hand, "and I know it was difficult to tell me."

"Is there any way we can reach her? Anything we can do?" Abel heard the tone of desperation in his own voice.

"We must be patient and keep trying, Abel. When Wilma brought the new baby over to your house, I thought I saw a flicker of life in Judy's eyes. But if it was there, it was gone before I could be sure."

Abel sighed. "I must be honest with you, Vi. I don't know how much longer I can stand it. She's there—I can reach her and touch her—but she's not there." He felt a reassuring squeeze of his hand.

"I know how difficult it must be," Vi said. "And I won't ask you to stay with her. You are a strong, handsome young man, Abel. You need not bear such a burden—"

"That's just the problem, Vi. Judy is the only woman I want, have ever really wanted. I'll not leave her. There must be some way, somehow, that her shell can be broken." Abel felt the sting at the corner of his eyes. "I want her back, Vi. And it must be soon." His voice trailed off.

"Or what, Abel?"

"I live with this constant fear that the anger building up inside me is going to explode. And some innocent people, the Indians or the soldiers under my command, will pay the price for my own weakness. I may crack under pressure; it isn't uncommon among officers in combat. And if I give the wrong order, lose control of my senses at the wrong time, blood will be spilled, and all that we've worked for among the Indians, all we have accomplished, will drown in blood."

Vi rose, walked to Abel, and touched her lips to his stubbled cheek. "I think you underestimate yourself, Abel Hubbard. You have established a reputation as a conscientious, highly capable leader. Among the Indians it is said that when Major Abel Hubbard speaks, his words are true and the Indian will do well to listen." She hugged the young officer. "Now, I suggest that you go and try to get some sleep. I know you are not a particularly religious man, Abel, but this is one time we must trust in something. We must keep the faith that the Creator will bring Judy back to us."

Vi watched her son-in-law walk listlessly across the moon-drenched compound, shoulders slumped in weariness. And it was not a weariness of the body, she thought, but the spirit. She choked back the lump in her throat. To lose Bill was almost too much to bear. To be with his unresponsive daughter, the young woman she so wished to hold and love, only to gaze into eyes that held no flicker of emotion, cut Vi's heart deeper each day. But to lose Abel as well . . .

Vi looked up toward the ceiling. "Lord, I don't ask this for myself entirely. If you see fit to help those young people . . ." Her voice trailed off, the remainder of the prayer spoken only in her mind.

She gathered the dishes and began her preparations for bed and another fitful night of sleep. She felt uncomfortably warm and closed in, and she went to the open window to try and capture whatever cool breezes might be lingering on the summer night air.

Across the way, she saw a candle flare in Wilma Henderson's window. It must be time for young William's midnight feeding, she thought. She felt the corners of her mouth lift in a slight smile at the thought of her robust young godson.

At least Major Ted Henderson would have a family to ride home to, sitting proud in the saddle, when the Indian wars in the Southwest had ended.

Lieutenant Kevin O'Reilly had been sent into Navajo country as part of Major Emery Church's advance unit. This assignment delighted the big Irishman since it meant he would most likely see the beautiful Navajo girl again. But so far there had been only the endless patrols into the countryside, chasing down bands of Navajo, parleying with them to get them to move to the reservation. There had been no sign of the girl . . . until perhaps today.

Kevin yanked his horse to an abrupt stop. The distant crackle of army carbines was shattering his concentration on the tracks of the Navajo band he and his six-man patrol had been following. The sound of the rifle fire alarmed O'Reilly, for among the footprints beneath his mount's feet were the small, dainty impressions left by the passage of a young woman—and the tracks led in the direction of the rifle fire!

He turned to Private Mike Connor, the broad-shouldered Irishman riding alongside. It was Mike who, at the last meeting with the Navajo chiefs some time ago, had prevented O'Reilly from striking out at the ugly Navajo brave that had accosted the lovely Indian girl. Kevin now noted that Mike's face wore a frown as he cocked an ear to the slight northerly breeze.

"How far away is the shooting, Mike?" O'Reilly heard the tension in his own voice.

Connor glanced at his friend. "Mile and a half, maybe two miles. Sound carries far on a day like this. Now, Kevin, we don't know what it means. Could be a hunting party. And even if 'twas a skirmish, we don't know your Navajo maiden is in it. Try to relax and have some faith. Believe in the luck o' the Irish. After all, there be many Navajo women." His voice trailed off as O'Reilly touched spurs to his horse and moved at a swift lope toward the sound of the gunfire. Mike kneed his own horse into motion, waving the other troopers forward. "By the saints, let it not be his Navajo," Mike muttered to himself. "If Kevin is to find her, let it not be this way."

They covered the distance in a very few minutes. Kevin already was off his mount and moving among the huddled bodies in the shallow ravine when Mike and the other troopers caught up. The scene before them shocked the veteran soldiers. Eleven Navajo bodies, including four women and two young children, were sprawled about the ravine. Two of the adult men wore the robes of tribal chiefs.

Kevin looked up, face pale. "She's not here, Mike. But, my God, why? We were supposed to parley with the Indians, not wipe them out. Yet here are eleven Navajo slaughtered like so many sheep—and not one of them is armed." O'Reilly sank to his knees, gently lifted the dead body of a young girl, perhaps eight years old, and cradled the bloody head against his jacket.

Mike Connor stepped from his horse, moved from first one body to another, then straightened. "I know the two chiefs," he said, aware of the tightness in his own voice. "Cuello and Castellito. They sought peace. They were going to come to the reservation willingly. And this is what they ran into. . . ."

Kevin O'Reilly carefully placed the dead girl on the sand, then covered her with a blanket that had been wrapped around the frail shoulders. He felt the tightening in his chest as the sickness gave way to a growing fury.

"I'll know who did this, Mike. And when I do . . ."

Connor saw the powerful hands of his Irish friend clench and unclench. He knew that when the explosion came, someone would pay. "All the work we've done," O'Reilly said through lips drawn thin, "all the effort to convince the Indians to come in peacefully. Gone in a volley of rifle fire in an ambush. The rest will never come in now, Mike."

"'Tis the truth you speak, my friend," Connor said. He turned to a pair of white-faced young troopers. "Bury them as best you can," he said. "I'm going to ride a small circle to see what I can find."

Connor returned in less than a quarter of an hour. He slid from his mount in front of the lieutenant, who was wielding a trenching tool alongside the troopers.

"Kevin," Connor said, "I'm no threat to Kit Carson at reading sign. But this was an army patrol that did in the Navajo. And it don't take no expert scout to put a name on a horse that moves with a left hind foot turned out so sharp."

Connor sighed to ease his own growing fury. "I didn't see it happen, Kevin, any more than you did—but that hind foot belongs to a Tennessee walker that's rode by just one man. It appears our Major Emery Church was the man who set this ambush up."

Kevin straightened. "Then, by God," he said, the edge of his voice as keen as that of his trenching tool, "the major will pay!"

Mike sighed. "Hold up a minute, you hot-tempered Irishman," he said. "Do you think Church's report will be the truth of what happened? Will Carleton take your word and mine—a junior officer and a single trooper—against that of a major? No, my friend. Trouble you don't need,—neither you nor your young Navajo woman."

Connor fetched his own trenching tool from his pack and

turned to digging hard and deep as he talked, welcoming the exertion. It would help to burn away his own disgust. He tossed a spadeful in a growing pile at the mouth of the small grave. "No, Kevin, let us not speak of this to the major, as we have no proof. The damage has been done."

Kevin straightened after placing a tiny bundle in the bottom of a grave.

"There's fact in your words, Mike. But, by God, someone will know of this besides us. Colonel Carson is on his way to take over the Navajo campaign, I hear. And Kit Carson will need no proof!"

VIII

With the subduing of the Apache in the eastern portion of the territory, the campaign against the Navajo began in force. Assuming full command over Major Church's smaller advance units, Kit Carson moved to Fort Wingate, located just on the fringes of Navajo country in Arizona. General Carleton, meanwhile, remained in Santa Fe, overseeing the relocation of the surrendered Apache to the Bosque Redondo and eagerly waiting for Colonel Carson's reports about the patrols that were being sent out to subdue the Navajo and bring them to the reservation with as little bloodshed as possible.

A hot summer turned to fall, and for his part, Ted Henderson still awoke each morning feeling the distance of the miles between himself and Wilma, the awful loneliness, the homesickness. He had learned about the birth of his son, and that only made his distress worse. He had nightmares now, nightmares that had long been stilled. He dreamed of how his first wife and daughter had been brutally murdered while he was away on a hunting trip, and he woke up each night in a sweat, petrified that the same thing might happen to Wilma and little William Ted.

Many times he considered handing in his resignation to Kit Carson so that he could go home. But each time he realized that he could not leave, that there was an important job to be done. Moreover, Wilma, understanding what her husband must be feeling, had written a line in her last letter that Ted remembered whenever he was in doubt about what he should do. She had written, *Remember, dearest, Indians have babies, too*.

* * *

"So that, gentlemen, is our plan," Kit Carson concluded, his eyes moving around the table, lingering for a moment on the face of each officer gathered at the Fort Wingate command post. "On the surface it may seem harsh. But in the long run it will save lives on both sides and bring a relatively quick end to the Navajo problem. Our purpose here is not to kill Indians, but to subdue them. Thus, by destroying their homes, burning their crops and orchards, gathering their sheep from them, and providing them food, medical aid, and clothing, we can get them to surrender."

"Suppose we meet resistance, sir?" one of the officers asked.

"Then return fire, and make sure your aim is true. The Navajo must see we mean business. If they kill, we reply in kind; if they raid, we raid. But if they surrender peacefully, they will be treated with honor."

"And when do we begin, Colonel?"

"It already has begun," Carson said. "Our Ute scouts have been dispatched to ask all major leaders of the Navajo nation to a parley. The first group should arrive by sundown. At noon tomorrow, the talks begin. If there are no more questions, you may go and carry these instructions to your men." Carson turned to the officer at his side. "Major Henderson, would you remain for a moment?"

Carson waited patiently until the last of the officers had left the building, then lifted eyebrows in Ted's direction. "Ted, I want you as my second-in-command for this campaign. As such, you will wear the rank of lieutenant colonel." Carson's voice trailed off as Ted quietly chuckled.

"You find the offer amusing?"

"No, Colonel Carson. Not at all. I was just thinking how far I've come since the Pony Express days."

"Then you accept?"

"Certainly, Colonel Carson. And I'm honored."

The former mountain man reached into a small box on the table and pinned Ted's new insignia of rank on his tunic. "Sorry it couldn't have been more formal, Colonel Henderson, but both of us are going to be awfully busy in the near future." Carson stepped back, snapped a salute, and Ted returned the courtesy. "Now," Carson said, "to avoid the confusion of an anthill full of colonels, let's keep it on a first-name basis—except, of course, in formal military settings and correspondence. But in the field, I'm Kit and you're Ted. Now, let's go get ready to meet some pretty powerful people around this neck of the woods tomorrow."

The two officers stepped from the command post into the afternoon sun, unaware of the scrutiny of a thin-faced major and a blocky lieutenant some twenty feet away. The major glared at the retreating figures for some moments, then spat into the dust.

"That's my rank he's wearin'."

Lieutenant Johnston shuffled his feet. "Sure is, Major Church. You shoulda been next in line for promotion, 'stead of some newcomer."

"What rankles my feathers more than anything else," Major Emery Church said, "is that neither one of 'em knows what fightin' Injuns is all about. All that highfalutin talk about feedin' and honorin' a bunch of savages won't hold water out here. Ain't but one good Navajo and that's a dead one!"

Kit Carson drew himself to his full height, glancing without fear at the bronze faces of the Indians who had assembled on the parade ground of Fort Wingate. Ted could tell from the slight frontiersman's stance that he was about to deliver the conclusion of his speech to the fourteen assembled Navajo leaders. Ted could only hope it would be a convincing one.

"For many years," Carson said, "the Great White Father has tried to live in peace with the Navajo. The Navajo promise peace, but their words are hollow. Instead of peace, they raid and kill and rob. Now the Great White Father has reached the limit of his patience. Now the Navajo must pay for his treachery." Carson's voice dropped slightly. "The Great White Father knows there are men among you who wish peace. When you leave here, you will have two choices. You can bring your people in, your families, your livestock, and go to the Bosque Redondo. Or you can return to the ways of war and be hunted like the wolf stalks the rabbit. Choose peace, and the Navajo shall live and once more be a proud and respected people. Choose war, and the Navajo will die."

Carson abruptly sat down. The decision, Ted knew, was now in the hands of the most powerful leaders of the Navajo nation. He glanced around the circle of Indians and noted the grim lines on some faces, placid expressions on others. Neither he nor Carson had hoped to convince all the chiefs to lay down their weapons. As it was said on the frontier, two Indians could not even agree on the price of a pony—let alone the price of peace.

At the center of the group, a thin, middle-aged Navajo stood.

"I, Toshoneshe, know of the fate of the Mescalero Apache." The voice, Ted thought, was surprisingly deep for such a small body. "Toshoneshe also know Kit Carson keep word, not massacre Indians. The people of Toshoneshe will come in peace."

The Navajo turned to the other Indian leaders, speaking in his own tongue. Both Carson and Ted Henderson, each with some mastery of the language, listened intently to the words.

"The man named Carson speaks the truth," Toshoneshe said. "The Navajo will suffer much if war rides the wind. Now it has come to this. Toshoneshe chooses peace for his people, and will carry the word to others. Toshoneshe goes now. Perhaps one day he and his people shall return to their lands."

At the edge of the semicircle, a powerfully built Indian leaped to his feet, dark eyes flashing.

"Toshoneshe speaks as a squaw." Ted winced at the venom in the tone. "And others sit and nod, as though he speaks for all the Navajo. Gallegos will fight for his freedom, for the lands which gave birth to the Navajo, the great sacred canyons, the mountains where the spirits live! Are the Navajo to walk like sheep from the resting place of the very bones of his ancestors? Have not the spirits been good to the Navajo? Do the plains, the hills, and the valleys not fill his belly, give him shelter in the winter, shade him in the summer? Have his tribes not prospered?"

Ted felt his concern grow as heads began to nod in agreement around the circle of Indians.

"And as for this talk of peace without reprisal—Gallegos asks his brothers: Would they have the kind of peace that now cradles Cuello and Castellito? They went to the white man in peace. And in their faith they were butchered as so many cattle"—Ted and Kit Carson exchanged alarmed glances—"and this talk of no war against women and children? Ask the wives and sons of Cuello and Castellito when they are greeted in the land beyond the darkness! See if they do not laugh at the Navajo's blind stupidity!"

The chief turned toward Carson and reverted to the white man's tongue. "Here is my answer to your Great White Father." Deliberately, Gallegos spat in Carson's direction. The mountain man remained expressionless as the glob of spittle struck his boot. "You will see Gallegos again, man named Carson—over the bend in his bow!"

The muscular chief turned abruptly and strode from the meeting place.

Ted heard Carson's sigh as, one by one, other chiefs rose to follow. Soon only the military men and just six of the Navajo leaders remained.

"Those of you who choose peace," Carson said, "are wise. You will be treated well. Go now and spread the word among your people. The Great White Father does not hate his red children, as you do not hate the small ones who nuzzle your women's breasts. He would not see the Navajo vanish as a race, as a people with a rich heritage and pride. Those who come in peace shall know this; those who do not shall feel such pain as the Navajo have never felt before."

As a group, the remaining Indians nodded, then rose, trickling away toward the clusters of family members brought to the talks.

Kit Carson watched them go, a heaviness growing in his heart. He felt a tug at his sleeve and turned to face the twisted visage before him.

"What is it, Major Church?"

"Colonel, you give me a couple of companies of cavalry and I'll take care of that Gallegos right here and now. Wipe out the ones who don't surrender and you've won the war!"

Carson yanked his sleeve free of the grip. "Major," he said, his tone icy, "the Navajo came to this meeting under a promise of truce. They did not break that promise. And neither will you! Am I understood?"

Unable to cope with the stern glare in the colonel's eyes, Church finally nodded. "But you're makin' a mistake, Colonel. I could drop that troublemaker from here with one shot!"

Ted Henderson was unaware that he had moved, but suddenly he found himself staring into the narrow face. "If you so much as touch a rifle, a pistol, or your nose, Church, if you even blink before those Indians have gone, I will personally teach you a lesson in behavior. One you will not soon forget. Take yourself back to your quarters, on the double, and don't even look back! Dismissed!"

Church glared at Henderson for a moment, then spun on a heel and stomped away. Ted watched the major vanish from sight. Finally, he turned to Carson.

"Kit," Ted said, "Church could be trouble. He shows all the signs of being an Indian-hater. I think we would do well to keep a rather close watch on our Major Church."

"Agreed, Ted. And in the meantime, let's see what we can learn about the deaths of chiefs Cuello and Castellito. I have a feeling we aren't going to like what we find."

After an afternoon spent filing the reports from returning patrols and discussing possible solutions to the show of defiance on the part of Gallegos and some of the other Navajo chiefs, Ted and Kit had their dinner. Then they returned to Carson's office, where Ted made a startling discovery. Located in the back of a drawer in the desk Emery Church had used before Kit Carson assumed command of the fort was a crumpled pile of papers. Among the muster rolls and the payroll sheets were copies of the reports Major Church had sent to General Carleton shortly after he arrived. As he read, Ted's jaw muscles began to twitch, and his teeth clenched in growing anger. He glanced up at Kit Carson, whose eyebrows arched.

"Ted, you look like a man who's just found a salamander in the bottom of his last canteen. If you're going to sit there and get mad, tell me what it's about. Then we'll get mad together."

Ted took a deep breath, hoping the level of fury would ease. He tried to keep his voice as calm as possible as he spoke. "Listen to some of these reports, Kit. These are just excerpts—paragraphs here and there—from copies of the drivel Church has been sending to General Carleton. Here's an example:

> "'Sir: I have the honor to report that on this date, fifteen hostiles were killed by one of my patrols. Send me a thousand troops, General, and I will sweep this area clean of all Navajo within three months.'

"And another:

> "'Sir: In response to your order, I must report that while we attempted to detain some fifty hostiles who had come to the fort in the guise of surrender, the Indians crept into our herd at night with the intention of stealing mounts. My soldiers, displaying great gallantry, thwarted the attempt and all but a dozen Navajo were slain.'"

Ted glanced up and saw the deepening frown lines in Carson's face, concern slowly giving way to anger. Ted tossed a couple of papers aside and picked up another. He paced the rough-planked floor as he read:

> "'Sir: I have the honor to report that on the afternoon of this day, two of the most powerful chiefs of the Navajo nation came to their just end. Tipped off by my scouts that Indians lurked in ambush, I led a flanking maneuver that resulted in the bodies of the chiefs Cuello and Castellito as food for the coyotes; we suffered not a single casualty.'"

Ted flung the report down in disgust. It fluttered to the floor near Carson's feet. The commanding officer made no move to retrieve it, and Ted saw fury flash in the piercing eyes.

"Damn it, Ted, that has to be the most incredible collection of stupidity I have ever heard! Not only does the man have no grasp of the reality of dealing with Indians, he rates the Navajo as something less than animals, and he can't tell a war chief from a peace chief! I'll court-martial that fox-faced little—"

A knock on the office door cut short the epithet.

"Come in," Carson snapped.

The door swung open. Ted noticed that the lieutenant almost had to duck to clear the upper frame of the doorway. The broad-shouldered young officer saluted, his fingers trembling slightly against the campaign cap.

"Lieutenant Kevin O'Reilly, sir, respectfully requesting an audience with the commanding officer."

Carson casually returned the salute. "Come on in, Lieutenant. Sit down. What's on your mind?"

O'Reilly swallowed, his nervousness now obvious to Ted.

"Sir, I could be—brought to court-martial for this, but— well, sir, my conscience just couldn't take it any longer." O'Reilly cleared his throat. "Major Church," he said, "is guilty of serious crimes against the Navajo."

Ted saw Carson's eyes narrow even more, and he felt sympathy for the lieutenant. The young officer did not know that Carson was angry when he had walked in, and from the worried expression and the twisting of his campaign hat, it was clear that O'Reilly mistakenly believed Carson was angry with him.

"There was the matter of an ambush, sir. Two chiefs—"

"Wait a minute, Lieutenant O'Reilly." Carson bent to retrieve the paper at his feet and handed it to Ted. "Colonel Henderson, will you please read the official report for the lieutenant's benefit?"

Ted did not need to look at the paper; the words were etched into his mind. He quoted the report, watching as the husky lieutenant's eyes widened in disbelief.

"But—but sir, that's not how it happened," O'Reilly stammered.

"Then why don't you tell us what did happen," Ted said.

O'Reilly shuffled his feet. "There was an ambush, all right, sir. But it wasn't the Navajo chiefs. Cuello and Castellito were not even armed! It had to be Major Church's patrol that staged the ambush, not the Indians!"

Carson sighed, sank heavily into a chair. "Will you swear to that under oath?"

O'Reilly scratched an ear nervously. "Yes, sir. And so will Private Connor. But it would just be the word of me and Mike against that of an officer commissioned in the United States Army. But if you ask, sir, of course, I will testify. And I will have the satisfaction of knowing I've told the truth, even if no one else does. But, Colonel Carson—"

"Yes, Lieutenant?"

"There may be even more mischief afoot, sir. Just before sunset, sir, Major Church and about thirty of his men rode out on patrol. I—I'm afraid they have something more in mind than just checking out the country."

Ted saw alarm flash into Carson's eyes. "Which way were they headed, Lieutenant?"

"North, sir."

Carson turned to Ted. "Any chance of catching up with them, Colonel Henderson?"

Ted shook his head. "There's no moon tonight; we would be searching on blind luck. And they have fresh mounts and a head start."

"Then," Carson said with a sigh heavy with dread, "I suppose we will just have to wait until sunup." He turned to the young officer and held out a hand. "Lieutenant O'Reilly, you did the right thing in coming to us with your story. It took courage for a junior officer to complain about the field conduct of his superior officer. I thank you. And when Major Church returns, your name will not be mentioned in our—uh—discussion."

O'Reilly released the smaller man's hand and saluted. "Thank you, sir." The lieutenant turned toward the door, then hesitated. "Colonel Carson," he said in a tentative voice, "I am assigned to Major Church's command. Sir, I can't tolerate his cruelty any longer. Several of the men in my platoon feel the same way. I would like to request a transfer, Colonel, along with the other men. We're horse soldiers, but we are also trained to fight on foot if you have no place for cavalry. And I'll take a reduction in rank, sir—back to private, if need be."

Carson turned to Ted. "What do you think, Colonel Henderson?"

Ted did not hesitate. "I would welcome Lieutenant O'Reilly and such of his men as wish to join my command. But we are short of horses. O'Reilly, would you honestly be willing to walk through this campaign? At your current rank?"

"Yes, sir." O'Reilly's nod was eager. "Anything to get away from Major Church, sir."

Ted raised an eyebrow. "Do you fear for your safety under his command, Lieutenant?"

O'Reilly's answer was deadly calm. "No, sir. I fear for Major Church's. I have an Irish temper and an army pistol."

Carson's sigh was audible. "I'm almost tempted to deny the request and supply you the ammunition," he said. "But I don't want to waste a good lieutenant. O'Reilly, as of this moment, you have your transfer."

"Thank you, Colonel Carson, Colonel Henderson."

The powerful figure stepped through the door into the deep night.

Carson clapped a hand on Ted's shoulder. "It looks," he said with a hint of a smile, "as if we've found a kindred spirit."

"I agree, Kit. And if I drank, I'd pour myself a glass of whiskey right now. I can't shake the feeling it is going to be a long night."

The bedlam of yells, whoops, and fast-moving hoofbeats jarred Ted from a fitful doze in the soft gray light of early dawn. He hastily pulled on his boots and, strapping his pistol belt about his waist, stepped from the small room that served as his quarters near Carson's command post. Ted felt the muscles in his jaw tighten, the hair on his forearms stiffen, as he watched the mass of riders whipping their mounts across the parade ground. He glanced at Carson's quarters. A light burned in the window, and Ted was sure the colonel had been awake the entire night.

With long, angry strides, Ted crossed the few feet to Carson's combination office and living quarters, fighting the growing tension in his stomach. He stepped onto the small porch as Kit Carson, his blond hair askew, opened the door. The two officers stood rigid and silent as Major Emery Church brutally yanked his lathered horse to a halt before them. Ted's heart skidded as he saw the blanket-wrapped bundle clutched in Church's right hand.

Church tossed the reins of his exhausted mount to a nearby trooper, then delivered a sardonic salute in the direction of the two officers. Neither Carson nor Ted returned the gesture.

"Come into my office, Major Church." Ted heard the flinty edge on Carson's voice. Waiting until Carson had stepped into the room, followed by the major, dusty and grinning, Ted entered and carefully closed the door. The heavy wood muffled the babble of excited voices from the parade ground outside.

"Explain yourself, Major. I ordered no night patrols." Carson's controlled voice did not match the expression in the narrow eyes illuminated by a single oil lamp on the commanding officer's desk.

Ted noted the ill-concealed glitter of contempt in the major's eyes. Knowing a clash was more than possible between the two, Ted casually stepped off to one side, placing himself a pace away from a point between the two men.

"Somebody had to do something besides talk," Church snorted. "So I did it."

With a flourish, the major flung open the blanket, spilling the bundled, grisly contents on the floor at Carson's feet. Ted heard his own sharp intake of breath. A gory pile of Indian scalps lay at his feet.

Church casually flipped a small scalp over with the toe of his boot. "That," he said, "is the only way to tame Indians."

Ted moved by instinct, catching Kit Carson's arm in a powerful grip as the colonel drew back to swing at the major. "Kit! Don't do it! Striking a junior officer will cost you the command, and we need you now more than ever! This animal isn't worth it!"

"Well, well," Church's sarcasm rang in Ted's ears, "the famous Kit Carson has a bodyguard now."

The slender thread of control that held Ted's own temper snapped. He whirled to face the major and advanced a step. Church instinctively retreated. Ted glared into the smaller man's eyes, pinning him to the spot like a bug nailed to the floor.

"Major Church," Ted said, surprised at the even, conversational tone in his voice that belied the fury now churning in his belly, "but for the fact that we are both in uniform, I would give you the damnedest beating you have ever seen in your miserable life." He noticed Church's hand ease toward the holstered pistol at his hip.

"Go head, Church! Try it if you've got the guts! You'll find out you aren't going against weak old men and kids. Go ahead, please. Pull a weapon on a superior officer, and I'll kill you on the spot!"

Ted advanced a step, then another, until the retreating major's back came into contact with the wall. Ted found a small measure of satisfaction in the sudden flash of fear in the major's eyes as Church suddenly realized the infuriated officer before him meant every word. Ted pushed his face close to Church's.

"Major, your stupidity is equaled only by your gutless taste for Indian blood. This butchery has turned what could have been a negotiated peace into a long and bloody campaign that will cost many lives! There was a chance the Navajo would have listened to reason—but now they won't accept a string of beads from us, let alone an offer of peace and friendship!" Ted reached out and plucked Church's pistol from its holster. "You wanted blood, Major," he said, cocking the weapon, "well, by God, you have it. And it might very well be your own."

Church's eyes, now bright with fear, followed the path of the pistol muzzle as Ted raised it slowly from waist level, pointing it at Church's forehead. Then, deliberately, Ted lowered the weapon.

"Major Church, you are confined to quarters until your superior officers decide on your punishment," Kit Carson commanded. "As for myself, I would prefer to hang you in the center of the parade ground to show the Navajo how white man's justice really works!"

Kit stalked to the door. He flung it open with such force it almost left the hinges. "Get Sergeant Major Armbrister over here, on the double!" he yelled to a nearby trooper.

He stepped back into the room, noticing that some color was beginning to return to Major Emery Church's face. "If you so much as poke your nose from your quarters, Church, I will personally bite it off. Do I make myself clear?"

Church turned to Ted. "You haven't heard the last of this, Henderson," he said, hate dancing in his eyes. "I'll get you for this."

"Any time, any place, Major—but out of uniform. I'll not disgrace the United States Army by smashing a snake in blue!"

Frank Armbrister, stepping through the door, took in the situation at a glance.

"Frank, I want you to escort Major Church back to his quarters. Arrange for a guard at his door at all times. If he wants to go out for anything other than the latrine, I am to be informed at once," Carson said.

"Yes, Colonel. I'll take care of it."

"And Frank," Ted added, "should Major Church make any attempt to escape or ignore your instructions, I would not be at all surprised to receive your report that he had met with a severe accident."

"Yes, sir. A man can get hurt real bad around here if he isn't careful," Armbrister said, one eye closing in a slow wink. "Now, Major, will you come along with me?" Armbrister took the major's arm. At the door, Church turned and glared at Ted for a moment, eyes flashing hatred.

"I'll kill you for this, Henderson—mark my word."

"Sergeant, did you just hear this officer threaten the life of a superior?"

"Yes, sir. Spoke right up and said it, he did."

"Don't forget that, Sergeant. You might have to repeat it under oath one day."

Armbrister nodded, then escorted Church through the door and into the light of a new day. Ted turned to Kit Carson, noting the hot fire still burning in the colonel's eyes. "So what do we do with this loathsome Indian scalper, Kit?" he asked.

"I know what I'd like to do—hand him over to the Navajo as a gesture of goodwill," Carson said, "but we might as well face facts. No court-martial panel is going to take action against him. In their view, what Church did would be an action against the enemy in time of war." Carson sat heavily in the rawhide chair behind his desk. "But if you will write out the report stating exactly what happened and its probable impact on the campaign against the Navajo, General Carleton should find it interesting reading. And if it's fighting Church wants, fighting he will get. I'll recommend his transfer to the East. I hope the general will go along. It would be interesting to see how the courageous Major Emery Church reacts when the enemy shoots back."

A tentative knock on the door brought Carson's voice to a halt. Ted called, "Come in," and Kevin O'Reilly, face lined in worry, stepped into the room.

"Begging your pardon, Colonel Carson—I heard what happened. I—I must examine the scalps that were brought in. I understand there were women and children killed by Church and his men."

"Certainly, Lieutenant," Carson said, "and from the tone of your voice and the expression on your face, I hope you do not find what you search for. After that, would you please see that the remains are given a decent burial?"

Gingerly, O'Reilly picked his way through the scalps, hoping he would not be sick in front of his two commanding officers. At length he looked up.

Ted could see the relief in the young officer's eyes despite the pale face.

"It—it isn't here, sir," O'Reilly said. Carefully and with a reverent touch, the big Irishman began placing the scalps back onto the blood-stained blanket in which they had arrived.

"For your sake, Lieutenant, I'm glad to hear that," Carson said. He turned to Ted.

"Colonel Henderson, we have a most unpleasant but necessary duty before us. I need you to assemble some messengers, people the Navajo may listen to. I must send my personal apologies to the various Navajo chiefs for this atrocity and all others committed by Church—and my personal promise it will never happen again." Carson sighed. "I don't think they will listen," he said, "but I must try. I will go in person to the chief of the band massacred in this most recent incident. You take charge here. Your patrols can work in the vicinity of the fort."

Ted nodded. "Myself, Yellow Crow, Frank Armbrister, and Albert Jonas will carry your message. I will find others as well."

"Sir?"

Ted looked up as Kevin O'Reilly stood, the blood-stained bundle held respectfully in his arms. "Yes, Lieutenant?"

"I would like to volunteer to deliver one of the messages."

"Do you speak Navajo?"

"Pretty well, sir. I've been spending a lot of time learning."

Carson nodded. "Very well, Lieutenant. Take no more than a couple of troopers with you—and you realize, of course, that the Navajo may kill you on sight?"

"I'll take the chance, Colonel Carson. And thank you." O'Reilly turned to go.

"Lieutenant," Carson said, his voice soft, "if you tell me which Navajo you search for, perhaps our other men might be of help."

The lieutenant paused at the door. "I don't even know her name, sir," he said, "but I have reason to believe she is with Gallegos's band, possibly a relative. She's—the most beautiful woman I've ever seen."

"Then go with God, Lieutenant. And I hope you find her."

Wind Flower gently brushed a stray strand of black hair back into place behind an ear. She breathed deeply the crisp, cedar-scented air of the secluded branch of the Canyon de Chelly, and felt the spirits that guarded the sacred place flow about her, bringing comfort.

Pride swelled in her breast as she listened to her father near the conclusion of his speech. Few bands of the Navajo, she thought, were so fortunate as to have as strong and just a leader as her father, Gallegos. His rich voice carried easily to where she sat, a respectful distance from the circle of braves around her father. Wind Flower never ceased to be impressed with Gallegos's ability as an orator. It was said among the Navajo that none spoke more eloquently than Gallegos, that none fought so well, and that no other seemed able to conjure up small miracles. Only he, it was said, could locate a herd of antelope when meat supplies were low, could predict a shower when the sun threatened the crops and orchards dotted about the canyon.

"You have heard the words of the white soldier," Gallegos concluded, "and they are the same words the Navajo have heard before, words that meant no more than the passage of wind through the trees. Now the Navajo must prepare for war! The spirits shall guide his arrows, and from the sacred grounds of this canyon he shall ride against the soldiers, strike hard and fast, and drive the blue-coated ones from the land of the Navajo!"

Wind Flower heard the mutters of assent from the braves, then suddenly felt a discomfort deep within and knew she was being watched. Fifty feet away, the squat, ugly figure of Choshay stood, his eyes glaring at her. Wind Flower felt a chill settle about her shoulders.

Choshay had become obsessed, she thought, since her father had banned him from the ranks of his warriors and warned him never again to approach Wind Flower. So far Choshay had kept his distance, yet Wind Flower continued to carry the thin, razor-sharp skinning knife in its sheath strapped against her thigh. The old ones, the gossipy grandmothers who knew more of tribal intrigues than the leaders themselves, had spoken of Choshay's growing band of warriors—mostly outcasts like himself—and their killing of white women and children on frequent raids from the holy canyon. His cache of big guns, even horses, continued to grow, and the whispering ones said he had accumulated much dried meat and corn in a spot known only to himself.

Wind Flower knew that she was wise to worry, for one day Choshay might become strong enough to challenge Gallegos for control of the Canyon de Chelly and its inhabitants; only his fear of Gallegos had kept him at a distance so far. But when Gallegos led his warriors from the canyon to defeat the soldiers, then Choshay might seize the opportunity to gain control. She suppressed an inward shudder. Choshay, she vowed, would never touch her body; Wind Flower would plunge the skinning knife into her own breast first. Death would be more welcome than his filthy touch.

Wind Flower rose, brushing the loose sand from her soft deerskin dress. Gallegos had finished his oration, gaining the enthusiastic support of his braves, and now they would be planning the details of their war against the white man. That left much for a woman to do. Meat and parched corn must be prepared for the warriors, crops had to be gathered, sheep had to be tended, blankets had to be made to shield the Navajo bodies from the cold that would come.

Making her way back to her own hogan, she paused at her grandfather's lodge to see if he was in need of anything. But the sight that greeted her stilled her tongue.

The old man sat hunched over the sacred sand paintings, wrinkles of many years deepening in the weathered, tired face. Wind Flower had seen that expression before, and she knew the sand paintings spoke to the revered old one of troubled times to come.

Sergeant Major Frank Armbrister took one final look at the charred remains of the two freight wagons, then swung aboard his gaunt bay gelding. Kneeing the animal back in the direction of Fort Wingate, he turned to the trooper riding alongside.

"Looks like this may go down in the history journals as the year of the smokes. We burn their fields and orchards; they burn our wagons. One of the lessons for you to remember about Indian campaigns—you spend three weeks looking and ten minutes in battle. To win a war, you have to find the enemy—and an Indian can make himself awfully hard to find."

Armbrister eased the reins as the bay suddenly stumbled, almost going down. The sergeant expertly shifted his weight, helping the horse regain its footing, then patted the animal on the neck, a signal of reassurance. "I know, fella," he said to the bay, "I'm tired out myself. Fifteen days on patrol, and all we have to show for it is dust in our ears and some grave-digging practice."

Armbrister glanced over his shoulder at the patrol—a dozen slouched, saddle-weary men on exhausted mounts. He felt a mixture of sympathy and pride for the men. Sympathy because he knew that if one Frank Armbrister, ex-Pony Express rider who had spent most of his days in the saddle, was feeling the effects of the long ride, his men must be numb from the waist down. And pride because even though they were worn out, thirsty, and on quarter-rations, they never complained. And they did their best.

It was the condition of the horses that worried Armbrister. This campaign, he thought, is going to end up being fought on foot; no amount of personal care could help a horse eat when there was no fodder, little grass, and only the small amount of grain they could salvage from the Navajo fields. Indian raids had cut into their horse herd, and a couple of incompetent soldiers had managed to lose half a forty-horse replacement remuda to white rustlers by sharing a bottle on guard duty.

Armbrister suddenly checked his mount, raised a hand to the patrol, then cocked an ear to the wind.

"You hear that, Willis?"

The trooper at his right shook his head.

"Gunfire. Big-bore rifles, one volley and then a few single shots, good ways off."

Armbrister sighed heavily and turned his horse in the direction of the gunshots. "We'd better check it out, Willis. Be like pouring sand in a gopher hole, though. On fresh horses we could get there quick, but as it is, we'll just be in time to bury the dead—soldiers, settlers, and Indians—before the coyotes do much damage."

He patted the bay on the neck again, keeping the pace to an easy walk. "Wouldn't help much to go home anyway, fella," he said to the bay. "Nothing for you to eat at Fort Wingate either."

Colonel Carson eased himself into a chair, exhaustion etching the lines deeper in the weathered face. Ted saw the heavy layer of trail dust streaked by sweat and an expression of hopelessness in the former frontiersman's eyes.

"Rough trip, Kit?"

Carson sighed. "We covered nearly five hundred miles in just ten days, Ted. Lost one man to snakebite, another when his horse fell. Four horses just gave out, lay down, and died. In exchange, we took five prisoners, all women." Carson snorted in disgust.

"Ted, this thing is turning into a test of endurance, thanks in no small measure to the stupidity of Emery Church. But for him, we might have negotiated a peace by now. What is our status here, Ted?"

"Since you left, Kit, another hundred or so Navajo have come into the fort, thanks mostly to Chief Toshoneshe. That Indian has accomplished more among his own people than our whole regiment. We have about seven hundred Navajo at Fort Wingate now, and it's taxing our supplies to feed them. They aren't allowed to kill and eat their own sheep, because when they move to the Bosque Redondo they will need stock to begin building again."

Ted paused, then flipped through copies of reports filed in Carson's absence. "The Navajo have accounted for twenty casualties among our troops and thirty-five settlers. Two soldiers and about fifteen civilians appear to have been killed by big-bore rifles, probably fifty-six-caliber Spencers as near as I can tell."

Carson muttered one of his rare curses. "I just pray we get our hands on whoever is supplying the big rifles and ammunition to the Navajo. We've got to put a stop to it once and for all."

Ted well knew that the death of the agent Colin Dibley and the defeat of the Confederates at Glorieta Pass did not mean an end to the presence of Confederate diehards in the West. Lieutenant O'Reilly had shown him and Kit Carson the cotton-boll medallion he had found near the Salt River, and it was certain that some of the Indians were being supplied with guns in order to cause havoc for the Union Army. Still, Ted was mildly surprised at the bitterness in his commanding officer's voice.

"The territorial newspapers aren't making our job any easier, either," Carson continued. "They've convinced their readers that Fort Wingate is a permanent post, the country hereabouts is safe, and land is here for the taking. The more settlers move in, however, the harder the Navajo fight. We're getting no support from the army, no replacement troops, no horses, supplies are finding their way to civilians instead of to us, and I doubt that one man in this campaign has had more than four hours' sleep out of any given day."

Carson sighed. "At the rate we're going, Ted, we won't win this war against the Indians and neither will the Navajo. Sometimes I feel like going down to the corral and banging my head against a post."

The door swung open, and Yellow Crow entered the small room. He nodded to his two friends. Ted noticed the slight droop of the heavy shoulders, the first sign of fatigue in the Cheyenne.

"Greetings, brother," Ted said. "You have ridden long?"

"Yellow Crow and corn-color horse both stumble," the Indian said. "But we find where Navajo raiders come from."

Both officers straightened in their chairs.

"In last moon, Yellow Crow backtrack many raiding parties. All sign lead to big hole in ground called Canyon de Chelly. Catch one Navajo brave. After a time, he talk to Yellow Crow. Two bands make most trouble. One led by Gallegos. He raid soldiers, not harm settlers, take no women or children prisoners, not kill them. Other band led by outlaw called Choshay. He have sixty, seventy braves, good horses, plenty food. He kill anything—soldiers, women, children, even babies. Where Choshay go, only death rides away."

Yellow Crow sighed. "Canyon de Chelly sacred ground to Navajo. Ground grow much corn, many orchards, gardens.

Other Navajo suffer from much hunger, get worse when cold weather and snows come. Canyon de Chelly Navajo still strong. Indians there eat better than soldiers."

Ted and Kit exchanged glances.

"Navajo say spirits guard canyon from white man," Yellow Crow said. "They say no soldier enter and leave alive. Yellow Crow go now, tend horse." With that remark, the Cheyenne strode from the room into the late-autumn sunshine.

"Ted," Kit said as the door closed, "I think your Cheyenne brother may have just handed us the bullet that could end this war. We'll attempt to burn them out of the Canyon de Chelly!"

"That may work. The burning of fields, driving off the Indians' herds of sheep, and keeping patrols constantly in the area to prevent the Navajo from settling down to plant new food crops has worked well in the Fort Wingate area. There is no reason to believe that the same procedures at the Canyon de Chelly wouldn't also meet with success."

Carson paced the floor, tugging at an ear. "Let's hope they do," he said. "If they don't, we'll have no choice but to make a direct attack on the Canyon de Chelly, even though it will cost many lives on both sides."

The former mountain man walked to the window and glanced over the parade ground. "The days are getting shorter, Ted," he said over his shoulder. "I have a feeling we are in for an early winter and probably some heavy snow. If we have to attack, it's going to be awfully hard on men, and we have only enough healthy horses to mount four companies. The rest will have to walk, and full rucksacks are awfully heavy—especially for cavalrymen without horses who aren't used to the sheer physical misery of the infantryman." Carson sighed. "But at least the snow will work in our favor. The Navajo won't be expecting us to mount a full-scale assault on their sacred canyon in the winter."

"Let's just hope," Ted added, "that there won't have to be a full-scale attack. Maybe our advance units can succeed in driving them out without getting cut to ribbons themselves. I'd hate to lose men as good as O'Reilly, Yellow Crow, Armbrister, and Albert Jonas. But when you have a tough job to do, you send your toughest men."

Carson nodded and slowly returned to the desk. "Any dispatches come in for me?"

Ted half smiled. "A long letter from Josefa. And two messages from General Carleton. Rather strongly worded. He seems upset that you led a patrol into the field and did not stay at your desk to file reports personally."

Disgust snapped in Kit Carson's eyes. "Tell the general," he said, "that he did not hire a company clerk or a desk rider when I signed on for this job, and that it is becoming easier to post dispatches from the middle of Navajo country than it is to get support from headquarters. Of course, I'll trust you to phrase the reply in the properly humble military form."

Ted grinned widely. "I'll see to it, Kit." He plucked a single letter from the stack of dispatches atop the desk and handed it to Carson.

"Your letter from Josefa," he said.

"Thanks. Maybe I could prevail upon you to read it to me after I rest up." The colonel hesitated, then looked at Ted. "Am I getting too old to be in the field, Colonel?"

"No, Kit. I'd say we both may be slowing down a bit. But I think we can rely on experience and common sense to compensate for our aching bones. Now if you will accept an order from a second-in-command, go get some sleep."

The rays of the early afternoon sun slanted through the window as Wilma Henderson sat at the table, writing a letter to Ted. The baby was with Anna and her adopted daughter, Ellen, as he was almost every afternoon, and, indeed, Wilma was now describing to Ted her delight at seeing their son and the Indian child sharing new experiences together, smiling and giggling. Ellen enjoyed her role as big sister and devised ingenious toys for little William Ted, improvising them from almost anything available.

By late fall, Wilma had completely regained her figure after giving birth, exercising both herself and Ted's stallion either inside the compound or, when they were permitted, outside the fort's walls within the immediate vicinity. Wilma smiled as she wrote: *When you see me, dearest, I'll be wearing again that dress you like on me so well.*

Suddenly the door slammed open, causing Wilma to jerk pen from paper in surprise. She looked up into the anguished face of Vi Robinson.

"Vi! What is it? What's wrong?"

"It's Judy," Vi said, the strain obvious in her voice as she fought to control her panic. "She's gone!"

"Gone? I don't understand. . . ."

"She was just sitting there rocking, and I went to get some

more wood for the fire. But when I got back, her chair was empty. I can't find her anywhere on the post, Wilma!"

Wilma bounded from the chair and placed a comforting arm about her friend's shoulders. "Is there any place you might have overlooked, Vi?"

Vi shook her head. "There's only one place she could be, Wilma—outside the fort!"

Wilma felt the alarm rise in her breast as she suddenly remembered the broken post in the stockade wall behind the stable. She had reported it, but just yesterday, as she had ridden by, Wilma had noticed that it still remained unrepaired. Certainly a slender person like Judy could slip through and get outside the fort. "Is Abel still out on patrol?"

"Yes. There's no telling where he is."

Wilma made an attempt to keep her own voice calm and reasonable; Vi was upset enough as it was. "I have an idea where she might have gone," Wilma said. "Do you remember the grove of trees about a mile north, where we all went to gather nuts a few weeks ago? Even in her state, Judy might remember the way." Wilma dashed for her shotgun, checked the loads, then plucked the big army pistol from a desk drawer and shoved the gun into the waistband of her riding skirt.

"Go find the corporal of the guard, Vi. Organize a search detail. Ted's stallion is saddled and waiting outside. I'll try to find her while the soldiers are getting organized."

"Wilma, no!" Vi grasped her friend's arm. "You can't go out alone! If there are Indians about—"

"All the more reason to move quickly, Vi. And I have the shotgun and I know how to use it. Now move! Get the corporal!" Wilma jerked free, dashed through the door, and swung onto the broad back of the powerful stallion. The high-strung animal pranced nervously, but quickly calmed under Wilma's firm but gentle touch. The stallion seemed to sense the urgency in her body and took off in a hard run. As horse and rider sped past the surprised sentry at the gate, they ignored the shouted cry to stop.

Shotgun cradled over her left elbow, Wilma reined the stallion toward the north and the grove of trees a long mile distant. Breathing a silent prayer that the stallion would not stumble on a stone or a badger hole, she gave the powerful animal his head, then scanned the landscape as the horse ran. A hundred yards from the grove, she brought the animal to an abrupt stop. She saw a small figure dressed in white among the shadows of the grove.

Wilma kneed the stallion back into a trot, relief flooding through her body. She had found Judy. In the girl's disturbed state, however, Wilma did not intend to go barreling full speed into the grove of trees. She did not know whether Judy would feel fearful or not, but she would take no chances.

Sixty feet from the grove, Wilma suddenly heard a sound that sent a chill up her spine: the snuffle of the stallion. Ted had told her of that quiet warning.

She slid from the saddle, knotted the reins, and draped them across the horse's neck. In the event of trouble, the stallion would be free to dash home to the safety of the stable.

Wilma had taken only a few steps when she heard the low murmur of voices in the grove—and the words were Arapaho!

Cautiously she made her way to the edge of the clearing in the center of the trees. The sight that awaited her jarred the breath from her lungs.

Only a few feet away, Judy Hubbard stood trancelike, staring at an Indian with a ragged scar across his forehead. The Indian, eyebrows arched in apparent surprise, stood for a moment, then smiled a twisted grin. Over his shoulder, he said something in Arapaho to his half-dozen companions. Although Wilma spoke some Arapaho, she needed no grasp of the language to understand the intention. The sight it conjured was not a pretty one.

The Indian slowly reached for the scalping knife at his belt. Breathlessly, Wilma cocked both hammers of the shotgun.

The heavy, metallic click of the gun was heard across the clearing. The Arapaho braves froze at the familiar sound, knowing any sudden move might bring a charge of buckshot from close range. It was an injury from which one did not recover.

The Indian standing near Judy slowly turned his head in Wilma's direction, the fear fading to mild amusement as he saw the woman behind the twin muzzles of the weapon.

"A squaw," the Indian snorted in derision.

Wilma replied in the Arapaho tongue. "Does it make a difference to the brave if a woman pulls the trigger? Would the brave be less dead than if a man were the one to shoot?" Wilma now moved a step closer to the motionless Judy Hubbard. "If any brave so much as sneezes, he will be blown in half."

Concern rippled the Indian's scarred brow as the woman's calm, controlled voice floated in the deathly silence of the clearing. Wilma glanced at Judy. The young woman's eyes seemed fixed at a point just below her assailant's neck. Then at the corner of her vision Wilma saw one of the braves move, and she swung the shotgun in his direction.

A sudden, sharp intake of breath beside her startled Wilma and almost caused her to squeeze the triggers.

The first sound Judy Hubbard had uttered in months began as a low moan, then climbed the scale of inner agony to a full-fledged, piercing scream as the small figure hurled itself at the Indian standing in front of her. One hand grasped a metallic object at his throat and yanked as the fingers of her other hand curled into a claw, nails aimed at the Indian's eyes. Instinctively, the brave ducked, but the fingernails slashed red welts on his cheek. He staggered back, hands held outward to ward off another blow instead of reaching for the knife at the belt, the brown eyes wide in sheer terror.

For a moment Wilma stood confused at the Indian's defenseless reaction, then the answer flashed through her mind. The superstitious Indians were terrified of "possessed ones"—crazy people.

But Judy's charge and the movement of the Indian had placed her between Wilma and the brave. Wilma felt a surge of sudden panic. If the Indian went on the offensive, she would be unable to shoot for fear of hitting Judy!

She sensed rather than saw the motion to her left. She wheeled as an Arapaho brave raised his war ax overhead, poised to throw. Wilma instinctively swung the shotgun muzzle, squeezed the front trigger, and saw the Indian lifted from his feet and thrown backward by the impact of buckshot. The recoil slammed the shotgun stock heavily against Wilma's shoulder and spun her halfway around, the muzzle of the weapon momentarily pointing skyward, the roiling smoke of the black powder obscuring her vision.

She regained control, swung the muzzle back, and felt her mouth drop open in astonishment. All the Indians were gone except Judy's would-be assailant, driven back almost to the edge of the trees under the young woman's relentless screaming and slashing attack.

Wilma watched in disbelief as Judy somehow wrested the knife from the Indian's belt, raised it high, and slashed. The point ripped across the Arapaho's chest. The Indian's heel struck a large root, and he tumbled onto his back. Judy raised the knife for the fatal strike.

"Judy! No!"

Wilma heard her own sharp cry pierce the rumbling thunder of approaching hoofbeats. The knifepoint stopped, trembled—and then sunlight flashed from steel as Judy tossed the weapon aside, shoulders heaving in uncontrollable sobs.

Wilma was at her side in an instant, the shotgun barrel lined squarely on the Indian's chest, now bloody from the savage knife attack.

"The Arapaho has two choices," Wilma said, aware of the quaver in her voice. "Die now before the purification rites and walk the darkness forever, or return as a captive of two women to wear leg irons at the white man's fort."

The shaken, terrified Indian finally regained his voice. "Stalking Horse go to fort."

The sounds of Judy's sobbing were muffled by a nearby volley of gunfire, then two single pistol reports. Suddenly Vi appeared at Judy's side, wrapped the young woman in her arms, and began to rock her as a mother would rock a baby. Judy's sobs slowly subsided, and Wilma saw her raise her eyes toward Vi.

"Vi—my God," Judy said weakly, the first words she had uttered in months. "I—it's all my—fault—can you ever—forgive me?"

Vi's tears mingled with Judy's as the two women embraced, then dropped to their knees in the clearing.

A corporal called out, then stepped into the clearing. Confused, he glanced from Wilma to the Indian, then to Vi and Judy, then back to Wilma. Finally he regained his composure and gently took the shotgun from Wilma's hand.

"I'll take care of this one, Mrs. Henderson," the corporal said, "if you will see to the others. Indians I can handle. Crying women, I can't. Oh, we got the other braves."

Wilma crossed the few feet to Vi and Judy and wiped a tear from the younger woman's cheek. Noticing a shiny object clasped in Judy's hand, she gently pried the medallion from the stiff and unyielding fingers.

Carved into the silver circle was a strange shape, an incomplete fleur-de-lis. Then Wilma made the connection—it was the same design Ted had showed her in the medal taken from the dead brave who had attacked the ranch: a stylized rendition of a cotton boll.

"Co—Colin Dibley," Judy sobbed. "It's all—coming back—now. Oh, God—I killed Daddy!"

Vi Robinson stroked Judy's long, tangled hair, continuing to rock her back and forth. "Shush, Judy. It's all right now. Let's go home."

They walked back to the fort, the soldiers on horseback riding at a slow gait as they led the Arapaho and the captured horses. Vi's horse was also in tow now, for the stallion, as Wilma had guessed, had run back to the fort during the skirmish with the Arapaho.

When they arrived at Fort Laramie, the three women went to the Hubbard living quarters, where Judy washed and changed clothes and settled down with her stepmother and Wilma in the parlor. They talked quietly, Vi and Wilma allowing Judy to unburden her soul and speak whatever came into her mind.

When she finally arrived at her own house, Wilma immediately sat down and, exhausted as she was, continued her letter to Ted. *Dearest*, she wrote, *this letter has just been interrupted by little less than a miracle.* . . . As briefly as she could, she related the story of Judy, the Indian, and the medallion, touching only briefly on her own role in the episode.

> *I believe, Ted, that it was the sight of the cotton boll—Colin Dibley's symbol—that finally jarred poor Judy back to reality. It was as though a storm that had been building for weeks suddenly broke, and then the sun shone through once more. Judy must have locked the unbearable truth deep inside her mind, buried herself with guilt because her actions had, she believed, directly led to Colonel Robinson's death. Her father was the one man she loved more than she loved Abel Hubbard. And Colin Dibley, the man she had so naively trusted, had used her, deceived her, beaten her—and worse. Once Judy began to talk, the words just tumbled out between the tears, one atop the other, and finally Vi and I began truly to understand. And when Judy took off her dress, we knew the reason she would not let Abel touch her or make love to her.*
>
> *You see, Ted, she wears the brand of Colin Dibley and all the guilt and horror it holds. On the*

inside of Judy's left thigh, that horrid beast had burned the sign of the cotton boll.

Of course, the true test will come when Abel returns from patrol and finds that his wife has broken free of the twilight world of the living dead. Judy is convinced that Abel will leave her, that he will explode in fury when he sees Dibley's brand stamped forever on her leg. I firmly believe she underestimates the love Abel has for her and his solid strength. It will not be easy for them in the coming months, for Judy must still learn—and Abel as well— to cope with the horrible memories. I have faith, however, that the bond between them will be even stronger once the healing is complete.

Perhaps one day, my dearest, their bond will be almost as strong as ours.

If I don't stop now, this letter will break the back of the army's strongest pack mule. May the Lord ride with you and protect you from harm until we are together once more.

With deepest love and devotion, Wilma.

P.S. Our baby snores almost as loud as you do, dear.

Lieutenant Kevin O'Reilly forced his leaden legs to carry him the final few steps to the top of the high mesa overlooking one end of the Canyon de Chelly. He raised a hand, signaling the footsore and bone-tired infantry company behind him to halt. He scanned the countryside with care and saw the smoke from numerous fires, the blackened, charred land where fields of corn once stood. Apparently Jonas, Armbrister, and the Cheyenne were meeting with as much success as he.

Satisfied at last that no Navajo warriors lay in ambush, he waved his soldiers forward. Tall stalks of heavily eared corn stretched over several acres before them. This was the Indian corn that grew late in the season and remained on the stalks right up until the first snow.

Kevin O'Reilly did not need to tell his troops what to do; by now they were ruthlessly efficient in the destruction of Indian crops. At his hand signal, they deployed in the familiar skirmish line at the edges of the cornfield. Within minutes, flames licked at the sun-dried stalks, and with the gusting winds, the field soon would become a short-lived and raging inferno. All that would be left would be another scar upon the face of the land.

A glimpse of movement within the cornfield caught his eye. He stared through the steadily growing circle of flames, hoping an innocent deer or antelope had not been trapped in the ring of fire.

His heart leaped in dismay as the movement suddenly snapped into focus through the heat waves shimmering above the field—a slightly built figure, long hair swirling, raced from one point to another, seeking a way to escape the nearing flames. It was a woman trapped there, O'Reilly realized.

The lieutenant reacted without thinking, tossing his rifle aside and plunging through a small opening in the ring of flames into swirling, choking smoke. He stood for a moment, confused and disoriented by the smoke and shimmering heat, eyes watering in protest. Then he spotted her again, only a few feet away.

O'Reilly squared his bull-like shoulders and plowed through the cornstalks. The slender figure, taken by surprise, tried to twist free of the powerful grip on her arm. O'Reilly shouted in the Navajo tongue above the growing crackle of flames: "Man help!" He momentarily released his grip, stripped out of his greatcoat, tossed the heavy garment over the small body, and scooped up the girl. He glanced about, feeling the first wash of fear, looking for a break in the circle of flames. He found none, and there was no time to search. Running at top speed, he dashed toward the nearest flames, felt the slap of fire against his body, and then broke through into the fresh clean air, stumbling into the arms of a sergeant.

Ignoring the hands that slapped at his smoldering clothing, O'Reilly whipped the greatcoat from the slender figure.

Recognition hit him with a jolt—the high cheekbones, chiseled face, brown eyes wide with fear—the girl from Salt River! Unable for a moment to speak, O'Reilly simply stared. The object of his long search was now within his arms! The woman's eyes softened as she touched his face and his forearms, and O'Reilly became aware he had suffered some minor burns in his dash through the flames. The touch broke his trance.

"Daughter—daughter is safe now," he said in his good Navajo. "No harm will come to her from the fire or the soldiers."

She bowed her head slightly, and O'Reilly was pleased

that the flames had not scorched her thick black hair, which fell almost to her waist. He reached out as though to stroke it, then checked the impulse as the girl once more raised her eyes.

Wind Flower felt her heart pound within her breast as she looked into the strong but gentle face before her.

"Twice now," she said, her voice musical in the flowery Navajo tongue, "white brave has saved Wind Flower. Once from the ugly one, Choshay, and now from the fire. The daughter of Gallegos thanks the brave soldier not once, but twice, for the gift of life."

Through the daze of a swirling brain almost overwhelmed by the beauty of the woman and the just-ended struggle to save her life, Kevin O'Reilly heard a low whistle at his side.

"The daughter of Gallegos," the sergeant repeated. "Lieutenant, you don't realize what a prize you have here."

"Sergeant," O'Reilly replied in a choked voice, "no man alive realizes just how much of a prize . . ." He could not seem to pull his eyes away from her face, her beauty, the tenderness he saw in her large, long-lashed brown eyes.

"If Gallegos will negotiate for anything," the sergeant said, "it's this girl. He'll pay almost any price to get her back."

"No!" O'Reilly's sharp tone surprised even himself. "It will be her choice; I'll not hold her captive!"

"But, Lieutenant!"

O'Reilly cut the protest short with a quick wave of the hand. "Wind Flower is free to choose," he said in Navajo. "It is white brave's hope, his dream, that Wind Flower will come with him, that she will join her people who have already come to the white settlement. But if she wishes to return to her people, no white hand will be raised against her."

Wind Flower looked steadily at this big soldier in blue with the gentle eyes; she knew he was a good man. But she also knew what she had to do, and she shook her head.

"Wind Flower must return to her people," she said. "Soon there will be no food, babies will cry, perhaps there will be sickness. Wind Flower will be needed. The daughter of a chief remains so when her people are in need."

Kevin reached out with trembling fingers and lightly touched the bronze cheek as he struggled with the tightness in his chest. "Then go, if Wind Flower must. A daughter of a chief must perform her duty. But part of white brave will be with her, suffering even as her people suffer.

"Please," he said, "tell Gallegos the white man does not

kill Navajo for sport. Take this message to him, for they are the words of Kit Carson. 'No Indian need die, as no white blood need be spilled. Those who come in peace will not be robbed of their animals nor tortured nor killed, but will be fed.' If Wind Flower can convince Gallegos of this, many lives will be saved—perhaps hers, perhaps the white brave's. And certainly many old ones and children."

Wind Flower nodded solemnly. "Wind Flower will carry these words to her father. She believes them to be true." She turned and, moving with the agility of a deer, was gone.

Kevin stood for a long time, staring in the direction she had taken. One by one, the soldiers drifted away to rest.

The sergeant, having worried a chunk of tobacco from his plug, now bit into it with a vengeance. "Dumb," he muttered. "Just plain old dumb, lettin' a hostage like that go."

The trooper at his side looked at the sergeant for a long moment.

"He's not dumb, Sergeant—at least no dumber than any man in love is."

IX

Major Abel Hubbard squatted near the small fire in the center of the Comanche chief's tipi, confident that his eyes would not reflect the jangle of his nerves. He sat in silence, a gesture of respect in the Comanche culture, painfully conscious of the number of lives that rested upon the outcome of the meeting with the barrel-chested and bowlegged warrior chief known as Two Fingers.

At length, the chief broke the silence.

"The Long Knife known as Hubbard is as brave as the stories told of him," Chief Two Fingers said. "Few white soldiers would be willing to ride alone and unarmed into the camp of Two Fingers's hunting party."

"No one other than the spirits knows better than Hubbard of the power of the Comanche nation," Abel replied, "and of the skill and courage of the great Chief Two Fingers. It also is known that Two Fingers prefers a life of peace, even though songs are sung to his honor as a warrior. Hubbard had no fear for he knew that when Two Fingers was approached in peace, he would repay in kind.

"Hubbard has come to discuss with Two Fingers the buffalo his hunters follow. He has come to say to Two Fingers, go and pursue the buffalo, for women and children must eat. The soldiers in blue will not interfere. This hunt shall be as the hunts of centuries past."

The Comanche glanced quizzically at Abel. "And what," he asked, "does the white soldier demand in return?"

"Nothing," Abel answered. "But he would welcome your word that the Comanche will seek only the buffalo, that white people will not be harmed."

Two Fingers fell silent for a moment, then nodded. "Agreed. But does it not strike you as strange, Hubbard, that such an agreement must be reached?"

"No, Two Fingers. Not strange. Only a sad comment on the times."

"Hubbard and Two Fingers will smoke to the agreement," the chief said, producing a pipe and pouch, "and while one day they may do battle, for the moment they will each follow their own paths in peace."

After he smoked with the chief, the weary Abel Hubbard rode from the village and rejoined his waiting patrol. As he and his men headed back to Fort Laramie, Abel turned in the saddle to face the lieutenant riding alongside.

"It's been a good patrol, Smitty," Abel said. "Except for a few renegade Arapaho, it now looks as if all the major tribes in the area will keep the peace."

As the patrol neared the top of the rise overlooking Fort Laramie, the lieutenant suddenly broke the silence by crying out and pointing in the direction of the fort. "Major! Look!"

Abel stared into the distance and suddenly stiffened in the saddle. He could just make out a small, slender figure waving a hand high overhead. "It's Judy," Abel muttered. Without taking his eyes off the distant woman, he said, "Smitty, take the patrol in from here; I'm going to ride on ahead."

Without waiting for the lieutenant's reply, Abel touched spurs to his mount. The horse, eager to be home to fodder and grain, broke into a gallop. Abel felt the sting of moisture at the corners of his eyes as he neared the animated figure. Then he skidded his horse to a stop, dismounted, and instantly Judy was in his arms.

"Abel—Abel—" The sobbing voice was muffled against his shoulder as he stroked the carefully combed hair cascading down her back. He made no attempt to check the tears that trickled down his own cheeks.

"Judy, I—don't know what happened or why, and right now I don't care." He heard the huskiness in his own words and held her tight.

"Abel, darling, they told us your patrol was coming in, and I had to come out to see you, to tell you—everything's all right now—it's all right." She looked up at him. "Abel, I—I'm sorry. I was—foolish and a—child and weak—and all I can do is pray for forgiveness."

He stoked her hair again, luxuriating in the thick richness

of it, the fresh smell of the woman who had been such a stranger when he had left on patrol.

"Hush, Judy, you're back home. And that's all that matters."

They went into the fort together, Abel leading his horse with one hand, his other hand around Judy's waist. He barely heard or saw the private who took the horse from him, paid no heed to the stares of the men and women living in the fort under his command. He forgot all protocol entirely as he walked with Judy to their house, his hand never leaving her waist, his eyes fastened on hers.

They embraced repeatedly and continued to look at each other, and it was a long time before Abel would allow Judy to speak. Her eyes, which had been blank for so long, now told him all he needed to know.

At last, Vi and Wilma knocked at the door, and Abel and Judy welcomed them inside. Suddenly the air was filled with excited chatter as the story of the encounter with the Arapaho and Judy's rescue and recovery came out into the open. The fact that the last of the renegade Arapaho Indians had been captured and brought into the fort was good news enough, but right now Abel's mind was filled with nothing but Judy.

The bitter winter winds pierced the protective walls of the holy canyon, slicing through small cracks in the hogan, burrowing through the thin and ragged blankets to stroke the huddled body beneath.

Wind Flower awakened from a fitful sleep at the touch on her shoulder and shuddered, partly from the cold and partly from the vivid dreams still swirling about her mind.

"Wind Flower cries out in her sleep," Gallegos said. "What troubles you, daughter?"

Wind Flower wrapped her arms about her breasts, trying in vain to use the heat from her own body for warmth. She sighed, the soft sound lost against the howl of the wind.

"Visions, my father." She watched her breath turn to smoke in the chill of the lodge, and remembered the old days when she was but a child and the breathing-of-smoke times were good, for there was food to warm the belly and blankets for the body and trinkets and playthings. Now the breath-smoke held a different meaning.

"In the visions Wind Flower saw young children with thin arms and swollen bellies, women with hungry eyes and breasts with no milk, and Wind Flower held one baby to her own breast but could not feed it, and as she watched, its face withered and the flesh fell from its bones." She fought back the tightening in her chest as the memory of the dream flared anew.

"These are not good visions for a young woman to have," Gallegos said with a shake of the head. "The spirits have promised to protect the Navajo here in the sacred canyon. But perhaps one stray evil spirit has made its way into the hogan. A small sacrifice of corn will drive it away, and Wind Flower's visions will be those of comfort."

"No," Wind Flower said. "There is no corn to spare for an offering, not in the hogan of a chief who gives his own food to those more needy; this is as it should be. But there are more visions. In the sleep world Wild Flower saw Choshay"—she noticed the involuntary grimace of her father's mouth—"and Choshay's belly bulged with corn and venison and squash. In one hand he held a rifle pointed at Gallegos's back; with the other, he held Wind Flower down, and the rocks were sharp."

Wind Flower sighed, then shuddered as a sudden blast of cold air penetrated the hogan. "And then there were men in blue, marching through the Canyon de Chelly, past the very door of this hogan. But they fired no shots; instead they handed food to the Navajo. One of them wore the face of the big man who saved Wind Flower first from Choshay, then from the flames."

She stared for a long moment into her father's face. "Is it not possible, father, that these visions hold truth? Have not many of the Navajo already surrendered to the white soldier named Carson?"

Gallegos's face twisted in hate. "These are not true visions Wind Flower sees, daughter. For the winds have spoken to Gallegos. The Navajo will never leave this sacred canyon! They will starve first! And the white man shall never enter here, either! If he does, he will not leave alive!"

As was his custom, Kit Carson sat astride his horse outside the gates, watching as his soldiers filed past into the relative safety of the compound. They were moving into the isolated and long-abandoned Fort Defiance, in the heart of Navajo country, to commence the campaign that Colonel Carson had talked about earlier and was now putting into action. The repeated attempts of the advance units to subdue Gallegos's hostile braves and get them to surrender and go to the reservation had failed, and even with the burning of the crops, the Indians had refused to budge from their fortress. There was no choice now but to attack the Canyon de Chelly.

From time to time Carson nodded or spoke to one of the soldiers slogging past in the calf-deep snow, then he turned to the officer at his side.

"Look at them, Ted," Carson said, the pride obvious in his tone. "A march of a hundred miles by nearly four hundred men on short rations through snow, and one in four is on foot. And not one word of complaint have I heard."

"I know," Ted replied. "I had to give one soldier a direct order to report to the surgeon for treatment of frostbite. The young man was afraid the physician would forbid him to take part in the raid on Canyon de Chelly. They are a rather remarkable bunch."

Ted watched as the final cluster of men struggled through the gate. The troopers quickened their steps despite the numbing clutch of snow against their boots, knowing their two commanding officers would not seek shelter themselves until their soldiers had been accounted for.

"The politicians and the generals are the ones mentioned in history," Ted said, "but soldiers like these—tired, hungry, cold—these are the men who win battles and conquer nations. Every child above the age of ten knows George Washington's name, but I'll bet not one in a hundred can name one private in the revolutionary army."

"You're right, Ted. It's a pity those soldiers will never have their true place in history." Carson reined his horse into the fort and glanced around. "I was afraid Fort Defiance might be in even worse shape than it is," he said. "At least the men will have some protection from the wind and a chance to dry their blankets. We're short of fuel—and everything else except Indians—but I think we can spare enough for two hot meals a day for the troops until they have regained some strength. They will need it when we march on the canyon."

The two officers dismounted before a structure that obviously had served as the fort commander's post in days past, and they handed the reins of their mounts over to a trooper for care.

The door creaked on its hinges, and the chill bit through the dusty smell inside the small room, but Ted welcomed the protection of the four walls and the roof overhead. Even though he was toughened to long marches and bitter cold, he felt the numbness in his fingers and toes, and he delivered a mental salute in the direction of the soldiers outside, marveling at their capacity to endure pain and misery.

Kit Carson placed his dispatch bags on a table. "After the evening meal, Ted, call the ranking officers and noncoms above the rank of corporal here for a meeting. We've some final plans to go over. We're going to rest for a few days and send out some patrols before we actually march on the canyon. Maybe—just maybe—we can convince some of these stubborn Navajo to come with us into the fort before it's too late."

The patrols were organized that night. Lieutenant Kevin O'Reilly would continue to lead his infantry patrol, and Kit Carson decided to lead a patrol himself. Ted's scouts, of course, formed the core of the mission, with Albert Jonas, Yellow Crow, and Frank Armbrister each taking charge of a unit. Both Kit Carson and Ted were delighted when the fully recovered Private Bernie Christian showed up, asking to be assigned to Frank Armbrister's company. The little private had proven himself over and over again, and his presence seemed like a good omen.

The patrols rode out early the next morning, heading in the general vicinity of the Canyon de Chelly. It was bitter cold, and the going was slow because of the snow and ice. They encountered Indians who had refused to surrender earlier, but were now willing to accompany the soldiers to Fort Defiance and eventually go to live on the reservation.

Kit Carson rode alongside his weary patrol, feeling the bite of the north wind, and glanced at the handful of captive Navajo. He felt a stab of pain at the sight of the emaciated women and exhausted children stumbling through the snow. On impulse, he reached down, scooped up a shivering child, and placed the boy in the saddle before him. Unbuttoning his greatcoat, he wrapped it around the youth. Gradually the shivering stopped as the child snuggled against the warmth of the former frontiersman's body.

Carson's spirits lifted as he looked around the column escorting the captives. One by one, the soldiers followed his lead. At least some of the children would ride. He became even prouder of these men in blue who rode with him; the same hands that could pull a trigger and take a life could also reach down and lift a child to safety. And Kit Carson was sure he saw the drawn face of one woman brighten, a brief flash of gratitude in the normally stoic eyes.

Perhaps, he found himself thinking, the Navajo would soon begin to believe they would be safe and well treated upon their surrender, that there would be no more men like Major Church in charge.

Meanwhile, just below the crest of a hill a mile from the eastern edge of Canyon de Chelly, Lieutenant Kevin O'Reilly abruptly raised a hand, bringing his half-frozen patrol to a halt in a jumble of boulders. He glanced at the burly trooper at his side.

"You hear, Mike?"

Mike Connor nodded. "Rifle fire. And not all that far off, my friend. Couldn't tell for sure, but it didn't sound like army rifles to me. Maybe one of our patrols got jumped and didn't have a chance to fight back."

O'Reilly waved the patrol in close. "Trouble up ahead, boys," he said. "We'd best move it out double-quick and see what's going on. Lord, what I wouldn't give for some horses right now."

He turned and, moving in such long-legged strides that some of the troopers had to trot to keep up, led the patrol in the direction of the gunshots.

Thirty minutes of fast movement through calf-deep snow had taken its toll on O'Reilly's patrol, but despite the exhaustion, Kevin could see the grim determination in the troopers' eyes as they surveyed the scene.

Several bodies lay in the snow, drifts already beginning to form in the bitter wind whipping about the still forms. They were Navajo and appeared to be one family, Kevin thought. There were an old man and older woman, four other adults including two females, and six thin young bodies. All had been shot down, apparently from ambush, by big-bore rifles.

Staring at the scene, teeth clenched in fury and stomach churning at the sight of death, Keven did not notice the young trooper nearby raise his rifle at something in the distance. The trooper started to call out, but a big hand clamped down on the weapon, forcing the muzzle aside. "Easy, trooper," Kevin heard Mike O'Connor say. "That Indian is one of ours."

Through the swirling snowflakes, the form of Yellow Crow on his tough palomino gelding gradually took shape. The Cheyenne said nothing, but slipped from the saddle and walked a circle about the bodies, stooping from time to time to brush away small snowdrifts and stare at some mark or to pluck an object from the icy ground. Finally he approached the patrol and nodded to Kevin.

"Yellow Crow hear shots," the Third Cavalry's chief scout said. "Soldiers not do this to Navajo. Navajo do this to Navajo. Try to make it look like work of soldiers. Indian learn tricks from white man pretty good."

He opened a hand to Kevin. Three shiny cartridge cases lay in the bronze palm. Kevin recognized them at once—Spencer rimfire, .56 caliber. Except for Yellow Crow himself, no man in Carson's expedition carried such weapons as far as Kevin knew.

"But why?"

Yellow Crow shrugged. "Maybe to make Navajo have more fear of soldiers. Maybe just plain mean. Know this one's sign. Warrior name Choshay. Bad Indian. Want be chief one day. Big belly, bad teeth, scar half close one eye."

Kevin felt the jar of recognition; he had met Choshay before, on the Salt River. It was clear now that the cotton-boll medallion he had found there belonged to Choshay. Obviously, the ugly Navajo brave was in league with the Confederates. He would have to tell Carson and Henderson, but for now he listened as Yellow Crow continued.

"Yellow Crow follow ugly one's trail. Gallegos's band not far from here. No good those two meet." Yellow Crow moved toward his horse. Kevin fell into step, and the two men talked quietly for a few moments. The Indian mounted and vanished into the snow. Kevin made his way back to his own men, calling Mike off to one side.

"Mike, Yellow Crow told me where Gallegos's band is. I'm going there to see Wind Flower if I can." He waved off his friend's protest. "I have to, Mike. I must see her again. I have something I must tell her. If I'm not back in two hours, take the patrol back to Fort Defiance."

Connor nodded, then clasped the lieutenant on the shoulder. "Then go, you dumb Irishman, but do nothing foolish. If you're going to lose your head over a woman, just make sure you don't lose your hair as well."

Kevin pushed himself through snow as fast as his legs could move, but a mile or more later, he finally sagged against the support of a sheltering boulder, knees trembling with fatigue. He wiped a gloved hand over his eyes, reddened from lack of rest and the constant search for signs of movement in the side branch of the Canyon de Chelly below. Disappointment lay heavy in his belly. His lone foray had brought him no sign of Wind Flower or others of Gallegos's band.

His time was running out; soon he must leave to rejoin Mike and the rest of the patrol. But first, a few minutes of rest.

A movement in the brush below caught his eye. Squinting against the snow, he made out the figure of an old woman, grubbing for roots with a sharp stick among the scraggly and leafless branches of a small thicket. He rose, silently making his way to within a few feet of the emaciated old woman. He watched as she worried a root from the earth and wiped the soil away with a tattered cloth. She stared longingly at the tuber before placing it in a pouch slung across a withered shoulder. Kevin felt a surge of pity. He, too, had known hunger, yet the old one had not eaten the root but had saved it, probably for the others.

"Grandmother," he called softly in Navajo. "Do not fear. White brave wishes you no harm. Does Grandmother know the girl called Wind Flower?"

The Navajo nodded. "She is near."

Kevin reached into his knapsack, produced one of his treasured biscuits, and handed it to the woman. "Please eat," he said. A wizened hand gripped the biscuit, then slipped it into the pouch. "Young ones need it more than old ones," she said.

"Will Grandmother tell Wind Flower the big lieutenant from the Salt River and the cornfield waits for her here?"

The old woman nodded. "She has spoken of big soldier. Grandmother will tell her you wait. She will come to you."

A few minutes later a slender, familiar form approached, and Kevin went down the trail to meet her. He was momentarily stunned at Wind Flower's sunken cheeks and thin limbs, and the thought of her suffering tore at his heart.

"Wind Flower still walks in beauty and pride," he said. "White brave has come to declare his love for Wind Flower, to beg her to return to the safety of the fort with him. One day, he hopes she will be his wife."

The luminous brown eyes softened, then dropped from Kevin's face. "Wind Flower is honored by the tall soldier. But she cannot leave her people. There is much hunger, and the children suffer so from the cold. She must follow the path of her people, share their fate. Wind Flower's heart is heavy, for she feels warmth at the sight of the tall soldier, yet knows she cannot go with him. Duty is a thing not limited to the warrior or the chief, and the needs of Wind Flower's people are many."

"Then," Kevin said, "if Wind Flower will not return with tall soldier, carry this message again to her people. If they will come to the fort, they will be fed and clothed. The soldiers will come soon. White brave cannot bear the thought of death or injury to Wind Flower or her people."

She touched his arm, and impulsively, he gathered the frail young woman in a firm embrace. They stood so for a long moment before Kevin finally stepped back. "May the spirits walk with Wind Flower until she and white brave meet again," he said. Kevin reached again into his knapsack, produced the rest of his field rations, and handed them to Wind Flower with trembling fingers. "For the children," he said.

Wind Flower felt the warmth of his embrace still flooding her body, an emotion she had never before felt in her breast. "For the children," she repeated, tears in her eyes.

She watched as the tall soldier turned reluctantly to leave, then called out. "Wait. Wind Flower will pray to the spirits for the tall soldier—but it would be easier if she could say his name."

Kevin felt a surge of emotion. "Kevin O'Reilly. An Irishman with love in his heart for a beautiful woman." He turned back to her, gripped her shoulders, and his lips brushed her own. The strange gesture sent shudders of warmth and a sensation Wind Flower had never before known flowing through her body.

O'Reilly stared for a long moment into the brown eyes. "When the soldiers come, go to a safe place where no harm will come to Wind Flower. When the fighting is at an end, Kevin will find Wind Flower once more."

The lieutenant turned again and made his way back up the path. At the crest of the canyon ridge, he raised a hand. Wind Flower returned his wave. Then, with the warmth of his touch still flowing through her body, she clutched the packet of food closer to her body and started back down the trail to her people in the sacred Canyon de Chelly.

Despite the soldiers' pleas, despite the near-starvation and the threat of an attack on their sacred canyon, the Navajo led by Gallegos still held out. Gallegos's fierce braves managed to attack the soldiers on patrol and to escape retaliation by riding back into the safety of their fortress. And they would continue to attack, for they had nothing but hatred for the white man who could not be trusted, who so often broke his word. The death of the Navajo family not far from the canyon—the same Indians O'Reilly's patrol had come upon—was just one more example of the treachery of the whites. There was not one brave among Gallegos's band who recognized that the shots were not fired by army rifles, that the death of the Navajo family was at the hands of one of their own members—Choshay.

The snow finally stopped, but the bitter winds still blew. Colonel Kit Carson issued the commands that established his camp near the western entrance of the Canyon de Chelly, and that initiated the final stages of the campaign against the Navajo.

Carson turned to the officer at his side. "What do they call this place, Ted?"

"It's known among the Navajo as *Chinle*, 'The Coming-Out Place,'" Ted replied.

"I pray that name holds true," Carson said, a wistful tone in his voice. "If they would only come out, so much suffering could be saved." Carson sighed. "Ted, I'm counting heavily on you and the success of our initial penetration of the canyon. You will be going in as far as you can with reasonable safety. The Navajo must be convinced that they will be killed if they resist, but treated with kindness if they come out. Have you picked the men for your patrol?"

Ted nodded. "Yellow Crow, Albert Jonas, four of my own scouts, and a half-dozen others hand-picked for their horsemanship, fighting ability, and common sense," he said. "I wish I had Frank Armbrister and Bernie Christian."

"I wish we had a thousand like them," Carson replied. "But they were needed on the force invading from the eastern branch of the canyon. They will be in position in two days. At that time, the invasion of the canyon will begin. Until then, it's up to you and your patrol."

"We'll be moving out within the hour, Kit. And we will soon know if the Navajo spirits do indeed protect the sacred canyon."

Kit Carson busied himself for the next few hours seeing that the needs of his men were being attended to. Then he went about setting up his command tent, turning down several offers of assistance. It was a task he preferred to do for himself, and besides, preparing the troopers to attack from two entrances of the canyon had spread his forces so thin there was more than enough work to keep every man in camp busy.

At last, he placed the oil lamp on the folding table, then settled into his campaign chair, silently envious of Ted Henderson. Ted, at least, would have something to do on horseback for a couple of days, even though his mission was highly dangerous and his patrol could come under attack at any moment.

A call from outside the tent brought him to his feet. He stepped into the cloud-muted light of the afternoon and tried to hide his surprise.

Ten Navajo were approaching the camp, waving a tattered rag. Carson went out to meet them, shaking his head at a soldier who had unconsciously cocked a carbine.

Carson felt a shiver go up his spine as he raised an arm in greeting. The braves' cheeks were gaunt, their eyes sunken; their clothing hung loosely from once-muscular frames now withered from starvation.

"Welcome to the camp of Kit Carson," he said in fluent Navajo. "Braves displaying a flag of peace need have no fear. They will not be harmed."

A middle-aged Navajo, apparently the spokesman for the band, stepped forward.

"It is said among the Navajo that the soldiers come to kill all those who surrender or fight," the Indian said. "But in the canyon mouth below was one who seemed to be a chief of soldiers. He said to us, 'Any who go to Colonel Carson will be welcomed and warmed and fed.' If Navajo die here, they die. If they do not, they will die from want of food or from the bullets of the soldiers. Braves place their lives in the hands of Colonel Carson."

Carson nodded, feeling the first glow of hope brighten in his chest; Ted Henderson had wasted little time in sending back the first captives from the sacred canyon of the Navajo. "The soldier chief spoke the truth. Come; share the soldiers' meat. If braves are sick, soldiers' medicine men will make you well. Braves will have new blankets, and then are free to return to gather families and animals. If the soldiers come before the task is complete, braves will not be harmed if they do not resist. Within ten suns, be at Fort Defiance with women and old ones, animals and children.

"There is no need for death or suffering. After braves have

eaten and warmed themselves by the fires, they will be given food for their families. Do the young ones and the old suffer?"

"Their pain is great," the Navajo said. "There is pain in their bellies from want of food, and pain in their hearts that the spirits have forsaken the Navajo."

Kit Carson shook his head. "The spirits have not forsaken the Navajo but have chosen to lead them in this manner. Perhaps the Navajo's spirits, like the white man's, are tired of the many years of fighting between red man and white. Perhaps this is how they have chosen to end the bloodshed."

Carson signaled for a corporal and issued orders that the braves be escorted to the cooking fires, where they would be fed and their other needs would be attended to. He turned back to the Navajo spokesman. "When brave returns, he must tell others that the treatment he has received will be theirs as well. The white soldiers wish no harm to those who join with them."

The Indian nodded. "This will be done, and some will listen. Others will choose to fight. What is to become of them?"

In a firm voice, Kit Carson replied, "Those who resist, who choose the way of war, shall be killed. It is that simple." He stepped aside. "Now, if the brave will follow the soldier, he will lead the way to the cooking fires."

Kit Carson watched the small band retreat toward the smoke from the camp cooking pots, then found his gaze drawn back toward the direction of the canyon. Perhaps, he thought, the returning captives would be able to swing sentiment against those whose talk was of war, that starvation and tribal pressure might bring even the fiery Gallegos to the camp under a flag of peace.

A mile deep into the *Chinle*, the Cheyenne scout Yellow Crow suddenly lifted a hand, waving it in a half-circle. Ted Henderson caught the warning immediately, turned, and shouted to his patrol, "Skirmish line formation! Rifle volley first, then individual pistol fire! You know what to do!"

He wheeled his mount into the open stretch of meadow, slipped his carbine from its saddle boot and cocked the hammer, then loosened his greatcoat to expose the butt of the pistol at his side. He heard the growing volume of approaching hooves. He estimated the attacking Indian force at about forty—not bad odds for his seasoned Indian-fighters—and watched Yellow Crow knee his palomino into position. Despite the cold, Ted felt the nervous perspiration of impending battle dampen his palms.

The mounted Navajo rounded a bend, thundering toward the patrol. Ted dismounted, knelt on one knee to steady his rifle as he knew the others would be doing, and lifted the muzzle of the weapon. Whoops and yells sounded among the Navajo as the braves, sighting the blue-clad soldiers ahead, hammered knees into their thin ponies for more speed.

Ted chanced one last glance around. To his right the huge Albert Jonas, carbine held like a child's toy in massive hands, waited patiently. To his left, a scout leisurely wet his thumb, wiped the front sight of his rifle, and cocked the weapon. Ted shook his head in silent wonder; in the face of death, the veterans were as calm and workmanlike as stagecoach ticket sellers.

The charging Indians were less than sixty yards away when Ted lined the sights on the chest of one warrior and squeezed the trigger. The rifle bucked against his shoulder, billowing smoke, and the brave tumbled backward over the rump of his horse. The rolling volley of shots from the other members of the company came close upon his own. Seven Indians went down in the deadly blast that raked their ranks, and Ted vaulted into the saddle, holstered the carbine, and gripped his pistol. The rifle volley had slowed the Indian charge, and the line of scouts remounted and, with revolvers at the ready, spurred their own horses forward.

Ted, feeling an arrow whip by his ear, snapped a shot toward one brave and missed. But the Indian's horse went down as Ted heard the blast from Albert Jonas's pistol. A steady roar of gunshots poured into the Indian ranks, and the Navajo who survived the unexpected and accurate counterattack rode wildly through the skirmish line of scouts. Those who had time to check their mounts wheeled their horses and fled back toward the canyon depths.

Ted sensed rather than saw a horse bearing down from his left. He twisted in the saddle and parried a lance thrust with his left forearm. He felt the bite of steel against bone, but his arm had deflected the point, and at point-blank range Ted touched off the pistol in his right hand. The brave stayed in the saddle for three lunges of the frightened horse, then toppled into the snow.

Through eyes watering from the acrid gun smoke and the

sting of the lance cut on his arm, Ted watched the furious battle near its close. The Navajo, their ranks shattered by the patrol's calculated fire, scrambled for safety. A few simply put down their weapons and awaited whatever fate was to befall them.

At the far right edge of the meadow, Ted saw one Indian sprint on foot for the relative security of a jumble of rocks and scrub trees. Albert Jonas, seeing the Indian at about the same time, kneed his horse to begin the pursuit. The fleeing Indian suddenly straightened, spun around, and pitched forward as the sound of a big-bore rifle rattled the air. The downed brave now struggled to his feet and, grasping his side, lurched into the rocks and bushes. Ted thought the Indian looked vaguely familiar, but he spent no time wondering; that shot had come from above, on the rim of the canyon.

Some three hundred yards away, on the top of the sheer wall, Ted caught a glimpse of an Indian, rifle in hand, dashing between the rocks—a short Navajo with a ponderous belly that bounced as he ran. It was the treacherous Choshay, whom Ted had learned about from Yellow Crow and Kevin O'Reilly. Ted instinctively reached for his rifle but realized that the running Indian was out of effective range. He wondered why Choshay would shoot a fellow Navajo when he could just as easily have dropped a soldier from that range with a rifle, then dismissed the incident as he turned his full attention to the chore of mopping up in the aftermath of the battle.

The stinging sensation in his arm gave way to a growing fire of pain, and Ted felt the blood trickle down his fingertips. He stripped back the sleeve and examined the wound; it was a clean cut, not deep. The blade had glanced off the outer bone of his forearm, and Ted silently offered his thanks. Had the angle been slightly different, he could have suffered a broken bone—or had his arm severed between wrist and elbow. He stripped the kerchief from around his neck and bound the wound tightly to stop the bleeding.

Yellow Crow appeared at Ted's side.

"My brother is injured?"

"Not seriously," Ted said. "And you?"

"Spirits still work," the Cheyenne replied with the hint of a grin. "Navajo arrow make hole in shirt, but not touch skin."

"What is our situation, Yellow Crow?"

"One scout catch war ax alongside head, another stick leg in front of lance. Both live but not fight again soon."

"The Navajo?"

"Count twelve dead. Four captives, two with bullet holes."

"You saw the Indian reach the rocks with Jonas after him?"

Yellow Crow nodded and said soberly, "That one Gallegos."

Ted pursed his lips in a whistle. One of the two most dangerous Navajo rebels would in all likelihood be captured on the first day in the canyon! Now if only they could apprehend Choshay as well.

"I go help black soldier?"

Ted glanced in the direction Jonas had taken in pursuit of the Indian chief. He shook his head. "No. Albert can take care of himself. And we have some dead Navajo to bury, others to escort back to Colonel Carson as captives. You and a couple of the scouts take the prisoners back. See that their wounded are treated. I'll stay and oversee the burial and wait for Albert to return."

Albert Jonas approached the tangled thicket quietly, pistol cocked and ready, and felt a grudging admiration for the brave he had been tracking for three hours, moving ever deeper into the canyon. But the Indian had been seriously wounded and Jonas had trailed him easily, following a crimson splash here, a drop of red there. The man's courage and endurance bordered on the superhuman, Jonas thought to himself.

A shuffling sound close by brought Jonas's senses to full alert. He eased his way around a fallen log and found himself face to face with the wounded Indian. Less than ten feet separated them. The Indian clasped one hand to his side, attempting to stop the flow of blood, yet defiance blazed in the dark eyes and a knife rested in the fingers of the other hand. Jonas aligned the sights on the pistol, then slowly lowered the weapon; he could not bring himself to pull the trigger on a dying man, especially this one. Even weakened from blood loss, knowing death was near, the Indian maintained a stolid dignity.

Jonas holstered his revolver. "One who fight so brave," he said in broken Navajo, "should be free to die as he chooses. Black soldier is called Albert Jonas. He offers his hand to red brother during his final hours."

"Gallegos, chief of the Navajo," the wounded man said. His voice, though weak from pain and loss of blood, impressed

Jonas with its note of pride. "Gallegos asks only that the black soldier not take his scalp so that his soul will not walk forever in darkness, and that Gallegos's body not be taken from this sacred canyon."

Jonas nodded. "It shall be so. Put aside knife, brother, for the fight is ended. Black brother will do what he can to make Gallegos's final hours more comfortable."

Gallegos let the knife slip from weakened fingers.

"Fifty paces from here," Gallegos said, "there is a small cavern. It is in that spot, known only to Gallegos and his daughter, that Gallegos's bones must lie." The Navajo grimaced in pain, then looked up at Jonas, the eyes seeming to reflect a deep inner peace despite the agony of the torn body. "Help Gallegos there, black soldier. He will tell how to cover the entrance so that the final resting place of Gallegos not be disturbed. The spirit of Gallegos will then be free to forever roam his magic hills and the holy canyon."

Albert Jonas nodded. The chief coughed, and a trickle of blood flowed from the corner of his mouth. "One day when this has ended, and if black soldier can find her, tell Wind Flower that her father lies forever in the cougar's cave. Her mind will then be at rest."

Gallegos attempted to pull himself to his feet, but his strength was fading rapidly. Albert Jonas slipped an arm beneath the chief's shoulders and gently assisted the Navajo to stand. For a moment they stared into each other's eyes. "The spirits move in strange ways," Gallegos finally said. "Many soldiers and settlers have died at Gallegos's hands, yet the one who leads him to his long sleep is a soldier." The chief pointed out a dim trail leading along the canyon wall. He stumbled from time to time, leaning heavily against Jonas's body.

Gallegos died even before they reached the opening of the cave. Carefully, Jonas carried the Indian's body inside. The last of the weak light of evening was painting its flat gray wash over the sloping hillside as Albert Jonas heaved the final rock into place, covering the entrance to the small cavern Gallegos had called the cougar's cave. He stood for a moment, then said quietly, "Your wish will be respected, Gallegos. Only your daughter and a black soldier shall know of your final resting place. May the spirits be kind in the life beyond."

Albert Jonas squared his shoulders, turned, and in rapid strides made his way back in the direction of the meadow of the *Chinle* where his comrades in arms waited.

* * *

The bitter snap of the night air nipped at the heels of dawn as Kit Carson mounted his horse and glanced about the camp. Satisfied that the three squads and single surgeon left behind would be adequate to guard the more than a hundred Navajo now in camp, he kneed his horse toward the Canyon de Chelly, where his own main force and the patrol led by Ted Henderson awaited his arrival.

The horse chomped at the bit, eager to increase his pace, but Carson held him to a fast walk. Glancing toward the east, he noticed a distant break in the gloomy skies, a single ray of morning sun silvering the edge of the clouds.

At the edge of the canyon he pulled the horse to a sudden stop, momentarily stunned at the panorama which unfolded before him, the vastness of the gash in the earth below. Wide valleys embraced streams that glittered in their cover of ice. Sheer walls rose hundreds of feet from meadow to rim, broken here and there by the openings of side canyons. And to the east in the distance, he saw the broad valley which led to the entrance of *Cañón del Muerto*—the Canyon of the Dead.

To the mountain man sensitive to the glories of nature, the Canyon de Chelly was a thing of beauty, a master touch of the Creator's hand. But to the commander of an invading force, it was a formidable fortress. And, Kit Carson reminded himself, he did not know whether a few hundred or more than a thousand Navajo lay in ambush among the rocks and trees. He stroked the horse's neck, a signal of reassurance, and found himself wondering if the gesture was meant for the horse or for the rider.

"No wonder that they fight so hard against leaving this land," he said aloud; "it is worth fighting for. And if only the Navajo had kept their end of the many treaties, here they might yet remain." He sighed. "Well, they made their own bed. Now they must lie in it or leave it forever."

He kneed the horse down the narrow trail toward the canyon floor, where his troops waited. An hour past sunrise, he would raise a gloved hand, motion his soldiers forward, and at the Canyon of the Dead they would run yet another gauntlet.

Regardless of the outcome, he thought, there was no turning back. The invasion of the Canyon de Chelly was about to begin!

* * *

Sergeant Major Frank Armbrister and his mounted patrol, Bernie Christian at his right stirrup, led the advance of the infantry between the narrow walls of the Canyon of the Dead. He turned in the saddle, glancing toward the foot soldiers slogging behind, rifles held nervously at the ready. But at least the snow was not deep in the canyon itself and the footing was better.

Passing a field of still-standing corn, Armbrister waved a hand, and within moments smoke curled skyward as the soldiers torched the stalks. To his left, Kevin O'Reilly set his men to chopping away at the long-since harvested peach orchards, destroying trees descended through generations of Navajo cultivation.

Where they passed, fields were left in flames, abandoned hogans were torched, and bands of sheep were corralled by the advancing infantry. From time to time a shot would sound, to be answered by a blistering volley of small arms fire. But they had met no massive resistance, and that did not in the least reassure the wiry former Pony Express rider.

An exclamation from Bernie Christian snapped Frank Armbrister's head around. The little soldier pointed ahead. There, in an open area of the canyon, a half-dozen Navajo braves stood, watching the approach of the soldiers. Then, one by one, the Indians laid down bows, lances, and other weapons. Frank raised a hand as one trooper leveled his carbine.

"No shooting, men, unless we're fired upon ourselves! It's surrender we want, not dead Indians!"

The braves fell into step in the center of the advancing army without protest. From time to time Frank saw one of the Navajo take a long look at some part of the canyon which must have meant something special to him. But heads remained erect and proud.

In the distance, Frank saw smoke roll above the skyline as the column led by Carson and Henderson laid waste to the Navajo homes and crops at the western entrance. Idly, Frank Armbrister wondered if Carson was meeting as little resistance as was his own invading force.

Kit Carson morosely fed another peach tree limb into the small fire before his campaign field tent. He watched the end of the stick blacken, begin to glow, and then burst into flames. He found no consolation in its warmth. Becoming aware of a presence beside him, he turned to face Ted Henderson. The one-time scout had approached silently and now squatted on his heels beside the fire.

"Something troubling you, Kit?" The words were touched with genuine concern.

Carson sighed heavily. "From a military standpoint," he said, "I should be the happiest field commander in the army. So far, we've met only minor resistance in our invasion of the canyon, and there's been little loss of life. But I find myself in the role of a destroyer, a scourge, a pestilence riding through a beautiful canyon and turning it to ashes." He plucked the peach tree limb from the fire, holding it aloft. "Look at this, Ted. This tree has stood for scores of years. Its ancestors were brought by the Spanish fathers to the Hopi, the cousins of the Navajo, and I am burning it in my campfire. By what right do I do this? Four days we have been here, playing God." He tossed the limb back into the blaze.

"If there were a better way, Kit, I would be the first to abandon this duty," Ted replied. "I don't feel exactly comfortable with it myself. But then I remember the ambushed fuel patrols, the teamsters murdered, the civilians butchered by the Navajo. It doesn't justify my feelings exactly, but it makes the pain seem less."

Carson nodded. "I believe doing it this way is still the quickest and least bloody way to end the hostilities of a hundred fifty years. But at night, I don't dream of whooping savages torching wagons and killing defenseless settlers. I see Navajo children with bellies bloated from starvation, arms no bigger than my thumb. I see warriors so weak they can barely walk, yet holding heads erect in pride."

Carson sighed heavily. "This is a place of bad memories, Ted, for me at least. Now I just want to get it over with, move these people to the Bosque Redondo, and go home to my own wife and children who have never felt hunger or cold." Carson abruptly rose and strode into the darkness.

Ted watched the reluctant warrior move away, wishing there were something he could say to comfort Kit Carson. But Carson's dreams were too much like his own.

On a high ledge above the canyon floor, Wind Flower stood and watched as Navajo, singly and in families and in groups, filed onto the canyon floor from their hiding places, joining the white soldiers in surrender.

Five suns had gone since the first smoke from the Coming-Out Place, and in those five suns Wind Flower had felt a pain in her heart that cut deeper than the knife, burned more than the flame of the torch. She knew she was a witness to the end of a way of life. She felt the pain of grief for a defeated people but also the hope that one day they would return to rise from the ashes of a foolish war and again become comfortable and wealthy. The Navajo would, at least, survive.

She turned and entered the small cavern where the old man lay huddled in tattered, soiled blankets, his eyes hot with the fever.

"Grandfather?"

Tired eyes fluttered open. "Yes, Wind Flower?"

"Grandfather cries out in his sleep. Is he troubled?"

"No, child of my daughter. This time the night visions were good." The voice, though weak, seemed suddenly more happy, Wind Flower thought. "There were two visions," the old man continued. "First were the dreams of the old days, as a wind of the past rustling the leaves of the trees of the mind. When your grandmother and grandfather first met. When they walked by the waters of the stream in the valley and talked of the future. The pride they shared when the fine young chief Gallegos chose our daughter for his wife. The day of Wind Flower's birth in the springtime when the air smelled sweet from the wild flowers covering the canyon floor."

The old man paused and gestured feebly toward the cavern entrance. "The second vision was of the future, and in the canyon were the Navajo, once more nourished by the spirits, once more wealthy with many sheep and much corn, squash, and fruit."

"Then the Navajo shall return?"

"Yes, Wind Flower. The visions have been repeated from the sand paintings. But Grandfather will not be among those who return. He is in the time when the leaves fall from life on this world. Is there word of Gallegos?"

Wind Flower shook her head. "There have been rumors that he was taken prisoner by the soldiers. Other rumors say that he died in battle, yet his body has not been found. Wind Flower will continue to search for him. One day she will know the truth. Today she goes to the Valley of the Quail. He often went there in times of trouble to seek guidance from the gods."

A shudder wracked the old man's body, then was gone.

"What is it, Grandfather?"

"A chill wind. You must go, Wind Flower, but beware. An evil spirit is about."

Sergeant Major Frank Armbrister trudged alongside the big Irish lieutenant, leading his weary and limping horse and once more marveling at the endurance of the steady infantrymen. He had been walking for less than a day, but the muscles in his legs protested with each step.

Kevin suddenly raised a hand, bringing the three squads of soldiers and the handful of captive Navajo to a halt. Frank took the opportunity to lean his weight on his right boot, away from the blisters his high-heeled cavalry boots had made on his left foot.

"What is it, Lieutenant?"

"Something here doesn't seem to fit, Frank," O'Reilly said. "Look up ahead."

Through the widening neck of the canyon they followed, Frank Armbrister saw a half-dozen tired-looking Navajo braves standing in a broad meadow, a stack of bows and an occasional ancient musket piled in a heap before them.

"Just looks like another bunch of Navajo wanting to surrender," Frank said.

Kevin shook his head. "Something about the way they're standing—no pride about them, just a hang-dog look. It's not like a Navajo to bend his head before the soldiers. And there's many a rock cluster and piñon grove about." The lieutenant turned and spoke in Navajo to one of the captives, then translated for Frank Armbrister.

"This place is called the Valley of the Quail," Kevin said, "and the band up there is one our captured friend has not seen before. An Irishman develops an instinct for which tavern not to enter, my friend, and this has the feel of such." Kevin shrugged. "Irish instincts have been wrong before. Still, I think a squad should go ahead and check this one out."

The lieutenant called over his shoulder, "Mike, bring your squad along." He turned to Frank. "If anything does go wrong, Frank, you bring the rest to bail us out of trouble."

Frank watched as the eight men and the lieutenant cautiously approached the gathered band of braves. A glint of sunlight on metal from amid a clump of boulders caught Frank's attention and set the alarm to jangling in his brain.

"Kevin!" he shouted. "Watch out!"

His words were drowned in a sudden volley of big-bore

rifle fire from the boulders. He saw Kevin O'Reilly stagger, then fall to the ground. Then another soldier slumped with an arrow in his hip. Others scrambled for safety, but caught in the open, one after another went down. Mike Connor knelt by his friend, Kevin, firing his pistol at the rocks.

Frank vaulted into the saddle even as the echoes of the first shots rolled over the small plain. He yelled instructions to the soldiers behind and, hoping his crippled horse could hold up for another run or two, dug spurs into the animal's side. Frank felt the weakened muscles below give at each stride, but soon the game horse was at top speed, carrying the slender rider toward the cluster of rocks ahead. He felt rifle balls fly past his ears as the soldiers behind him laid down a covering fire, while the other troopers sent slugs into the piñon trees on the other side of the trapped soldiers.

Frank felt his horse stumble as a heavy rifle bullet plowed a furrow along his own shoulder. Revolver cocked and ready, Frank did not flinch at the pain of the tear in his muscles. He waited until the gelding had regained its feet, then burst through a ragged volley and into the ambush spot where the Navajo crouched.

Frank fired his revolver, and a brave slammed back against a boulder, a Spencer rifle sliding from his grip. Frank's second shot took down a second Indian, and he leveled his weapon toward a fat, ugly Navajo frantically trying to chamber another round in his rifle. At a range of six feet, Frank pulled the trigger—and nothing happened. The usually reliable army pistol had misfired, the result of a faulty bullet.

He slammed spurs into the horse again, the charge carrying him through the cluster of Indians, and felt the crackle of the air as rifle slugs sped past. He kneed his horse to the right, angling toward the safety of a cluster of rocks, and glanced back over his shoulder. The fat Indian lumbered from the boulders and, with dirt kicking over his feet, ran through a storm of bullets into the cover of a piñon grove. Other Navajo, their confidence shattered by the sudden charge of a lone soldier, broke and ran, only to be cut down by the devastatingly accurate rifle fire from the infantrymen a hundred yards distant.

Frank checked his mount in the piñon grove, letting the exhausted and trembling animal gasp for a moment's air as he reloaded his revolver. Calmly and with a calculating eye, Frank examined the terrain between himself and the spot

where the fat Indian had disappeared. From the descriptions
he had heard, Frank Armbrister knew the fat Navajo was the
treacherous Choshay.

"Okay, Choshay," Sergeant Major Frank Armbrister muttered aloud, "this is just between the two of us now."

With a full-throated Arapaho war cry, Frank Armbrister
dug spurs into the trembling gelding's flanks and kneed his
mount in a zigzag pattern toward the piñon trees. He saw the
belch of smoke from a rifle and snapped a wild shot in reply,
but at the same instant, he felt the slug take his horse in the
chest. The animal, dead on its feet, made three more strides
before it went down, giving Frank time to kick free of the
stirrups and roll into the tucked position which would keep
him from falling hard to the earth.

A slug kicked sand in his face as the forward roll began to
carry him to his feet, and for an instant he saw the flash of
brown flesh in the trees ahead. He snapped a shot and heard
the audible grunt over the ringing blast of his own handgun; he
was sure he had scored a hit. Then, a stride later, a heavy blow
caught him just below the belt; lifted from the ground, he
folded at the middle, then fell to the earth.

He raised his eyes and, through a growing red mist, saw a
fat Indian, side covered in blood, scrambling up the side of the
sheer canyon wall. Frank tried to raise his handgun but found
himself unable to lift the now anvil-heavy weapon. Then the
Indian was gone, and Frank heard the growing roar in his ears,
a rolling wall of noise like floodwaters nearing, ever louder.

Halfway up the wall of the canyon overlooking the Valley
of the Quail, Wind Flower buried her face in her hands,
shaking her head back and forth as though to deny what her
eyes had seen. Huddling deeper into the small cluster of
boulders, she fought back the cry of grief that pushed against
her throat.

Slowly, she raised her eyes once more. Through the film
of tears she could see at a distance the form of the soldier
named Kevin O'Reilly stretched in the meadow below, head
cradled in the arms of a trooper, unmoving. The sight was yet
another knife point slicing through her heart; she was over-
come with the memory of his face, his gentle eyes, the warmth
of his embrace. The agony of loss was not one of self-pity, for
that could not be in the daughter of a chief; it was grief for the
soldier himself, for the future that would never be. Suddenly

she became aware of the scuffing sound of footsteps approaching rapidly. She glanced toward the trail below and heard her own sharp intake of breath.

Laboring up the steep incline, nearing her place of concealment, was Choshay, broken teeth exposed in a grimace of pain and the effort of drawing air into heaving chest.

Wind Flower felt the surge of a new emotion, a combination of fear and hate, and her hand slipped to the knife at her thigh. For a moment, the urge to kill the man responsible for so many deaths was almost overpowering. But common sense told her she was no match for the strong, heavily armed warrior. She forced her slender body deeper into the boulders, knife gripped in a firm hand, cutting edge turned upward. If Choshay saw her, she thought, he would kill her on the spot— or worse, take her captive.

Wind Flower tried to calm the pounding of her heart. She vowed that if Choshay neared, she would take either his life or her own. His hands would never touch her body.

She watched as Choshay struggled nearer, noticed the splash of red along his side, then breathed a silent sigh of relief as the renegade brave suddenly changed direction and passed some thirty feet away from her hiding place, then vanished into a jumble of trees and rocks. She fought back the urge to call out to the soldiers below, to show them where Choshay had gone. But the battle in the Valley of the Quail had already broken the strength of Choshay's band. Perhaps the spirits would cause the wound in his side to slowly and painfully snuff the life from Choshay, that he might know the agony he had caused so many others.

Wind Flower returned the knife to its sheath. Then once again she lowered her head into her hands in silent and overwhelming grief.

Private Bernie Christian was not ashamed of the tears that streaked down his face. He knelt beside the body of the first true friend he had ever known, pounding his fist again and again into the ground in frustration. From the moment he had rolled Frank Armbrister onto his back, Bernie had known there was nothing he could do except place his own coat beneath Frank's head—and wait for the moment of death.

Bernie became aware of a touch on his arm, a weak squeeze from a hand that had held the reins of scores of horses and had led scores of men also. He lifted his eyes. Frank's face was gentle, a peaceful expression in the wounded man's eyes.

"Don't let it—get you down, Bernie," Frank said, his voice faltering. "Had to—happen sometime. Soldier's lot. Tell Ted I'm sorry—I won't be there to meet him—when the forces join up. . . ."

Bernie lifted Frank's callused hand in his own, rubbing it, trying to force some of his own life into his friend's failing body.

"Frank—don't die on me now. I need you more than I did when you stood up for me. The men need you."

"How many—casualties do we have?"

"Two dead, Frank. Three wounded. The lieutenant was hit but not bad. If you hadn't broken up that ambush, we'd have been wiped out to a man."

"Then it—was worth it. One life more makes a—three-for-twenty trade. A good day's work—for a soldier."

Bernie Christian had difficulty pushing the words through his tightened throat muscles: "The Indians will pay for this, Frank."

"Bernie—don't hate. No revenge. It won't help either of us—not all Navajo are bad. Just—follow the plan—keep after them, but don't kill unless you have to." Frank's voice was fading rapidly and Bernie had to lower his ear close to the lips to make out the words.

"Bury me—here, Bernie. It's a pretty place to lie forever." Frank's voice was laboring now, just to get the words out. "And Bernie—see after my horses, will you?"

"Frank—" Christian lowered his head as the last breath of life left the body of Sergeant Major Frank Armbrister.

Then Christian's grief, his fury and frustration broke loose. He scooped up Frank's fallen revolver and, ignoring the calls of other troopers sprinted toward the canyon wall where the ugly Indian had fled. Alternately running and crawling, he scrambled up the steep trail, pistol cocked and ready, trying to wipe the film from his eyes.

A form suddenly appeared on the trail before him, and Bernie swung the weapon into line, about to squeeze the trigger, when suddenly he realized the figure was that of a woman.

He lowered the revolver and stared into eyes that reflected his own grief. The woman stepped forward, saying something in a language Bernie did not understand. He tried to remember the sounds of her words, the inflection, and then she touched his arm gently, turned, and disappeared up the trail toward the canyon rim.

Exhausted, his hate and grief burned away for the moment, Bernie Christian turned and slowly made his way back down to the meadow in the Valley of the Quail.

Soldiers already were at work with shovels, preparing three graves. Bernie felt the sting of tears at the sight, fought them back, then turned and looked in the direction the woman had gone. There was something about her, he thought, something he couldn't explain. It was as if he had been talking with a princess. He wondered if he would ever see her again.

In the small cavern above the floor of Canyon de Chelly, Wind Flower filled a small pouch with a few more precious belongings, then turned to her grandfather.

"It is time to go, Grandfather, to join the others in the soldiers' camp. There is no other way. Wind Flower will help you."

A shadow suddenly fell across the cavern floor, and Wind Flower spun, grabbing at the knife against her thigh.

"Be not afraid, woman," a lithe, tall Indian said. "Yellow Crow of the Cheyenne tribe, blood brother to the subchief of Colonel Carson, will help. It is a painful day for the Navajo, and Yellow Crow shares your sadness. He would consider it an honor to escort the shaman and the woman to safety. Soldiers mean no harm."

Wind Flower, hearing the sincerity in the tone, turned to her grandfather.

"The shaman has heard of Yellow Crow," the faltering voice said. "His reputation as a warrior and scout are legend through many tribes. It is said that his words are true when he speaks. The granddaughter and old man would welcome his help, for the old man is weak and the granddaughter is not strong."

Yellow Crow stepped into the cavern, crossed to the old man, and offered a hand. The shaman gripped the Cheyenne's forearm and, with Yellow Crow's help, struggled to his feet. He looked around the cavern, rheumy eyes watering, and Yellow Crow suspected the drops were not all from the sickness in the thin body.

"It is time," the medicine man said. "The old one leaves the sacred canyon for the last time, yet it goes with him in his heart."

With Yellow Crow supporting the old man and the woman trailing a step behind, they made their way to the canyon floor. A family stopped to wait for them to catch up, and Yellow Crow yielded his place alongside the shaman to a young Navajo.

"Go in peace now, brothers of the sun and moon," the Cheyenne said. "And may the spirits ride upon your shoulders."

Wind Flower watched as the powerful but lean Cheyenne trotted away from the group, back toward the Coming-Out Place. Despite the heaviness in her heart, Wind Flower raised her head with pride; she was, she reminded herself, a Navajo woman.

Colonel Christopher Carson turned for one last look back at the sacred canyon of the Navajo, now reduced to blackened ruins. He watched the scattering of Indians making their way toward the campsite of the expedition, then turned to the officer at his side.

"Ted," he said, "I share your grief at the loss of Frank Armbrister. He was a good man, a fearless soldier. His actions saved many of his comrades. It was men like Frank Armbrister who kept the casualties on both sides to a minimum. Their lives cannot be restored, and history may overlook them. But those of us who were here will know, and we will remember."

Carson touched knees to his tired mount. "Let's leave this place of bad memories behind," he said. "In a few days, when the stragglers have come into our camp and surrendered, we will move back to Fort Defiance."

He turned in the saddle once more and stared for a long moment at the Navajo families making their way along the path toward camp. "But I'm afraid that the suffering isn't over yet. It's a long walk from Fort Defiance to the Bosque Redondo reservation."

They returned to the camp they had established at the outset of the campaign and dismounted. Ted fell into step with Kit as he wandered among the Indians already gathered here. Snow crunched beneath cavalry boots, and a bitter wind swirled flurries into the faces of soldier and captive alike.

Carson stepped from time to time to speak briefly with a Navajo. Finally he turned to Ted.

"By the latest count," Carson said, "we have more than two hundred Navajo here, and, of course, others are on their way. How are our supplies holding up?"

Ted shook his head. "We're short of everything, Kit, and most of these Navajo have nothing. Before we left the canyon, I sent Albert Jonas and Bernie Christian ahead with a squad to Fort Defiance for supplies, but we need food, blankets, and medicine for the Indians right now. All we have left is our soldiers' rations and a few broken-down horses and mules that could be butchered. We'll have to move out soon and hope to meet Albert and Bernie on the way back."

Carson nodded. "We must hang on for two more days somehow, or the stragglers coming in to surrender will be left to die for certain. I'm afraid we'll have to cut the troops' rations again."

Ted tugged his greatcoat tighter about his neck. "That will put the men on quarter-rations," he said, "but I've seen the way they look at these Indians. I don't think they'll mind."

Carson stomped his feet, trying to force some circulation back into near-frozen toes. "I'm going to check on the surgeons," he said. "When you fill out the reports, Ted, be sure to put the medical team in for commendation; no one has worked harder or longer or with less equipment, yet saved so many lives."

"I agree. There are good men in this group, but the medical team may be the best and most dedicated among us all."

"In two days, then, we pull back to Fort Defiance. By the time we get there, most of the Navajo, having learned of the routing of Gallegos's tribe, will have come in to surrender. Then Fort Defiance will have served its purpose. From there, it's only four hundred miles to the Bosque Redondo."

Ted caught the bitter irony in Carson's comment. "I wonder, Kit," he said, "how many of them can we keep alive?"

Kit Carson's frown was obvious even in the growing darkness of nightfall. "As many as we can. Coming along to visit the sick and wounded with me?"

"If you don't mind, Colonel, I'd like to prowl about among the Indians for a few minutes. How is Lieutenant O'Reilly?"

"In some pain, but fortunately he wasn't hit too hard. He will recover; he'll probably be back on his feet after a few days in the surgeon's wagon. But he won't be moving around very fast after that. A hip injury tends to slow a man down some. Takes away his enthusiasm for walking."

"I'll join you in your tent in a few minutes," Ted said, then watched the small figure slide away in the darkness.

Ted moved from one group of Navajo to another, trying to reassure them that all was well, offering blankets to those in need.

A tiny, bundled figure caught his eye; the sound of a child whimpering drew him to the small fire where a group of women huddled.

"Do not fear, mother," he said to the woman holding the child. "Soldier wishes only to check on the little one." Carefully, Ted unwrapped the tattered blanket covering the face of the dark-haired Indian baby. He winced at the sight of the small and almost fleshless limbs. The child—if he lived—would soon be of toddling age.

He stroked the baby's cheek. "Mother has a fine son," he said. "Soldier himself has one of about his age. Are you in need of food for the child?"

The woman, old for her years, shook her head. "The soldiers bring food."

"It is sad that the young ones, who have harmed no one, must suffer," Ted said. "Perhaps one day soldier's child and Indian mother's will hunt side by side." He replaced the worn blanket about the baby's face, shrugged out of his own greatcoat, and draped it about the shoulders of the mother, tucking it securely around the child.

Shivering in the bitter wind, the former Pony Express rider listened to the crunch of snow beneath his boots as he made his way back toward the command tent, wondering about his own child. How would he react to his father, a man he had never seen? They were not father and son, Ted reflected; they were strangers, and the thought of rejection by his own son brought more fear to Ted than facing a renegade Apache with a drawn bow. But he comforted himself with one thought: At least little William Ted Henderson was warm, healthy, and safe in the arms of a loving and wonderful mother.

Wilma Henderson snapped awake, unsure for a brief moment what had jolted her from a sound sleep, heart pounding. Then she heard the sound—a soft wheeze from the small form beside her on the bed. Instinctively she reached out, touched the baby's head—and jerked her hand away in surprise and alarm.

The child was burning with fever.

Wilma placed her fingertips gently on the small chest and felt the tiny muscles laboring for air. Fighting to maintain her self-control, she lowered an ear to the child's chest. She bit her lip in fear at the sound of the labored breathing, little more than the rustling of a fingernail across canvas. Without thinking, she gathered the child against her breast, feeling the heat of his fever even through her thick nightgown. The movement brought a whimper from little William Ted.

For a long moment, Wilma merely held the baby, rocking back and forth, trying to force her own runaway panic back into a measure of common sense. She glanced toward the window and noticed the pale gray of the early dawn. She must go to the post surgeon to get help. Yet even as the thought formed, Wilma found herself torn between the fear of leaving the child alone and carrying him into the cold morning air. After a brief hesitation, she carefully wrapped the baby in a down comforter, placed him on his side in the center of the bed, and, still clad only in her nightgown, dashed across the compound.

Blinking against the tears, she pounded on Vi Robinson's door. It swung open almost immediately.

"Wilma! What is it?"

"The baby's sick, Vi! Please, get the surgeon for me, quickly!"

Without awaiting a reply, Wilma ran back across the compound, slipped through her own doorway, and crossed quickly to the bed. The child still lay where she had left him, small chest pulsing in labored breaths. She stoked the fire against the chill in the room, then gathered the baby to her as she slipped a pan of water onto the coals of the fireplace. She had to bring the fever down somehow, she realized, swallowing hard against the lump in her throat. It seemed an eternity before the water in the pan warmed slightly, yet Wilma knew only a few minutes had passed. She dampened a clean cloth with the slightly warm water, then bathed the baby's forehead and neck.

The door swung open, and Vi, Judy, and the post surgeon, unshaven and rumpled, crossed quickly to mother and child.

Dr. Mason opened his bag, placed it on the table near the bed, then reached for the baby. Reluctantly, Wilma handed the child over. She felt Vi's arm around her shoulders, Judy's hand on her forearm, offering silent reassurance and hope as the physician carefully examined the baby.

"Has he been showing any signs of troubled breathing before this morning?" The surgeon's voice was calm and controlled, but Wilma could see the concern in the light gray eyes.

Wilma shook her head. "He was fine last night, happy and laughing." Her voice cracked, and she made a determined effort to regain control of her emotions.

"Any coughing, runny nose?"

Wilma shook her head. Dr. Mason lifted the damp rag from her hand, carefully bathed the small body from head to toe, wrapped the baby in his comforter, and cradled it in his arms.

"What is it, Dr. Mason? What's wrong?" The tone of Judy's voice betrayed her deep concern.

"I don't know, to tell you the truth." The surgeon sighed lightly, rocking the infant. "Sudden fever and chest congestion could be caused by any number of things—a spider bite, a sickness that suddenly strikes. We can set broken bones and patch bullet holes, but there is so much we don't know yet." The gray eyes drifted from Wilma back to the child. "You hang on, little William Ted. I delivered you, and we'll see you through this." He handed the child back to Wilma.

"What you were doing is the best thing at the moment," the surgeon said. "Frequent baths in tepid water may help control the fever. I have some drops that will help him rest. The more he sleeps, the better." Dr. Mason reached in his bag for the bottle of drops, then squaring his shoulders, he turned to face the three women.

"I'll be perfectly frank. It's very serious. These sudden high fevers in infants may last a short time, or . . ." He left the remainder of the thought unspoken. "Only time will tell, Wilma. Keep him warm and close to you; a mother's touch can do wonders for a sick baby. Bathe the child with a wet cloth every half hour. In the meantime, I'm going to check out some relatively unused sources for help."

Wilma felt Dr. Mason's reassuring touch on her arm. "Worry as much as you want, Wilma. The next twenty-four hours are going to be critical."

Kit Carson shifted his weight in the saddle and glanced down the long line of Navajo captives and tired soldiers trudging through the snow toward Fort Defiance. He could almost feel the effort in his own muscles as he watched men, red and white, and women carrying babies, forcing legs shaky with fatigue to take first one step, then another. He kneed his horse in Ted's direction.

Ted rode to meet his commanding officer, noting the deep worry lines in the former mountain man's face.

"We're running out of time," Carson said. "We've still got twenty miles to go before we reach Fort Defiance, and we don't have enough food to keep a woodchuck alive. We can't feed the Indians, and a forced night march would kill them just as surely. We're lost if Jonas and Christian don't show up soon with supplies."

"I'm well aware of that," Ted replied. "I'd trade my commission and half my private horse herd for them to arrive right now. But let's keep the faith in Sergeant Jonas for a few more hours, then get down to some serious worrying."

The distant crack of a rifle brought both men erect in the saddle. Ted lifted his field glass to his eyes and peered hard at the horizon. A line of tiny dark shapes snapped into sharp relief, moving in the direction of the Navajo expedition.

"Jonas and Christian," he said. "Even from this distance I can make out those two, Kit. But I don't see any wagons. Looks like a half-dozen soldiers under heavy packs." Without waiting for a reply, Ted spurred his horse toward the distant men, his concern growing as he neared the squad.

As Sergeant Albert Jonas waved a hand in greeting, Ted noted the heavy field packs across each man's shoulders, save one whose arm was in a sling.

"What happened, Albert?"

"About five miles out of Fort Defiance, we got jumped. Managed to fight them off. Three of 'em won't bother anybody now, but they shot both the team horses."

"Indians?"

Jonas shook his head. "White men. Just plain bandits, near as I could tell. We packed up what we could carry and came on. Thought you might be gettin' a little on the hungry side by now."

Ted nodded. The amount of supplies the men carried may not amount to much, he thought, but it could mean the difference between life or death. He noticed the pack strap cutting into Bernie Christian's palm, frozen blood darkening the fabric. The little ex-Confederate carried almost as heavy a load as the big black sergeant. Ted leaned down, and with Albert Jonas's help, managed to transfer the pack from Christian's back to the pommel of his saddle.

"Thanks, Colonel Henderson. I'd about tuckered out."

"You men rest if you can. I'll see if we can't find some people to take over for you. We'll find a couple of horses and go get the wagon; we need the rest of the supplies desperately. If they're still there."

"They will be, Colonel," Albert Jonas said. "We hid that wagon so good it'd take a fine black-and-tan houn' dog with a hot nose to find her. Bernie and me'll lead you back to it. Somethin' we need to talk about on the way." Jonas held out a hand. In his palm rested two silver medallions, each engraved with the cotton-boll symbol. "Bernie took one of these off a dead Navajo from that bunch that jumped Frank in the canyon. I got this one from one of the bandits back there. Got lucky and took him alive, though he was pretty badly wounded. He still managed to say quite a lot before he died. Colonel Henderson, I think he gave me enough names, dates, and places to knock a big hole in this bunch that's been dealin' guns and whiskey to the Indians."

To Ted, this was very good news. If they could smash the Confederate organization once and for all, there would be a much greater likelihood of peace in the West. Indeed, if the Confederates had been stopped before this, the war with the Navajo might never have come to pass. As it was, there were still braves like Choshay receiving guns and supplies; and Ted just hoped that the information Jonas had learned could lead the Third Cavalry to the Confederates' next base of operations.

Ted reached out and clasped Jonas's shoulder. "Sergeant Jonas," he said, "if you knew how badly I want to stop those responsible, you'd appreciate the enormity of the service you've just rendered the people of the West. You just stay alive until I get back with some help."

Ted checked the urge to spur his exhausted mount; the rail-thin horse already had done more than his share, and he need not pay the cost of the fury, the frustration, and the anxiety of the man on his back.

Kit Carson instinctively checked his horse and nearly cried out as he viewed the scene from the top of the bluff overlooking Fort Defiance. Jonas had said there were a lot of Navajo, but Carson was not prepared for the shock. At first glance it looked as if the fort area was overflowing. There must be over a thousand Indians down there, he thought. And in the distance, he could see specks against the snow, moving toward the fort.

Carson raised a hand and waved the ragged band of prisoners and soldiers forward through the narrow pass below. "I remember telling General Carleton it was cheaper to feed them than to fight them," he said aloud to himself, "but how on God's green earth are we going to find supplies enough for that herd—and how am I going to keep them alive all the way to the Bosque Redondo?"

After they arrived at the fort, Kit returned to the office he had occupied earlier and watched as the Indians continued to stream into the compound. By nightfall, literally hundreds of campfires had been lit, and they reflected a strange red-yellow light against the low-lying pall of smoke that seemed to constantly fill the shallow valley surrounding the fort.

Carson shook his head in disbelief and turned to his second-in-command, who had just joined him in his office. "Ted," he said, "I expected this campaign to bring the Navajo to their knees. But never in my wildest dreams did I expect such a wholesale surrender. There are almost three thousand Indians here now."

"And more will arrive every day," Ted added. "As usual, we are short of food, blankets, medicines, and almost anything else you can think of."

Ted walked to the window, stood for a long moment to look over the panorama outside. "When the Navajo began to realize we were not killing captives and when the enormity of the problem of survival became clear, they had no real choice," he said. "The Navajo are, for the most part, a proud but realistic people. Like you, I must admit I am stunned at the sheer numbers that have come to the fort. I had no idea this country could support such a population."

"And we can't," Carson said. "We must begin moving the Navajo to the Bosque Redondo. Ted, I want your Third Cavalry Regiment—and such others as you may choose—mounted. Act as scouts and hunters as well as provide protection to the captives and the remainder of the soldiers." Carson sighed. "It won't be an easy job, and much of it will leave a bitter taste in your mouth. We're going to lose some Navajo to cold, illness, and exhaustion. And raiding parties will be tempted by a lightly guarded column of potential slaves. We must cover ten to twelve miles a day in order for our supplies to last through the trip. Normally that distance would be no problem for an Indian. But these aren't normal situations, Ted."

"Have all the tribal chiefs been informed?"

Carson nodded. "They will have their people as ready as can be expected. They already have given the trip a name. The Navajo are calling it the Long Walk."

Wilma paced the floor in nervous frustration, pausing from time to time to glance out the open window toward the hastily constructed Arapaho tipi in the center of the parade ground. Steam drifted from the opening at the top, and every few minutes a trooper would approach to hand a pail of water through the heavy elk skin, which served as a door.

Wilma heard the low, indistinct chants of the aged medicine man, and frequent puffs of smoke told her the old one had added another handful of herbs to the heated stones inside. Her nostrils still held the traces of the pungent aroma in the dense fog of steam inside the hogan. The medicine man had been there for almost twelve hours now. Vi and Judy had joined Wilma inside the hogan, taking turns holding the feverish baby, and it was Judy who was there now, spelling the other women.

There were those on the post, Wilma knew, who thought she and Dr. Mason had taken leave of their senses, placing a seriously ill infant in the care of an old and wrinkled Indian. But she remembered the doctor's comment when he had returned after his first visit to suggest another remedy to cure the feverish infant. The doctor had said, "The white man's medicine is of no help, but the Arapaho shaman's knowledge goes beyond magic—I have spent hours with him learning of the curative powers of native plants. We must place little William Ted in his hands."

The irony of the situation was notable, Wilma thought. An ancient Indian called on his gods as the white women prayed to their own, and a highly trained surgeon turned to what his colleagues called superstition, all in the effort to try and save one small life. That the old Indian had agreed to make the long ride from his own tribe to Fort Laramie was little short of a miracle in itself. Wilma knew that regardless of the outcome, she would feel forever in debt to the ancient one who answered a cry of desperation.

The tipi flap suddenly opened, and Wilma saw Judy, her wavy hair now falling straight under the weight of the steam and her dress plastered against her sweat-drenched body, step into the cold, clear air.

"You had better come in here quickly," Judy called, as Wilma opened the door of her house. "I think little William Ted is hungry!"

Tears of elation and gratitude flowed down Wilma's cheeks as she dashed out of the house to the tipi, flipped the elk skin aside, and stepped through the swirling steam to the small, lustily crying bundle in the brittle brown arms of the old Indian. The medicine man was peering intently into the baby's eyes.

The Arapaho glanced up. "The fever is gone now," he said. "The child breathes well. He will be weak for a few days, then will live a long and healthy life. You must feed him." He handed the baby to Wilma. Noticing the exhaustion in the wrinkled face, she took the child and cuddled him to her breast.

"Wilma's heart is filled with gratitude for the life of her child," she said in fluent Arapaho. "Anything the shaman wishes is his, and it will not be enough."

A gnarled hand waved from side to side. "Shaman wants nothing," the medicine man said. "It is enough that the little one lives, that the spirits smiled upon him. One day he will become a great man, perhaps a chief among his people. It is enough."

Wilma placed a hand on the withered forearm, making no attempt to check the flow of tears down her cheeks. "The young one will often hear of how the Arapaho shaman saved his life," she said. "He will remember, as will his mother. Now the shaman must rest and eat. The Henderson home is yours, now and at any time in the future."

The old man shook his head. "Shaman will rest for a few hours, then return to his people." He waved a hand about the tipi. "It must be burned, for the evil spirit from the little one's body now lives in the walls and will return if not destroyed."

"It will be done. There is no way to repay the debt except in friendship."

The wrinkled face suddenly parted in a gap-toothed smile. "The spirits walk in strange ways," the old Indian said. "The white man and the red combine their medicine and their prayers; an Arapaho attends to the sickness of the godson of his tribe's enemy, the Cheyenne, and also the son of the chief of scouts who has sent many of the shaman's tribe to the world beyond. And it matters not, for a child is saved."

X

The Long Walk had begun. Fort Defiance was once again abandoned as soldiers and Indians, horses and wagons, left the fort and headed for the distant Bosque Redondo reservation.

Lieutenant Kevin O'Reilly grimaced with the sudden jolt of pain as the hospital wagon's rear wheel jounced over a rock concealed beneath the snow. In one way, he welcomed the pain, for it was a reminder that he was lucky to be alive and fortunate that the campaign had a talented surgeon along. The .56 caliber slug they had dug from his hip would leave him with a slight limp for the rest of his days, but the wound was healing well.

And in only a few sunrises, O'Reilly told himself, he would be able once again to move about. And he would try to find, among thousands of blanket-wrapped Indians strung out over miles of icy, windswept terrain, one beautiful Navajo woman.

Kevin was aware of the odds, even if she were still alive, of finding her amidst that sea of humanity. But he felt no lack of confidence; a man who could find Wind Flower in the vast Canyon de Chelly could locate her once more. And as he made his way through the captives, he would leave word that he wished to speak with her again on urgent business. He would not tell them the urgent business was an affair of the heart.

Less than a hundred yards away, Wind Flower felt her spirits sink. In the center of the column of captives, she tried to support her aged grandfather with one arm and hold a baby firm against her hip with the other.

With each step in the snow and the bitter wind, Wind Flower felt the strength drain from her grandfather's weakened body. Her own muscles cried out in the pain of fatigue and cold, even though the passage of the soldiers and captives in front had packed the snow and left the walking easier. It was, she told herself, only the second day of the march, the Long Walk, and many more such days lay ahead. For the moment she was satisfied just to be able to place one foot before the other. She had given up her place in one of the wagons to an ancient grandmother. In such a difficult time, the young should defer to the old that more of the total number might live.

She did not regret her decision.

She felt the tears come to her eyes as the old man at her side began to chant softly. The words, though barely whispered, were his death chant.

"Grandfather," she said, her voice soft, "why does the most powerful of the medicine chiefs of the Navajo chant the last song?" She fell silent, knowing he had heard and would answer when the chant paving the way to the Other Side was complete.

At length, the old man fell silent for a moment, then turned his head toward Wind Flower. Through the exhaustion in the bloodshot eyes, Wind Flower could see a calm acceptance, the warmth of peace, reflected in the depths.

"Grandfather has seen his final sunrise in this world, child," the medicine man said. "His soul is at peace with the spirits. It was the final vision in the sand painting—the body of an old man lying in the snow. Then the old man's spirit rose from the body it no longer needed and took wing as a bird in the air, and the bird was warm and happy and found delight in its freedom." The old man stumbled, but righted himself with Wind Flower's aid.

"His life has been rich, Wind Flower, and full. While most of the Navajo fear death, he does not. Soon the bird shall soar in the breeze of the time when the land turns green. It is time he went to join the others who have fallen during this walk." Gently, the old man lifted his granddaughter's hand from its supporting position about his waist, holding it for a long moment.

"Grandfather—"

"Hush, child. Do not grieve for the old one, but remember—if a man's vision remains in the eyes of those left behind, his spirit dwells forever untroubled."

Wind Flower swallowed the painful lump in her throat. "Grandfather shall always be remembered."

"It is good. He leaves you with these words: Beware of the ugly one called Choshay, for the visions tell Grandfather the ugly one yet lives and plans to do you harm. The visions also say your tall soldier lives; perhaps with him you will one day find your peace." With that, the old one drew away with dignity and, without looking back, threaded his way through the crowd toward the fresh new snow outside the trail.

Wind Flower followed at a respectful distance, making no effort to conceal the tears that now trickled down her cheeks.

Some twenty paces from the edge of the main body of Navajo, she watched her grandfather sink to his knees in the snow.

"Farewell, Grandfather," Wind Flower said, her voice broken by quiet sobs. "May the sun shine forever upon your spirit."

Then she turned away and drifted to the center of the column once again, where the child would be partially protected from the bitter wind by the bodies around them. The column would not stop for funerals, not even for the death of a medicine man of great power and vision. There was no time to spare.

"How many have we lost so far, Ted?" Kit Carson's voice reflected his concern.

"Since we left the fort two days ago, about thirty Navajo have died," Ted replied. "To date, the losses have been the very old, the wounded, and the weak. In our own ranks, we have lost one trooper whose horse slipped on a snow-covered rock and crushed him; three others have been placed on the medical wagons suffering from exhaustion, frostbite, or both.

"And in the meantime, about a hundred more Navajo have joined the column. I've asked the chiefs to supply their best hunters to augment our own hunting parties, but I fear we will find no game until we reach the Rio Grande valley—"

The snow-muffled sound of approaching hoofbeats cut Carson's statement short. The two officers turned to see a trooper swaying in the saddle, trying to spur more speed from his tired mount. Ted and Kit mounted as soon as they saw the horseman and rode to meet him. Ted reached out, caught the bridle, and pulled the trooper's horse to a stop, then noticed the smear of blood on the young man's shoulder.

"What happened, Private?" Even as he asked the question Carson, still on horseback, began stripping away layers of clothing to examine the soldier's wound.

"Navajo, sir—jumped us—left rear of column. Rode in—all bundled up in blankets—ugly, fat one raised hand. We thought they wanted to surrender. Had rifles under blankets—caught us by surprise. Killed three soldiers, stole two women—"

"Which way did they go, trooper?" Ted noticed the sharp, tightly controlled anger in his voice.

"Northwest, Colonel—I'll show you—"

"You'll do nothing of the sort, soldier," Carson said. "Colonel Henderson is an expert tracker, and you're going straight to the surgeon's wagon. That shoulder doesn't look good." He watched as Ted, already spurring his horse in the direction of the attack, yelled for Yellow Crow. The Cheyenne seemed to materialize from nowhere, and before the two riders passed from view, a third joined them. Even at that distance, Kit Carson could identify the massive bulk of Albert Jonas, riding at Henderson's stirrup. Carson fought back the urge to follow; he and Ted had agreed that both of them would not ride into potential danger except when necessary. There were competent officers available, but continuity of command was a necessity under such harsh conditions.

He placed an arm about the wounded trooper's waist and turned the horses toward the surgeon's wagon a hundred yards distant. "Don't worry, young man," Carson said. "With those three on the trail, the Navajo raiders will taste of the cup of justice."

But the next afternoon, a grim-faced Ted Henderson, accompanied by Yellow Crow, Albert Jonas, and two sad-eyed Navajo women, rode back into the column. Though Ted had learned valuable information from Jonas about the Confederates' whereabouts—information that he had already sent by messenger to Abel Hubbard—the fact remained that Choshay's well-supplied raiding party had been able to wreak havoc with the column.

Kit Carson kneed his horse in the direction of the approaching riders. "What did you find, Ted?"

"There were six of them." Carson wondered at the barely contained fury in Henderson's voice. "The two women," Ted said, "were mothers of young babies. The raiders killed the babies—just smashed their heads with rifle butts and tossed them aside. Then they stopped to play with the women.

"We caught up with them just before nightfall. One got away. It was Choshay. Two of the Navajo were killed in the gunfire. I personally executed the two who tried to surrender—I could find no reason for mercy toward baby-killers. How is the trooper who was shot?"

"With some help from the Almighty, he will make it. He lost a lot of blood. If the surgeons can keep him alive until we reach Santa Fe, he has a good chance. Were any of you three hurt?"

Ted shook his head. "Not in the physical sense, but my God, those babies . . ." Ted slid from his exhausted horse and helped one of the young women down from her perch in front of the saddle. "Young mother will be returned to her people," he said, speaking quietly in the Navajo tongue. "White soldiers grieve for the little ones."

The two officers watched as Yellow Crow assisted the other Navajo woman from Albert Jonas's saddle, then led the pair toward the main body of captives in an attempt to locate their families.

Finally, Ted turned to Carson. "Kit, I'm beginning to let it get to me. We need three times as many men to protect these people—even from their own. And still they don't complain. They just plod along through the snow and the sickness, accepting their fate. I just wonder if my strength can match theirs!"

The next day they neared Fort Wingate, and Carson, Ted, and a small squad of men left the main column to go to the fort to resupply. As they rode, they passed scores of Navajo, waiting stoically to join their tribesmen in the Long Walk.

"It is beginning to look as if our supply depot here is giving us as many more mouths to feed as it is bread to put in them," Carson said as he and Ted entered the gates of the fort. He turned to the quartermaster sergeant at his side. "Sergeant, gather all the supplies and wagons you can lay hand on, leaving just enough for the garrison here to maintain itself. The officer in charge of stores here knows our situation and his own. Work with him. But anything he doesn't need for subsistence, take it unless it's nailed down or red-hot."

"Yes, Colonel." The sergeant moved off toward a nearby cluster of wagons and buildings. Carson and Ted continued toward the camp commander's quarters. "Guess it's time we catch up on some correspondence and find out what General Carleton plans to do with Emery Church."

They entered the office of the commander of Fort Wingate, a captain whom Carleton had assigned to take over when Kit Carson left to begin the campaign in the Navajo country. The captain handed Carson a large packet of papers sent from General Carleton, and then waited to receive further orders from the colonel and his second-in-command.

Carson handed the packet to Ted with a wan smile, and in minutes Ted found the letter they sought. He scanned it briefly and felt the muscles in his jaw twitch. He read it aloud to Carson.

"*Colonel Carson: It appears that in the matter of Major Emery Church, based upon your reports of his activities in the Navajo campaign, I may have made an error in judgment as to his capabilities and intentions. There are insufficient grounds, however, for convening a court-martial board, as his actions were directed against an enemy in a time of open warfare. Nevertheless, I am enclosing herewith orders for Major Church, instructing him to report to me in Santa Fe for reassignment in a noncombat post at Fort Riley in Kansas Territory.*"

Ted snorted in disgust. "That still puts him too close to the Indians to suit me," he said, "but I guess it will have to do."

Carson turned to the captain standing at the door. "Is Major Church still confined to quarters?"

"Yes, sir, as per your orders."

"Please have him brought here at once."

After a few moments the door swung open, and Major Church, eyes flashing, stepped into the room. He did not salute nor stand at attention.

"Your new orders, Church," Carson said, handing the thin-faced officer a packet. Ted saw the close-set brows furrow as Church read the document.

Hatred glittered in the major's eyes as he stared at Ted Henderson.

"Damn you, Henderson," Church said, voice dripping venom, "you and your Indian-lover friend! You haven't heard the last of Emery Church!"

Ted stepped forward, unaware he had clenched his right hand into a fist. He glared into the hate-filled eyes. "Major, the fact that we are both in uniform is the only thing that stopped

me from beating you senseless before. Don't count on your
luck holding."

Carson sensed the growing tension in the air. As much as
he wanted to turn Ted loose on Church, he could not afford to
lose the services of his second-in-command.

"Captain," he said to the officer who had assumed
command of Fort Wingate, "please prepare an escort detail of
three men to take Major Church to General Carleton in Santa
Fe. Once there, his arms may be returned to him. I would
appreciate it if the detail could be in the saddle within the
hour."

"Yes, sir. Major Church, if you would come with me,
please."

"Henderson," Church said, his voice tight with fury, "the
next time I see you, it will be over the sights of a gun."

Ted calmly returned the glare. "In that case, Church, I'll
be watching my back—because I don't think you have the guts
to try me face to face."

"Henderson, you're a dead man."

"We'll see about that. I've stomped vermin before."

Ted watched, trying to control the grinding fury in his
stomach, as the major spun on a heel and stalked from the
office.

Kit Carson sighed. "I'm not sure you have seen the last of
that one, Ted. I would watch my back, if I were in your boots."

Ted let the tension out in a rush. "I'll be ready when he is,
Kit. But in the meantime, there are the Navajo to worry
about."

The bitter winds of March gave way to the gentler days of
April, and Lieutenant Keven O'Reilly felt his strength growing
by the day. Two weeks into the new month, he eased himself
over the tailgate of the hospital wagon and, clutching the
rough-hewn walking stick Mike Connor had made for him,
took his first hesitant steps since the battle in the Valley of the
Quail. His hip still hurt, but it was tolerable, he decided, and
the need in his heart was greater than the protests of torn flesh
mending itself.

He blinked in the unaccustomed brightness of the
afternoon sun, feeling the muscles in his eyes strain to readjust
themselves from the dim interior of the canvas-shaded wagon.
His breath caught in his throat as his vision slowly cleared. For
mile upon mile, a broad sea of Indian bodies threaded along

the trail. And somewhere among those thousands, he must find Wind Flower.

Kevin glanced at the thunderclouds building up in the west and knew that by nightfall a spring storm would be pelting down, adding to the misery of red man and white alike.

But in the meantime, he could begin his search. He would not accept in his mind the possibility that she might be dead, and the odds of finding her did not deter his resolve. The Irish, he thought, may have a reputation for a quick temper—but they also had a streak of stubbornness as wide as a wagon track.

Kevin limped toward the nearest group of Navajo, realizing that a blind search would produce only disappointment. When you wanted to find someone in a crowd, you went to the doctors and the gossips. He knew he would have little trouble finding the medicine men, and an Irishman's instincts inevitably led him to the town gossips—for better or for worse.

He stopped a wizened, toothless old woman. "I search for Wind Flower, daughter of Gallegos," he said. "Do you know of her?"

The old woman shook her head.

"Would you ask your friends? Tell them the tall soldier wishes to speak with Wind Flower?"

"I will speak of this. Perhaps someone will know." A half-smile added another score of wrinkles to the old woman's face. "From the look in your eyes," she said, "I hope you find her, soldier."

Judy Hubbard leaned back against the pillow, luxuriating in the warmth that still spread throughout her body. Gradually, her breathing returned to normal. She reached out, stroked Abel's chest, and felt his hand resting lightly and comfortably on her leg. For the past few weeks, even though her reunion with Abel had been a joyous one, Judy had been unable to make love to him. Finally, tonight, something happened within her. She knew she would be able to give herself freely to her husband from now on.

"Thank you, Abel," she said, her voice still husky with passion, "for being so patient and gentle and understanding."

"You are worth waiting for, Judy," he said. "We both knew it was only a matter of time until you were able to break through that last barrier."

"But," she replied, "a lesser man would have simply given

up long ago. I am so fortunate to have you, Abel. Because of you, I can cope now with my foolishness and its consequences."

"What you did, Judy, you did for love of me. I hope you see that now."

"I will feel guilty for the rest of my days, Abel, but now I believe I can live with it. And I don't think the nightmares will return, or at least not as often."

She felt his fingers trace the scar shaped like a cotton boll on the inside of her thigh. Although Abel seemed not to be bothered by it, she wondered if she would ever get over her distress about having the mark there.

"Judy, I must go away again for a few days, perhaps as long as three weeks." He felt an involuntary twitch in her fingers, and then her hand relaxed once more.

"I can cope with that, Abel—now."

"What we hope to do won't remove this scar from your leg," Abel said, "or the scars from your mind. But we have a chance to crush this cotton-boll ring, or at least set them back for a long, long time. I received a letter from Ted. During the Navajo campaign, they were fortunate enough to capture one of Colin Dibley's lieutenants. From him they obtained names, dates, and meeting places where the Confederate sympathizers trade whiskey and guns to the Indians. One of the biggest shipments yet should be nearing the exchange point in a valley along the Belle Fourche River near the Black Hills. My scouts already have confirmed the movement of the supply train toward the meeting place."

Abel paused for a moment. "Tomorrow, I will lead a force of every available soldier in Fort Laramie toward that valley. If our timing is right, we will destroy the supply train and capture most of the remaining trouble-making Indians in the process. At the same time, Union spies and intelligence agents will arrange the sudden disappearance of a banker in New Orleans, a secret manufacturing plant in Boston will blow up, and two frigates will be sunk in the Gulf of Mexico. Soon the back of Colin Dibley's organization should be broken."

He felt a reassuring squeeze on his forearm. "Just promise me one thing, Abel."

"What might that be?"

"Stay out of the way of any stray bullets." She reached across, grasped his shoulder, and pulled him to her. "I've just found you again, Abel, and I'll not let you go until our grandchildren have grandchildren!"

Kit Carson slowly looked around the circle of medicine men and tribal chiefs of the Navajo, letting his eyes rest for a moment on the face of each. Mud squished beneath his boots as he shifted his weight.

"Leaders of the Navajo," he said, raising his voice that all might hear above the distant rumble of rushing water, "it is time once more to call upon the courage of the mighty nation that fears no man. The halfway point of the Long Walk has been reached, and it is here that the spirits have chosen to test our strength."

An aged medicine man leaped to his feet. "Does Colonel Carson mean the wide water called the Rio Grande?"

Carson nodded.

"Too much water flows down the Rio Grande sea," the medicine man said. "It is impossible to cross. The Navajo do not swim. They will not go."

Mutters of agreement swept around the council. Carson raised his hand.

"Brothers," he said, "listen—there is no choice. Across the river are needed supplies, food, blankets. It is unfortunate that so much rain falls this greening season, that so much snow melts, that the river swells as a sheep at lambing time. If the people stay here, they will starve. Cross and they will live. The Navajo have been tested by fire and have survived. The Navajo have undergone the test of the ice and have survived. The Navajo have mastered the earth and brought forth fine crops and many sheep.

"Perhaps," Carson continued, "crossing the big water will be the last test of a proud race. White Commander has sent his best people to the river to search for the easiest crossing place. The women and children and old ones will be carried across in our wagons."

"And the others?"

"They must make the crossing as best they can."

"Many will die."

"If they do not cross," Carson answered, his voice firm, "they will die. The soldiers will assist the Navajo in all possible ways. Now, go and prepare the Navajo. The crossing will begin when the sun rises."

As the Indians grudgingly left the meeting place, Kit

Carson muttered to himself, "And may the gods of both red man and white ride with us."

He turned at the sound of approaching hoofbeats. Ted Henderson and Yellow Crow checked their horses and dismounted. Ted shook his head.

"It's worse than we feared, Kit," the grim-faced Ted said. "We found only one place where this many people and wagons might cross. And it's still very dangerous."

Yellow Crow nodded his agreement. "Not good. We lose many Navajo, I think."

"Any chance the water level will drop over the next couple of days?"

"No, Kit. In fact, it will get worse than it is now. Thunderstorms are building over the mountain watersheds, and the snow runoff hasn't yet reached its peak. Like it or not, we must go now."

The next morning, Colonel Carson rode his big gray gelding to the edge of the red, swirling, muddy waters of the Rio Grande. He studied the place where Ted and Yellow Crow had suggested they should cross. Dread grew in Carson's belly. Even his riverwise horse, born and bred in the wild herds that roamed the Canadian River country, snorted nervously and seemed reluctant to set foot in the eddying floodwaters at the ford.

Here the river was wide, so the currents would not be as strong as in the narrow passages, yet Carson knew it would be deep enough to drown a horse. Stumps and driftwood rushed past in the red waters, some large enough to knock a hole in a wagon, and many of sufficient size to hurl a man from his feet into the raging waters a hundred yards downstream.

Carson suppressed an inward shudder. He had crossed the Rio Grande many times, but never had the river seemed this angry. He listened to the rush of floodwaters, then turned to listen to the commotion behind him as the troopers prepared the Navajo for the crossing as best they could. He stared for a long moment into the wide brown eyes of braves who would calmly and without fear ride outnumbered into the very heart of an enemy camp. Now, sheer terror danced in their eyes. Kit Carson understood. Fear of nature was much more difficult to handle than fear of other men.

Ted and Yellow Crow rode up alongside him and sat looking for a time at the turbulent waters. Behind them the booming voice of Sergeant Albert Jonas shouted commands as the troopers formed up the column for the first passage. Carson noted that Ted and the Cheyenne rode their best high-water horses, strong, long-legged animals not prone to panic when a hoof struck quicksand or slid in the mud. Carson wished he had about four thousand such horses; then each captive could ride.

"How is the footing, Ted?"

"Could be better, Kit, but it's reasonably firm, and I don't believe we will hit any deep holes or quicksand. But you know as well as I how fast a river can change in flood stage."

Albert Jonas, on foot, stopped at Carson's stirrup.

"First crossing party ready, Colonel," the burly black man said, whatever fear he himself felt well concealed.

Reluctantly, Carson raised a hand, waved the column forward, and spurred his own gelding into the water. Ted and Yellow Crow followed suit. Each man held a braided Mexican lariat at shoulder height, keeping it free of the water for the moment. Carson took the point, letting the skittish army mules follow the path set by his own horse, while Yellow Crow angled off a few yards downstream and Ted took the upstream flank.

Carson felt the push of the current against the gray's strong legs as the water steadily rose. He felt it spill into his boot tops, then creep up to the skirts of his saddle. The riverwise gray suddenly stopped, angled to one side a bit, and a half-submerged log spun by beneath the bit. Then the animal seemed to become more sure of its footing. Carson felt the waters recede, and finally his mount was on dry ground again. The big horse shook itself, flinging off excess water and jarring Carson's teeth. The ex-frontiersman fought back a quick surge of anger at the horse, then turned the animal back toward the river.

The sight chilled him more than the wind against his wet clothing. Panicky army mules lunged against traces, working against each other. Wagons drifted dangerously sideways, threatening to swamp. First one, then another sheep tumbled downstream, as they struggled in vain to swim, and Carson felt his heart sink as a brown arm tenaciously clung to one sheep until both sank from view beneath the red waters.

As they crossed from one bank to the other, Navajo desperately hung on to ropes that had been stretched from one bank to the other, as well as to the tailgates of wagons, the manes and tails of troopers' horses, anything that might help them in the passage. Carson watched as a chunk of driftwood knocked one Indian down. The brave surfaced briefly, flailing, only a few feet from Carson. Shouting in Navajo to grab and hold on, Kit tossed his lariat to the Indian, felt the rope become taut—and then go slack as the panicked brave released his grip on the lifeline.

Kit spurred his horse back into the center of the maelstrom a few yards downstream from the crossing, frantically trying to grab one of the tumbling bodies. He felt something bump into his horse, reached down, and grabbed a slender arm. A Navajo who was scarcely more than a teenager was hoisted to safety on the gray's strong back. Another Indian managed to grab a stirrup. Carson leaned down, grasped the wrist firmly, and spurred his horse toward the far shore. He deposited the half-drowned pair on solid ground and plunged his horse back into the river.

Some twenty yards away, he saw a teamster suddenly stand, pulling at the reins in an attempt to bring a four-horse hitch back under control. The wagon lurched as a wheel jounced over a submerged rock, tossing the driver into the waters. Completely out of control now, the lunging team turned upstream. The current caught the rear of the wagon, and the vehicle slowly began to topple. Carson bit his lip in frustration; from such a distance there was nothing he could do.

From the corner of his eye, Yellow Crow had seen the driver fall from the wagon barely a dozen feet away. Instinctively, he kneed his horse toward the wagon. When the horse was within a yard of the lunging team, Yellow Crow leaped from the animal's back onto the wagon seat, scooped up the reins—and realized he was too late to help as the wagon began to tilt dangerously. Still, he pulled at the reins, and to his surprise, he felt the wagon stop its slide toward destruction. He glanced around and saw a soaked tunic, split beneath bulging black muscles. His feet braced against a boulder, Albert Jonas had grabbed the side of the wagon and, against the powerful force of the sweeping current, was managing to hold his own. Then the wagon began to stabilize as Yellow Crow regained control of the team, got the horses settled and working in unison, and both men felt a surge of relief as the wagon wheels found firm ground once more.

Safely on the bank, Yellow Crow set the brake, tied the reins, and sprinted around the side of the wagon. Jonas was leaning against the wagon, shoulders heaving as he gasped for air.

At Yellow Crow's touch, Jonas looked up and smiled through his exhaustion. "For a minute there," he said, gasping, "I thought maybe we were in trouble. Now let's see if anybody's hurt inside."

Jonas peered in over the tailgate at more than a dozen pair of frightened eyes. "It's all right now," he said. "You are all safe and on solid ground." Despite the shadows cast by the canvas over the wagon, Jonas found his eyes drawn to a far corner, where a young woman grasped two children to her. She was, he thought, the most beautiful girl he had ever seen. But the thought was interrupted by a string of expletives that did rather admirable justice, Jonas thought, to the English language. He turned and watched as a soaked teamster, reddish-brown water squishing from his boot tops, approached the wagon. The teamster clambered aboard, kicked the brake loose as he unwrapped the reins, and slapped them with authority on the horses' rumps. "Damn jarhead, no-account, buzzard-baits—I'll show you a thing or two. . . ." The voice trailed off as the team drew away toward the gathering place a hundred yards from river's edge.

By late afternoon, the crossing was accomplished. The Indians and soldiers set up their camps to rest and dry out, and an exhausted Kit Carson sat on a campaign stool, eyes downcast, as the smoke from hundreds of fires cast a pall over the river encampment.

"How many did we lose, Ted?" Carson did not look up when he asked the question.

"There is no way to be sure; possibly a hundred Navajo, mostly men, and maybe four hundred sheep and goats. What are your plans now, Kit?"

Carson sighed. "Camp here for a few days and replenish our supplies as best we can. Let the Navajo warm themselves and dry their possessions, grieve for their dead. Then we will push on to the Bosque Redondo." Carson removed his hat and ran his fingers through the graying blond hair. "Ted, I am going to do a selfish thing. I am going to Taos—to Josefa."

Ted half smiled. "I don't blame you one bit, Kit. If we were at all close to Fort Laramie, you can bet I would already be saddled up and headed for Wilma."

* * *

General James Carleton tugged at his muttonchop whiskers and stared across the mahogany desk at the trim, crisply dressed woman.

"Josefa Carson," the general said with a sigh, "you can be more stubborn than any Apache war chief I've ever met." There was admiration in his words, though he was trying his best to be stern. "Here I am, begging, asking, demanding, and pleading with the army and the government to furnish supplies for seven thousand or more Indians who soon will be at the Bosque Redondo. I'm having to send troops into Navajo country again, this time to keep the settlers and raiders in line. And you talk to me of a school?"

The general's bluster brought only a slight smile from the woman. "It would be the smallest and best investment you could make, General," Josefa said.

Carleton snorted. "Do you honestly believe the people in this territory would tolerate sending Indians—enemies for hundreds of years—to schools? Do you think they will buy books, pay teachers, build a schoolhouse? Josefa, with all due respect, I don't think you truly understand the political climate here."

"The school would not be for Indian children only, but for Mexicans, whites, even adults who are unable to read and write," Josefa said, her voice firm. "And, General, which would you rather have? Comfortable politics and an illiterate, restless population, or positive contributions from educated natives of the area? We must not lose their rich culture, their knowledge of the land. And we cannot force them into our way of life. But we can bring them new choices and trust to the innate decency of the human spirit."

Carleton sighed. "I find no flaws with your argument, Josefa. But the national budget is sorely strained with the war and the Indian troubles. Money is impossible to come by in sufficient quantity to meet all our needs. No—it's simply impossible."

Josefa leaned forward, placed her elbows on the edge of Carleton's desk, and cupped her chin in her hands. "Is it possible, General, that you depend too much on the Great White Father in Washington? Kit and I will donate two acres of land for the school and an adjacent garden plot, where students may learn cultivation of plants along with their numbers. The women of Santa Fe and Taos have raised the money to equip the school and employ two teachers, qualified and fluent in several languages, including the Indian dialects of this region. As far as the building is concerned, I have received a grant of two thousand dollars from the territorial governor—"

"Begging your pardon for interrupting, Josefa, but how on God's green earth did you squeeze money from that miser?"

Josefa's smile was conspiratorial. "Let us just say that I am aware of certain—uh—indiscretions regarding personal use of government funds, and the editor of *The New Mexican* is a friend of mine."

"Josefa, that is blackmail."

Josefa shook her head. "I see it as restitution. The money is coming from his own pocket."

Carleton barely suppressed a smile. "I apologize for my earlier remark about your grasp of politics. But if you already have this school lined up, why come to me?"

"Because, General Carleton, the backing of the military and your personal support of this project will sway many who might not otherwise participate with either their time or their money."

Carleton leaned back in his overstuffed chair, made a steeple of his fingers, and looked at the ceiling. "I suppose," he said, "that you are going to tap my own pocketbook while you are here?"

Josefa's laugh was musical. "The thought has crossed my mind, General."

Carleton finally allowed his own smile to break through. "Very well, Josefa. You will have my letter of endorsement and my contribution by tomorrow afternoon." He rose as Josefa stood.

"Thank you very much, General Carleton. Perhaps someday I can repay the favor."

"You owe me nothing, Josefa. In fact, your hospital has more than indebted our government to you."

Josefa shrugged. "One does what one must. I will show myself out, General Carleton."

Riding back to Taos the next day, Josefa Carson was delighted with the outcome of her meeting with General Carleton. But her delight quickly turned to astonishment and joy when she arrived at her house. There, already waiting for her, was Kit, who had bypassed Santa Fe and rushed home to be with her. He had arrived only hours before she did.

They embraced and kissed longingly. Josefa explained that she had been absent in Santa Fe seeing about the school, and

Carson chuckled aloud. "Remind me, woman, never to get in a poker game with you," he said. "I have a feeling you would go in with the deck stacked."

They fell silent for a moment, savoring each other's presence. After a time, Kit spoke. "I must return to the column, Josefa. My men are struggling. I leave tomorrow."

Her sigh was quiet. "I know, Kit. It would not be like you to leave unfinished a job you had started."

"This time, Josefa, I'll not be gone long. The next time I ride home, it will be to stay. I've had enough of fighting and cold and heat and bugs, and not enough of you and the children."

She pulled him to her and placed a finger on his lips. "Hush about that," she whispered. "I will make dinner, and you can take a long bath. Afterwards, there is something else you must do before you leave. . . ."

The smoke, dense and acrid, lay heavily on the battlefield in the valley of the Belle Fourche, obscuring most of the scene from Abel Hubbard's eyes. The fight had been brief, barely a quarter hour in duration, but intense. Abel turned to the lieutenant at his side.

"Casualty figures, Lieutenant?"

"We lost two men, sir. Seven others wounded, one seriously."

"And the traders?"

"Thirty-four dead, Colonel. Twenty-six of them Indian, mostly Arapaho. Eight freight wagons destroyed, some two hundred Spencer rifles either burned or captured. We took one hundred and six prisoners, and all but about a half-dozen of them are Indians, sir."

Abel pushed his hat back and wiped a dusty sleeve across his brow. "The Confederate leaders of the trading ring—did we get them?"

"Two captured sir, all ready for the hangman. Two others were killed. I think it safe to say, sir, that we dealt a heavy blow to Indians and Confederates alike today."

Abel nodded. "The settlers should sleep better tonight," he said. "Line up the prisoners and rope them in columns of twos. What we cannot carry in the nature of weapons and supplies, put to the torch. And, Lieutenant, please convey my compliments to our gunnery officer. That was some of the finest cannon work I have ever seen."

The lieutenant snapped a brisk salute. "Yes, sir."

A sudden gust of wind swept the smoke from a portion of the valley, and Abel Hubbard felt nauseous at the sight of the carnage below. Bodies littered the battlefield, and wagons still blazed. An occasional crackle of exploding small arms ammunition punctuated the roar of flames and the cries of the wounded. He turned from the scene, balancing the destruction below against the havoc raised by the cotton-boll consortium and its gunrunners—and against a brand seared upon a white thigh.

Abel felt no surge of elation for the battle won, only a quiet satisfaction that some atrocities had been avenged. The gunrunners may not have been dealt a mortal blow here today, he thought, but at least they had been handed a temporary setback. The expedition from Fort Laramie had bought some time—and time, on the frontier, meant lives.

Ted Henderson squared his shoulders, ignored the southwest wind which kicked fine grains of sand into his face, and looked about the cluster of Navajo medicine men and tribal chiefs.

"Brothers have asked for a meeting. Talk now of what troubles the Navajo."

A young, barrel-chested subchief stepped forward and waved a hand in a sweeping gesture. "The Navajo," he said, "do not like this land of no trees, of the strange grass, of the bushes that move and tumble with the wind spirits. There is not enough to eat, not enough water to drink. The people weaken and die. It is a time of darkness for the Navajo. They have been forced to leave their homes and their gods, to walk through snow, to drown in rivers, and now to breathe the sand in this land of no mountains. Many of the young braves grow restless and angry. The Long Walk started in peace, but it may not end so."

Ted raised a hand as a mutter of assent rippled through the Indian ranks.

"The soldiers know of the suffering of the Navajo. Do not they eat of the same slim rations, feel their own tongues swell with thirst? And is it not true that the Navajo are a brave and strong people? Are the Navajo going to give up when they are but ten suns from their new home, where there is water and crops to be planted?"

He paused for a moment, then fixed his eyes on the

barrel-chested one's face. "Send the restless and angry young warriors here," he said. "Those who wish will be equipped with guns. The soldiers trust their brothers enough to have no fear that the weapons will be turned against the soldiers. Perhaps the brothers' anger may be turned to the good of the tribe, as hunters."

"Would white soldiers place weapons in the hands of those who have come to hate the white man?"

"Yes," Ted replied. "It is true that in the past, promises have been broken by both the Navajo and by the white man. But soldiers no longer fear their Navajo brothers. They will listen to the wisdom of their leaders who counsel patience. Carry this message to those who are discontent: Soon the Long Walk will end, and the Navajo nation will begin its rebirth."

An elderly man wearing the raiment of a medicine chief rose slowly from his cross-legged position on the wind-whipped sand. He turned to face the other members of his tribe.

"What the white chief of soldiers says is true. Let no Navajo hand be raised in anger. All have seen the soldiers' wagons throughout the night, bringing such water as can be found while the Navajo rest. The Navajo have come this far. They can last another ten suns." The shaman, his joints twisted by arthritis, turned and made his way back toward his tribal group. One by one, others followed. The last to leave was the barrel-chested one. When he had gone, Ted Henderson finally allowed himself a relieved sigh. The gathering, he thought, could have spelled a lot of trouble had not the aged medicine man taken control.

At the same time this meeting was taking place, Kevin O'Reilly was trudging alongside the outer edge of the column of weary Navajo, trying to forget the pain in his hip, scanning the sea of Indian faces in hopes of spotting the one for whom he searched. Day upon day of searching, questioning, and coming away empty had not dampened his resolve. He had found out from one old Indian squaw that Wind Flower still lived, and for the moment, that knowledge fanned his fire of hope.

A dozen feet away, a young Navajo boy drifted from the edge of the crowd. Suddenly Kevin heard a flat, dry buzzing sound and opened his mouth to shout a warning, but the child's cry came with the strike of the rattler. Kevin saw the snake dangling from the calf of the child's leg, fangs imbedded in the flesh. The boy stood, frozen in terror, staring down at the wriggling reptile.

Instantly, Kevin broke into a shambling run as the snake fell away. He raised his walking stick high, slammed it down on the reptile's head, then reached for the child.

"Fear not, small one," he said, easing the wide-eyed boy to a sitting position. He whipped the kerchief from his neck and tied it tightly below the knee and above the twin holes oozing blood on the boy's calf. "It is time to be a brave warrior now," he said, drawing his knife. "Sometimes it is necessary to make a small hurt to avoid a much bigger one." The razor-sharp edge of the knife traced a half-inch-long cut across the two fang marks. Kevin heard the boy's sharp intake of breath, but the youngster did not cry out. Two more quick strokes of the knife left bleeding crisscross tracks over the puncture wounds. As the blood flowed freely, Kevin placed his mouth over the cuts, sucked the blood and venom from the wound, then spat the mixture into the dirt. He repeated the procedure a number of times before finally straightening from his kneeling position.

He placed his large hand on the boy's shoulder and smiled into the frightened brown eyes. "What a strong young brave!" he said. "The leg will be swollen and sore, and it may have the sensation of fire. Possibly there will be sickness, but the young brave will live."

Only then did Kevin become aware of the crowd of Indians at the scene. A young woman dropped to her knees and held the boy's head to her breast. Kevin rose, went to the dead reptile, and sliced off the tail. He handed it to the pale child, whose small, trembling fingers closed around the rattlers.

"Keep them always as medicine," Kevin said. He uncorked his canteen, offered the boy a few swallows, then rinsed his own mouth and spat the water into the dust. He turned to the young woman.

"You are his mother?"

The Indian nodded.

"He must not walk for a few days, and he should have all the water he wants. But it is probable he will live, Mother. He is a strong young boy. Perhaps the Navajo medicine man should look in upon him from time to time, and the white medicine man will do the same."

An elderly woman knelt beside the woman and child,

whispered softly for a moment, then looked at Kevin. The big Irishman could see the gratitude in her eyes.

"The white soldier gives the gift of life," the old woman said. "The Navajo has nothing to give in return."

Kevin pulled himself erect, the pain in his hip flaring anew. "The white soldier wishes nothing but for the boy to be well."

Then, deciding he had nothing to lose, Kevin said, "Perhaps there is a way Grandmother might help. Is the maiden named Wind Flower, daughter of Gallegos, known to Grandmother?" To his amazement, the old woman nodded. Kevin felt his heart skip a beat. "The white soldier would speak with her."

"Tonight when the moon rises," the old woman said, "come to the big wagon the color of grass where the sick ones go."

Near the center of the column of captives, an ugly, potbellied Indian attempted to copy the shuffling, exhausted gait of those around him. From time to time he glanced up, keeping in sight the small frame of the woman a few yards ahead. By the time the column stopped for the night, he would know where the daughter of the hated Gallegos slept. And then he would fulfill the blood oath; he would take the woman first—and then kill her.

Choshay had recovered from the wound he received in the Canyon de Chelly, and had continued to lead his braves on raids against soldiers and Indians. But the blue-coated ones had proved to be too much for his band. His warriors either had been killed or had left to join the march to the reservation, and Choshay was on his own.

The fat Navajo heard his belly growl but made no effort to reach into the dried venison-laden pouch beneath his shirt. Though he felt thirst, he did not drink but took comfort in the nearly full, sheep-stomach water pouch in his bedroll. There would be plenty of time to eat and drink once the sun went down. He glanced around with contempt at the stumbling soldiers scattered about the column. To slip by them and join the band had been no more difficult than snapping a rabbit's neck.

He stared for a moment at the slender, black-haired figure ahead. He felt again the surge of lust against the sea of hate in his breast. Perhaps, Choshay told himself, he would never be a chief of the Navajo now. But this woman, along with her father, whose bones now fed the creatures of the night, had conspired against him and humiliated him, and soon she would feel the vengeance of Choshay.

That night, at the conclusion of the day's long march, Wind Flower lay in her blankets on the hard ground, trying to sleep. Not far away, other Indians were also wrapped in their blankets, already sleeping, exhausted from their exertions. The camp was deathly quiet, and finally Wind Flower herself dozed.

The touch of cold steel against the base of her throat jarred Wild Flower from a fitful sleep. She lay still for a moment, confused, until she felt the skin split at the point of the knife. She choked back a cry—there, silhouetted against the soft moonlight, was the familiar, potbellied figure of Choshay! His face was close enough that she could smell his rancid breath, coming now in excited gasps as a rough hand shoved her skirt aside. She knew she could not reach the knife strapped to the inside of her thigh.

Wind Flower remembered her vow even as the raw terror surged through her body—this man would never take her. The terror gave way to a calm, almost peaceful resolution as she prepared to thrust her head forward and cut her own throat on the knife held by Choshay—

A sudden cry and the flare of a torch cut through Wind Flower's silent preparation for death. Choshay sprang to his feet, knife at the ready, and Wind Flower heard her own involuntary gasp of surprise. There, illuminated by the flickering flames of the torch, a tall soldier leaned upon a makeshift cane, flanked by an old woman.

Choshay lunged toward the soldier, who seemed to be standing immobile in surprise. Instinctively, Wind Flower swung her left foot out and hooked her instep against Choshay's ankle. The ugly one staggered at the unexpected blow, swiped downward with the knife, and Wind Flower felt the icy track of the blade along the side of her calf. Choshay, his face twisted in fury, turned back toward Wind Flower and raised the knife high for the thrust that would end her life. From the edge of her vision, she saw something dark and heavy in the tall soldier's hand.

A streak of fire seemed to touch Choshay's back as the flat blast of the big pistol hammered against her ears. Choshay suddenly stiffened, reaching toward his back with his free hand. Kevin thumbed the hammer again, squeezed, and saw the blocky body jerk. His third shot sent the lifeless form of Choshay tumbling into the dust.

Then Kevin was at her side, holding her tenderly in his arms. "Wind Flower—are you all right?"

"Yes, Kevin." She pronounced his name Key-van. "I am fine now. I was—afraid you had been—killed in the Valley of the Quail."

"You won't be rid of me so easily, my beautiful Wind Flower—" Kevin's voice stopped in midsentence; he was staring at a dark stain on his hand. His eyes drifted down her body and saw the blood on her leg.

"You've been cut!"

"It is nothing, Kevin." But before she could protest further, he had scooped up her small form and began pushing his way through the growing crowd toward the hospital wagon.

The throng of excited, jabbering Navajo, awakened and drawn to the scene by the sound of the shots, respectfully cleared a path for Kevin and Wind Flower. Those nearest the pair fell silent, gazing with open curiosity as the big, limping soldier gently carried the daughter of their chief in strong arms.

Kevin sensed a presence alongside, and Albert Jonas fell into step at his side.

"The girl—is she badly hurt?"

"No, Sergeant," Kevin replied, "but she does have a nasty cut on one leg. Is the surgeon about?"

Jonas grunted. "That one never sleeps. Do you need some help? I mean, with your hip and all—"

"Thank you, Sergeant, but no. This is one bundle that is mine alone to carry."

Jonas leaned forward and peered at the girl's face in the weak moonlight. "The woman in the wagon," he muttered.

"I don't know about any wagon," Kevin said, "but this is Wind Flower, daughter of Gallegos. Wind Flower, meet Sergeant Albert Jonas."

Wind Flower nodded her head slowly in Jonas's direction. "It is nice to know the name of the dark man who saved Wind Flower and her people from the red waters."

They were within a few strides of the surgeon's wagon when Jonas reached out and placed a gentle hand on Wind Flower's arm. "I have a message from your father," he said. "Gallegos's last words were for you. He asked me to tell you that his spirit still walks the canyon, that his bones rest forever in the cougar's cave."

In the growing light from the surgeon's lantern, Jonas saw the quick flash of pain in the woman's eyes. "He did not die at the white man's hand," Jonas said. "The ugly Indian lying dead in the dust back there was the one who shot him."

"Thank you for telling me of this," Wind Flower said. "I had sensed my father was dead; he would have so chosen rather than leave his beloved mountains. Perhaps one day I shall return to visit his resting place and speak with his spirit." Wind Flower winced as Kevin lifted her up to the waiting arms of the physician.

Albert Jonas touched the brim of his hat in tribute to the woman, then withdrew, convinced that this was neither the time nor the place for a crowd.

Kevin held Wind Flower's hand as the surgeon worked on the cut. From time to time he felt the slender fingers twitch involuntarily in pain, but she smiled throughout the ordeal.

"Wind Flower," Kevin said, "I know this may be an awkward time and place, but it will have to do." He sighed, gathering his courage. "Wind Flower has captured my heart. I ask her to be my wife."

For a long moment she did not speak, and Kevin geared himself for the worst. The pain in her eyes, he sensed, was not from the gash along her leg. Finally, she spoke.

"Kevin, the time is not yet right. As the daughter of the chief of the Navajo, I must do what I can to help my people through these troubled times. And what would your people and my own say to the marriage of a white man and an Indian woman? We would find ourselves outcasts."

"Hang what people think!" Kevin snorted. "It's not approval I want! I want you!"

"We must be patient, Kevin," Wind Flower said with a shy smile. "Perhaps by the time you have gained the army's permission to marry an Indian"—she cut off his protest with a wave of a hand—"the Navajo should be well settled in their new home. Then, if you would ask again?"

The Irishman sighed heavily, his disappointment obvious. "As you wish, Wind Flower. I have waited this long. I can wait many more moons, as long as there is hope I will hear the right answer."

And in Wind Flower's eyes, Kevin O'Reilly found all the hope he needed.

* * *

On a low ridge overlooking the shallow waters of the Pecos River, Ted Henderson and Yellow Crow rested their horses and watched as the first of the Navajo column entered the confines of the barren and wind-swept Bosque Redondo reservation, a scattering of hastily erected buildings known as Fort Sumner clustered a half-mile from the eastern bank of the lazy stream. Nearby a meadowlark broke into song, its five-note melody a strange counterpoint to the whisper of sand stirred by winds.

At length, Ted sighed. "So the Long Walk has come to an end," he said. "Almost three months of suffering, hunger, exhaustion, cold, heat, and rain. Yellow Crow, we are watching the end of a historic journey—but I wonder, are we also witnessing the end of a proud people?"

"It may be so, my brother," Yellow Crow said. "The Navajo are a strong and determined people. One day they may return to their sacred canyon and their mountain gods. But the old ways will be gone. And who is to say what makes a people? Does the simple act of staying alive, even at the price of one's heritage of centuries, make a people?"

"These are questions I cannot answer, Yellow Crow. And contemplating them only makes me very sad."

The approach of a small figure on horseback interrupted the conversation. Kit Carson, returning from Fort Sumner, checked his horse, kneed the animal about, and joined Ted and Yellow Crow in watching the procession of Indians and soldiers into the reservation.

After some time, the former mountain man turned to Ted and his Cheyenne blood brother. He studied their faces for a long moment, then nodded. "I know how you feel," he said. "God, if there only had been any other way, if there only had been a little more trust and understanding on both sides. . . ." Carson let the sentence trail away, took off his hat, and wiped the perspiration from his forehead with a sleeve.

"Ted," he said, "your job here is done, and your people have done it well. The Third Cavalry Regiment is free to return home."

"Kit, what of your future now that the campaign is over?"

A slight smile lifted the blond mustache. "I am considering an offer to become the Indian agent for this area," he said. "It is a job I have done before, one with many challenges and a few rewards. And it would keep me close to Taos and Josefa."

"You take job," Yellow Crow said, surprising Ted. "You best man to watch after Indians."

Kit Carson touched his fingers to his hat brim. "Yellow Crow, that may be the highest compliment I have ever been paid. Now if you will excuse me, gentlemen, I have much work to do." The man who helped map the West turned his horse back toward the fort, then hesitated. He called back to Ted. "One of your men, a Lieutenant Kevin O'Reilly, has asked to stay behind at the fort." Ted saw the twinkle in Kit Carson's eye. "I think it has something to do with a young Navajo woman. I told him I didn't think you would mind."

"Not at all, Colonel Carson," Ted said. "I hate to lose a good man except for a solid reason. And from what I've seen of Wind Flower, she is reason enough."

They watched as Kit Carson rode back toward the fort. Ted turned to face his Cheyenne brother. "Yellow Crow seems troubled."

The Cheyenne nodded solemnly. "Last night I have a vision that Yellow Crow and Ted Henderson have but few rides left together. One day our trails shall part, and I fear that day come soon. Yet we shall remain brothers, even should the white man come to take the hunting grounds of the Cheyenne."

Ted fell silent for a moment. Finally he reached out and grasped the Cheyenne's forearm. "I, too, have had the same vision," he said. "Let us put such matters from our minds now, brother. For we have at least one more long ride at each other's stirrup.

"Far to the northwest," Ted said, "there is a woman who has been from my reach too long. There is a son I have never seen—your godson, Yellow Crow."

Ted waved toward the fort below. "We have been away from Fort Laramie and our own sacred mountains for too many suns. And our duty here is done, even though it leaves a foul taste in the mouth like bad whiskey."

"We have paid a price, brother," Yellow Crow said, his voice barely a whisper. "Many prices remain to be paid. But we face future when future comes. For now, we ride home together."

* * *

For the dozenth time, Wilma Henderson carefully unfolded Ted's last letter, read it slowly, and savored each word, especially the simple phrase, "The Third Cavalry is coming home." She refolded the paper, returned it to an apron pocket, and walked to the window. She stood for a long time gazing toward the pass in the southeastern hills, where the Third would first appear.

"Watching won't make them move any faster, Wilma," a voice beside her said.

"I know, Vi. Lord only knows where they are. I'm anxious—and in a way, I'm frightened." She let her eyes drift to the corner of the compound where little William Ted and the Arapaho girl called Ellen played outside. "I don't know if Ted has changed or if I have changed. But most of all, I'm worried about how little William Ted will react to seeing his father for the first time."

She felt a comforting hand on her arm. "I wouldn't worry too much about it, Wilma," Vi said. "These things have a way of working out."

"Still," Wilma replied, "I worry about it."

Vi shook her head. "Never fear, Wilma. Their response to each other will be natural and unrehearsed. That is as it should be. Now I've got to run along—there is so much to be done, preparing for their welcome home. At least Abel and Carl solved one problem for us with their successful hunt. We'll have plenty of tender young elk and antelope to feed a hungry mob of soldiers."

"I'll be along in a moment to lend a hand," Wilma said. She watched her friend move across the compound, steps quick and sure, head held high. A thought suddenly struck Wilma—Vi had no one coming home! Perhaps, she thought, that is why Vi has thrown herself so wholeheartedly into preparations for the regiment's return. Keeping her hands busy could help conceal an emptiness in her heart.

A quarter-mile below the low pass leading into Fort Laramie, Colonel Ted Henderson raised a hand. The column came to a stop.

"Sergeant Jonas, form the column up by threes. Strictly parade-ground formation from here on in. We wouldn't want to make our homecoming a sloppy one, would we?"

"No, sir!" The black sergeant wheeled his mount. "By the threes! Look sharp, men!"

The excitement among the troops was a thing one could almost touch, Ted thought. He felt a quickening in his heartbeat; after all these months, he was only a mile or so from Wilma and his new son. Brushing the trail dust from his tunic, Ted once again found himself wondering how the boy would react to him, and how he would respond to the boy.

"Colonel?"

"Yes, Jonas?"

The black sergeant pointed at the tattered Third Cavalry banner. "We have a new one, sir," Jonas said. "Should we break it out for the homecoming?"

Ted studied the regimental flag fluttering in the breeze, its edges ragged from winds, colors faded slightly from the sun, with jagged holes made by a half-dozen rifle balls and arrows.

"No, Sergeant," he said, noticing the slight catch in his voice. "She's flown with us this far; she deserves her own homecoming."

A broad grin split the sergeant's face. "I was hoping you would say that, Colonel. I'm kind of proud of the old flag myself."

The cries began from the back of the column, then moved in waves toward the front ranks.

Jonas turned to his commanding officer. "Column formed up and ready, sir."

"Very well, Sergeant. Let's go home."

"Here they come!"

The cry from the sentry sent Wilma's heart leaping. She scooped up William Ted. "Daddy's home," she said to the child, giving the youngster a firm hug. Still carrying the baby, she moved to the window. In the distance, she saw Ted, riding easy in the saddle, Yellow Crow on a big palomino at one stirrup and a huge black man at the other. Wilma blinked back the tears that formed in her eyes, wondering if she could control her emotions, conduct herself as an officer's wife rather than a silly schoolgirl greeting a lover. Then she felt a twinge of loss as the column moved into full view. In the middle of the troopers, about thirty riderless horses were roped together in a final salute to members of the Third who had died in battle.

At the gate, the United States flag dipped to half-mast as the riderless horses passed, and soon the last of the mounted men had entered the compound.

As the gates swung shut, Wilma caught a quick, longing glance from her husband. She savored the moment of homecoming as Ted smoothly directed the Third into rows of horsemen, each sitting tall in the saddle. A volunteer brass band, making up in enthusiasm what it lacked in talent, broke into a lively song.

Ted waited until the band had quieted and the cheers of greeting began to die away, then lifted a hand.

"Gentlemen of the Third Cavalry," he said, his voice carrying sharp and clear over the nearly silent parade ground, "we have just concluded a long, hard campaign—so we will save the speeches until ten o'clock tomorrow morning with full-dress uniform. Now, welcome home and dismissed!"

The chorus of applause began with a single handclap, grew to a roar as the cavalrymen of the Third surrendered their mounts to the care of the stable detail, and then all semblance of military decorum fell apart as soldiers dashed to greet friends and loved ones.

Ted stepped to the rough plank porch where his wife and son waited. He stared for a long time into Wilma's eyes. "My God, woman," he finally said, "you get more beautiful by the day."

Wilma tried to blink back the haze of tears, battling against the urge to throw herself into Ted's arms. But there was one more important thing to attend to first.

"Ted," she said, holding out the baby, her voice cracking with emotion, "may I present your son, William Ted Henderson."

Wilma felt the tension grow inside her as father and son looked intently into each other's eyes. Then little William Ted grinned and waved his arms happily—and was swept into his father's embrace. Wilma was not far behind.

The crisp clear notes of the bugle sounded over the compound as Ted, flanked by Abel and other officers of the post, surveyed the assembled members of the Third Cavalry standing at attention beneath a bright, warm sun.

"Soldiers of the Third Cavalry Regiment," Ted called, "no officer has ever had the pleasure of commanding such a courageous and outstanding group. You have my personal gratitude and that of an entire nation for your efforts in a long and arduous—and frequently distasteful—campaign.

"You have endured hardships beyond belief, yet no one

complained. I will not inflict still more hardship by dragging out these proceedings with my personal comments." He unfolded a roll of parchment. "This document," he said, "bears the seal of the President of the United States. It bears the signature of Abraham Lincoln. It reads, in part:

> "*To the men of the Third Cavalry Regiment: On behalf of the citizens of the United States of America, I express my own and the nation's gratitude for your contributions above and beyond the call of duty. History may little regard your accomplishment, your courage, and your devotion to a cause on a remote field of battle. Yet no regiment, no battalion, no army has contributed more to the cause of freedom. It is with great pleasure and extreme humility that I bestow upon your number, those who survive and those who have fallen in combat, this, the Presidential Citation for Valor. Gentlemen, an entire nation is in your debt.*
>
> > *Your obedient servant,*
> > *Abraham Lincoln.'*

"In addition," Ted went on, returning the scroll to its container, "the Third has been singled out for unit citations on three occasions during the campaign, and many among us have received individual commendations. I now present some individual awards of conspicuous merit.

"Private Bernie Christian, please step forward."

The slightly built former Confederate stepped smartly from the ranks.

"For Bernie Christian, the Badge of Military Merit." Ted pinned the decoration onto Christian's tunic, stepped back, and saluted. Christian returned the salute.

"Please remain in place, Bernie," Ted said quietly.

"For Sergeant Major Frank Armbrister, posthumously"— Ted detected a quaver in his voice—"the Congressional Medal of Honor for courage above and beyond the call of duty."

Solemnly, Ted handed the five-pointed star and ribbon to Christian. "Bernie," he said, "Frank had no family. I would be honored if you would keep this in memory of our mutual friend." Ted noticed Christian's eyes blinking rapidly and placed a hand on the slender shoulder.

"For Lieutenant Chad Clark, posthumously, the Badge of

Military Merit and Individual Commendation for Valor." Ted cleared his throat and went on.

"The following promotions are hereby affirmed: Sergeant Albert Jonas, to the rank of sergeant major. Private Bernie Christian, to the rank of corporal. . . ."

At the conclusion of the ceremonies, the Third had four new noncommissioned officers and one new lieutenant, all promotions earned by gallantry on the field of battle.

"Tonight," Ted concluded, "in honor of our return, the garrison of Fort Laramie has planned a feast. For the duration of that event, all rank is suspended for social purposes. Enlisted men are welcome to share bread with the officers. After all, we've done it for months now. Dismissed!"

Long tables groaned under the weight of smoked elk, fresh beef, trout from the high country streams, and a bountiful supply of fresh vegetables from the garden kept by the women of the fort. Kegs of brandy and rum, enough for one glass for each man in the fort, were opened for the celebration.

Throughout the compound, campaign tables hosted gatherings of enlisted men, officers, scouts, and wives.

Ted held his sleepy young son on his lap and raised his token glass of wine to the radiant woman seated at his left.

"To you, Wilma. No man should be so lucky."

"To us, Ted. And to the future we will have together."

They sipped the wine, an unspoken promise to leave the banquet early touching them both with its electricity. Wilma placed a warm hand on his arm. "Look, Ted," she said, nodding her head toward a nearby table. There, an animated Judy Hubbard, radiant in a new indigo gown, clung tenaciously to her husband's arm. Across the table from them, Sergeant Major Albert Jonas was smiling and talking with a pretty, young black woman.

"Looks as if the sergeant is having a good time," Ted said. "I don't recognize her."

"She came in on the last wagon train," Wilma said. "She's a fine seamstress, and already has more work than she can handle. A sweet girl, too."

Ted did not try to suppress a smile. "As many shirts as that big man splits across the shoulders," he said, "he'd best find himself a good seamstress."

Ted noticed a curious expression, a wistfulness, in Wilma's eyes.

"Something bothering you, dear?"

"I was just wondering—what is to become of Vi Robinson? She couldn't have much money left since Bill died."

Ted sighed. "I've been somewhat concerned about her myself," he said, "but she's a strong woman. She has proven that enough, God knows. I believe she will not only survive but prosper as well. She knows she has many friends, if she should ever be in need, and she's certainly welcome to stay on at the fort, in light of her husband's rank."

Ted glanced up at a touch on his shoulder. "Yellow Crow go now," the Cheyenne said. "Too many people here; mountains call."

Ted handed the sleeping boy to Wilma and fell into step with Yellow Crow as the Indian led his big palomino toward the gate of the post and the wilderness beyond.

Outside, beneath a blanket of stars, the Cheyenne and the white man clasped forearms.

"When will I see my brother again?" Ted asked.

"Before snow falls, Yellow Crow return." A sudden smile split the normally stern face. "Need to make sure godson learn right ways, not pick up any bad habits from white man." Then the Cheyenne vaulted onto his horse, lifted a hand, and kicked the horse into a trot toward the nearby mountains.

Ted leaned for a moment against the gatepost, watching the Cheyenne ride into the night.

"I hope, my brother, that we have not yet made our last long ride together," he said quietly.

Slowly, Ted turned and began to make his way back to the hubbub inside the fort and the murmur of excited voices. If only it could last, he thought. But he knew that lasting peace would be long coming to this wild and wonderful country. As long as one man craved land that another claimed, there could be no freedom from fear, no escape from the battles yet to come.

Ted shook the thoughts aside. For the moment, at least, there would be calm waters. And he had a woman waiting and a new young son to discover.

Coming in
1987...

WINNING THE WEST
BOOK TWO

LARAMIE
by Donald Clayton Porter

Though Colonels Kit Carson and Ted Henderson have successfully turned back the Confederate invasion of the West and subdued the Apache and Navajo in New Mexico, their work of taming this rugged land has only begun. A half-breed Seminole known as Long Walker, supplied with Southern weapons, is rousing the Plains tribes to drive the white man from their ancient hunting grounds and sacred places. And Ted's friend, Yellow Crow—his loyalties challenged by fellow warriors—rides with the Indians fighting against his white brothers.

Meanwhile, Kevin O'Reilly and his Indian bride, Wind Flower, take over management of the Henderson ranch and face the hostility and violence of their Indian-hating neighbors. And Judy Hubbard risks her marriage and her life to play up to a suspected Confederate spy, who—working with Long Walker—arranges the kidnapping of Ted Henderson's young son.

The stakes are high in the epic struggle to bring peace and justice to a land torn asunder by civil war and by the bloody confrontations of Indians and whites.

Read LARAMIE, on sale April 1, 1987 wherever Bantam Books are sold.

AMERICA 2040

A daring new series of original stories filled with action, adventure and excitement. These are moving, prophetic tales of America's future pioneers ... the unforgettable men and women who dare to explore the stars.

AMERICA'S NEW FRONTIER. It stretches out beyond the planets to the vastness of infinite space. The time has come again for America's best and brightest men and women to become pioneers, to carry freedom's precious message to a new wilderness more dangerous, more lawless, and more exciting than any travelled before.

THE MISSION. It will determine America's destiny. Locked in a final deadly struggle with the Soviets, the free world trembles on the brink of nuclear holocaust. But whatever the Earth's fate, the spirit of America must not be allowed to die. The dauntless courage of those who first challenged the uncharted regions of the Old West now returns to blaze a new trail into the unknown.

☐ AMERICA 2040 #1 (25541 • $3.95)
☐ THE GOLDEN WORLD #2 (25922 • $3.95)